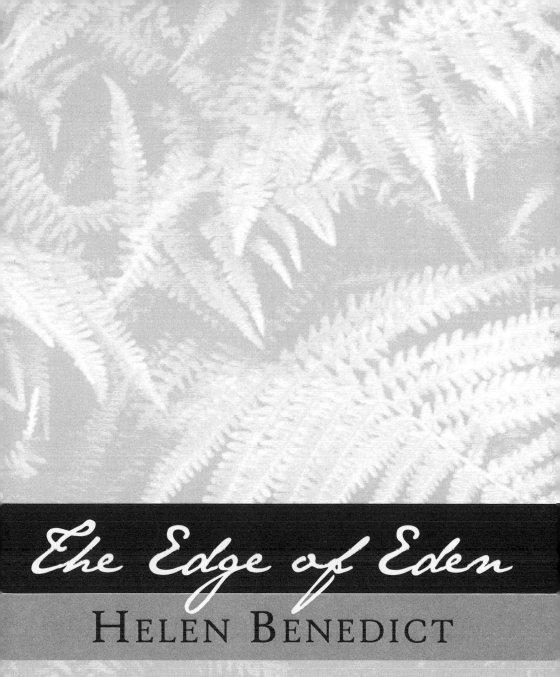

The Edge of Eden

HELEN BENEDICT

Published by Soho Press, Inc.
853 Broadway
New York, NY 10003

Library of Congress Cataloging-in-Publication Data

Benedict, Helen.
The edge of Eden / Helen Benedict.
p. cm.
ISBN 978-1-56947-602-4 (hardcover)
1. British—Seychelles—Fiction. 2. Seychelles—Fiction. I. Title.
PS3552.E5397E34 2009
813'.54—dc22
2009014772

10 9 8 7 6 5 4 3 2 1

To Burton and Marion Benedict

AUTHOR'S NOTE

The language of Seychelles is a French Creole, although nowadays all Seychellois also speak English. In the 1960s, Creole was written with French spelling, but today it has its own phonetic spelling, which is still being standardized and which I have used here. Readers who know French only have to say most of the words aloud to understand their meaning: *Leker* is *le coeur* ("heart"); *dye* is *dieu* ("god"); *ser* is *soeur* ("sister"); *rouz* is *rouge* ("red"), *dibwa* is *du bois* ("of the woods").

The strict meaning of the word *gris-gris*, or *grigri* in Creole, is the amulet or charm used in witchcraft to plant curses or spells. However, in Seychelles it is also commonly used to mean sorcery itself. The spells mentioned in this book are taken from accounts by the Seychellois people.

The art of being a slave is to rule one's master.

—Diogenes of Sinope

Tell me whom you love and I'll tell you who you are.

—Seychellois proverb

PROLOGUE

1960

The ship was as big as a world to Zara. She explored it all day long, tumbling through corridors and stairwells while the SS *Kampala* lumbered through the Eastern seas. The cabin she shared with her sister seemed a magician's box, full of hidden drawers and locking compartments. The ballroom was a vast rink, its polished wooden floor so slippery she could skate from one side to the other in her socks. But best of all was the upper deck pool, cool and slappy on its surface, weighty and secret below.

Zara was eight and heady with new independence. The self-contained universe of the ship, free of traffic and schoolteachers, had enticed her parents into a neglect she had never experienced before and she relished it. She was free to be bad or good or neither—to just be, however that took her from moment to moment. Her mother stayed in bed most of the time, too seasick to move, her father hobnobbed all day, and her London school seemed eons away, with its hurtling boys and the headmaster who liked to beat them with a long, white cane. There, Zara had spent her time hiding in a corner to avoid those boys, or wincing at the sound of their beatings. Here, she did what she wanted and made her little sister Chloe into her servant.

It began with words. A three-year-old is so easy to frighten with words. "There's a lady, long and skinny, who lives in the smoke-stack," Zara told Chloe one morning. "She's watching you. If you don't do what I say, she'll come out to pinch you all over." Zara demonstrated and Chloe went wailing to their mother. But she couldn't find their mother, so she had to turn back, wailing doubly to Zara. "Don't worry," said Zara. "Just do what I tell you and I'll keep you safe."

Zara loved Chloe's dimples, two on one side, one on the other; her bubble cheeks and bright curly hair; her little round bottom, perfect as two peaches. She liked to dress Chloe up in her frilly frocks, cuddle and kiss her, then take her between the lifeboats where no one could see and make her pull down her knickers and bend over to be spanked. Chloe would resist. "You're not my mummy," she would protest, but a reminder of the lady in the smokestack took care of that. After the spanking, Zara would feel high and strong, guilty and dirty all at once. Excited between the legs, ashamed between the ears. The cure was to go swimming and later, to do it again.

Zara felt at home as a tadpole in the water. She would put Chloe in the paddling pool on the side and tell her to stay. Then she would jump in, expel her breath, sink to the bottom and sit cross-legged for as long as she could, watching her black hair float about like smoke. The sky—too big and too blue out there over the Indian Ocean— would be tamed then, a shimmering ceiling patterned by bubbles. The water would fill her ears, cutting off the sharp noises, the things she didn't want to hear. Zara made up her mind to grow gills. If she stayed underneath long enough it would happen, she was sure. Once she stayed under so long one of the deckhands jumped in to grab her, plucking her out like a captured frog. Zara kicked him hard in the chest, shooting out her leg, thin and straight as a bone.

The children's mother, Penelope, heaved herself queasily out of bed every evening just long enough to take them to dinner and then to their very own cabin to sleep; Rupert, their father, they hardly saw at all. Penelope was always dressed for the ship's formal dinners then, long and slender in a sparkly gown, her back exposed to reveal vertebrae like a row of chipped pebbles. She reeked of cigarettes and perfume, a sickly, cloying smell that made Zara turn away even as she was kissed.

Penelope with sprayed brown hair teased into a high bun, a shiny fringe low on her brow, clumpy mascara weighing down her vague blue eyes, and red, red lipstick, sticky as paint. She had to climb the ladder to the top bunk to reach Zara, awkward in her long skirts.

"You're turning black as a crust in all this sun," she said one night in her new seasick voice. "You remind me of Kitty." Kitty! Their black cat, white paws, a curling tickly tongue. Penelope had given her to the cleaning woman in London because the family would be gone so long. Zara had cried all day over Kitty and already she had forgotten her! She clutched her toy kangaroo and forced the tears to come, wanting to feel the loss again. And so, lying against the white pillow, her sharp face thin and browned, her walnut eyes crumpled, she did indeed look like a cat.

Penelope brushed her hand over Zara's long hair, smiling weakly. "Do you know how lucky you are, darling, to be adventuring about on a ship like this? When I was your age, I was stuck in a freezing little cottage in Devon with Nanny O'Neill."

Zara looked up at the shadowy face of her mother, the red lips almost purple in the dark. "That was in the war, wasn't it, Mummy? Were you very brave?"

Penelope tucked the sheet into a crisp fold under Zara's chin and stroked Kangy, the child's threadbare plush kangaroo. Bravery was not exactly what sprung to mind when Penelope thought about the war. Fear did, of course, and that shrieking in the air. Ear-bursting explosions and years of lonely exile. "No, I don't think I was very brave. Go to sleep now, poppet," and she stepped down to Chloe's bunk beneath.

Zara heard the muffled sounds of complaint, whimpering, a soothing kiss. "Yes, dear," Penelope cooed. "Do as your sister says. She's a good little mother."

"Where's Daddy?" Zara said to her mother's bony back as Penelope picked her way out of the room. "I want him."

"Oh . . . somewhere. Good night, dears. Kiss, kiss, sweet dreams."

As soon as her mother had left, Zara decided to count to one hundred and when the coast was clear, go find Daddy herself. She was not afraid of the night but she didn't like the porthole beside her bed, the glass thick as the seat of a bottle, nor the darkness outside of it. Daddy would make it better. She tried to look out—she wanted the porthole to behave like a real window—but she only saw her own face as a phantom, some flickering lights moving maybe behind her, maybe in front, and a solid black that seemed to go on forever. She didn't like that, but she was not afraid. Zara was not afraid of anything, she told herself every day, not even the headmaster's white cane because he never used it on the girls.

After she reached one hundred, she tucked Kangy under her pillow and climbed down the ladder to the floor. The ship was rocking more than usual, the floor heaving up and down as if someone were trying to shake her off it. Zara staggered, hitting her ankle against the bunk's sharp metal leg. She gasped.

"Thara?" Chloe said in her baby lisp.

"Shh. Stay here. I'm going to find Daddy."

"I'm thcared. The ship's all bumpy."

"Don't worry. Go to sleep. I'll be back soon." Zara slipped out of the cabin.

The ship was different at night, bigger, more frightening, but also more beautiful. The inside corridors were the same dim beige as in the daytime, but outside the ship had been strung with so many lightbulbs it looked like a fairground. She made her way to the promenade deck, the floor tilting beneath her, sending her careening from railing to wall and back again. She had to zigzag and run to get anywhere. To the right, run run crash. To the left, run run crash.

When she reached the promenade deck, she saw some grownups leaning over the railing, some in pairs, some alone. Long legs stretching upwards, the jackets of the men crisp and white as paper, the skirts of the women full as curtains, billowing in the wind. Their heads somewhere up there, bobbling in the sky. She staggered again, laughing because the wind was so strong and the stars were so big and the gaps between the railings were wide enough to swallow her whole.

The ship was rolling harder now and even the grown-ups were weaving as they made their way back inside, clinging to whatever they could. Her daddy—there he was! He was clinging too, but to a person. A lady with yellow hair. Zara zigzagged over to him. Her daddy, tall and straight as a lamppost, beard like a woolly pillow. Zara crashed into his legs.

"Bugger!" her father yelped. The lady squeaked.

"Zara! What are you doing here?" His voice sounded wobbly.

"Hello, Daddy." Zara held onto her father's lamppost legs and looked up into his face.

"Rupert, is this is your daughter?" the yellow lady said. "Oh dear."

"Oh dear," mimicked Zara.

Rupert frowned and bent down, his hands on Zara's shoulders. "Don't be impudent. Now what's the matter, muffin, you can't sleep?"

Zara shook her head. "The ship's gone funny." Her father's breath smelled acrid and sweet—wine and pipe. "I wanted to find you."

"You shouldn't be out here, a storm's blowing up. Come, I'll take you to bed." Without looking at the yellow lady, Rupert strode off, holding Zara's hand, the two of them tossed side to side by the heaving ship. After banging into a wall twice, they managed to get through a door and she recognized the ballroom. During the day the room was empty—her rink of bare floor—but now it was cluttered with chairs and people, and tables laid with white linen, glass and silver. Zara stared. Nothing was as it should be. Chairs lay on their backs in the middle of the room as if they'd somersaulted across the floor. Glasses and bottles were knocked over. Grown-ups were sitting on the ground, looking surprised. Everything was higgledy-piggledy.

The ship tipped over so far they both sat down, plonk, Zara between her father's legs. "Hold tight!" he cried, clasping her around the tummy, and they slid across the polished floor, all the way from one side of the room to the other. With them slid the tables and chairs, gliding in a curious slow motion. "Duck!" Rupert called as a table sailed over them and crashed into a wall. No sooner had they hit one side of the room, the ship rocked back again and everything slid to the other side in the same stately procession, plates and glasses skimming across tabletops as if they'd come to life, while the ship's stewards balanced on their sea legs, collecting the breakables as best they could. A woman in a ball gown shot past, her legs splayed like a doll's, her eyes and mouth open in astonished O's. A man in a tuxedo floated by, his legs straight out in front of him like a plank. A waiter twirled around a central pillar, one arm hooked to it, the other still holding up his tray. People shrieked. Rupert clung tight to Zara and both of them laughed till their bellies ached.

Finally, they managed to half stagger, half creep back to the cabin, where Rupert stowed Zara safely into her top bunk. "Are you all right, lovey?" he said in his wonderful rumbly voice. "Not frightened?"

"No. Are we going to sink, Daddy?" Zara pictured the ship sinking, with its ladies in long dresses swimming like mermaids, chairs drifting about as if they could fly, chandeliers and wine goblets twinkling as they spiraled to the bottom of the sea.

"No, we are not going to sink. This is a British India ship. Sound as a bell. Now go to sleep."

The next morning, Zara was awoken by the ship's steward, a sour-faced man in a white uniform, bearing a tray of the hot chocolate and croissants he brought to the children every morning. Perched up there on her throne of a bed, the silver tray on her knees—a saucer of jam, a swirl of butter, two fluffy croissants and a whole teapot of hot chocolate all to herself—Zara gazed out of the porthole, no longer dark but bright now with sky, and saw that the sea had calmed to a glossy blue-black, like the back of a sleeping fish. She decided she had to swim, that instant.

"Chloe?" She pushed aside the tray, spilling chocolate on her sheets but not caring, and climbed down the ladder. "Chloe, get up! We're going swimming." But Chloe was not there. Zara shrugged. She was probably in their mother's cabin, cuddled up in bed to hide from last night's storm.

Zara was relieved. "You must watch Chloe every minute, darling," her mother was always saying. "Babies have been known to drown in even two inches of water." The image of Chloe lying face-down, still and dead, had the habit of invading Zara just as she was settling at the bottom of the pool to grow her gills. It would force her to the surface, spoiling everything.

She wriggled into her bathing suit—blue smocking with a little skirt she hated—and ran barefoot into the corridor, stopping now and then to investigate the discarded breakfast trays outside cabin doors. She found a half-finished chocolate croissant, which she gobbled, and a miniature packet of Cocoa Krispies only half eaten. She shook the rest into her mouth and dropped the box into someone's shoe, left out to be polished.

Nobody was on deck yet, it being early, so Zara made her way alone to the square pool, which lay still and green under the morning sky. She sat on the tiled edge to watch the surface for a moment before disturbing it. She had noticed before that the pool on the ship, a pocket of water within water, moved as if solid, shifting from side to side like newly-set blancmange. If she jumped in, maybe she wouldn't even splash or get wet; she would only sink silently, like a knife slicing through jelly. Would she be able to eat her way out? Or would she get caught halfway down, trapped the way that poor baby starfish was trapped in the glass paperweight on Daddy's desk? Splayed and still, like Chloe drowned in two inches of water. Zara jumped up. The railing was only a few steps away. She ran to it and looked over the edge. With one lurch of the ship last night, Chloe could have slipped through as easily as Zara shot across the ballroom in her socks. Chloe shooting overboard, forever.

Zara grasped the railing and climbed up to the second rung so she could see better. The sea, vast as the sky here, stretched until it dipped over the edge of the world. She leaned far over, staring at its gleaming black surface, flashing silver under the white morning sun. A few foamy crests winked here and there, each resembling Chloe's curly head. Zara balanced on her stomach and strained over further to watch the water near the hull, churning like a boiling pot. Was that Chloe, that yellow bubble in the middle? Or was that her over there? If only Zara had finished growing her gills. With gills, she could climb over the railing, spread her arms like wings and dive into the bubbles, deep, deep into the water, following a sun shaft to the bottom of the sea. And there she would find Chloe, curled like a shrimp around a coral fan, waiting for her. Zara would tuck her under an arm and swim up and up, flying into the embrace of her mother and father. *Oh Zara*, Daddy would say, *I am so proud*. All the people of the ship would cheer, holding her above their heads, her father glowing, her mother weeping with relief. . . .

"Zara, get down!"

She felt herself seized by the back of her bathing suit and yanked off the railing. "What are you doing? You could have fallen! Never do that, never!"

Zara looked up into her mother's frightened face, makeup smudged into black wedges under her eyes, her body lumpy in a pink velour bathrobe. How much Zara would have liked her mother not to be this mother, this one on the ship who was too pale and too smelly and too everything. Zara wanted her old mother back, the one who used to make up games for her and tell her about animals, the one from before they put everything in boxes and gave away Kitty and had to walk through each of the empty rooms of their flat to say good-bye. "You must bid farewell to every home you leave," that mother had said. "Otherwise it will haunt you forever."

Penelope dropped to a crouch, eye level with Zara. "Where's Chloe? She's not in the cabin. I thought she was with you."

"She's a fish," Zara said, still in her dream, and sucked in her cheeks to make fish lips.

"Stop that!" Penelope gripped Zara's thin shoulders. "This is serious. Where is your sister?"

"She's swimming in the sea," Zara said, undulating her arms the way she'd been taught in ballet class.

Penelope shook her hard. "Don't act the baby with me! Tell me where Chloe is!"

Tears welled up in Zara's eyes. "I don't know," she stuttered. "She—she was gone when I woke up."

Near panic now, Penelope stood and dragged Zara by the hand to the nearest uniformed presence. "I can't find my little girl! Curly blond hair, three years old. Alert the captain, quickly!"

She locked Zara in the cabin, told Rupert what had happened, and ran all over the ship crying out Chloe's name. The ship seemed to grow around her as she searched, like a Hydra sprouting neck after neck, head after head, shooting out corridors, ladders and sinister cupboards and doors. Death traps lurked everywhere: Machines in the hold, their cogs murderously sharp, their belts designed to mutilate; portholes suddenly huge and open, sucking like vacuums. And the railings—how could she not have noticed how wide apart the railings were? And Rupert, damn him! Why, they wouldn't even be on this lethal ship if it weren't for him. Ever since he'd received this infernal posting he had turned hard and selfish, blind to both her and the children. He hadn't even consulted them about the move. He'd simply announced that they were to give up their old life with no more fuss than shrugging off a coat and follow him to the ends of the earth, where they were to stew for an entire year, or perhaps even longer. And when she'd objected, all he'd had to say was, "But everybody tells me Seychelles is paradise."

Penelope and Rupert looked everywhere. Over all five decks of the ship, inside lifeboats, kitchens and gaming rooms, the dining hall, ballroom, cocktail bar, smoking room and cabin after cabin. Penelope ran and wept, calling for Chloe until, hit by another wave of nausea, she collapsed in a deck chair, only to be up again as soon as she could, crying out, running. Rupert steamed through the corridors and over the decks in dread, shouting out Chloe's name and wishing he could, through sheer force of will, conjure her safely in front of him. He only remembered Zara at one o'clock in the afternoon, when the ship's chime rang out for luncheon. "Poor little pea, shut up like that all morning," he muttered, hurrying to her cabin. Unlocking the door, he pushed it open.

"Daddy!" Zara looked up at him, flushing a little. She was sitting on the floor, naked, her legs spread. And opposite, in the same position, as trusting as ever, was his golden bundle of a Chloe.

"We're giving names to our peepee places," Zara said.

"I got a peepee place!" crowed Chloe.

Rupert shut his eyes, the ice draining from his limbs. "Girls, get up now and put on your clothes," he just managed to say. Then he crumpled to the ground and pulled Chloe to him. "My God, where were you?"

"Nowhere," Chloe said, cuddling up in her father's smell of beard and pipe. "You're thcratchy."

Rupert looked over at his dark daughter. "Where was she?"

Zara shrugged, and clamped her mouth as tight as a seam.

Exile

PART ONE

I

Penelope lay in bed for two days after they arrived in Seychelles, sweating in the equatorial heat. She knew she should get up and help the children settle, but she just couldn't. She felt too sick from the boat, too exhausted and too damned angry at Rupert.

The journey had been insufferable—all twelve days of it. Propeller planes bumping about in the sky. Those lurching ships, first one from Mombasa to Madagascar, then another from Madagascar to Seychelles. Rupert's shameless flirtation on the ship and that terrifying episode when Chloe had gone missing. Yet even when it was over and Penelope had stumbled onto solid land at last, she had found no relief. She'd looked up at the mountains looming above her, massive heaps of lush and tangled forest, at the myriad black and brown faces staring at her from the dock, and her heart had trembled. She'd felt shanghaied—just as she had on the ship—bound and gagged and dropped into this strange and blaring land, as will-less as a sock.

Rupert and the children, of course, were enthralled. "Look at that!" they'd cried over and over in the taxi that took them to their new home, pointing and jabbering as they craned out its window. "Oh, isn't it lovely!" And, Penelope had to admit, it was. Palm trees bold against fathomless blue skies. Sands white as teeth. The sea a dancing turquoise. Huge round rocks crowning the mountains, swathed in rolling mists—and all of it lit by a bright and spangling sun. But what had it to do with her? It seemed so outlandish, as if she'd stepped onto a stage set. She could imagine putting a hand out of that taxi window and pushing over one of those palm trees, or even the Technicolor mountains as easily as if they were made of cardboard. I don't understand, she thought. What am I doing here?

Penelope had never left England before. Having spent most of her childhood exiled from her family, first in that Devonshire cottage she'd mentioned to Zara, where she'd lived with her nanny throughout the war, then at a Kent boarding school until she was eighteen, she had always clung as close to home as she could. She had certainly never imagined ending up in a place like Seychelles, so tiny and remote one could hardly see it on the map. It was ridiculous, when she thought about it. Africa was a thousand miles away on one side, India almost two thousand on the other, yet Seychelles didn't even have its own aeroport. It was barely a country, really, but rather a cluster of a hundred or so miniscule islands tucked under the equator like an afterthought, most of them inhabited by nothing but bird excrement. Even Mahé, the biggest of the islands and where Rupert had set them up to live, was only seventeen miles long and seven across at its widest. But the final straw, as far as Penelope was concerned, was that although Seychelles had been a British Crown Colony for over a century and a half, nobody she knew in England had ever heard of it.

So the minute they reached the house Rupert had rented for them, she crawled into bed, even though it was still early morning, as sick with resentment as she was from the sea, and lay there watching a wicker fan wobble dangerously in the ceiling and trying to muster the strength to face it all. "Stay away, little ones," she told Zara and Chloe when they poked their heads around the bedroom door. "Mummy's still not feeling well." Rupert, she sent to stay in the study.

The house was soon all a-bustle. Marguerite Savy, the combination maid and nanny the office had hired for Rupert, cleaned and clucked, humming hymns as she watered the potted plants, uprooted every sign of grass from the front courtyard and swept its pink dust into graceful, symmetrical patterns with a broom of bundled sticks. Sylvie Ballon, the rotund and very dark cook, put together mysterious concoctions in the kitchen. Zara and Chloe explored wildly. And Rupert bossed and grinned, disappearing for a couple of hours to introduce himself at the government office, then returning to direct the unpacking of bags, the arrangement of furniture, the placement of pictures. After which he sat in a high-backed straw chair on the veranda, ran long fingers through his woolly beard and marveled at his good fortune.

Rupert had been plucked from a lowly and ineffectual position in the British Colonial Office for this job in the Seychelles, a posting some might have regarded as banishment but he saw as hard-earned recognition of his worth. His assignment was to produce a report on the Seychelles' economy and how to improve it—a Herculean task, as his superiors well knew, because the islands were crushingly overpopulated and had suffered over a century of spectacular neglect. Seychelles had long been an unwelcome burden to the British, so removed from civilization that nobody but birds, turtles and pirates had noticed it for hundreds of years. The place wasn't even settled until 1770, and even then only by a motley group of fifteen Frenchmen, their seven African slaves, five Indians and one solitary black woman. ("Given how crowded the place is now, that one woman must have been kept awfully busy," Rupert liked to say.) The French had governed the colony in a desultory manner until the British took it off them during the Napoleonic wars, after which it had prospered for a time, being rich in timber and fertilizing guano. But once the Emancipation Act of 1835 had freed all the slaves and thus the labor from British territories, the islands had plummeted into poverty. Now Seychelles was in debt up to its very tall mountains, produced nothing of interest to the world but a sprinkling of cinnamon, vanilla and the dried coconut meat known as copra, and was regarded by Her Majesty's Government as unfit for anybody but junior civil servants and lepers.

If Rupert's post was undistinguished, it was nonetheless a step up from the one he'd had in England. Yet, as he sat on his breezy veranda, listening to the rhythmic warbling of the local doves, he found himself hard-pressed to care. He was too thrilled at having exchanged the gloom and push of London for a tropical paradise to think of anything as bothersome as steps up to anywhere. Instead, he sat in his straw throne, sipped at a cold Tiger beer and surveyed, with some astonishment, the unexpected beauty of his new Seychellois house.

He and the children had fallen for the house the minute they'd seen it. Built a century earlier by a French landowner, it looked as un-English as possible, with nary a blackened brick or gray stone in sight. Made entirely of wood, it was painted white from top to bottom and was as fanciful as a cream cake. It had a wraparound veranda, rows of open doors and windows on every side and an oversized sloping roof like a sun hat. The veranda was fenced in by an ornately carved white balustrade, above which hung bamboo shades, pale green and rolled up like lizard tongues, ready to be unfurled against the afternoon sun. The edge of the corrugated iron roof was fringed with lacy Indian carvings. Every one of the tall, glassless windows was protected by a nut-brown shutter that levered open at the bottom to let in the evening breeze. In front of the house was the dusty pink courtyard, behind it a riotous garden of tropical plants, and all around it a dense and verdant forest.

The children loved the house for its secrets. Their bedroom upstairs had a narrow closet that ran behind the entire back wall like a smuggler's tunnel. Their beds were tented with gossamer mosquito nets, which to Zara looked like spiderwebs and to Chloe like princess curtains. Instead of a basement, the house was perched on stone pillars to protect it from rats and termites, leaving a crawl space full of satisfying dangers: red ants that bit and burnt, mysterious holes plunging deep into the rust-orange earth. And in the back of the house was an extra-wide veranda with bamboo deck chairs crouching like grasshoppers and a round, glass-topped cocktail table.

Zara liked to lie underneath it and pretend she was trapped in a fishbowl. "Let me out, Chloe, let me out!" she would beg, laughing. Marguerite, small and sturdy and rusty-skinned as the local cinnamon bark, scolded her for leaving fingerprints all over the glass.

The children played all day long. Zara was queen, Chloe anything Zara made her—servant, horse, prey or punching bag. And if they missed their mother, no matter, they had Daddy. When they tired, he put a daughter on each knee and told them their favorite stories, featuring them as heroes rescuing babies from evil wizards and witches with names like Flappy Flopbottom and Snotty Snootnose. He didn't make them do much about quotidian affairs such as eating or washing. Zara, already brown as a rabbit, turned darker than ever from scrabbling in the dust, her long hair so matted no comb could get through it. Chloe's pink skin grew smutty with dirt. But Rupert wasn't bothered. After all, they were free of the old conventions now, free of all those dull rules that so mummified the British—wasn't that the point of coming to a place like this, really? So why make the children fuss with tedious things like baths and hairbrushes, the way they had back in London?

Penelope stayed in bed. Marguerite brought her food—a curry, a row of tiny bananas, a mango—but Penelope still felt too queasy to eat anything much. She could only lie there and wait out her paralysis, watching the translucent house geckos cling to the walls and rock back and forth on their gluey splayed feet. Once in a while she would drag herself up to look through the window at the tangle of foliage in the garden: the banana palms, their shaggy leaves as long as oars; the great spread of mango tree, its fruit dangling from strings like orange kidneys; the fan-shaped palm leaves the size of baby blankets. But the mass of greenery, so fleshy and alive, would drive her back to bed, stomach clenching, heart afraid, just as she had felt in the war.

Penelope had been only six when her mother and Nanny had packed her clothes into a brown cardboard suitcase, hung a hideous gas mask around her neck and taken her to Paddington Station.

They'd told her they were going to the family's summer cottage for a holiday, but the minute they'd walked into the station she'd grown alarmed. All around her were hundreds of children, some afraid, others excited, address labels pinned to their overcoats, their own gas masks dangling. Mothers were weeping. Harried grown-ups in armbands were blowing whistles and herding the children this way and that, and the din of voices and cries, train hisses and whistles cut through to Penelope's bones.

"Why are all these children here?" she'd asked, squeezing her mother's gloved hand in fear. No answer. "Why are the grown-ups crying?" No answer to that either. When they reached the train, Nanny climbed on first, then lifted Penelope inside. But when she called, "Hurry up, Mummy!" her mother wouldn't move. The porter blew his whistle but still her mother remained fixed to the platform. "Aren't you coming?" Penelope cried. "You said you were coming!"

"I can't." Eyes skittering, mouth tight. "I must stay here to work for the war. Now don't cry. Mind Nanny and be good. We have to keep you safe from the bombs."

"Mummy!" Penelope screamed as the train chugged away. "I don't care about bombs!"

For five years and nine months, Penelope was kept in that Devonshire cottage, her only contact with her parents their letters and crackly telephone calls. "Why don't you visit me?" she would ask her mother. "There are two boys in the village whose mummy visits them."

"No, darling, I'm busy making you a little brother." Penelope missed the birth of that brother, James, and then of a second as well, Roddy.

"Why don't you sent the babies away like me, to keep them safe?"

"Because they're too young. Don't worry, poppet, we've put a Morrison Shelter in the sitting room. It looks like a giant rabbit hutch. We sleep in it together every night to keep your brothers safe."

Penelope's longing for home, for sleeping like rabbits with

Mummy and Daddy, became a permanent part of her, following her to the village school, where she was considered too glum to make friends, to the fields she roamed alone for hours and to her cold room under the cottage roof, where she lay shivering each time a German plane rumbled overhead. Otherwise, she remained in the clutches of Nanny O'Neill, who filled her with Catholic prayers and ghost stories, slapped her hard and scrubbed her with icy water the many times she wet her bed, and left her alone night after night to weep for her mother.

Penelope was beyond weeping now, but she was not beyond outrage. How could her own husband, who had promised never to do to her what the war had done, have torn her away from home like this?

For a long time in that cottage, Penelope had comforted herself with the assurance that she still had a home. She allowed herself to hear welcome in her parents' rare telephone calls, and to read affection into the occasional letters and presents they sent through the post—once a rag doll but most often books. "Mummy, I'm frightened you'll all be hurt," she wrote during the Blitz. "Mummy, can I come home now?" she said on the telephone once it was over. "Mummy, can I speak to Daddy?" She pushed aside the gentle denials, the hurrying off the phone, hearing instead, "As soon as the war is over, darling, of course you can come home."

But the war refused to be over. The London Blitz might have ended, but in Penelope's little corner of Devon the worst was still to come. It began in April of 1942, when Lord Haw Haw, the German propagandist, declared that Hitler was going to bomb the nearby cathedral town of Exeter until its streets ran with blood. The Nazis were angry, Nanny's radio explained, because the RAF had bombed the cathedral in their town of Lubeck. Nanny reinforced the burlap she'd glued onto the cottage windows, checked the blackout curtains for traitorous holes and made Penelope come down from her attic bedroom to sleep in the cellar amongst moldy potato sacks and piles of maggoty wood. Then it began. The thud of approaching bomber planes like blows to the chest. The howls of air raid sirens growing to a great desperate scream. The whistle of incendiary bombs dropping all around them. "Jesus, Mary and Joseph," Nanny muttered in her rough Irish brogue, crossing herself frantically as she hunkered down next to Penelope, who was curled tight on the floor, hands over her ears. "And your daddy t'ought we'd be safer here than in Richmond, Lord help us." Penelope was nine years old by then, but each of the seventeen air raids that devastated Exeter made her wet herself. And after the worst night of all, she emerged to find the woman next door sitting beside her flattened house, rocking and screaming for her children, and the school hall filled with the wounded and the dead.

Please God, please don't kill any more people, Penelope prayed every night. Please let the war end.

And then, at last, it did. VE day—victory! Freedom and quiet and sleep. Bees buzzing over flowers, yawns in the sun, the jubilant songs of blackbirds in the morning.

People came from all around to fill the village green with long tables draped in sheets and to cook whatever they could scrounge for an all-day feast: sandwiches and chickens, cakes, jellies and trifles, even homemade ice cream—a wildness of riches in those half-starved times. Posters went up in shop windows, surrounded by gay red, white and blue rosettes. Flags snapped in the wind. Bunting streamed from trees and lampposts. The boys brass band squawked and blared, and effigies of Hitler and Mussolini were burnt in a bonfire. The grown-ups got drunk on beer and relief, and the children ran and laughed under the May sky. The Jerries are done for! Hitler's defeated! Even Nanny allowed herself to be pushed about by a burly farmer in some form of a dance.

Penelope sat at the corner of a table, a thin, long-legged eleven-year-old, sucking a strawberry ice lolly and watching the scene with lonely blue eyes. A few of the children from school asked her to play, having grown used to her sadness and bookish ways over the years, but she shook her head. She could think of only one thing: Home.

They returned to London by train the next week. Penelope hunched in her seat, heart squeezing at the thought of seeing her mother and father again, and stared out of the soot-grimed window. Nanny sat opposite, her swollen hands knitting. Devon in spring was a palette of colors, of undulating green hills, fields of sunny buttercups and dandelions, pale primroses and summer blue violets. But the closer they drew to London, the more the color drained away, until Penelope could see what war had really done. The Germans may have almost burnt Exeter to the ground and flown their terrorizing bombers back and forth over Penelope's village all the war long, but that was minor compared to what they'd done to London. She stared out of the window in shock. Blackened brick and rubble. Rows of sooty houses with every fourth one or so missing, like gaps in a mouth of rotting teeth. Buildings in shreds. The city looked frightened and broken, as if a giant's foot had stamped down and crushed it. Maybe Mummy's dead, she thought. Maybe the voice on the phone wasn't Mummy at all. Maybe it was somebody else, pretending.

When she arrived at Paddington Station, she stepped onto the platform, her legs gangly in their ankle socks and heavy brown shoes, and looked about her anxiously. All through the war she had nursed a black-and-white photograph of her parents, her mother in a boxy suit and waved hair, her father sly in a thin mustache, but she realized then, facing the bewildering crowds, that she had no real idea of what her parents looked like. She turned for reassurance to Nanny, lumbering off the train with a bag in each hand, her square face red and her mouth pinched into a rectum of wrinkles. She resented Nanny with all the ferocity of an unloved child, but at least she knew her.

"Penny, is that you?" she heard a voice hoot. "Goodness, how tall you've grown." A large woman loomed before her, hair dark and glossy, sharp blue eyes examining.

Penelope looked up. "Mummy?"

"Take your suitcase from Nanny now, don't make her do all the work. Come along. The boys are waiting to see you." And the woman turned, her tall back grim between firm padded shoulders, and marched away.

Penelope followed, squeezing first one eye, then the other, as if she couldn't see.

In the tube to Richmond, she sat on the scratchy seat, clutching her old suitcase on her lap, unable to think of a thing to say. Her mother sat beside her on one side, Nanny on the other, conversing over her head, but Penelope couldn't hear, her ears deafened by the hum of fear.

"Penny?" Her mother's voice penetrated. "I want you to understand something. Your uncle is in hospital and your father is quite upset, so I expect you to help me look after your brothers, all right?" And when they arrived and walked all the way from Richmond station to the front door, Nanny once more carrying the bags, her mother said something else. "Nanny is going to say good-bye here, darling. You'll be off to boarding school soon, so she's going home."

"Boarding school? But I don't—"

"We'll discuss that later. Say good-bye now."

Penelope turned, an awkward, aching girl face-to-face with a worn stump of a woman. "You're leaving now?" she said, and her voice unexpectedly trembled.

"So it seems," Nanny replied as she placed Penelope's suitcase on the ground with a grunt. "Good-bye to ye, girly. Look after ye-self," and hitching up her battered carpetbag onto her swollen hip, she trudged off down the street, never to be seen again.

"Right," Penelope's mother said, "in you go, then." And she pushed open the dark and unfamiliar front door.

On Penelope's second evening of lying in bed, her anger at Rupert still steeping inside her like an over-brewed tea, he waltzed in without knocking. (Another sign that he thinks he owns me, she thought wearily.) "Penny, get up," he said in exasperation. "You can't be this sick, or whatever it is you say you are. You should be enjoying yourself. This place is stunning."

"Is it?" she said sourly.

Rupert ignored that. "Anyway, it's time to start mingling. The governor's having a cocktail do to introduce us. You know the sort of thing. It's on Saturday and I want you to pull yourself together and make a good impression."

"Be the charming wifey?"

"Exactly. At least pretend. Come on, Penny, please. The children need you."

That had an effect. "All right, I'll try," she said with a sigh. "It's just that I feel so ill. Ask Suzanne to make something digestible, would you? Not, for God's sake, a curry. I'll join you for supper."

"Sylvie."

Penelope looked at her husband in irritation. Back stiff as a cricket bat, brown hair thick and unruly, whatever was left of his charm hidden in that smelly bush hanging off his chin. "Sylvie what?"

"That's the cook's name, not Suzanne. You better get it right, or we'll lose all the servants in a day."

"You know, Rupert, if you could ever think of anything to say to me that wasn't either a scold or a command, we might actually be able to converse."

"God, Penny, you should hear yourself." And he left.

That hurt, as he so often hurt. For she didn't really want to snipe at him like this, she didn't really want to go about seething and resentful. No, in fact she yearned to bring Rupert back to the way he used to be in London, to the days when he had been kind.

So she sat up, woozy and layered in sweat, and with an effort swung her legs off the bed. I'm here now, she told herself. I shall just have to make the best of it.

The first family dinner in the new house was a chaotic affair, despite the airy dining room, the careful white tablecloth and fine Minton china unpacked from London. Marguerite shuffled in and out whenever she pleased, snatching plates and slamming down others, regardless of whether a person had finished. The ceiling fan failed to cool them much at all, although it did succeed in blowing the candles until they splattered wax all over the linen. And the children, unkempt as chimney sweeps, interrupted constantly, hurtling into Penelope's knees at every opportunity, making her already weakened stomach lurch. How had they become so savage so fast, she wondered. Chloe, in particular, kept trying to jump onto her knees like a puppy, wiggling and knocking her. Penelope looked down at her youngest. How terrifying it had been when she'd gone missing on the ship! And Zara had never explained, the minx—she had probably locked the poor mite in a cabin cupboard and just wouldn't admit it. Penelope lifted Chloe onto her lap. "Sweetie, you're filthy!" she said in surprise. "Rupert, what have you been doing to these children?"

He shrugged. "Don't fuss. Let's just enjoy ourselves. It is our first supper in our new home, after all. As a complete unit, that is."

Penelope had, in fact, been aware of this, which is why she'd taken half an hour to dress. She did want to please Rupert, really, outdo any vulgar blonde on a ship. So she'd bathed off the sickbed sweat, teased and pinned up her dark hair, carefully blotted her ver-million lipstick and put on the slim green frock she'd had tailored in London, one of several she had designed herself to show off her long waist and limbs. She had also applied the usual perfume, although it did smell a bit strong in the cloying humidity of this climate. She glanced at Zara scowling at her from across the table. Zara looked most disagreeable with her hair a mat of tangles like that. It was time to get this family into shape.

"Rupert, what's your new office like?" she said, offering him a smile.

"Shabby but tolerable. I certainly have my work cut out for me, though. The economy here is a frightful mess, Penny. As far as I can see, the only thing to do is either pour in even more aid, which we're bloody unlikely to get, or goad the Seychellois into starting up a tourist industry. . . ."

But Penelope couldn't listen. Why did Rupert natter on like this, she found herself thinking, when he knew that wasn't what mat-tered? What mattered was that he'd sabotaged everything they used to have and wouldn't even talk about it. For things had been all right in London before he'd received this posting, hadn't they? She with her friends and charity work, her shopping and dinner parties, school meetings and the children; he with his government job and his pipe in the evenings? Their times alone after the girls were in bed, when they would have a cozy talk about the events of the day, she would sit on his lap by the fire and remove first his pipe, then his waistcoat, then his trousers? Things had been orderly then. Zara in school, uniformed, tidy—nothing like the ragamuffin she had become here. Chloe in nursery school or with an au pair. They'd had a good, loving, family life—tea and biscuits in the afternoons, picnics on Sundays, cuddles and closeness—a private life, not this embarrassment of scowling servants watching their every move. And it had all happened so fast! One minute, they were in South Kensington, and the next in the wilds of Africa! Why, in Nairobi, they'd had to sleep in a thatched hut, smothered in mosquito netting like Burton and his explorers, while elephants lumbered about outside as loose as pet dogs! Rupert relished all this, she knew. He felt free and brave; she could tell by the bounce in his stride and the new boastfulness in his voice. But what role, what place was there for her here? Had he thought of that? Of course not! And then the way he'd behaved on the ship, as if he had purposely set out to humiliate her—

"Penny, I'm talking."

"Oh, are you, darling?"

Rupert glowered. "I was saying that tomorrow I want to show you around, now you're on your feet. You need to know how to get to town, where the shops are and so on."

"Shops? Do they have shops here? How charming."

"Stop it."

"Stop it," Zara mimicked, with that irksome parroting she had taken up lately.

Penelope closed her eyes.

"Don't annoy Mummy," Rupert said. "She's not feeling well."

"Mummy's always thick," Chloe lisped, cuddling into Penelope's breasts and sticking her thumb in her mouth.

Marguerite wandered in just then to clear the plates. The girls had been perfectly happy to eat the rice but hadn't touched the fish curry or any of the vegetables, for which Penelope could hardly blame them. Rupert, on the other hand, had gobbled up everything, popping pimentos, chilies and unidentifiable objects into his mouth like sweets and swilling it all down with gulps of beer—leaving the heat-spoiled wine, she noticed, to her. Penelope had taken three bites of her curry—yes, curry—and pushed the rest into little mounds. It tasted raw, powdery and dangerous. Never mind, she would try the mangoes Rupert had brought for dessert. She liked mangoes, she had discovered whilst lying in bed, a fruit she'd never set eyes on in London. She looked over at the maid.

"You can tell Su—Sylvie we will have the mangoes now. Thank you."

The woman's hard little face was expressionless, her brown eyes penetrating but unreadable. Penelope couldn't tell how much she understood because she mostly spoke the island's French Creole, with only a smattering of English. Nor could Penelope place her race, for Marguerite seemed as much Indian as African, her skin that rich cinnamon, her face snub-nosed but delicate and her body short and strong. Each morning she arrived at work in a variation of the same homemade dress, a full-skirted frock of sun-bleached cotton, often gaping at the breast where a button was missing to show a rumpled white brassiere, clearly too big but very clean. Her black hair, thick and straight, was done up in a plait and wound about the top of her head like a crown. And on her feet, which were crusty with calluses, she wore rubber thongs that slapped all day as she walked about the house, setting Penelope's teeth on edge.

Marguerite stacked the plates willy-nilly, squashing the remaining food and spilling quite a bit onto the white linen tablecloth, and snapped out of the room, returning a second later with a rough wooden bowl full of whole and no doubt unwashed mangoes.

"No, no, I'm afraid this won't do," Penelope said wearily. "We must have them peeled and cut into edible cubes. Mangoes are much too messy to eat on a linen tablecloth like this. And please, tell Sylvie to wash them first."

Marguerite looked at her, unblinking. Penelope sighed and tried the same command in her schoolgirl French, but it made no difference. "Rupert?" she said, already exhausted.

"Please wash the mangoes, if you don't mind," Rupert repeated in English, enunciating each word with excruciating precision. "Thank you so much."

"Please, if you don't mind and thank you so much," parroted Zara, managing to capture the exact tone of her father's groveling.

"Zara, must you behave like an utter nincompoop?" Penelope said once the woman had gone.

"Utter nicapoop." This time it was Chloe who echoed, giggling and wriggling on Penelope's lap.

Marguerite chose this moment to return with four plates of mangoes, still unpeeled or cut, but now curiously shriveled. Penelope picked hers up. It was hot and smelled of soap. "What's this?" she said sharply.

Marguerite stood by the door, looking sturdy and self-righteous.

Zara sniffed her mango. "She gave them a bath!" she said, laughing.

Penelope turned to Rupert. "Is the woman mad?"

"Really, Penny, we don't eat the damn skins, do we? And the rain washes them every morning. I can't see what you're fussing about."

Penelope plucked Chloe from her lap and put her on the floor. "I'm sorry, I just don't feel well. Do excuse me, darlings. And Rupert, perhaps you could point out to Marguerite and Susan, or whatever their blasted names are, that I won't put up with any tricks."

"But Mummy, you said to wash them," Zara protested.

Ignoring her, Penelope stood up, stilettos teetering, and clicked out of the room.

2

Zara loved the mango-washing rain. It came almost every morning, so heavy and hard it was as if someone were tipping huge vats of water out of the sky. It drummed down on the iron roof, hammering relentlessly, sometimes bringing with it the crash of a dropped coconut, bone-rattling as a bomb. Her mother shuddered at the rain those first days, but Zara liked to run out and twirl around in it, her only shower of the day. Then, as instantly as it had arrived, the rain would stop and the sun reappear, as burning as ever. Raindrops as big as her fingernails would rest, shivering, on the giant palm fronds, the leathery mango leaves, and cling to the tips of the scrubby grass, suspended for a moment before sliding down to the orange-pink earth.

But Zara liked the spider web best. It was there after every rain, stretched across the garden between the trunks of two coconut palms, as long and wide as a badminton net. The web's elaborate strands were bejeweled with raindrops, and splayed in the middle was the spider itself, its body the size of Zara's fist and its black and yellow legs so long they could have wrapped around her neck. Zara would stand in the grass, staring up at it. The spider frightened her, of course, for it was monstrous—Chloe refused to go into the garden at all if it was there—but Zara was fascinated by it. On the days her mother snapped at her to leave her alone or quarreled with Daddy, Zara would wish she had the courage to pluck the spider off its web and place it on her mother's sleeping face.

Zara had taken to Mahé as if she'd been born there. Most of the island was cloaked in tropical forest and many an English girl would have found the giant plants and trees frightening, never mind the ginger-headed fruit bats that hung chattering in their branches or the myriad roots that writhed along the forest floor. But Zara welcomed the way the outsized plants made her feel as small and spry as an ant. She loved that a single palm leaf was big enough to shelter her from the sudden rains, and that she could run around in the garden using one as an umbrella. So she clambered happily about, unafraid of the twisting roots and prickles, the swooping bats or the bright, enticing berries Marguerite told her were poisonous. It was all Marguerite could do to make Zara keep her shoes on.

"The children here, they have worms from walking in bare feet," she would scold (her English being much better than she had let on to Penelope). "You know why their bellies, they are so big? Bloated from hundreds of worms squirming inside."

That image did the trick when Zara remembered it, for she had seen those children, their limbs like twigs and their bellies like balloons, their eyes resting dully on something in space. Maybe they were listening to the worms squiggling in their tummies, she thought. But then she would forget Marguerite's warnings, kick off her shoes—horrid leather things, hot and heavy—and run barefoot as a mouse over the poisonous prickles.

Chloe was more cautious; she had been subjected to enough physical punishment from her sister to risk any more. Her skin was softer than Zara's anyway, pink and vulnerable compared to Zara's tanned hide. Chloe would dutifully wear her sturdy leather sandals, bought for her by Penelope back in London. On the other hand, she loathed her clothes. It was not unusual to find her naked out in the courtyard, a dimpled putto but for white socks and shoes.

The girls made a nest in the kapok tree. There was one on the edge of the garden, its roots swirling around its trunk like the skirts of a vast ball gown. They cleared out pebbles and dung beetles from between two of its folds, lined their nest with banana leaves and brought out supplies: a packet of galettes, baked by Sylvie from cassava flour and smeared with tinned butter; a mug of sweet and creamy condensed milk, the only kind Penelope would let them drink; and their favorite toys, Kangy for Zara, a little stuffed lion for Chloe and a pile of picture books. "Read me a thtory," Chloe would demand, and they would curl up like fledglings to read and feast, while the sun played hide-and-seek in the leaves.

Zara never questioned the lack of school, for life in Seychelles had become a sort of extended summer holiday and she'd hated school anyway. Nor did she miss London, for how could dreary routines and dank skies compare to exploring a jungle or swimming in the balmy sea? But she did miss her mother's cuddles on rainy days, just as she missed the family life that seemed to have dissipated here like the morning mists. On the days when this missing was particularly acute, when her mother was shut up in her room and her father was at work, Zara either huddled in her kapok nest with Chloe, read for hours in the long cupboard behind her bedroom wall or sought the company of Marguerite.

Marguerite was the saving of the children in those early days. She was protective of children, for she'd had six of her own. She knew you needed them at the end, just as they needed you at the beginning. And she liked these two girls, these *ptit blans*. The pink one was so loving, so uncomplicated, still at the age that knows no resentment and harbors no ill. And Zara, yes, the quiet observer, the scamp, the girl who hid behind walls for hours with a book. Yes, Zara had a power, perhaps even the Sight. Marguerite would wait and see.

Her youngest son, Francis, helped when he wasn't in school. Fourteen, a good boy, strapping and strong, with a handsome, friendly face, smooth coppery skin and a head of curly reddish-brown hair. Every day, he would bring his mother fresh catch from the fishermen and jackfruit or guava from the trees. Zara adored him. He made her kites out of leaves and bamboo, and carved her little boxes from kapok wood, which she hid all over the garden and under the house. (The boxes frightened Marguerite when she discovered them, for they looked like the work of a sorcerer, but she assumed the little white girl knew nothing of that.) Best of all, Francis would whisper stories to Zara, stories she loved about ghosts and magic, the *bonnonm dibwa, Ti Albert* and *grigri.*

"What's a *bonhomme du bois*?" said Zara, who pronounced the Creole she was learning as if it were the French she'd been taught at school. "What's *grigri*?" Francis crouched down to tell her in a whisper that sent chills up her arms.

"The *bonnonm*, he is a mighty wizard. He can put a curse on somebody, he can cure the worst sicknesses, he can make someone love you forever. And the spells he uses, some call this *Ti Albert* and some call it *grigri.*"

A real wizard, just like in Daddy's stories! Right there on their own island! Zara could hardly believe her luck.

Francis soon became Zara's favorite companion. She would abandon Chloe at first sight of him and trot around at his heels all day. He got her to help him do the odd jobs of the house: fill the paraffin lamps for the many times the power went out, replace the cylinders of Calor gas for the stove, polish doorknobs and oil hinges, dig in the garden. Or he would put her in a wheelbarrow and push her about while she squealed, then shimmy up a tall and spindly coco palm, a huge knife between his teeth, knock down the resident tree rat, cut off a green coconut and toss it to her, calling out in Creole, *"Tansyon! Zetwal pe tombe!"* ("Watch out, a star is falling!") And after he had slid down the tree trunk as smoothly as if it were a fire pole, he would open a hole in the nut with one blow of his knife and give her its tingly coconut water to drink and spoonfuls of its jellied flesh.

"When I grow up, I'm going to marry you," Zara said.

Before long, Marguerite began taking the children to her own home as often as she could. At home, where she did not have to feign respect for fools and take orders from moping white women, she could put the girls safely in the care of Francis or her teenaged daughter Lisette and go about her own business: looking after her plants, her hens and her pride and joy, her coconut tree, whose sap fermented into the highly alcoholic drink known as *kalou*, the palm toddy to which so many island men were addicted.

Zara and Chloe didn't much like going to Marguerite's house, though. There was nothing to do there. Her house was nothing but a simple rectangular shack, divided in two by a bamboo partition, one side the bedroom, the other the salon, but she wouldn't allow the girls to play with anything in it, not even the plastic-wrapped dolls and knickknacks given her over the years by her employers. "These things are for looking only," she told them sternly. She let them play on the covered veranda, which was cluttered with old chairs, and in the dusty front courtyard, but she forbade them even the bedroom because it was so filled with beds you couldn't cross the room without stepping on one.

Marguerite had not always lived in a house this poor, propped up on wobbly slabs of stone, with a roof of rusting iron, walls of government-issued Masonite and no plumbing, just as she had not always swept other people's courtyards or wiped the bottoms of their babies. No, she had once been married with a fancy, middle-class house and a husband who earned. Love and *grigri*, however, had conspired to undo her luck, piece by piece.

Like most Seychellois, Marguerite was descended from a mix of rapacious white slaveholders and their African slaves, along with, in her case, a visible strain of South Indian, and the blend had made her a beauty. She had the light skin so valued by her countrymen and that long black hair Zara loved. Her face, broad in the brow, tapered to a small, fetching chin. Her eyes, when not narrowed in suspicion, were a wide and warming tea-brown, and her muscles were hardened by a lifetime of labor. As a result, by the time she turned thirteen, she was the object of many a man's desire and many a woman's envy. But her looks were not all they coveted, for her father, Charles Savy, was a harbor policeman, and this was a rare and privileged position for a Creole in the Seychelles.

Officer Savy, as he liked even his family to call him, was proud of his job but perhaps even more so of his uniform, every item of which was a dazzling white: the sea-captain hat, the short-sleeved shirt, the flared shorts, the knee-high socks and even the shoes. He was so proud of it, in fact, that he made Marguerite whiten those shoes, then starch the shorts with cassava flour every day, ironing them until they stood out like a tutu, exposing the knobbles of his dry and scrawny knees.

Marguerite's mother, formerly one Adèle Joubert, was more level-headed. Descended from slave and master on her father's side and a Bombay tradesman on her mother's, she had been a nurse in Victoria Hospital until she'd had babies, and had maintained a hospital-like regime in her household ever since. Strict and deeply Catholic, she made sure her daughters never missed school, attended church every Sunday and never walked out with a boy. The minute Marguerite entered puberty, therefore, the mothers of respectable young men came flocking, eager to snap up a girl who could not only give their sons light-skinned babies and money but was even, her mother assured them, a virgin.

But Adèle Savy was no fool, so whenever these suitors came courting, whether mother or son, she subjected each one of them to grueling interviews over cups of deliberately sugarless tea, while Marguerite, a fidgety teenager, eavesdropped from behind a door. Adèle grilled them about their assets and bad habits, screened out anyone who seemed diseased, lazy, poor or mad, and after three months made her selection. Marguerite was given no say in it at all.

The husband Adèle chose for her daughter, Henri Malbrook, was a man of forty, much too old for Marguerite's thirteen, as everyone knew, and ugly as a blowfish. But he had an excellent job managing a coconut plantation. And even more significant, he had a big house, which he'd been given by his employer, a *gran blan*, as the locals called the French landowners. And what a house it was! It was the best Marguerite would ever live in: a big white block of a place, with two floors, four shuttered windows and, to her great pride, a fifth under the red iron roof.

So the wedding day was set, and Marguerite was delivered to Henri trussed up in a white gown, ribbons and a veil. Henri's rotund body was inserted into a double-breasted blue suit, crowned by a matching fedora, his pudgy hands encased in filmy white gloves. Firecrackers were set off at the end of the church ceremony, and as the guests filed up the hill to the reception hall, they were preceded by no less than twelve fiddlers, one guitarist, a drummer, an accordion player and a little boy tinging on a triangle, all playing "Auld Lang Syne." Then, in a hall overlooking the sea, Marguerite's father and Henri's brothers gave long, erudite speeches in French, after which everyone tucked into a delicious cake and plenty of beer. The whole thing was beautifully arranged, all agreed, and the family had reason to be proud, not only because the wedding had been impressively pompous and Madame Savy most generous to the guests but because few Seychellois could afford a wedding at all, let alone one like that. As repulsed as Marguerite was by her old and hideous husband, therefore, she accepted her fate. Even at thirteen she understood the importance of weddings, houses and husbands, and then her mother had warned her not to expect physical pleasure in the beginning. "It will take time, *pti gate*," Adèle had said, "and if you are lucky, you will benefit from the experience of an older man. Wait and see."

But then Henri began to beat her. Isn't that always the way? Blind to the fact that she was still only a child, neither ready for him nor anyone else, he was convinced she was cuckolding him every minute, being so much younger than he and so pretty. He beat her until she wept and begged. And finally, after one terrible scene when he'd flung scalding soup at her in a rage, driving her to hide under the house all night among the rats and ghosts, she went to her mother.

"*Manman*," she said in the thatched kitchen shed behind the house, where her father and five siblings could not hear, "please help me." And in tearful whispers, she told of being chased around the house by Henri while he attacked her with a stick of bamboo. "I am sorry, I know I am disappointing you. But look." She opened her dress to show the burns and welts. "What should I do?"

The next day, just before dawn, Marguerite put on her newest cotton frock of coral pink, packed her basket as her mother had instructed (a small bag of copra, a papaya and three rupees), covered it with an embroidered handkerchief and crept out of her parents' house. Her chest tight with apprehension, she made her way up Morne Seychellois, Mahé's principal mountain, in the dark. She was not used to the climb because only the poor ever went up there, where they lived crushed together in shambly shacks, their thatched roofs falling down, their walls patched and their chickens skinny and tough, hopping about with one leg tethered to a broken coconut shell. Marguerite had been taught to despise these poor by her mother and so never visited them. They were the blackest of the Creoles, Adèle had said, the women slovenly and desperate, the men addicted to *kalou* and the fermented sugarcane juice known as *baca*. It was only later, when Marguerite had to work as a servant, that she grew sympathetic.

So she climbed the steep dirt road in the early heat, underneath an arch of thick-leaved trees—spreading mangos and bushy jackfruit, fat sang dragons that oozed blood red if you cut them, breadfruit hung with the yeasty globes that fed the island—wondering what she would find. For a whole hour she toiled under the rising sun, midges buzzing at her neck, until, panting and dripping, she reached the hidden path her mother had described, a path that plunged deep into the forest. She hesitated. Animals she did not fear, not even snakes, for none on the island were venomous. It was men she feared, the drunken no-goods who might waylay and molest her. She stood still and listened. The wind rustled through the trees with the sound of running water. A bulbul bird squawked like a jay among the branches. A fruit bat clucked nearby. But otherwise, silence. No, the men were still sleeping off their drink; she was safe. So on she trudged, clutching her basket to her flat teenaged stomach.

At last she saw it, an ornate wooden house almost hidden by a breadfruit tree with leaves like a crowd of giant hands. The house was perched upon cement pillars so tall she could have stood underneath without stooping, and a stone staircase led down from the veranda to an immaculate front courtyard of raked orange earth. All this indicated competence and success.

Pulling off her wide-brimmed straw hat to pat down her hair, which had frizzed up in the morning humidity, she replaced it, straightened her dress and stood in the courtyard, waiting for her panting and apprehension to subside. Finally she called, gently, like the cooing of a dove. She felt like a crazy person but that's what her mother had said to do. "Coo-ooo," she called.

A door opened a crack and the white gleam of an eye peered out of the darkness. "*Kwa?*"

"*Bonzour Imsye Bonnonm,* I am hoping you are free?" She held out her basket.

A dark hand extended from the doorway and beckoned.

She mounted the tall front steps with trepidation. This was much more serious than going to the fortune-teller in town, Madame Hélène, whom everybody consulted for little troubles here and there. A *bonnonm* or *bonnfanm dibwa* was a great deal more dangerous. It took years of your life to become such a person, to inherit or win the position from the one currently in power. Marguerite had heard it said that to qualify as a sorcerer like this, you had to murder somebody you loved.

The door remained ajar but the figure within had disappeared. Marguerite stepped over the threshold, then stopped to allow her eyes to adjust to the dark. When they did, she saw a parlor so cluttered with side tables and chairs she could make out no clear path between them. The wooden walls were festooned with old calendar pictures and postcards and dominated by a large portrait of a somber young Queen Elizabeth, whom everybody in Seychelles affectionately called *pti tantine*—little aunt. The parlor was stuffy, unlit and hot.

"Come, I haven't got all day," the *bonnonm* croaked. "In the back, quick!"

Marguerite wove her way through the furniture, following the voice into a back room.

There, sitting in the light of a slatted window shade was a dark-skinned creature so fat and shapeless that Marguerite couldn't tell whether it was a man or a woman. The sorcerer bore the name of a man, France Puissance, but in town some said he was really a woman and others that he was an hermaphrodite. Marguerite's mother said nonsense, it was only old Hortense, whom her own mother had known at school, but gazing at the creature now, Marguerite could not believe it. This person not only looked sexless but much too young to be the age of her grandmother.

"Well?" said the voice, deep as a man's, yet so rasping it could have been a woman's.

Marguerite held out her basket of riches. The *bonnonm* scooped them out without a glance, stowed the loot under a chair and gestured at her to sit. Outside, it had begun to rain.

She took a chair opposite the sorcerer, who was seated behind a small wooden table, and waited to see what would happen. On the table was half a coconut shell filled with twisted roots, a stack of worn playing cards, a clutter of tiny medicine bottles and tins and a small pile of freshly-cut wooden sticks, each three inches long. She was close enough to smell the *bonnonm* now, a sharp scent of sweat and ginger. It's a man, Marguerite thought. Only a man smells like that.

"How old are you, young lady?" *Bonnonm* Puissance rasped, sweeping his eyes over this nervous young girl: Pretty face, long rope of hair, body as compact as a calf's.

"I am fourteen, *Bonnonm*."

"And you have man trouble already? Is that why you have come?"

"Yes, Doctor."

The *bonnonm* shook his small, shaven head. Women were always coming to him like this with complaints of cruelty at the hands of their men, of being cheated or robbed, or simply because they were sick or desperate for love or revenge. But it was rare for a girl as young as this to seek his help.

"Come, then. Tell me."

They talked for some time. Marguerite told of how Henri took her brutally at night, paying no attention to her needs or pain; of how he beat and chased her and of how she wept every day for home and her mother.

"You have no children?"

"No, Doctor, it has not happened yet."

"And you have been with him how long?"

"One year."

"You have found no *grigri* against you?"

"Oh yes, I found some stones in a pattern outside my front steps the very day after I married, and my hair comb, it was gone."

The sorcerer clucked disapprovingly. "This explains it. You should have come to me a long time ago, *Manmzel*. You know who did this against you?"

Marguerite nodded. Many girls were jealous of her, of her cinnamon skin, her family and her rich husband, but none so much as the Lagrenade sisters, Charité and Alphonse and their baby sister, Joelle—bad, greedy girls who had never liked her.

"And the blue bottle, you have not found the blue bottle?" A bottle filled with blue water and hidden in your home signified a powerful curse, guaranteed to crush whatever happiness you might have scratched out of life.

Marguerite shook her head. "No, *mersi adye*." Her face grew hot. It felt blasphemous to thank God in the presence of a *bonnonm*, whom

everybody knew to be in league with the devil, despite the promise
to be good embedded in his name.

Bonnonm Puissance nodded, got up and hobbled across the room,
moving his bulk with difficulty, as if he had something wrong with
his legs. He wore baggy brown shorts and a huge blue shirt, which
made his bare head looked small and knobby. Taking first one jar,
then another from a set of dusty shelves, he returned to the table.
Pulling out a piece of tin, which had been hammered into bumps
with the point of a nail, he used it to grate a root of some sort into a
coconut shell, added some dry substance from the mysterious jars,
mumbled and fiddled, and finally produced a black powder. This
he folded into a small square packet of brown paper.

"You must burn this powder with three lumps of charcoal and
a clip of his hair in a broken pot," he said. "As the smoke rises,
you must stir it and say, 'Take the anger out of him so he cannot
beat.' Say this three times as you stir, you understand? After that,
you bury the pot and the ashes by the steps of your house, where
your husband passes every day, and he will grow calm as a cat with
its belly full. Understand?"

Marguerite nodded, wondering what was in those jars. She had
heard that sorcerers used the eyeballs and genitals of a bat, or the
bones of dead people, burned black and crushed.

"But do not put this powder in his food, *Manmzel*, or you will
make him weak. His member, it will sleep like a baby's." Puissance
winked. "And, *pti ser*, if he does try to beat you again, run to your
mama and tell the whole village until he is shamed."

On the way back down the mountain, Marguerite smiled to herself. She couldn't wait to make Henri weak as a baby.

Over the next four years, Marguerite bore Henri two children, no
more, for the *grigri* powder did indeed render his member reluctant
(she fed it to him quite often), along with her new willingness to

tell on him when he caused trouble. The first child was a daughter, Lucille, on whom Henri doted. He petted and fussed over her, sent her to school with a new uniform every year, and bought her a sewing machine and a pig for a dowry. Lucille now lived in Mauritius with her husband and four sons, where she worked as a seamstress. The next child was Marcel, Marguerite's first boy, who suckled at her breast until he was five. Marcel adored Marguerite the way she had always longed to be adored, but he drowned in the sea when he was only eight because he was foolish and reckless and would not listen when she told him to stay away from the water, but most of all, she was sure, because of the Lagrenade sisters' envious curse.

With no Marcel, the house did not matter to Marguerite any more. The five windows, the rush mats, the plastic-wrapped teddy bears Henri used to buy her after a beating—none of it meant a thing. So two nights after her son's death, her heart stricken with such pain she could barely breathe, she said goodbye to ten-year-old Lucille and walked away with nothing.

After that, Marguerite grew devoted to the *bonnonm dibwa*. She continued to go to Madame Hélène for little troubles, such as aches in the stomach or the womb, because the fortune-teller was nearer and cheaper and a good herbalist. But for the big troubles, those that made her life unendurable, Marguerite depended on Dr. Puissance. She went to him for the pain of Marcel's death, for protection against further curses and for revenge on Joseph, the man she lived with after Henri, when he was unfaithful. And in return she spread the word of the sorcerer's efficacy and wisdom. For Marguerite had learned that you could pray to God for help with every last breath in your body and yet never know what would happen. The help of a *bonnonm* you could buy.

After leaving Henri, Marguerite had to earn her own living, so by the time she started working for the Westons she had been a nanny for four European families already: one French and three British. While Penelope and Rupert were caught up in the shock of adjustment, therefore, she took over with a calm and watchful efficiency, mildly curious to see how this particular family would cope. That tall Monsieur Rupert with his hot, messy beard—he was weak, she could feel it. He strutted and puffed too much, like a cock afraid of losing his hens. And he was already growing fat with beer and pent-up lust. Oh she knew, for what secrets does a maid not know who washes the sheets and makes the bed, a bed in this case always unstained? Ripe for the plucking, was he. But Madame Penelope, she was a puzzle. She may have been wearing the shell of a snail for now, hiding in her room, feigning helplessness, but Marguerite sensed that inside that shell was something dangerous, something sly and lethal. So Marguerite put her head down, watched over the adults and guarded the children, and waited with Seychellois patience for time to reveal what would happen.

3

The cocktail parties of British diplomats were always the same, no matter where you were, Penelope mused as she and Rupert drove up to Governor's House on their first Saturday in Mahé. She surveyed the mansion without enthusiasm: A long white building, big as a barracks. Two floors of pillared verandas shaded by dark green blinds. And the whole packet perched on a terraced rise of shaven grass withering in the sun. It reminded her of the yacht clubs to which her old school friends belonged, full of stuttering gentlemen who thought they ruled the world. She sighed. She had been to enough of these affairs in London to know the routine. The wives were looked over like sides of beef, the men tested for their mettle, and everybody tootled in accents that showed off their pedigrees while they talked about nothing at all.

"God, it's hot," she said to Rupert as they climbed out of the car. "I don't think it's dropped below ninety since we got here."

"You're exaggerating. It was eighty-two yesterday. I find the climate quite temperate myself."

"How jolly for you." She tugged at her tight linen dress.

Earlier that day, Penelope had invited Zara and Chloe to help her choose an outfit for the party, knowing they loved to dress her up. Chloe, of course, had wanted her to wear one of the glittery evening gowns she'd worn on the ship, quite unsuitable for a cocktail party in the tropics. But Zara, old enough to be more practical, had settled on a pencil-slim linen dress of navy blue, with large white buttons marching down the front and a wide belt of white patent leather. "Wear these too, Mummy," she'd said, and held out the huge, white-rimmed sunglasses that Rupert thought made Penelope look like a mosquito. A becoming straw hat, high heels and a matching handbag—all in white—completed the outfit, which Penelope hoped would appear both fashion-plate elegant and alluring. "What do you think?" she'd asked the girls, twirling around in front of the bedroom mirror.

"You look like you used to at home," Zara said, her voice wistful.

Chloe pouted. "Don't want Mummy to go."

Back in London, Penelope's first act upon having been commandeered by Rupert to move to Seychelles was to visit a dressmaker. She had designed six smart frocks in linen or Liberty print poplin—each, she thought, suited to a government wife condemned to the tropics—with miniature versions for her daughters that, so far, they had refused to wear. As Rupert seemed unable to advance his career anywhere but in this remote outpost, she, at least, would try to help him by dressing like the wife of a man of consequence.

The door of Governor's House swung open the minute Penelope and Rupert approached to reveal a dark-skinned Creole in perfect butler uniform, save for the large beads of perspiration rolling down his forehead. He looked at them stonily, took their names and said in deep local accents, "Go get in now," which Penelope thought startlingly rude. Turning his trim and upright back, he led them into a huge drawing room full of people, where he deposited them like two cats in a litter box.

"Ah, Weston, we meet the wife at last," squawked a short, rotund man with orange hair and red-rimmed eyes scurrying toward them through the crowd.

Penelope held out her fingers and shook the man's sweaty hand. He looked, she thought, like a boiled toad.

"This is Roger Talbot, darling, my superior at the office," Rupert said in his usual ingratiating tones. "Talbot, my wife, Penny."

The man winked, running his eyes over her breasts. "Lucky beast, Weston. Come on, you two, time to pay your respects. The governor always likes to look over the wives." He winked again at Penelope, which made her badly want a drink, and led them over to the thickest clump of women in the room.

Penelope could see why the women were so gathered, for Governor Michael Toynbee was shockingly attractive. Tall and fair, with a trim, military bearing, an Etonian accent and the perfect manners of the powerful, he reminded her of a film star—Olivier, perhaps, or that new actor, Peter O'something. "My God, what a beauty you've brought us, Weston!" he said, shaking Penelope's hand and crinkling his long gray eyes into a smile. His crisp face was lightly freckled, his bony nose imperious. He beckoned over a servant to hand her a strong pink gin. "I hope to see a great deal of you two in my house. It will be a pleasure to gaze at such a handsome young couple." He turned back to Rupert. "Now, tell me the worst—how's it looking so far?"

Rupert shook his head with glum self-importance, which embarrassed Penelope so much she downed her gin in two swallows. "Mauritius has been hiking the prices of our imports quite out of reach, sir. They bear no resemblance to the original bills, and with our production as low as it is, we're hopelessly out of balance."

"Yes, yes." The governor sighed. "It's always been like that. Seychelles is the victim of its own location, I'm afraid, and until we build our own aeroport I don't see that changing."

"Yes sir. I know. It's awfully difficult."

"That, plus the attitude of the Seychellois, of course, who don't seem to give a damn about anything but toddy and women. But your poor wife, we must be boring her silly." Toynbee turned once again to Penelope. "I do apologize for talking shop, Mrs. Weston. Have another drink."

Thanks to a succession of such drinks, offered on small silver trays with pleasing punctuality by the servants, Penelope managed to do her duty as a government wife. She accepted an invitation to play tennis—although she couldn't quite remember from whom—flirted with a balding man here, an old codger there, and listened with apparent humility to the outpouring of advice each woman in the room seemed compelled to offer. The only moment that penetrated her gin-cushioned calm was when one unpleasant sack of a woman, who exuded evil intent the way other women exude perfume, said to her, "Darling, one word of warning: your husband will be chasing the native girls within the week. They all do. Nothing you can do about it." The woman, who was round, loud and so overcooked by the sun her cleavage had turned black, laughed the sort of laugh one hears at funerals. "Come for cocktails on Sunday. We must get to know you."

Nevertheless, by the end of three drink-laden hours, Penelope was enjoying herself. The high-ceilinged room was impressively spacious, the glasses and chandeliers blended amusingly when one squinted one's eyes and the gins were passed around with a speed that quite dazzled. The food was a bit sparse, she noticed, a few nuts, some canapé-like blotches on a tray, but who had any appetite in this heat anyway? No matter, the gins were well freshened with bitters and nobody was counting. And she had the further satisfaction of knowing she was the best-dressed woman in the room. I wonder what on earth happens to these government wives in the colonies that they so lose their sense of style, she mused, surveying the dumpy bosoms and gaudy patterns of the summer frocks around her. Rupert, of course, was nowhere to be seen, which was annoying, for Penelope would have liked him to notice her success. He was probably off in a corridor with some woman, flirting, as usual. (Oh Rupert, she thought with a pang, what has happened to us?) But at least she had the attention of plenty of other men. The governor especially seemed to have taken to her. I do like confidence in a man, she thought, it sets off the shoulders so well. Toynbee had such a masculine build, upright and taut, with no incipient belly like Rupert's and no silly beard, either. At one point, he took her elbow and bent toward her ear. "Mrs. Weston, I think you'll find this interesting. Allow me," and he steered her out of the room and along a stuffy corridor lined with portraits of previous governors, where he stopped.

"You see that man?" he said, pointing to a frightened-looking gentleman in a tidy gray wig. "Chevalier Jean Baptist Quéau de Quinssy, commandant of Seychelles for thirty-three years. He was one of those fellows who blows with the wind, Mrs. Weston, I'm sure you know the type. Under the French he was Quinssy, as you see by his name on the plaque there. But once we took over, he changed his name to Quincy, ran down the tricolor and hoisted up the Union Jack without a blink!"

"But why did he stay here so long?" Penelope said, her mouth flapping oddly. "What did he like about the place? It's so . . . far away."

Toynbee smiled down at her. "You've only been on the island a few days, poor child, you're still in shock. You'll become as addicted to the warm seas and gentle clime as the rest of us soon enough. Our islands are most seductive." Toynbee dropped his baritone voice to a purr when he said that, and swept his eyes over her entire body. "Now, come along with me and I'll show you a governor who had real integrity."

He took her elbow again and steered her past several other stiff gentlemen to one who, being wigless, looked considerably more modern. "Now here is my favorite of my predecessors, Dr. Percy Selwyn-Clark. He was made governor in 1947 and was quite a reformer. Up until then, I'm ashamed to say, we Britons hadn't done much for the Seychellois. We more or less left them to their own devices for a century and a half, which is why they've stayed so damnably French."

"Yes, I've noticed. All those Catholic schools, and that peculiar patois they speak." Penelope hiccupped.

"Well, it's Creole, actually. Mostly French, but with a mix of Malagasy, English and Hindi stirred in. But indeed, as you say. They still have the Napoleonic Code, which is quite absurd for a British territory. But it's our fault, really. We left them to rot, more or less, until this fellow came along. He not only built houses and started schools, he reformed the hospital and the leper colony."

"Are you going to do something like that?" Penelope peered up at him blearily.

Toynbee smiled. "I'm doing my best, my dear, doing my best."

Perhaps Rupert could make something of himself if he hooked onto this man, she thought—a man of true ambition.

"Now, if I may, I'll show you the other gallery," Toynbee said, "the one with the real pictures." He led her around a corner to another corridor, this one lined with lush paintings of ships tossing on green, pasty seas. "Ships are a passion of mine. In fact, I spent quite a few years in Her Majesty's Navy before taking this job. Now I merely collect paintings of ships, alas for me—vicarious sailing, you might say. Speaking of which, how was your voyage here? You came on the SS *Kampala*, I believe?"

Penelope swayed on her high heels, the mere memory of the voyage enough to make her a little seasick. "Awful. We got caught in a storm and the ship bounced about like a cork."

"Yes, I heard about that. Bit of a hurricane, I gather—unsettling. But I am fond of a British India ship. Good seaworthy vessels, and pretty, if modest in size. Not unlike that delicious little ear of yours." And the next thing she knew he was nibbling it—the ear, not the ship—and the seasickness was getting worse. She swayed again, the gin heaving inside her with its own wavelike action, and found herself leaning against him, a little fuzzy about precisely where she was and who, exactly, had his tongue in her ear. It tickled, sending a hot tingling down her spine. She moaned.

"You must visit me, soon," Toynbee murmured, sliding a firm hand over her buttocks. "I shall send my chauffeur," and he led her back to the cocktail party.

But did any of that happen? Penelope wondered in the car on the way home that evening, her head spinning. She couldn't be sure, sitting there in the ridiculous Austin Mini they'd rented, the size of a pea pod, with Rupert folded up beside her, smelling of whiskey and sweat. For at the end of the party she had found herself standing by a window, not quite remembering where she was, gazing at the stretch of lawn, which looked like a transplanted English park in the dusk, except for the palm trees. "Lovely people," she said aloud in the car, or thought she did. "Very welcoming."

Rupert clenched his teeth. "God, Penny, did you have to drink that much? You were an embarrassment."

"No, no, that wasn't me, sweetie, that was you," she slurred. "I have many invitations already. I shall show myself a great asset to you here, I believe. Help you climb the proverbial ladder. Isn't that why we came here, darling, so you could climb the ladder? Please slow down, you're about to slaughter a native."

Gaggles of brown and black people along the dusty road, eyes white or bloodshot in dark faces, wide straw hats, baggy shorts and sundresses, colors everywhere one looked, bright, happy colors. Placidity and joy—so different from the crooked-toothed rat faces of the English poor. How do these people do it? Penelope wondered. How do they laugh in the streets in their bright whites and yellows, their oranges and blues, their smells of spices, their multitudes of skin shades, banana bunches slung over their shoulders, huge baskets of fruit on their heads . . . how do they stay so vital? I, she thought, feel about as vital as a dead leaf.

"Rupert," she said aloud, or perhaps in her head, as he pulled the car up to the house, "I have to lie down." And she entered the front door, weaving, one high heel kicked off, limping up and down like a piston until she found herself prostate on her bed, temples pounding. Who am I? she thought.

Marguerite watched from the veranda.

Rupert followed Penelope in and sat on the edge of the bed, looking down at her. "Can't you pull yourself together, Penny? You never made a spectacle of yourself like this at home. You can't be that unhappy, can you?"

She squinted up at him through the headache now clawing at

her temples. He'd turned bronze and hairier than ever during their voyage here, and had taken to wearing absurd khaki outfits, as if he were a Victorian big game hunter. Indeed, there wasn't much difference between a stuck-up Victorian husband and her own, she thought. He was living out some silly boy's adventure story, beetling around in pith helmets and governor's mansions, for God's sake, while he expected her to stay home and rot.

"What am I to do while we're here, Rupert, since you've taken me away from everything I'm interested in? There just isn't anything for me to do."

He shrugged and pulled his beard. "I thought we'd agreed you'd school the children and throw the odd dinner party. You know, whatever it is you do in London."

"How could we have agreed on anything when you wouldn't talk about it? And London was different, although I don't suppose I can expect you to understand that. You're too busy thinking about yourself."

"Oh, for Christ's sake. You really know how to be unpleasant, don't you, Penny?"

She ignored him. "I didn't spend seven years slogging at boarding school to sit about in the middle of nowhere with no friends and nothing to do. You didn't marry an idiot, you know. I would have gone to Oxford if I hadn't married you."

"But you said you didn't want to go to Oxford. You said a man was much more interesting than anything they could teach you at university."

"Well, it was true then. You were interesting. Now you're not."

Rupert sighed and stood up. "I'm not going to listen to you—you're drunk. But you know, we can't continue this way. You won't even let me sleep in the same room with you anymore. What's a husband to do?"

Penelope closed her eyes. A husband is to be someone to rely upon not to break his promises. A husband is to avoid humiliating his wife by dragging her halfway across the world while flaunting his flirtations under her very nose. A husband is to crawl out from his own skull once in a while and notice his wife is a human being. But all she said aloud was, "Oh, go away and let me sleep."

Rupert stood looking down at her. He didn't like the way her long, delicate face—thin nose, oblong eyes, the tight line of her mouth—blurred when she drank, and he certainly didn't like this new sharpness of tongue. She seemed nothing like the lovely and graceful girl of eighteen he'd met dancing at the Hurlingham Club a mere ten years earlier. He'd been smitten the instant he'd seen that Penelope, slender as a spoon, with a deep laugh and a saucy wit, and even more so once she'd waltzed and bantered with him for a week. He was twenty-one then and a student at Cambridge, but he'd thought her superior to all the girls he'd met there, lovelier and more self-contained by miles. In fact, he'd been almost frightened of her, which seemed quite odd to him now. After mustering up the courage to ask her out, he'd spent three nights tossing in bed, trying to plan every moment of the outing so nothing would go wrong.

The first part of the evening had gone fine. He'd arrived at her house, a drab semidetached in Richmond, exactly on time, where he was greeted by her mother, who proved to be large and forbidding, with a plummy voice and Penny's long legs. "How do you do, young man?" she'd said a trifle too eagerly, and ushered him into the sitting room to wait. "Now, have some whiskey and tell me all about yourself. What does your father do?"

"Um, he was in the Foreign Office," Rupert had replied, taken aback at her forthrightness. "That is, before he was wounded."

"Oh, I'm sorry. And you?"

"Well, I'm a second year at Cambridge."

"Jolly good!"

He did not mention the squalor into which his parents had slid since his father had come home crippled from the war: the walls stained with damp, the parade of tenants they'd been obliged to take in, the screams in the night and teacups hurtling at his mother's head, her voice drained of joy or verve. Perhaps that's why I'm so keen on Penny, he'd thought, staring at the avid pink countenance of her mother. Penny is bursting with verve.

Then at last Penny had appeared, smelling of the latest Chanel and dressed like a model in a flaring green skirt, tight pink pullover and steel-tipped stilettos. Everything about her was enticing: her enormous cerulean eyes, her flip of brown hair so cheekily modern, her conversation full of that very sparkle Rupert's mother so lacked. How proud he had been to walk down the bombed-out streets of London with her, the cold tweaking their noses! He took her to Leicester Square, where they sat in a freezing cinema with their overcoats on, holding hands and feeling wonderful.

After the film, they'd caught a bus to Kensington so Rupert could introduce her to his parents. He lived just off the Cromwell Road, on a street lined with pillared town houses, once elegant, now shabby. He led Penny past a bomb site, exposed wallpaper and naked fireplaces dangling off its walls, and up the front steps of his home, all the while plotting to avoid his parents altogether and seduce her instead. But when he saw her examining the soot-grimed facade of his home, and its chipped and peeling blue door, his confidence faltered.

"I live three flights up," he said meekly. "I hope you don't mind the climb." He ushered her ahead of him up the staircase, carpeted in old brown rug, the banister greased by years of tenants' fingers. The smell of frying sausage followed them up like a spy.

"Do your parents really live here?" Penelope said over her shoulder, her mellifluous voice full of doubt.

"Yes, on the ground floor. I have my own flat upstairs."

"But you said I was going to meet them."

"Well, I thought you were, but I forgot they went away for the weekend. I . . . um, here we are."

He unlocked his door, rattled by his lies, and switched on the light, a naked bulb in the ceiling that lit up his beige walls to unfortunate effect. Crouching, his overcoat hunched about him, he fed his last two shillings of the week into the meter and lit the gas fire with a match—three rows of ineffectual blue flames. The room was frigid.

Penelope stood, shivering in her green woolen coat, gazing about with what he assumed was dismay. Rupert knew his place looked like the lonely bed-sit of an old bachelor, not the cheerful home of a young man with a future. His bedspread was a fecal brown, his green linoleum floor bare and cold. He hoped she would at least be impressed by his several long shelves of books.

"How long have you lived here?" she said.

He flushed. "Since the end of the war."

"Lucky you, having a place all to yourself!" And to his relief, she smiled.

"Do sit down, please," he said quickly. "I have some gin. Would you like some?"

There was nowhere to sit but the bed. Penelope perched at the foot of it, her overcoat drawn about her. Her delicious long legs poked up from her skirt, the kneecaps whitening under the pressure of her nylons. "Yes please. Do you have any tonic?"

Rupert did. He pulled out a bottle from his sock drawer and poured the drinks into two blue enamel tooth mugs, hoping no toothpaste would show. Loping over to hand her one, he folded his six-foot-two frame beside her, still wearing his overcoat, too. "It'll warm up in a minute. Cheers."

"Cheers," she replied, giggling. They clinked mugs and drank.

At last, loosened by two gin and tonics, Rupert explained why he'd been living in the servants' quarters since he was fifteen. "You see, when my father came home from the war he had lost both his legs, so Mother said she couldn't look after the two of us anymore and sent me up here. My father's a bit difficult, I'm afraid. He shouts at Mother all the time. I thought I'd spare you the spectacle." He smiled bravely. "But it's all right. I'm used to fending for myself. It's made me old for my age."

Penelope looked impressed, then offered her own confessions, which Rupert found unexpectedly shocking. For one thing, it turned out her own father had died only a week earlier, on Christmas day. "He went out to the garage in the middle of dinner and gassed himself in the car," she said, her voice oddly flat. "I was the one who found him." Her uncle Keith, she went on quickly, had returned from the war unable to talk or eat meat, and wept inconsolably at the sight of his own hands. Her younger brothers were increasingly impossible—James, at eleven, already showing signs of juvenile delinquency, ten-year-old Roddy unable to stop fiddling with his privates in public. And finally, she said with a shrug, her mother kept on insisting that they all behave as if Daddy hadn't gone anywhere at all.

Rupert murmured sincere enough condolences as he listened to Penelope's story, but all he could really think about was tearing off her clothes. For two weeks now, as he'd stumbled around the Hurlingham Club ballroom with her, his long legs tangling beneath him, he had been trying to imagine what her breasts must look like under her bullet-shaped brassieres and tight pullovers. He longed to push up her skirt, undo her bra and suspender belt, pull down her knickers and examine every part of her. He longed to make her moan for him. But how to begin? She looked so impenetrable sitting there beside him, her lips and nose thin in her narrow face, her blue eyes so virginal. She looked so polished. He had no idea what to do.

For three hours, they sat in the dim little room talking and sipping gin but getting, as far as Rupert was concerned, nowhere.

Then, unfortunately, Penelope had looked at her watch. "Oh God, I have to go," she said, leaping to her feet. "I'll be stranded if I miss the last train!"

Rupert jumped up, too. "But—but you needn't leave yet," he stammered. "The station's not far. Why don't you take off your overcoat? It's warm in here now."

Penelope looked at him quizzically and headed to the door.

Desperate, Rupert darted in front of her and shoved her onto the bed. Flinging himself on top of her, he struggled with her overcoat buttons while she flailed beneath him.

"Ow!" she cried. "You're crushing me. Don't be ridiculous, Rupert. I have to catch the train. Ow!"

"Sorry, sorry, terribly sorry," he muttered, but he kept trying to burrow his way through her thick layers of clothing. Then something wet and sharp clamped down on his chin and squeezed.

"Bloody hell!" he yelped, and she took advantage of his surprise to shove him off her with such strength he landed in a heap on the floor. Rupert sat up, his hand to his chin, staring at her.

"Good-bye," she said crisply. And fled.

That might have been the end of it, had Rupert not come to his senses. He dashed from the flat, thudding through the dark streets, and caught up with her at the tube station. "I'm sorry, I'm terribly sorry," he panted. "I've been a fool. Forgive me, Penny, because I've fallen in love with you."

And now, ten years and two children later, here he was standing by Penny's bed a million miles away from London, not sure whether he loved her at all anymore—or what, in fact, love even meant.

4

Zara squatted on the wooden floor of the large and breezy kitchen, a heap of spiky pandanus leaves in front of her. Marguerite was crouched beside her, teaching her how to weave a mat out of them, crisscrossing the long thin blades and folding them over at the tips to prevent them springing apart. Biting her lower lip in concentration, Zara threaded one leaf over another and then under the next, over and under, until it held. Still, her mat came out crooked and full of holes, not a perfect tight rectangle like Marguerite's.

"Where is your sister?" Marguerite said in the mix of English and Creole she used now with the children.

Zara shrugged. "I fed her to the spider. Can I plait your hair?" Zara loved Marguerite's hair, so long and heavy. She loved the way Marguerite wore it, too, the plait circled around her head like a tiara, or dangling down to her waist in a rope. Sometimes Marguerite let her undo it, brush it and roll it up into an enormous bun, but usually she kept it tightly pinned to her head, like a Sunday hat.

Marguerite cuffed Zara playfully. "You must look after your baby sister, it is your duty. She is sad when you leave her."

"I don't care. She's boring." Zara shoved her mat away. "I can't do this! It looks horrid."

"Shush, shush. Here, give it to me." Marguerite tried to show her how to keep the lines of her leaves straight, but Zara grew too restless to pay attention. Casting her eyes about the kitchen for other entertainment, she spotted a column of black ants carrying granules of sugar from the kitchen counter to the floor, so she abandoned the weaving to set them an obstacle course.

"Look, I can make the ants walk over the treacle spoon till they get stuck!" She lay on her belly to watch them flail and drown, imagining herself their size, turning the world huge while she shrunk to a speck. What would she do if confronted by a lake of treacle? Eat her way through it? Spend three days finding a path around its edge? She watched an ant lumber into the sticky trap and then try to pull itself away, tearing off its leg as it struggled free, and it reminded her of the ship's swimming pool like a bowl of blancmange and of the starfish embedded in her father's paperweight.

Marguerite sat back on her heels and watched the top of Zara's head for a minute, that head of tangled hair nobody could brush, under which was a mind full of mystery and mischief. She wondered if the girl had only the Sight or if the Evil Eye had entered her, too. For the child could turn toward darkness if she so chose. She had a streak of it already—look at the joy with which she tortured those ants. Had Zara not been so young, Marguerite might have been afraid of her, a malevolent spirit like that, so full of cruelty and cleverness. Why, Zara had learned enough Creole in two weeks to understand a dangerous amount of what was said around her. She brought her sister to tears ten times a day. She played by herself for hours, humming and mumbling and scrabbling in the dirt. And most significantly, she read books deep into the night, and books, Marguerite had been taught, held the key to unfathomable powers. My task, she said to herself as she studied Zara, is to turn the child's powers from darkness to light.

Marguerite rose to her feet with a grunt, emitting a waft of the baby oil she used to smooth her skin and the curry with which she flavored all she ate. "I am going to find Chloe," she said and slapped out of the kitchen, the hem of her faded red dress swinging over the backs of her thick knees. Chloe worried her, for both

Madame and Zara had been neglecting the child so often of late—Madame sunk into her battle with Monsieur, Zara occupied with Francis and her own inner games—that the poor baby had grown listless and fretful.

Once Marguerite was gone, Zara propped her chin on the dark wooden floor, inhaling with pleasure its shoe-polish smell of fresh wax, and watched the ants carry away their dead, hoisting them onto their backs like coal sacks and marching off without a stagger. Placing a clean spoon over the treacle as a bridge, she baited it with sugar so the ants would climb to the lip of a bowl, heave themselves over it and climb down inside, where she crushed them with a pestle. Satisfied with that, she dug out one of Francis's kapok boxes from its hiding place in a zinc-lined flour drawer and opened its lid. In it she had hidden a dead dung beetle, the claw of a ghost crab—those speedy white crabs that scurried all over the beach, darting into their sand holes as quick as a blink—and a bright yellow curl she had snipped off Chloe's head. Carefully, she added a spoonful of crushed ant. She wanted next to include a cutting from Penelope's long fingernails, and then to take the box to the *bonhomme du bois* Francis had told her about, the sorcerer who would teach her how to use this medicine to cure her mother.

For Penelope had changed again. After two days of lying in bed, then sitting in long silences at the supper table, she had turned into a storm trooper. She raged about the house issuing orders, snapped at the children and at Rupert, on the increasingly rare occasions he was at home, and disappeared for hours every day dressed in bright tennis clothes, returning bronzed, muscular and bossy.

"Nana?" Zara had said the other morning while Marguerite was helping Chloe dress, for this was the children's name for Marguerite now. "What's the matter with Mummy?"

"I want Mummy," Chloe said, nodding.

Marguerite was sitting on the edge of Chloe's bed, holding her between her legs as she brushed her yellow mop of hair. "Nothing is wrong with your mama. What are you saying?"

"Don't be silly," Zara retorted, sounding just like Penelope. "Of course something's wrong with her. She's cross and horrid. And she's making Daddy not want to come home."

Marguerite sighed, buttoning up the back of Chloe's white sundress. "Well, perhaps your mother, she is homesick, you know? It happens to many English when they first get here. She will be better soon."

"I don't think that's what's wrong with Mummy," Zara said. "I think somebody's put *grigri* on her."

Marguerite glanced at Zara, startled. "What do you know about *grigri*?"

Zara shrugged. She had already dressed herself in navy-blue gym shorts and a sleeveless shirt, and was busy hunting for her sandals under the bed. "Nothing. But at home Mummy used to take us places and play with us. Now all she does is shout and stamp about. Francis says when people start to act different like that it's because they're under a spell."

Marguerite considered Penelope's changeability toward the children, hugging and reading to them one minute, ordering them out of her sight the next. "Yes, perhaps he is right. Maybe the Evil One, he has put a worm in her heart. Sometimes I think I do see a demon in your mama, a Somebody Else in her soul."

Zara stood up to look at her. "You mean you can see a worm inside Mummy's eyes?" Francis had told Zara about the worm you could get here, how it burrowed into your feet and crawled through your body until it reached your eyes. "You can only see it at midnight," he'd said. "That is when it comes out to swim in your eyeballs and look at the world."

Marguerite returned her look sharply. "Why do you ask, little heart? What have you seen in your mama?"

But Zara was thinking too hard to answer. In her mind she saw herself gazing into her mother's blue eyes to see another face staring out at her, a snake face with an evil expression. A chill dropped over her. "I want my old mummy back," she whispered.

"Do not worry, little one. We will find some medicine to help her. I will talk to the doctor."

"Don't like doctors," Chloe said, wriggling in Marguerite's hands. "Nana, let me go. I want pawpaw juth."

Ignoring her, Zara stared at Marguerite. "You mean the *bonhomme du bois?*"

Marguerite placed Chloe aside, frowning. "There is no *bonnonm*, this is only stories. I will talk to the doctor. Leave it to me."

But Zara was not the type to leave anything to anybody, not when she cared about it this much. She wanted to bring her mother back to the way she'd been in London, when they'd hunted silkworms together in Holland Park and brought them home on a mulberry leaf to watch them weave their silken cocoons. Those days Mummy had played Monopoly with her, and had found her books in the library about insects and birds. She had laughed and tickled, too, and served chocolate biscuits for tea. Mummy hadn't shouted at Daddy all the time then, but had welcomed him home at the end of the day with funny stories and a hug. She hadn't ignored Zara so much, either, but had cuddled her when she was sad and bought her lollipops when she'd had a miserable day at school. She'd been a proper mummy then, not sick like she'd been on the ship, and not like she was now, kind one minute, cross the next, marching about in her white tennis clothes and barking orders like a policeman.

So Zara took to stalking Penelope, catching her fingernail clippings and hair strands and snipping tiny holes out of her clothes, which Penelope thought were caused by moths. And she put them all in her little boxes, the way Francis said to do, waiting until she'd learned how to use them.

Having left Zara to her ants, Marguerite found Chloe asleep in Penelope's bed, which saddened her. The baby girl was always crawling in there when she felt lonely, curling up in her mother's leftover smell, sucking her thumb. At times Marguerite had watched her rocking and singing to herself in an off-key chant, "Mummy, Mummy, Mummymummymummy," until she'd fallen asleep. Marguerite didn't approve of leaving a three-year-old alone so much, with no playmates but her capricious sister and no adults but a nanny. Why, Madame had become so busy with her new friends and tennis that she never took the poor child anywhere, or bothered to find her other children to play with. And as for Monsieur, he rarely came home these days until dinnertime, and when he did, it was only to quarrel with his wife. So that afternoon, after Penelope had returned from one outing and was preparing to leave for yet another, Marguerite stopped her in the foyer, where she was pasting on lipstick in front of a long, teak-framed mirror, and ventured to speak.

"Excuse me, Madame," she said in the best English she could muster, "I would like to talk."

Penelope blotted her lipstick and peered into the mirror without looking at her. "What is it?"

"It is *ti koko*, the baby."

"If you're speaking about Chloe, use her name, for God's sake. It's hard enough to understand a thing you say as it is."

Marguerite suppressed a snort. Penelope's rudeness amused more than offended her. It was so clearly the product of weakness, so much an imitation of somebody else. Penelope always sounded like a child trying to mimic her teachers.

"Chloe, she is sad, Madame. She cry all the time. She calls for you. She needs other babies to play with. Zara, also. It is not good for little girls to be so alone like this."

"I really don't think it's your place to tell me how to bring up my children," Penelope snapped, although Marguerite's words, in fact, pierced her. "You presume too much."

Marguerite muttered and shrugged, flip-flapping out of the room. I see right through your fragile skin, Madame white woman, she said to herself. I see your cold little heart shriveling up to a stone. I see your sex wilting like an old flower. I see your fear turning you blacker than I will ever be. And I see your husband with another woman, an evil woman—Joelle Lagrenade, one of those sisters I have always despised.

Penelope dropped her lipstick into her handbag, annoyed with herself. Whatever had possessed her to be so rude? She was being much too bad-tempered these days, with both the servants and the children. It made her feel awful, but she didn't seem to be able to stop. Rupert was off in his pith helmet fantasy, spending more and more time away from home and treating her with open irritation. Her daughters were turning savage before her very eyes. And she was hopelessly distracted by sex with Governor Toynbee.

The governor had first summoned her two days after the cocktail party. "Weston, I have a favor to ask," he had drawled down the telephone. "Would you mind if I send the car for your wife tomorrow? I would like her opinion on some new pictures I've bought. She has a jolly good eye for pictures, did you know? Tell her to be ready by four, would you?"

"Yes, of course, sir. Thank you." Rupert was surprised. Could his inebriated wife have made a favorable impression after all? "Penny!" he'd called. "You've been invited to Government House."

Penelope received the news with inner gratification and outer nonchalance. Rupert might be ignoring her, but at least this Toynbee fellow seemed to find her worthwhile. Perhaps his attention would encourage Rupert to notice her again, to see her value through another's eyes.

She spent a good deal of time choosing what to wear. (She did not, this time, invite the children to help.) The sheer white voile blouse, she decided, with a full pink and white striped skirt, cinched at the waist with her patent leather belt. Hair up high on her head, the fringe sprayed and glossy; lipstick outlined in shimmering fuchsia. And to top it off, her most fashionable white high-heeled sandals, the ones that revealed a slightly obscene row of squashed varnished toes.

At the appointed time, the chauffeured car pulled up to the house and sat purring until she emerged. Rupert was at the office, of course, so there was nobody to see but Marguerite watching at the door and Zara peeking out from up in the kapok tree. Penelope was a little disappointed at the sight of the car, for although a Rolls-Royce, it was a scratched and mud-splattered gray—rather outré for a man people called His Excellency. Nonetheless, when she slid inside she found it luxurious enough, the backseat upholstered in cool maroon leather, the Creole driver uniformed and silent. When he shut the door behind her, the slam echoed against the house like a gunshot.

During the drive, Penelope gazed through the window at the bright and tumbling vegetation, tin-roofed shacks and the dusty road, wondering what Toynbee's wife did in this wilderness. For he had a wife, of course—a Kate or a Catherine or something— one could hardly be governor without one. There were children, too, and a tutor somewhere, she remembered dimly from the party. Perhaps if Toynbee liked her enough, she could persuade him to allow her children to play with his, because Marguerite was right, of course, the girls did need some company. Yet, as the car entered the long, elegant driveway, her plans gave way to dread. What am I to say? she thought in a panic. Who am I pretending to be? Why am I going to this man's house alone? If only Rupert would return to normal, if only we could be a family again, curled within our nest—if only he and I could be close the way we were those first years, then I wouldn't be spinning off like this, a stone flung into space. For she and Rupert had been close in their early years of marriage, much closer than either of them had thought possible. Young and desperate for intimacy, for something warmer than servant garrets and war-torn families, they had clung to one another in bed, on long walks and over dinners, confessing and re-confessing their pasts. Rupert admitted to the bullying he'd suffered at his Warwickshire school, where he'd been sent to wait out the Blitz, and the hurt he'd felt at being banished from his parents' flat on his return. Penelope described the years in Devon and her near-instant dismissal to boarding school right after the war. "We won't send our babies away like that, will we?" they'd agreed, even before Zara and Chloe were born. "We shall keep them with us, even if there's another war, and stay a family." Oh, the talks they'd had in those days! With her cheek on Rupert's reassuring chest, Penelope had found herself able to speak for the first time about Uncle Keith shaking and wetting himself like a baby, and of the night she'd found him in the bathroom trying to cut his throat with her father's razor. She told Rupert about her father, too, and how he'd wept every evening in his study, in deep, rend-ing whoops, hating himself for having been too asthmatic to fight while his little brother was sacrificed instead. She even told him about the night before her father killed himself—Christmas eve, 1950—when he'd crept into her bedroom, knelt at her feet, put his head on her legs and sobbing with shame and apologies, had begged her to let him treat her as wife. Yes, she had told Rupert all her secrets, as he had told her his, and he'd held her close and said, "Never mind, darling, it's all over now." But it wasn't, was it? It wasn't over at all.

Toynbee greeted her himself this time—no butler—his yellow hair flaring in the sunlight. "My dear, how kind of you to come," he said, drawing her arm through his and ushering her into a private sitting room she hadn't seen before. "I'm afraid Kate had to be in town today to attend a meeting. She works much harder than I do, having twice the brains."

Penelope laughed politely. She suddenly and urgently wanted not to be there.

"A drink, my dear? Pink gin, if I remember from the party?"

"Just a G and T, please." Penelope's voice wavered a little and she saw her long face flash at her in a mirror across the room.

Toynbee strode to the mahogany bar on one side of the room,

which was furnished just as one would expect of a tropical government house: stark and unimaginative, full of dull browns and beiges, save for the effervescent sunlight that insisted on slipping through the window shades. He loped back to her, a gin and tonic in each hand.

"Cheers, to a lovely woman!" He clinked her glass and she drank deeply. Her nerves were buzzing, and a light film of sweat clung to her limbs.

"Come, my dear, bring your drink and tell me what you think of my new picture." He hooked her arm into his again and marched her out a back door and along a bare back passageway, which she suspected was meant for servants. On the way, they passed a curious and vulgar sculpture, mounted on a pedestal between two windows. Penelope couldn't help stopping to look at it. Made of dark, gleaming wood, it was the shape of a plump woman's pelvis, with a patch of hairy substance precisely where one would expect. She peered closer, for the hairy substance looked uncannily natural, as if it had actually grown there.

"What on earth is this?" she said, trying to sound amused. "Not a Henry Moore, I hope?"

"No, no. Deliciously obscene, isn't it?" Toynbee replied with a chuckle. "Actually, it's nothing but a bilobed coconut. Not made by man at all. Purely the work of God. You haven't seen the *coco-de-mer* before?"

Penelope shook her head. Even the word *bilobed* sounded obscene to her.

"It's one of our Seychelles specialties. Grows nowhere in the world but on two of our islands, Praslin and Curieuse. The nuts are enormous, as you can see, the biggest seed on earth, in fact. This one's only a kernel, polished of course, so you can imagine how huge they are in their husks. They can weigh more than forty pounds, you know. When General Gordon, the one who died at Khartoum, was stationed here in the 1880s, he took this for the original apple of

Eve—you can see why—and decided he'd discovered the Garden of Eden."

"Must be awfully dangerous to walk underneath. I wouldn't want a forty-pound nut falling on my head," Penelope said with a nervous giggle. The thing was so aggressively sexual it made her blush.

Toynbee patted her hand. "The poor man was terribly excited by his find, though. He not only thought the *coco-de-mer* was the Tree of the Knowledge of Good and Evil but that the breadfruit was the Tree of Life. Everybody thought him a fool, of course, but he was convinced. Come, let's look at my newest ship."

Drawing her arm further into his, he led her down the passage to a hidden room at the end, a cozy study lined with teak bookshelves and stacks of paintings. Letting go of her arm at last, he picked up one and laid it flat on an enormous leather-topped desk. "Take a look at that. I think it's rather good." He plucked her glass from her hand, put it on a bookshelf and stood leaning over her shoulder.

"Look at that marvelous detail," he said, pointing to the meticulously painted crow's nest on top of the ship's mast.

She murmured approval, although in truth paintings of ships all looked the same to her, technical and dull, whether they were tossing in storms, lying in a port or sailing out to magnificent horizons. Who cared when there was no story, no emotion, no patterns or people? This was boy's stuff, like engineering and building sets; it was design, not art. The only thing worth looking at was the artist's rendition of the sea, whether it looked real and wet, threatening or magnificent, or simply like lumps of sticky oil paint.

Oh. For Toynbee had pushed her facedown over the picture and was lifting her skirt. In one swift tug, he'd divested her of her underwear, exposing her bare behind to his gaze. "Lovely," he murmured, running his hands over her, spreading apart her buttocks, her vagina, and the next moment he was in her, thrusting hard and fast, hurting her a little, his hands squeezing the wired shells of her brassiere. She had barely thought to protest before it was over, he was out, her knickers were up, her skirt down, and they were walking back to the sitting room where, he said, the chauffeur was waiting to take her home. "For I have an appointment, you know, terribly sorry. I'll send for you again on Tuesday."

And there she was, in the back of the car again, marooned on maroon seats, a new stickiness between her legs and a sense of shock turning her numb. Was that what she had come for? Was that what she had wanted? Had she embarked on the first extramarital affair of her life only to discover it was nothing but a gin and a poke? Yet that night, lying in bed awash in a confusion of guilt and triumph, she slid her fingers between her legs, thinking of what Toynbee had done to her, of herself bent over and exposed to this strange man's gaze, not shocked any longer but aroused.

And so it went, two or three times a week, with few variations, the act jarring and not particularly pleasant, the memory of it making her writhe with desire in the night. It gave her a routine around which to arrange her days, now that Rupert seemed to have no need of her. Her mornings consisted of tennis, consultations with Sylvie and Marguerite about dinner and the children, and gin-soaked lunches with the other government wives. Her afternoons were filled with sunbathing and swimming at the beach, followed by a duck into the bathroom to insert the pink and powdered disk of her diaphragm (recently legalized by Her Majesty's Government for married women only), a quick visit to Toynbee to be poked, teatime with children and, usually, preparations for a dinner party. Thus, Penelope told herself, I exact my revenge.

Marguerite had almost been right about Rupert, but not quite. He had not, in fact, slept with her old enemy Joelle Lagrenade since arriving in the Seychelles, although he would have liked to, but he had managed to become obsessed with her. Joelle was a high-toned *rouz*, as the locals called people with a light or reddish skin, who worked as a secretary and typist in his office. She had been recommended for her excellent English and speedy, obedient fingers by his immediate superior, Roger Talbot, the squashy man Penelope had met at that first cocktail party. Talbot had also made it clear that the women in the office were there for the taking, if one helped things along with a few little presents.

"What sort of presents?" Rupert had said to him over a whiskey at the British-only Seychelles Club a few days after his arrival. (He and Talbot had become friends of a sort because Talbot gave him a lift to and from work every day so Penelope could have the car.) "What do these island women want?" He genuinely didn't know, for Rupert was not used to buying women. He had fallen for Susan Winslop, his mistress in London (and, unfortunately, the wife of one of his office mates, Ian), because she was his sort, the type of girl he used to meet at the Hurlingham Club—well-bred and outspoken, if a trifle dim. He had only started sleeping with Susan because she adored him, God knows why, and because Penny seemed so uninterested in him in bed. After making love to Penny, he could feel her disappointment settling over them like an eiderdown, manifested in her silence and the rapidity with which she turned her back to him and fell asleep. They never even made love more than once a week; she always seemed more interested in talking. Whereas Susan squealed and squirmed, panted and scratched and did whatever he asked. Penny, he never dared ask to do anything but lie on her back, so afraid was he of her icy compliance.

Yet Rupert did not consider himself the philandering type. (Mrs. Slater, the blonde on the ship, was a mere flirtation.) He was much more interested in family and stability than sexual adventure. Look at how he'd loved Penny at first, and how he adored his two darling daughters. He had been faithful for his whole marriage until he'd met Susan, and he'd felt awfully guilty once that had begun, so much so that he'd welcomed this post in the Seychelles as a chance to put an end to it. No, he wasn't out to conquer and seduce. He only wanted what any man deserved: good sex and enough admiration to get him through life intact. The trouble was, Penny hadn't been giving him either of these things for years. And now, here he was, bewitched.

Rupert had felt impossibly flustered by Joelle from the first moment she had wafted past him to sit at her desk. A musky scent of coconut oil and some sort of island magic had drifted after her, settling around him like a cloud of gnats, bringing his attention inexorably to her body as she placed herself in the chair before him. She was tall and strong, with broad shoulders, majestic breasts and a long neck crying out to be brushed by his lips. Her sturdy thighs and high buttocks were enticingly outlined by her full yellow skirt, and her face was as sculpted as Nefertiti's, with long Egyptian black eyes and a mouth plump and inviting. But best of all was her dusty red skin, earthy and mouthwatering, smooth and supple. Rupert was struck dumb. He had never in all his life seen anybody, smelled anybody, longed for anybody so blatantly sexual.

"Good morning, Mr. Weston," she'd said that first morning in excellent English, her Creole accent rolling into a throaty purr. Rupert stuttered. She crossed her legs, showing a flash of rosy thigh, and poised a pen over her notepad. "I am ready," she murmured, a phrase he heard as full of promise.

"My dear boy, don't fret over the presents," Talbot had told him at the club, a third whiskey in hand. "These island girls are so poor they'll take anything. Cheap perfume, bottle of beer. Soap, a rupee or two. Whatever you have lying about at home and don't want, dear chap. Easy as taking a lollipop from a baby." He grinned, his pale, pinkish eyes looking a trifle devious. What he didn't say is that he'd tried to buy Joelle for himself and earned a resounding rejection.

"Really? It's that easy?" Rupert said, feeling encouraged. "Should I give it a shot, do you think?"

"Of course, old boy," Talbot replied disingenuously. "We all do."

So each evening when Rupert came home from his office, he would check over the cool, tree-shaded house to see whether Penelope was out, and if she was, ferret through her things looking for abandoned objects. He had tried the Indian and Chinese shops in town, but everything they contained was so much the same (mass-produced dolls and trinkets, embroidered handkerchiefs, baskets and hats, bolts of cheap cotton) that he felt stingy offering those to the delicious Joelle. And the perfumes and ointments they sold smelled terrible to him, like the cheap stuff of shopgirls. So he resorted to theft. This would have been easier in London, where Penelope surrounded herself with bric-a-brac, for there she shopped like an addict, bringing home sacks of clothes and jewelry, half of which she stowed away in a box and forgot. But to come to the Seychelles she'd had to be frugal and pack almost nothing, so the pickings were slim. Still, he found a ring he'd never seen her wearing, a tiny silver chain-link purse he'd given her years ago and a wispy silken scarf of vibrant blue. (He hesitated over that, for it did match Penelope's eyes exactly. On the other hand, when had she ever gone in for wispy scarves?) I wonder if Joelle will even like any of this? he thought as he pocketed his loot. If he were in London, he would have wooed her like a gentleman, taken her to dinner or the theater and sent her flamboyant bouquets of flowers—thrown himself at her feet, treated her like a queen. Here, he had to resort to bribery. And he flushed with something like shame.

If Joelle was pleased with the presents, she certainly didn't show it. She simply took the proffered object, which Rupert found himself presenting with ever-increasing blushes and stammers, slipped it into her basket without even looking at it and carried on as if nothing had happened. Rupert was flummoxed. She didn't even thank him. Could she tell he had stolen it from his wife? Were the gifts beneath her? Was she contemptuous of him, trying so blatantly to buy her like this? He had no idea.

What am I doing? he thought as Talbot drove him home after his third failed attempt to elicit some gratitude or warmth from Joelle. I steal from my wife, lie and cheat, and I can't even buy a woman who is there to be bought. If Penny knew, she would hate me.

5

Zara took a deep breath and dipped her face into the sea. She had persuaded Penelope to buy her a snorkeling mask and a rubber ring, and now each time she was taken to the beach she swam a little further out to watch the fish. And the fish were plentiful there in her corner of the Indian Ocean, fed by a coral reef and dotting the water in all the colors of confetti. Zara explored for hours, just as fearless as she'd been in the ship's pool, her little body afloat in its rubber ring, her flippers splashing quietly, her snorkel burbling in the warm and gentle waves.

Zara's mind flowed freely there underwater. No storming Mummy, no worry about why Daddy never told his stories anymore, no annoying Chloe, scolding Sylvie or clucking Nana underfoot. Only Zara and the fish, who had made her their monarch. She tried again to grow gills but the magic had gone out of that, so instead she became a mermaid queen with the powers of a *bonhomme du bois*. She designated each fish a role in her court. The yellow angelfish with the bright blue stripes were the horses who would pull her chariot, the blue and turquoise parrot fish were her footmen, the zebra fish her maids, the orange and white clown fish the cooks and the shoals of razor fish, who swam head down like rows of exclamation marks, were her soldiers. Her palace was an ever-shifting landscape of greens and blues, lit by the white sand below, sun sparkles above, and furnished by rocks, coral and shells in deep reds and oranges. Some of the fish would tilt upward to look at her, their little mouths in astonished circles, others would follow her, a whole shoal of them glittering and playing between her legs. Zara found she could reach out and touch one, they were so unafraid. Once she saw a barracuda, another time a shark, but as she didn't know what they were she had no fear. Zara was queen.

Chloe, on the other hand, was afraid of the sea. She would splash in the surf if someone stayed with her, but otherwise preferred to remain under the thick-leaved takamaka trees that bordered the beach, cuddled up against whichever adult had come with them: sometimes Marguerite but more often her daughter, Lisette. For the further Zara ventured, the more Chloe clung, as if her sister had sucked all the courage from her.

Finally, driven by hunger or thirst, Zara would wade out of the ocean to demand refreshment. *"Mon swaf,"* she would say imperiously in her newly acquired Creole, still in her mermaid-queen mode, and if Marguerite were there, her lack of manners would earn her a cuff. Lisette, however, would only shrug and hand her a bottle of Coca-Cola, expressly forbidden by Penelope, or some of the island's fresh passion-fruit juice. Then Zara would throw herself down in the soft sand, wiggle into it, along with pine needles and ants, coconut husks and fallen takamaka leaves, which looked like huge leather tongues, and gaze up into the swaying trees, trying to catch sight of a bird to tell her mother about. Most often she saw mynahs, which were everywhere, upright as robins, black with white flashes on their wings and yellow bandit masks around their eyes. Bulbuls were common, too, their bodies a murky green, their heads crowned by a cheeky tuft of black feathers—they liked to kick up a ruckus in the trees. But sometimes she would see a sooty tern in bold black and white, sometimes a Madagascar *fody*, exactly like a sparrow whose head had been dunked in red paint, and often, flying over the water, a white tropic bird, trailing long tail feathers like smoke. But best

she liked to spot a frigate, gliding high and black against the sky like
a jag of ink, its long tail straight as a stick and its enormous wings
as majestic as a pterodactyl's. I'll tell Mummy about that one, she'd
think. Mummy used to like hearing about birds.

Lisette was a dreamy girl of sixteen who never entered the water.
She preferred to sit under the drooping ostrich feather leaves of a
casuarina pine, or the solid shade of a takamaka, humming and
yawning. Like most people born in the Seychelles, she could not
swim. Also, like them, she was inured to its beauty. The mist-
swaddled mountains, alabaster sand and velvet-smooth boulders,
the palm trees bent by the wind, as if bowing to the summer blue
sea—to all this she was indifferent. She was more concerned with
her marks at school and with her dreams of becoming a teacher like
Michel Deschamps, the mathematics professor with whom she was
hopelessly smitten.

Lisette was a good student, quick, and ambitious in the class-
room. She had Marguerite's sturdy build and good looks, her eyes
large and clear, her smile dimpled and sunny. She also had her
mother's head for business, so was of great use in keeping track
of the family's income and expenses. But like Marguerite, she was
prone to falling in love, and for a year now had suffered a pain
ful crush on Deschamps, a strapping youth of twenty-two who was
the heartthrob of the school. During the daily mathematics lesson,
he would stride back and forth, waving his elegant hands as he
explained algorithms and theorems in his deep, thrumming voice,
while Lisette followed him with her eyes, moony and lost. To him
she was one of many pretty girls to flirt with (the nuns adored him,
too). To her he was fodder for endless dreams of romance, the principal one being that she would become as good a teacher as he, they
would marry, start their own school and become famous.

Lost in these dreams, Lisette often kept the children at the beach
all afternoon, heedless of Chloe's fretting or Zara floating out of
sight. But at last, when the daylight dipped into evening, turning

the sea a silvery pink, she would mutter, "Time to go," lift the sun-groggy Chloe onto her waist (Chloe was always peeling and sun-burned now, and covered with mosquito bites she wouldn't stop scratching), and saunter back to the Weston home, swaying her hips and swiveling her pretty eyes, on the lookout for boys who might admire her. Zara would scamper behind, collecting coconut husks, collecting shells and dead crabs and insects for her *grigri* until, sandy and exhausted, she and Chloe would stumble through the door barely in time for supper.

One evening, two months into their stay on the island, the children came home from just such a long day at the beach to find their mother in a rage. "Oh for God's sake, can't you look after yourself at all?" she snapped at the sight of Zara's salt-matted hair. "You're filthy!"

"I am not!" Zara said, wounded at her mother's words, but more at her neglect and weeks of bad mood. "You don't care anyway," she added, kicking a chair.

At that, Penelope seized Zara by the arm, hauled her into the bathroom and before Marguerite could stop her, took a pair of scissors and began chopping off the long, ratty tangles that framed Zara's face.

"Madame, stop!" Marguerite cried in horror at the bathroom door. "Let me take her to Monsieur Chanson the barber—"

"Absolutely not," Penelope snapped, cutting, cutting with a dreadful clashing sound. She bent over her and hissed, "That, my girl, is what you get for being so insolent and for never combing your hair when you're told!"

For the first time, Marguerite was truly angry at Penelope. What reason could Madame have for attacking the child so cruelly? Was it not enough that she slid off in the governor's car whenever her husband was out, which had set the whole island gossiping, and that she paid almost no attention to her own little girls? Perhaps she did have a worm in her heart, as Zara had said. Or perhaps she had

found out at last about her husband and that scheming *bordel*, Joelle
Lagrenade—for everyone else on Mahé knew by now that Rupert
was sleeping with his secretary. Even so, Marguerite thought,
Madame had no business taking out her troubles on the girl.

Yet even more disturbing was Zara herself. She did not cry. She
didn't even whimper. She simply shut her eyes, screwed up her little cat face and uttered not a sound.

Chloe wandered in then, as luck would have it, and when she saw
her mother slashing at Zara's head, her blue eyes grew large. "What
are you doing, Mummy?" she squealed. "Thara's hair's all gone!"

Marguerite picked up the child and whisked her away, for Chloe
was already sobbing with fright. "Zara's hair is not all gone, little
heart, do not cry. Your sister will have a new hairstyle, that is all.
Very chic, very pretty. She will look like a . . ." What would she look
like? Marguerite cast about for comforting words, but all she could
come up with was coconuts and dusty bare stones. "She will look
like a . . . like a little brown bird."

But this only set Chloe off more. "I don't want Thara to be a
bird. I want Thara to be Thara." Marguerite had to take her to the
kitchen and feed her condensed milk and some of Sylvie's special
coconut balls dipped in Lyle's Golden Syrup before she could calm
her down.

After Penelope had tossed the scissors onto the bathroom shelf,
pushed Zara out of the room and ordered Marguerite to sweep up
the chopped hair, she announced she was retiring to her room and
was not to be disturbed. "And Marguerite," she said in the crisp,
cold voice she had been using lately, "let this be a warning to you,
too. You were hired as a nanny, which means you are to see to the
grooming of these girls. They are an embarrassment. What do you
think other people will say? Who will have them to their houses
when they look so dirty? You hear?" And with that, she slammed
into her room and locked the door.

Without a word, Marguerite took Zara into her arms and hugged her for a long time. Still the child would not yield. She stood there, unbending as a stick, and waited in silence for Marguerite to be done with this demonstration and let her go.

"Come," Marguerite said finally, "let us see what Nana can do with your poor little head." She put Zara in the bath—although the girl was not at all dirty, whatever Madame said, having been washed all day long by rain and sea—and gently shampooed the remaining few inches of hair. Zara sat, a brown nugget in the tub, silent as ever, her eyes squeezed shut. But just as Marguerite was about to pour a bucket of water over her hair to rinse it out, Zara opened them and looked right up at her.

"Close your eyes!" Marguerite exclaimed. "The shampoo, it will sting."

"I want it to," Zara said. "I want the shampoo to wash out the worm. It will wash it out, right, Nana?"

"What worm, *choux choux*? You have no worms."

"I think I have the demon worm that lives in people's eyes, the same one Mummy has."

"No, no." Marguerite shook her head. "This is not true."

"Yes, it is. I can tell. I can tell because it's making me hate Mummy."

That night, when Marguerite put the children to bed under their mosquito nets, she sat in a rocking chair and tried to soothe them with an old story she remembered from her childhood.

"This one is about a clever servant of the king whose name is Kader," she began, settling a cushion into her back and stretching her tired legs out with a sigh.

"What's he look like?" Zara demanded.

"Oh. Well, he looks like Francis, of course. Are you ready?" Marguerite leaned her head against the back of the tall chair, smoothed out the old pink skirt of her dress and crossed her muscular arms.

"*Byen*. One morning the king called Kader to him and he said, 'Kader, go to the sun and ask him why he sets red and rises red.'"

"Which king?" Zara interrupted again.

"Uh, it was King George."

"King George would never have asked a stupid question like that," Zara muttered.

"Zara, shush and listen. So, Kader, he traveled far to reach the sun, and on the way he passed a fish who was stranded on the beach. He picked him up and threw him back into the sea. 'Thank you, Kader!' the fish cried. 'You have saved my life.'"

"Fishies don't talk," Chloe declared with a giggle.

"Then Kader continued on his way to see the sun, and he passed a baby bird who had fallen from her nest. He picked her up and put her back in. 'Thank you Kader,' the baby bird said, 'You have saved my life.'

"Finally, Kader got to the sun, just as it was halfway gone over the horizon. '*Imsye* Sun,' he said, 'My king has sent me to ask why you set red and rise red.'

"'I cannot tell you why I set red and rise red,' the sun answered. 'Go to church and ask a priest. And tell your king to pay off his debts, and that the queen of the fish is much prettier than his dead wife.'"

"Ooh, that's rude!" said Chloe.

"Chloe, will you shut up?" Zara snapped, for she was caught by the story now.

"So Kader, he traveled back to the king," Marguerite continued placidly, "and he told the king what the sun said. And the king, he said, 'Kader, I want to marry this fish queen. Go catch her for me.' So Kader, he went to the sea, but he did not know how to catch the fish queen. Suddenly, a fish jumped up. 'Remember me?' he said. 'You saved my life. How can I repay you?'

"'Bring me the fish queen,' Kader told him. 'The king, he wants to marry her.'

"So the fish brought the fish queen, and the king married her happily because she was so beautiful he could not stop kissing her. Her eyes were big and blue and her long, yellow hair hung all the way down to her backside."

"Fishies don't have hair!" Chloe interrupted again, and was once more hushed by Zara.

"The years passed, and the king and fish queen were happy. But then the king got old and the fish queen stayed young. 'Kader,' the king, he said one day, 'find me a *tizann* to make me young again, so I can please my wife.' So Kader went out, but he did not know how to find such a *tizann*. He was walking past a tree, when he saw two blackbirds. 'Kader, remember us? You saved our child when you put her back in the nest. What can we do for you?'

"'Find me a potion to make the king young again.'"

"So the mama bird flew up and took seven drops of water from paradise, and the papa bird flew down and took seven drops of water from hell. 'Take these both,' they said to Kader. 'You never know when you will need them.'

"Kader gave the king the water from paradise to drink, and he grew young and so handsome, the fish queen, she loved him again. But the years passed and once more, the king grew old. 'Get me another *tizann* to make me young again,' the king said, but instead, Kader gave him the water from hell. The king died and Kader married the fish queen himself."

"What a cheat," Zara muttered.

Marguerite leaned forward in her chair and dropped her voice to a whisper. "One day I was walking in the forest on the mountain, and I met this Kader. 'Ah, Monsieur Kader,' I said with a wink, 'I see you got yourself a beautiful fish wife.' He was so angry he kicked me all the way down the mountain until I landed right here with you."

Zara would have loved that story had she been in a better mood, especially the part about King George marrying a fish queen. But all she did was grunt, pull the sheets over her head and say, "Nana, you tell stupid stories. Leave me alone."

Clucking at this rudeness, Marguerite heaved herself up from the chair and kissed the girls good night on their foreheads, filled with indignation at their mother. Why did Madame have to make the poor children so unhappy? They had harmed no one. She closed their door and tiptoed downstairs past Madame's room. And inside, quietly but distinctly, she heard the sound of sobbing.

A few hours later, Penelope awoke to unbearable remorse. She had downed the wine left over from dinner and cried herself to sleep like a child, but now could no longer hide from what she'd done. It frightened her, this behavior, for she had never been like this in England. She'd never been gratuitously cruel to the children, and she certainly hadn't stormed about like a Medea, picking fights with her husband and collapsing into tears. It was all because of the way he had changed since they'd got here: his indifference, his short-ness with her, his long absences driving her into the arms of another and, she had to admit, not very nice man. Or perhaps it wasn't only Rupert but both of them. For what did either of them know, really, about how to be good parents, or even about marriage? Nanny O'Neill certainly hadn't taught her, nor had boarding school. And nothing Rupert had learned from his schoolmates and beaten down mum had helped him either. The war had stolen their childhoods, taken them away from everything normal, and perhaps they had only been playacting at happy families ever since. "Oh God," she thought, "what will become of us?"

Flinging herself out of bed, she ran upstairs to the children's room and yanked aside Zara's mosquito net. Zara bolted upright, startled out of sleep.

"My poor little Zouzou, I am so sorry," Penelope moaned in a whisper. "Are you all right?"

Zara looked at her warily.

"Oh God, I'm not fit to be a mother. I'm destroying everything, falling into negligence and depravity . . ."

Zara stopped listening. She didn't understand half the words her mother was saying and didn't want to understand the other half. She shrank back against the pillow, her eyes widening under her newly cropped hair.

"Come, darling, come with me and I'll try to make it better." Picking Zara up, Penelope carried her downstairs—quite easily now that tennis and swimming had strengthened her arms.

Chloe whimpered, peering hopefully at her mother from behind her mosquito net, but nobody noticed.

Penelope put Zara in her bed and lit the hurricane lamp beside it. She climbed in and drew Zara onto her shoulder, moving her as if she were fragile. "Now let's cuddle together, the way we used to," she said, her voice humble. "But first, sweet one, I really am sorry for cutting your hair so angrily like that. I should have taken you to a hairdresser in Victoria, if there is one, instead of doing it myself. It was beastly of me. Will you ever forgive me?"

Zara felt too confused to reply.

"I'll take you tomorrow, all right? We'll make you look so pretty! And think, no more tangles to hurt when you brush your hair! And after the hairdresser, I'll take you to the Chinaman's shop and buy you a present. Would you like that, little button?"

Zara still didn't answer. Instead, she lay stiff and wary, more certain than ever that something was wrong with her mother. This wasn't the helpless Mummy from the ship, the fun Mummy from home, the feeble Mummy from those first days in Mahé. This wasn't even the angry Mummy from the past few weeks. This was a Mummy she didn't recognize, a Mummy with the worm.

Summoning her courage, Zara sat up, climbed on top of her mother and leaned right over her face, staring into her eyes. It was dark outside, perhaps even midnight. Maybe now was the time the worm would come out and prove Zara right. She peered even closer into her mother's tear-and-wine-reddened eyeballs.

"What are you doing?" Penelope said uneasily.

"Mummy, open your eyes wide."

"You want me to make a funny face?"

"Yes, like me." Zara widened her eyes into a googly glare.

"All right," Penelope said, relieved that her daughter wasn't too angry to play a game.

Zara bent closer, placed her fingers around her mother's eye sockets and spread them wide. She stared so long that Penelope finally twisted her head away.

"Ow, that hurts, darling."

Zara continued to squint into her mother's face. The lamp wasn't bright enough to see properly. But she had caught sight of something in the corner of one of eye, a wiggly red thread. Could that be the demon worm?

The next morning, right after breakfast, Marguerite took the children to her own house to give them a reprieve from Madame, who seemed to have gone quite mad. "Nana?" Zara said as they walked down the hill, Chloe trotting beside them, her pudgy hand in Marguerite's calloused grasp. "If I went to see the *bonhomme du bois*, would he teach me how to kill Mummy's worm?"

Marguerite shook her head, tutting. "Shush, you are talking nonsense. That Francis, he has a big mouth and he tells a lot of lies." She should have warned him not to speak about the *bonnonm* within hearing of this English girl. The activities of a *bonnonm* were illegal, for one thing, a jailable offense, as were those of the fortune-teller she went to see all the time. But more important was that powerful secrets such as these were dangerous for children, let alone a child as absorbent as Zara. "Go catch the hen and see if she has laid any eggs," she said once they arrived, and slapped off in her sandals to tell Francis to keep his mouth shut.

Zara pouted, squatting in Marguerite's sun-scorched courtyard to scratch at the hot red dust with a stick. Why wouldn't Nana tell her about the sorcerer? Francis did, Lisette did, the women in the market talked about him all the time. Why not Nana? Irritated, she poked a hole in an anthill and watched the ants swarm up the stick, dropping it before they reached her hand. Zara liked digging for ants and termites, or crawling under houses to see what she could find. Marguerite always shrieked when she saw her there, shouting about spiders and ghosts and chicken *kaka*, but Zara wouldn't listen. She was hunting the way Mummy had taught her to hunt, and hunters weren't afraid of anything. She had captured a leaf insect so perfectly resembling a green leaf that its head was like a bud and its legs were nicked to mimic the bites of aphids; and a stick insect that had startled her when it moved because she'd thought it a twig. She had caught praying mantises, dung beetles, and giant cockroaches, too. Her favorite prey, though, were the geckos that lived in the house and the garden. The inside ones were so translucent you could see their hearts beating, while the outside ones were bright green. And all of them had the delightful ability to shed their tails if attacked and run off unharmed, leaving the tails writhing behind to distract predators. Zara had learned to capture those tails and hold them up to a shrieking Chloe. Once, she would have kept all these treasures to show to Penelope. Now, she put them in her kapok boxes to use for *grigri*.

"Thara?" Chloe came toddling up, her legs sturdy in their white saddle shoes, her yellow sundress smeared with red dust. "I want to go home. I want Mummy and Daddy."

Zara looked up at her. "Would you like to grow bigger?"

Chloe cocked her curly head to one side and thought a long time. She squatted next to Zara, her thick cotton knickers bulky between her pudgy thighs. "Bigger like you or like Daddy?"

"Bigger like me, silly."

Chloe rumpled her brow a minute, her eyes blue like Penelope's, not dark brown like her sister's. She nodded.

"Because I heard about a potion that makes you grow so fast, you wake up big the very next morning."

"Where?" said the ever-gullible Chloe.

"Come with me." Zara crawled under the house, Chloe following on all fours. When the two girls had settled in the back, out of Marguerite's sight, Zara said, "You see all the red in this dust?"

Chloe nodded. "It's red because it's magic. It's full of iron, Mummy told me, which makes you strong and big. And it tastes like cinnamon. See?" Zara scooped up a patch of dirt and pretended to eat it. "That's why I'm so much bigger than you. I eat some every day."

Chloe scooped up some dirt, too, for indeed it was the color of cinnamon, and took a tentative lick.

"Isn't it good?"

Chloe looked down at her hand dubiously.

"Well, some of it tastes better than other bits. You have to try different pieces to find the right flavor. Let's try the dry bit over here."

Chloe crawled over and sampled some dry red dust. "Better," she said.

"Good. Eat some more of that and you'll be huge in the morning. I'm going to find Francis." And Zara crawled away, trying so hard not to laugh her belly cramped.

Back out in the sun, she spotted Francis about to climb the coconut palm to collect the *kalou* for his mother to sell. *Kalou* was made by shearing off the growing tip of a branch and hanging bamboo cylinders off it to collect the dripping sap, which fermented into alcohol so fast that after only three days it was too dangerous to imbibe. Only householders over sixteen were allowed to draw *kalou*, as the government strictly licensed the heady stuff, and only men were supposed to climb the trees, which meant that if you were a woman you had to either rely on male relatives to climb your tree or pay a man to do it. This was an annoyance to Marguerite, especially as her second man, Joseph, had tended to drink more *kalou* than he sold—one of several reasons she had booted him out. On the other hand, owning a *kalou* tree was perhaps the safest investment a person could have. All Marguerite had to do was pay the police an annual license fee and sell the toddy; it needed no treatment other than a single day to ferment (sometimes she added a little sugar, too) and the tree produced eight to ten bottles a day. Furthermore, she was never short of customers. Men appeared every morning to buy and drink a full bottle on the spot, staggered off to work, then came back on their way home in the evening for more. It was money in the pocket and took almost no effort at all.

Marguerite's main worry was that because she was needed at the Weston house so often, she had to leave Francis in charge of selling the *kalou*, which at his age was illegal. Back when his father Antoine had still lived with them he had run the tree and the garden. But that was over now, alas. Antoine Dupuis, the only man she had ever loved, had left her for another woman and not even the *bonnonm*'s magic had been able to stop him. The thought still burned so fiercely it made Marguerite's chest tighten into a hard, aching knot.

Zara strolled over to the *kalou* tree and stood there to watch. She was fascinated by the way Francis climbed a coconut palm. He would stand at the bottom, jump onto the trunk and shimmy up it in little springs, his arms hugging the tree and his bare feet clinging to it like a gecko's. To get down, he held on with his hands and feet and simply walked backwards.

"Can I come up, too?" Zara asked, gazing at Francis, who was unhooking a foot-long cylinder full of *kalou* from the top. He didn't answer.

"Franceeeeees!" she yelled. "I want to come up, too!"

He peered down at her, this little white girl who'd turned almost as brown as him. What a troublemaker, he thought affectionately. He regarded her as a little sister now, if a rather naughty one. As Marguerite's youngest, he'd never had anybody trail after him adoringly before.

"No, *pti ser*, it is too dangerous," he called back. "Anyway, girls don't climb trees."

"I do." It was true. Zara was always up in the branches of kapok and wiry frangipani trees around her house.

"Girls should never climb trees. It is not decent." Slinging the rope handle of the cylinder over his shoulder, he virtually ran down the palm tree and landed with a little jump without spilling a drop. "I'm taking this in to Mama." He went into the kitchen shed behind the house. When he came back outside, Zara had gone.

"Zara, you little monkey, where are you?" he called, his voice already deep and rich, although he was barely fourteen. He looked around. "And where is Chloe?"

"Here me." Chloe waddled up to him, looking her typical mess. Her mouth was covered in red dust and she'd cast off her clothes, as usual, and was burning and naked in the sun, except for her leather shoes.

Francis sighed. "Where is your dress?" he said, as he had to several times a day. Chloe pointed under the house. "You went under there?" She nodded. "*Manman* and me, we have told you a hundred times to stay out of there. It is dangerous and dirty!" Chloe began to cry. Irritated, he picked her up and carried her to the edge of the house. "Go under and get your clothes, quick, before my mother sees." He wouldn't go under himself. He was too afraid of the house imps and devil spirits who lived there, not to mention the filth of animal excrement. "Perhaps the spirits don't like white people," he thought, as he watched Chloe's little pink bottom disappear. "These English girls don't seem to suffer from them."

Chloe came out a second later, carrying her dress and underpants scrunched up in her hands. The pants were soaked with urine—she had taken to wetting herself several times a day, which was one of the reasons she was always stripping off. With some disgust, Francis took her by the hand and led her to his mother, who was on her knees digging around her cassava roots, her arms flexing with the effort and her face shaded by a wide-brimmed straw hat.

"*Manman*," he said, "Chloe's pissed herself again."

Marguerite put down her trowel and sat back on her haunches. "You are too old for this! You think you are a baby still?" she scolded Chloe, slapping her gently on the buttock. She took her over to the water bucket to wash her down.

Having rid himself of one nuisance, Francis went to look for the other. "Zara!" he called. He wasn't in the mood for her silliness right now. He wanted to go play football with his friends before he had to come back to sell *kalou* to the men returning from work.

"Hee-hee," he heard. He looked around. Where could a child

hide here in the open courtyard? Had she gone off into the forest?

"Look up, stupid." So he did. And there she was, halfway up the sixty-foot coco palm, hugging the trunk with her arms and legs as if she'd been glued there.

"Ai!" he shouted. "*Merd*, you will get killed! Come down quick, before anybody sees you." He darted a look over his shoulder, hoping his mother hadn't heard. "Come down!" he hissed.

"How?" she said.

"The same way you went up, *enbesil*, however you did that." But how did she do it? She must be a lot stronger than she looked.

Zara peered down fearfully. Climbing up the tree had been one matter, her bare feet sticking somehow to its trunk. But getting back down was quite another. "I can't. It's too far."

At first Francis tried to coach her down, but Zara was afraid now and wouldn't budge. She had climbed almost thirty feet, determined to prove to him that girls weren't the saps he thought, but now the ground looked far away and very, very hard. Furthermore, she had used up all her strength in climbing and her muscles felt shaky and weak. It was all she could manage to cling to the treacherously smooth trunk and wait.

God, I'm going to have to go up and get her, Francis realized, and quickly, before *Manman* sees me. He wished he'd built a bamboo ladder up the tree, as his mother had been nagging him to do for years.

Hoping Marguerite wouldn't catch them, he shimmied up the trunk until he reached Zara. He couldn't carry her in his arms, as he needed both to clasp the tree. He would have to take her down on his shoulders.

"Sit on me very carefully," he said to her in a fierce whisper. "If you wriggle or scream or lean back or move, I will fall and we both will be dead. You understand?"

Zara nodded. Her throat had closed up and she couldn't speak. Slowly, with several gasps of terror, she lowered herself onto Francis's broad but bony shoulders, her hands still wrapped around the tree trunk. Francis grit his teeth. How could a child so skinny weigh so much? She felt like a great sack of yams.

"Now hug the tree and do not let go," he said. "I am going down slowly and you must let your hands slide down the tree. You understand?"

Zara whimpered.

Francis clung to the trunk as hard as he could, sweating. Normally, clambering up and down palm trees was as easy as walking to him, for he'd been doing it since he was six, but he'd never had to carry such a weight before, let alone a weight alive and terrified. He released his thigh muscles enough to slide with a jerk down six inches. Zara shrieked.

"Shut up!" he hissed.

Francis was now stretched out as far as his body would go, his arms clinging too high, his hips slung too low—he should have been bunched up and springy. The sweat poured into his eyes.

"*Ar mou dye, o syel*, Mother of God, Jesus Christ Almighty . . ." He mumbled prayers in his head, the prayers that had been drummed into him every morning by the nuns at school, and released his hands just enough to slide them down level with his shoulders. Zara swayed dangerously around his neck, but she made no sound.

The next time he lurched down, Zara teetered back, losing her balance, and almost tore them both off the tree, but she righted herself just in time. Francis froze, heart pounding, waiting for the strength to return to his legs. His thigh muscles were shivering, his palms stinging. Clenching his jaw, he slipped down another length, and this time Zara stayed steady. And so, inch by inch, he lowered the two of them until his foot touched the ground and she fell off his neck with a thud.

Dizzy, depleted, covered with sweat, Francis squatted on the ground, his head hanging, trying to catch his breath. But Zara, finding herself safe, couldn't resist the impulse to crow.

"See? I can climb the tree just like you, even if I am a girl," she boasted. He ignored her. "I came down on you like a monkey, didn't I? I'm a monkey, I'm a monkey." She capered around the tree, chortling with triumph.

Francis raised his head and gazed at her with a mix of fury and wonder. "I pity the man who marries you when you grow up," he muttered. "You are a devil."

6

Rupert had entirely misread Joelle Lagrenade; she had no intention of rejecting him. She was simply showing the dignity and good taste she had been raised to show. One did not make a fuss over presents or money, for to do so would embarrass the giver and make one look like a beggar. If Rupert had ever had occasion to pay anybody a wage (he left all that to Penelope, who paid Sylvie and Marguerite their meager five rupees a week), he would have noticed that the Seychellois received money without looking at it, counting it or even thanking one for it, just as Joelle received his presents. To do otherwise was tantamount to groveling.

In fact, far from being contemptuous of Rupert or offended by him, as he feared, Joelle thought him the most endearing man she had ever met. Not at all like that *makro*, Monsieur Talbot, who had so arrogantly tried to buy her with nothing but a pot of marmalade. No, Rupert had convinced her he was adorable the minute he had shut the door one day while she was taking dictation, knelt at her feet and kissed her fingers, one by one.

"I am besotted with you," he'd said in English (Rupert had no gift for languages, so couldn't speak a word of Creole, which sounded as foreign as Swahili to him). "I'm in a fever for you. I can't sleep, can't eat, I want you so. Please have mercy and take me." And he had meant every word.

So, by the end of Rupert's first two weeks at the office—and the most laissez-faire of offices it was—Joelle and he were lovers. They made love in his room when everyone else was out drinking—over the desk, against the bookshelves, on the bare wooden floor. They made love on the deserted beaches under the bowing palm trees, plagued by flies, ants and the powdery sand that had a way of getting into the most unwelcome places. But most often they made love back at her house, a two-room shack she shared with her mother and whichever sisters were temporarily at home, whom she had to shoo away each time she brought him in. And every moment of it was glorious.

Rupert could not get over his luck. Before Joelle, he had only been familiar with bony and drunken Englishwomen, never anybody so exotic, so passionate and luscious as Joelle. Even Susan Winslop, who, come to think of it, was rather bony and drunken herself, seemed clinical in comparison. And Joelle not only turned him vigorous in bed but treated him with such tenderness he felt dizzy from morn to night. He longed for her constantly, whether she was in his arms or out of reach. At home, he barely heard what was said to him by the guests at dinner parties, by Penelope, the servants or the children, for his mind was constantly sailing away on erotic memories. I do believe, he told himself after a fortnight of this, I do believe I am in love.

Joelle, too, was pleased. She had been with a few white men over the years, being in the position to get at them easily as a government secretary, but she had never had one like Rupert. All the others had made it clear that she was nothing but a fling, a "bit on the side," as Englishmen liked to say, with whom to pass a night as an exotic adventure. They had shown no curiosity about her life and had tolerated no questions from her. One or two had been considerate enough to slip her mother a few rupees, but none had been as attentive as Rupert. He showered her with gifts. He complimented her extravagantly, asked her all sorts of questions about her past and her three sisters and two brothers, and he was a superb lover, considerate and gentle, daring and sensuous. But best of all, he made her feel a delight she had never felt before. She would catch herself looking at him in appreciation, so tall and manly, with those big brown eyes and long, high-hipped legs. The way he stroked his beard (which looked better than it smelled), the way he smiled with his eyes as well as his mouth, the way he stuttered like a child whenever he tried to speak Creole—she found it all adorable. So each morning, when she woke up on her straw mat amidst whichever sisters, nieces and nephews had come for the night, she prayed for help to keep him. Let me bear his child, Mother Mary, she whispered to the candles in her room, to the Madonna on her wall. Let me swell heavy with his seed so I can keep him for my own. For Rupert was always talking about his two little girls. He was just the sort of man to be caught by a baby.

Joelle didn't know it, but she was benefiting from Susan Winslop when it came to Rupert's skill in bed. Susan, who was a good six years older than Rupert, was by far the most unrestrained person he had ever known, having managed to avoid the entire war and the worst of its depressing aftermath by living in America, where she had devoted herself to the study of sex. Or so it seemed to him when she told him about her courses in psychology and her immersion first in the Kama Sutra and later in Alfred Kinsey's racy book on female sexuality. "He wrote an entire book about that?" Rupert had exclaimed when she'd mentioned it in bed one clandestine afternoon. "But what is there to say?"

"My dear man, that's what I've been trying to teach you," Susan replied with a patience Penelope never would have shown. "They are quite advanced in America, you know, when it comes to sex. There's another American doctor who's been studying the female orgasm, and—"

"I'd like a job like that," Rupert interrupted. "Where do you think one applies? Here?" Susan giggled. "Or perhaps here?"

So Joelle got a Rupert who, at thirty, was a very different man from the one Penelope had found dancing at the Hurlingham Club when he was twenty-one. He was now a man who had learned to reckon his worth and know what he needed: a job that was stimulating without being taxing, enough travel to make him feel worldly, a home of modest luxury but easy comfort, and, above all, a woman both lustful and motherly who appreciated him not for whom he might become but for whom he was now.

All Joelle had to do was make him get rid of that stinky beard. And his wife.

Although Marguerite had been right about Rupert and Joelle, she had been mistaken in thinking that Madame knew, for Penelope's distrust of servants, born of her disastrous years with Nanny, along with her dislike of the other government wives had kept her too isolated from gossip to learn the truth. No, the reason she had stormed and slashed that terrible day of the haircut wasn't because of Joelle at all. It was because of Governor Toynbee.

Penelope had grown sick of Toynbee's quick poking. She didn't like the way he never undressed, never expressed affection or acknowledged their relations, never even caressed her, and she was tired of him always doing it the same way, bending her over and sticking it in from behind as if she were a sheep. Since she'd been reckless enough to embark upon the dangerous and morally corrupt voyage of adultery in the first place, she should at least be enjoying it. So she had chosen that day to rebel.

"Michael?" she'd said in his study, turning around before he could press her over the desk and lift her skirt. She blushed, for using his Christian name still felt overly familiar, if not outright cheeky. "Michael, could we try something else for a change?"

He stood back, narrowing his gray eyes in surprise. "Such as what? I do like my mistresses compliant, you know."

That chilled her. The dominating man of her fantasy, of the finger in the bed, was not at all the same as a dominating man in real life. "Well, I thought perhaps you could—um—kiss me."

"Don't be silly. If you want something different, kneel. I'll try your mouth."

Furious, she pushed him away. "I will not be used!" she snapped, and whirling around, stalked out of the room. Behind her, she heard him snort with laughter.

Damn him, she told herself while driving to Vicky Hubert's house a few minutes later for tennis and cocktails, damn him to hell! He's the only lover I've ever had other than Rupert and look at what I got. Pervert!

So much, she thought, for revenge.

Yet that wasn't the worst of it, it turned out, because later that very day, as if one humiliation per diem weren't enough, later that very day, as she sat on the veranda of Vicky's house (Vicky being the sun-blackened wife she had met at that first cocktail party), Toynbee had dropped in. There Penelope was, still in her tennis whites, grimy with tropical dust and sweat, drinking a large and welcome martini with four other government wives, when in he had strolled with all the insouciance of a shepherd among his flock. "Hello girls!" he'd said cheerily. Penelope had run her eyes over the other women—and that's when she had seen. By God, had she seen. Vicky Hubert, overweight and overcooked, turned as blotchy as a crab. Edith Talbot, wife of the boiled toad Roger, wriggled her rumpled little body like a schoolgirl. Nancy Simpson, gaunt and fidgety, flushed a terrible mottled purple. And Hannah Watkins, a pudgy, motherly type who was Penelope's favorite of these frightful women, blushed a liverish pink. My God, Penelope realized, he's had every one of us.

She'd looked down at her lap, her short, white tennis skirt suddenly obscene, her long legs glaringly naked beneath it. What a fool I am, she thought, for she had been so sure that Toynbee had selected her out of them all. Hadn't that been the best part of it, really, the thought that this masterful man had chosen her as the youngest, prettiest and by far the most intelligent of all these other cows? Oh shit shit shit. She was no better than a cow herself.

And then there was the awkward matter of the children. For she had just arranged their first visit to Governor's House to play with the Toynbee brats, a strategic move, both for their sake and for Rupert's advancement. If she refused to go to Michael Toynbee anymore or—and she had to admit the possibility—he refused to send for her, what was she to do about that?

"Oh dear, look at the time," she'd said, noticing that Toynbee was standing behind Hannah now, his hand resting on her plump shoulder with the casual possessiveness of a man holding his bicycle. "I must go. Rupert is expecting me." And out she'd walked, her legs exposed, her bottom seared by knowing glances. And as she'd driven home, scorched with shame, she'd thought, I must change, I must stop all this, I must win Rupert back. He, at least, is decent and not perverted—he, at least, knows how to love.

So in she'd come, full of resolution and remorse, longing to see Rupert, to fling herself in his arms with tears and capitulations. But Rupert hadn't been there. Only her changeling of a Zara was, looking unkempt, un-English, speaking Creole like a native, hair in a heap of tangles and knots, full of impudence and disobedience— evidence, physical evidence of all Penelope's mistakes.

The next day in the car, driving Zara to Victoria as promised, Penelope made a vow. She may have been raised by a backward and superstitious nanny with a heart like a prune pit, but the woman had at least instilled her with Christian values. Penelope had not, emphatically not, been brought up to embrace moral turpitude— let alone to be screwed like a sheep. So, as she wound the tiny car over the mountain, past rustling palms and giant yellow breadfruit dangling like udders from the trees, she determined to make up for it all. No more Toynbee, no more afternoons lost to cocktails. Let the rest of them pave their paths to hell, she thought grimly. I shall be loving to my children, patient with my husband and kind to the servants. I shall be a paragon.

When she reached Victoria, she parked near the clock tower, which was painted a tinselly silver and vaguely resembled a shrunken Big Ben, took Zara by the hand and set off down Market Street to shop. Marguerite had trimmed and styled Zara's hair that morning, so there was no need for a barber after all, thank God (Penelope dreaded the appraising eyes of Seychellois barbers), and now the child looked quite appealing, rather like a French gamin. Penelope glanced down at her daughter. She would never forgive herself for doing her such violence, but in fact it suited her, this tousle of short hair with its little fringe, even if it did make her look like a boy in a dress. "My poor muffin," she murmured, giving the back of Zara's neck a squeeze. "My brave little Zouzou. We will buy you anything you want today."

Zara skipped alongside her mother, basking in this unexpected generosity. In the new truce between them, she had agreed for the first time to wear one of the miniature frocks Penelope had ordered in London to match her own: red and white stripes, puff sleeves for Zara, sleeveless for Penelope, both tight at the waist and springing into full skirts. Zara had also been forced to succumb to leather sandals, which chafed, so used had she become to rubber thongs or bare feet. But she was too taken by the sights and sounds of Victoria to be much bothered. After her customary solitude around the house or at Marguerite's, and the silence of the sea as she snorkeled for hours among her fishy subjects, the bustle and laughter of people in the street enthralled her.

To Penelope, Victoria was more of a shabby village than a town, and she had been most disappointed when she'd first seen it, particularly as it was the only town in all of Seychelles. Aside from a couple of stone buildings near the clock tower, it was nothing but a sprawl of tin and wood shanties drooping in the sun, with only one significant street of shops. And even those shops were dilapidated, leaning against one another like exhausted drunks, their paint blistered and their rusting roofs sagging and lopsided. Ragged children played in the doorways, two open drains ran down either side of the narrow street—one had to step on little planks to cross them—and dust and sand layered everything in sight, as if objecting to the existence of a town at all.

Zara, on the other hand, loved it, for what could be more exciting than a street full of people, the women gay in bright dresses and bare feet, and the smells of spices wafting from the shops' open doors and windows? Everywhere there was life. Men in summer shirts and shorts, laughing and drinking beer as they squatted over banana leaf mats, slapping down dominoes with loud clacks. Transistor radios playing African beats, the music blending with the whoops of street vendors. Women undulating past, balancing baskets of fruit on their heads, or vast bundles of fluffy white kapok balls like heaps of cotton snow. And everybody wore the most wonderful hats: wide-brimmed straw hats like flying saucers, high hats like pudding bowls, round hats like teacups, felt and straw fedoras and pointy, cone-shaped hats like upside-down funnels.

Zara's favorite place of all, though, was the Indian shop. Penelope had taken her and Chloe there several times already, and now Mr. and Mrs. Raja, the shopkeepers, a kindly old couple with not enough teeth, pressed little gifts on them whenever they came: coconut biscuits in a rainbow of colors, macaroons or marzipan, Quality Street toffees imported all the way from England and half melted in the heat.

Zara followed her mother inside the shop and inhaled. She was just as thrilled by its smell, a nose-tickling mix of curry and coffee, as she was by its clutter. Burlap sacks as tall as her chest were lined up on the scuffed wooden floor, their tops rolled back to reveal heaps of coffee beans, lentils or hard, raw rice. The shelves along the walls were stacked two deep with jars containing orange saffron or long black vanilla beans, ant-red paprika or rust-colored curry powder, and tiny bottles of patchouli oil and perfumes. Other shelves held evaporated milk for babies, rows of red Carnation tins, bolts of bright cotton for dressmaking, pins and thread, needles and soap, hair oil and talcum, fish hooks and wire, string and glue and mysterious bottles of salves and potions, all so jumbled together that only Mr. Raja and his wife could find anything. The shutters and doors were open all day long, tea was served to favorite customers and Mr. Raja bustled about in his white cotton trousers and shirt, with his black hair gleaming and his clean clean hands, serving with a smile and just the slightest of bullying each customer who came by. "A little ginger with that flour, Madam? So good for the biscuit making, so good for the digestion in tea," he said to Penelope in English. "And these vanilla beans, yes, we grow the vines right here in the Seychelles, which we must pollinate by hand, and their beans are so fragrant you can smell them like a perfume." "Madam, you cannot want only one little bag of these wonderful coffee beans my brother sent me from Kenya? No, no, these are the very best, but I do not receive them often. The fragrance, the taste, ah, it will make you feel as if you are in Paris."

Penelope bought it all.

Back outside, they headed down the street to the open market, a collection of stalls and benches where one could buy fresh fish and vegetables, the little bananas that were so tangy and moist and the papayas Zara could eat by the pound. Penelope, who had grown to understand Creole quite well (helped by her years of French at school), haggled mercilessly with the fishermen, who could barely feed their families as it was, while Zara wandered off to look around on her own. She was fascinated by the things people sold here: not only food but embroidered cushion covers and handkerchiefs, salad servers carved out of tortoiseshell, woven baskets and mats made of pandanus leaves (like the mats Marguerite had tried to teach her to make, only so much better) and conches from deep in the sea, polished a thrilling pink, like the inside of a mouth. She found a shriveled old man sitting at a table, his fedora drooping with years of wear and the heat, offering to write letters for the illiterate. Further along was a woman selling seed and shell necklaces, and Zara wanted to buy a string of cowrie shells for Chloe because her sister loved sissy things like jewelry and because Nana had said cowries were good luck. Then she spotted a necklace of jequirity seeds, which looked just like ladybirds, bright red and glossy, with a black dot at one end. She wanted that not because it was pretty, however, but because Francis had told her that the *bonhomme du bois* used the seeds to poison evil spirits.

Penelope appeared at her side. "Ah, there you are, darling. I managed to bargain that poor man down by almost half—he was quite distressed!" She chuckled proudly. "What do you see here? Oh, look at those little red beads. Aren't they lovely?"

Zara smirked.

"What would you like, poppet? Remember I said I'd buy you a present today? Only one, mind you, we mustn't spoil you. But you don't like jewelry, do you? Let's go to the Chinaman's shop and look for a toy."

"No, Mummy, I would like that one, please." Zara pointed to the cowrie necklace. "I want it for Chloe."

Penelope looked at her in surprise. "That's very nice of you, darling. But don't you want something for yourself as well?"

"Yes, please. May I have the red one?"

"Of course you may. It *is* pretty, isn't it?"

Zara took the red necklace from the smiling woman who was selling it and heaped it onto her palm, where it glittered like a handful of rubies. "*Mersi bocou Madanm*," she said in her best Creole accent, and hung it around her neck.

For the rest of that week, Penelope pursued her plan of reform. She still went off in the mornings to play tennis or swim, but immediately afterward excused herself from the noxious company of the other government wives to see to the children and plan a nice supper for Rupert, should he deign to join them. After a few days, however, she found that she didn't want to go out at all. She felt more like staying at home to read a book and perhaps prepare a lesson for the girls, whose schooling she had neglected scandalously since arriving in Seychelles. So she settled into one of the a grasshopper–like deck chairs on the back veranda, cooled that day by a breeze from the sea, and turned her attention to the latest volume of Anthony Powell's gossipy opus, *The Music of Time*, which had come out in England just before she'd left. She had brought all five volumes with her because she'd anticipated having a great deal of time to read while in exile and reading was something she loved. It was a pleasure she'd discovered as a child, when she had needed escape from missing her mother and battling with Nanny.

There was another reason Penelope didn't want to venture away from the house, though: she wasn't feeling well. For several days now she'd had periodic bouts of the runs, and her stomach was tender and appetite down. It must be all that glutinous curry, she thought, or the coconut oil in which Sylvie insisted upon frying the vegetables. Or perhaps she had picked up some sort of germ. Never mind, she had no fever. It couldn't be serious.

What she didn't know was that along with her morning coffee and evening soups, she had been ingesting crushed ant, claw of ghost crab, gecko tail and burnt offerings of her own hair and fingernails, all pounded with a pestle into the finest of powders and finished off with one poisonous red seed.

I wonder if it's working? Zara thought, peeking at her mother from around a corner of the veranda. I wonder if the demon worm is dead yet?

A few nights later, Penelope and Rupert sat in the dining room over a rare dinner alone. Rupert had come home at a reasonable hour for a change and the children had gone to bed early, being exhausted from a day of swimming and a sweets-laden tea at the Toynbees', so Penelope had given both Marguerite and Sylvie the night off. She wanted to have Rupert to herself, like the old days, so they could talk and perhaps more. For not only had he been spending more and more time away from home lately, he had not come to her bed once.

There had been no problem about sending the children to Governor's House to play after all, for Mrs. Toynbee—or Kate, as she liked to be called—was naturally in charge of domestic matters and happy to have the children over, apparently knowing nothing of her husband's peccadilloes. Kate had turned out to be rather nice, much the most tolerable of the government wives, aside from Hapless Hannah. (Penelope had given all the wives silly names now.) It caused Penelope some regret, for she would have liked to make friends with Kate, both for Rupert's sake and because the woman seemed without the malice that had corrupted the others. But how could they be friends when every time Penelope looked at her, she found herself blushing at the memory of offering her bare behind to the woman's own husband?

"Rupert," Penelope said as they ate the dinner Sylvie had prepared earlier—curried fish soup with onions and lentils, accompanied by a green papaya salad—"I'm afraid Chloe has some kind of worm." She brought this up because the children were the one subject she and Rupert seemed to be able to talk about without squabbling.

"Worm?" he replied with alarm, squinting over the flickering candles at his long, thin wife. She's gone astonishingly brown, he noticed. Browner than Joelle, come to think of it. How odd. "What do you mean, worm?"

"Well, Marguerite told me today she caught Chloe scratching her behind rather a lot, so last night she had a look and saw some little white worms coming out of her bottom."

"Good God, how disgusting. You can't be serious."

"I'm afraid I am. Marguerite says not to worry but it's still awful, isn't it? I mean, as far as I know, people in England don't have worms in their bottoms."

Rupert guffawed, spraying his mouthful of beer all over the table. "God, Penny," he sputtered, laughing. "You're making me choke."

That gave Penelope a pang. For they used to laugh together a lot like this, didn't they? Over irreverence, over foolishness, over their own silly mistakes. When had that stopped? she wondered. It seemed like a long time ago now.

She gazed at him sadly. "Oh, Rupert."

He chose to ignore this. "But there must be some sort of powder Chloe can take to cure her?"

"Yes, I'm sure there is. I'll drive her to the clinic tomorrow." Penelope stared down at the large pink flowers circling her hand-painted Minton dinner plate, one of the few she had brought from London that had not yet been smashed. Like everything else precious we once had between us, she thought, smashing up piece by piece.

She looked back up at Rupert, who had gone off in a dream, as he did so often these days, stirring his soup absently as he gazed into the candle flames. She longed to call out to him, to take him by the hand and lead him gently to bed. Whatever had possessed her to insist on her own room when they had first arrived? She'd never done that in England, and now it had set up such a barrier she might as well have locked herself in a fortress.

"Rupert?" She had to say it again before he woke up and looked at her. "Um, how are things going with the job, you know, at the office? You never talk about it much."

Rupert blinked his large, liquid eyes (how Penelope loved his eyes) and scratched his horrid beard. "Ah, yes. Well, things are all right. The records are in a devilish mess, though. Most time-consuming. My . . . my secretary is a great help with that. Very good at alphabetizing and that sort of thing. Crack typist, too." He blushed. He couldn't help himself, couldn't help speaking of the woman who was on his mind day and night. He longed to say her name.

Why is Rupert blushing? Penelope wondered with alarm. Is he telling some sort of lie?

"Really? Is your secretary local?" she asked as she pushed a lump of fish around her soup bowl. The fish was very good, in fact, but her stomach virus, or whatever it was, hadn't quite left her yet.

"Um, yes, yes, she is. Born right here in Mahé. Mother a domestic, father dead, alas. Clever girl, though. Speaks French and English remarkably well."

"I must meet her some time. She sounds like quite a find." Penelope watched his face.

"Yes, well, I didn't find her. Talbot did. You know Talbot?"

"Rupert, we've had him to dinner at least twice this month with his vile wife, Evil Edith. Don't you remember?"

"Evil Edith?"

Penelope shoved aside her soup bowl and sat back. "Yes, I've given all those beastly women names. I wish I could find somebody decent to be friends with. I'm so bored here, Rupert."

As he didn't answer, she stood up and walked to his end of the table, where she stood beside him for a moment, stroking his thick auburn hair and the tender nape of his neck. "Darling," she murmured, pulling his head to her breasts. She bent down to tickle his ear with her tongue, sliding her hand down his chest toward his crotch.

Rupert pushed her away with the same unconscious gesture he used to push away the children when they annoyed him. "I'm sure there's something you can find to do here. Ask the other wives. Do stop breathing all over me like that."

She drew back as if he'd slapped her and returned to her chair, where she sat down, staring at her hands, too hurt to speak. Oblivious, Rupert went back to slurping his soup.

Finally, having recovered enough to talk, she said quietly, "Perhaps I could get a job at the office and work with you? It might be rather nice to work together, don't you think? I should be able to do something. After all, I did get into Oxford. What's your secretary's name again?"

"Joelle Lagrenade," he blurted, knowing instantly he shouldn't have. He blushed again, this time turning almost purple.

Penelope's heart was pounding and her hands began to sweat. But she managed to keep her voice steady. "You haven't answered my question, darling. Could I work there in some capacity, do you think?"

But Rupert was too flustered to reply, having spoken Joelle's beautiful name aloud right here in his home. God, he missed her. Her intoxicating smell, the cushion of her body as he settled onto it, the silkiness of her vagina as he slid into her. I am a man obsessed, he thought gleefully, for it was rather wonderful to come from a lonely flat off the Cromwell Road with a war-wrecked father and a mousy mother and be a man obsessed. I wonder if Penny has ever been obsessed? he mused. I bet not. I bet she's never even been in love, not deeply, not passionately like I am—not even with me.

Of course, he had once believed Penelope was in love with him, back during their courtship and the early days of marriage. She had seemed so open to love then, pretty and eager, not all spiky and forbidding the way she'd turned here. A fresh English flower she'd been then, and a rather willing flower at that. For after his first unfortunate attempt at seduction in his flat, when she'd taken that bite out of his chin, she had succumbed with startling rapidity, if unimaginatively, to his subsequent overtures. He felt a little sorry for her now, to tell the truth, for what had she known of sex and the erotic, she with her father newly dead, her desperate mum and that uncle screaming about ripped off faces at the mere sight of a beefsteak? The war had done that to them all, of course—destroyed the parents and terrified the children into rigid conventionality. And there was poor Penny in the midst of it, a frightened, middle-class virgin with no one to teach her anything about pleasure but him, and all he'd ever done was open her legs and stick it in. Of course, he probably would have stayed just as unimaginative himself if it hadn't been for Susan Winslop, because those Cambridge girls hadn't known anything, either. He shouldn't have succumbed to Susan, he knew that—it was very bad of him—but how could he have resisted? She was such a free spirit. That lucky blighter Ian, having a wife like that. No call for a mistress when you have a wife dedicated to the Kama Sutra, is there? Unless she was a mistress like his delectable Joelle, of course. Didn't need any textbooks with Joelle—put that in your pipe and smoke it, Alfred Kinsey!

"Da-da!"

Rupert blinked as a small blond blur whizzed into the room. God, the children.

"Chloe, my little muffin! Climb up on Daddy's lap. I thought you were asleep. Where are your clothes?"

"Don't know," Chloe said happily as her father picked her up and settled her, a plump cherub, on his knee. She pointed to the soup. "I want thome please. Bread, too." So Rupert allowed her to dip his bread into the soup and suck at it noisily. He pulled her close and gave her a squeeze. He had always loved how soft and pliable the bodies of his children were, like little pillows. He even allowed her to feed him a sopping piece with her fingers, dripping soup into his beard.

"Rupert," came the weary voice of Penelope. "Have you heard a word of what I've been saying?"

"Of course I have, darling," he replied, not even minding the soup splattering onto his shorts and bare knees. I can't even hear my wife anymore, let alone listen to her, he thought. Look at her over there, rigid as a broomstick. I've made a terrible mistake.

It wasn't until Chloe had been sitting naked on his knee for twenty minutes that he remembered the worms.

7

Penelope brought Chloe to the clinic in Victoria the next morning, where they had to sit in a hot and crowded waiting room for some time until the overworked doctor could fit them in. She was surprised at being made to wait. She'd assumed that, being English and government, she would somehow be able to skip the queue, but apparently Dr. Panyal thought differently. So she sat on a bench, fanning herself with a medical leaflet and trying to keep Chloe on her lap and away from the other patients as best she could. As for what Rupert had revealed over supper the night before, she couldn't bear to think about it. All she could do was give him the benefit of the doubt and quash the rising fear within her as quickly as possible.

Chloe seemed perfectly healthy as far as Penelope could see, sucking her thumb and fondling the toy lion she brought everywhere with her now, but who knew what sorts of diseases one could contract in a backward place like this, with those open drains in the streets and everyone practicing God knows what sort of hygiene? After all, this was basically Africa, and quite a forgotten corner of Africa at that. If Rupert only had a little more push, a little more ambition, he could have advanced his career back in London without ever having had to drag them all to this godforsaken place. Seychelles was obviously a dumping ground for incipient failures.

Look at Toynbee and that toadlike Talbot; it was clear to her now these were not men destined for greatness.

While she waited, she tried to avoid staring at the unfortunates around her, but this was not easily done. Several of the children had the swollen bellies and vacant eyes Penelope knew signified malnutrition, and one man in the corner must have been suffering from elephantiasis, for he had such grotesquely swollen legs that he had to be delivered to the clinic in a wheelbarrow. She had heard that venereal disease was common on this island, too, which made her eye the vigorous young fellows in the room with apprehension. She pulled Chloe to her and found herself wishing, for the first time in her life, to be in the familiar if hideous offices of her National Health GP.

"Mrs. Weston?" The Indian doctor poked his face through the doorway, blinking with fatigue behind thick glasses. He spoke in English, with the melodious, precise accent that Penelope always thought made Indians sound so polite.

She carried Chloe in, feeling the eyes of the other patients resting on her curiously. "Undress her, please, and lie her down on the table," Dr. Panyal ordered wearily, washing his hands at a sink. He was small and chocolaty brown, with a pleasing square jaw. He bent over Chloe, tickled her until she giggled and flipped her onto her stomach for a quick examination. Then he sat her up, washed his hands again and handed her a lollipop.

"Say thank you to the doctor, Chloe," Penelope told her.

Chloe licked the pink lollipop tentatively, decided she liked it, and only then said, "Thank you, M'thieur Doctor," which made him smile.

"Is it really worms?" Penelope asked as she pulled up Chloe's knickers.

"Yes, Madam. Pinworms. Small white worms that live in the intestines and rectum." He walked to his desk, hiding a yawn, and sat down behind it. "It is odd to see them in a child this old. I usually only find them in small babies. They catch the worms from one another, you see, or by eating sand or soil."

"But Chloe hasn't been seeing any babies," Penelope protested, easing a pink sundress over her daughter's curly head. "And she's such a fussy eater. I can't imagine her swallowing any sort of earth on purpose, she's too old for that sort of thing. It's not something dangerous, is it?"

"Why no, Mrs. Weston. Almost all children get them at one time or another. Please, sit down." He gestured to an old wooden chair in front of his desk and began to write out a prescription.

Penelope sat with Chloe on her lap, who was now intent on her lollipop. "Do you mean to tell me this isn't a tropical disease?" Penelope gazed into the doctor's solid face—a quite handsome face, come to think of it, even with his thick glasses. "Do you mean even English children catch this? At home, I mean?"

Dr. Panyal suppressed a snort. What did this woman think, the English were too good for worms? "Yes, that is what I mean, Mrs. Weston," he said as he handed her the prescription. "Although I must say, many Europeans do not realize how advanced we are here in the clinic when it does come to tropical diseases. There have been quite a few cases of *Entamoeba Histolytica*, for example, one of the dysentery amoebae, which we often recognize long before your Western doctors even know—"

"Yes, thank you," Penelope said crisply, standing up to go. "How much of this must I give her?"

Dr. Panyal, whose family had worked long and hard to earn the money to send him to medical school in Delhi, was too accustomed to the arrogance of colonials to show any offense. "One spoonful today and another in two weeks, that is all," he replied patiently. "And perhaps for your other child, too, to be on the safe side. Pinworm is highly contagious."

"Oh." Penelope looked disconcerted. "So adults can catch this, as well?"

"If they share food with a contaminated child or have contact with the worms, most certainly."

Penelope remembered Chloe on Rupert's knee the night before, feeding him soup. Serves the nefarious bastard right, she thought. I hope he gets the worms and his damn secretary does, too.

"Well, I do think you're wrong about how Chloe caught the worms, but thank you in any case, Doctor. Good-bye."

Dr. Panyal stood up, said a polite farewell and bowed her out of the room. What an insufferable woman, he thought, and returned to his desk.

The minute Penelope reached home, she summoned Marguerite.

"Yes, Madame?" Marguerite walked into the foyer, wiping her hands on an old white apron. Her hair was down today, in the long black rope Zara so liked to pull. "How is my *ti gate*, eh?" she said, bending down to give Chloe a kiss.

"She's quite all right, apparently," Penelope said, touched by this display of affection. "It's only pinworms—I don't know what you call it in Creole. But you were right, it's not dangerous. The doctor says it comes from babies playing with one another or eating earth. Make sure both the children take a spoonful straightaway, would you?" She handed the bottle of medicine to Marguerite.

"But Chloe, she has not been with other babies and she does not eat the ground, Madame," Marguerite said in surprise. She was used to seeing worms among the Seychellois children—roundworms, usually, or those hookworms that come out in your eyes at night. Some of the poorest children went untreated for so long they vomited worms in great wriggling gushes. But the children of *gro blan?* That was rarer. "You know this little one, she eat nothing but sweets, soup and rice."

"I know. That's what I said to the doctor." Penelope bent over Chloe, whose dimpled cheeks were stained pink from the lollipop. "Darling, can you remember any time you ate some earth or sand?"

Chloe cocked her head to one side in a gesture that always charmed Rupert but that Penelope thought rather affected. "Yeth," she said, surprising both adults.

"Yes? When?"

"At Nana's house." Chloe pointed to Marguerite, who looked shocked and frightened. But before Penelope could say a word, Chloe added, "Thara told me eating red dust will make me grow tall and big. But I'm not big." She shook her head, her little mouth pouting. "I'm just the thame."

Penelope stood up. "Zara!" she called, her voice sharp.

"Wait, Madame, please. Zara did not know."

"Didn't know what? I've told her over and over again to be careful of the germs here. Of course she knows not to let her sister eat dust! What was she thinking? Oh, you cope with it. I don't feel well."

Penelope stormed off to the toilet, feeling another bout of diarrhea coming on, and locked the door behind her.

Marguerite went to find Zara. Madame is right, she thought, what was Zara doing? Was she trying to make some type of *grigri*? Would she do that against her very own sister?

Rupert failed yet again to come home for dinner that night—the third time that week—so Penelope and the children had to eat in the large and airy dining room alone. Penelope found it embarrassing to sit at such a grand table with no company but the two little ragamuffins her daughters had become, while Marguerite served them in knowing silence. It was a humiliation, blatant evidence of Rupert's desertion, and the contrast with their cozy suppers at home struck her more cruelly than ever. The bamboo blinds rattled out on the veranda, Marguerite slapped around in her sandals, a gecko on the wall cackled like a dirty old man. Penelope shut her eyes. She couldn't bear what was happening to them. Hadn't Rupert promised to resist the sort of family shattering they had experienced during the war? Hadn't he listened to her when she'd told him of her loneliness with Nanny and her unwelcoming family? That had been their contract—to stand by one another and protect the family unit. And look at him now! He had broken every promise he had ever made.

"Mummy?" Zara said, penetrating her thoughts. "Mummy, you know that medicine we're taking?"

"What? Oh, the worm medicine. Yes, why?"

"Are you taking it, too?"

"No, darling. It's only for you and Chloe."

Zara frowned and chewed on her finger, a brown and very dirty finger, Penelope noticed too late. "I want you to take it, too, Mummy. Please."

"I don't see why you should care, poppet. Now if you're finished, go and wash. As you should have done before supper."

"Only if you promise to take it. I'll go get the medicine now. Will you? Please, please?"

Penelope wasn't a fan of medicines. As a child she'd spent half an hour every morning resisting with vigorous determination any attempt Nanny O'Neill had made to dose her with cod-liver oil. "But the doctor said it's only for you children. Why are you so concerned, darling?"

"I don't want you to get sick, Mummy. Please take it!"

Penelope was touched. "That's very sweet of you, Zouzou. All right, I will, if it makes you happy. Now off you go."

Later that evening, after Penelope had swallowed a spoonful of the revolting medicine under Zara's anxious eye and put the children to bed, she went into the kitchen, pulled out a chair from under the table and dropped into it with her head in her hands. Marguerite, who was cutting up a pineapple for the girls' breakfast the next day, looked at her in surprise. The kitchen was her territory, hers and Sylvie's, and Sylvie had left, dinner being over. The children were welcome, of course, but not the master or Madame. She felt invaded and tried to show it in the stiffness of her back.

"Marguerite?" Penelope said at last, her voice uncharacteristically meek. "Are you married?"

Here I have been under her nose every day for six weeks, and only now does she ask. But Marguerite was curious, so she replied with courtesy, as was expected. "No, Madame, not any more." She continued to scrape off the pineapple prickles at the kitchen counter, her sturdy back turned to Penelope, her tightly woven plait dangling straight to her hips.

"But you were before?"

Having shed the prickly skin, Marguerite sliced and cubed the pineapple, catching its acidy juice in a bowl. Pineapple season was short on the island, so while it lasted everybody ate as many pineapples as possible; at least those who could afford to eat rather than sell. So it was with most of the fruit: jackfruit (which grew straight out of the tree trunk, like a wart), papayas and *jamalac,* avocado and mangoes, oranges and passion fruit. One had to harvest and sell, pluck and eat as fast as possible before thieves or rats got there first. She held the sharp knife toward her, cutting expertly but dangerously, in just the way Penelope had been taught never to do.

"Everybody here has many husbands," Marguerite replied cautiously.

"Husbands?" Penelope sat up, like a dog with its ears pricked. "Have you had more than one?"

Marguerite blinked. She wasn't used to such direct questions. She found them rude.

"Yes, Madame. I have had three." In fact, she'd only married one of them, but Madame didn't need to know about that.

"Three! Ah, then you know."

Know what? Marguerite wondered. But she kept silent.

"I was married at eighteen," Penelope said then, talking in a low voice, as if to herself.

"You did not marry until eighteen?" Marguerite turned around, her eyebrows raised. "But that is so old!"

Penelope looked startled. "In England it isn't. Why, how old were you?"

"I was thirteen when I was married to my husband, Madame."

"*Thirteen?*"

"*Wi.* And my first child, she came when I was sixteen. I had six children, you know."

Penelope blinked. "Gosh, well done. Are any of them grown?"

"Yes, all but Lisette and Francis. I am forty-five and the grand-mother of eleven already," Marguerite added proudly.

"That's impressive. I can't imagine being anybody's grand-mother. But then I'm only twenty-seven."

Marguerite was surprised, although she said nothing. She had thought Madame much older, with those lines around her eyes and along her thin neck. White people wrinkle early, she had noticed long ago, their skins so papery and weak. She turned back to the pineapple.

Penelope stared at the wooden floor and at Marguerite's crusted heels, resting on her worn and lopsided rubber sandals. The wicker ceiling fan creaked above their heads and a dog barked down in the valley. In the silence that had fallen between her and Marguerite, she could hear the warbling of doves and the rattle of palm fronds out in the garden, and these sounds turned her mind back to her childhood years of wandering the Devonshire countryside alone. She had so loved the quiet welcome of the fields, the grass alight with butter-cups, the bluebells in the woods like carpets of sapphire velvet, the dots of white sheep on soft, distant hills. She had felt at home in those fields, despite the fear of German planes overhead. It was there she had learned to find pleasure in solitude and comfort in nature. It was there she had felt she belonged. She shifted her eyes back to Marguerite, still slicing away at the pineapple, and all of a sudden the curry-scented kitchen, the clattering palms and even Marguerite herself seemed so alien that a wave of unbearable homesickness washed over her. If only Rupert would wake out of his lotus-eater's trance and take her home!

"May I ask you something?" she finally said in the humblest voice Marguerite had ever heard her use.

"*Byensir*, Madame." Marguerite covered the bowl of pineapple with a plate, wiped her hands on her old apron and turned to face her, leaning against the counter and folding her thick arms.

"You've worked for quite a few English families before us, haven't you?"

"Yes, Madame. French, too."

"Well, I wanted to ask if you've seen, if you've noticed with those other families . . ." Penelope fell silent. I can't, she thought. I can't talk about this aloud. Flustered, she tried to change the subject. "I heard Zara talking about a person here, a sort of village wise man they call the *bonhomme du bois*. She seems to think he's some sort of wizard. Do you know anything about this?"

Marguerite shook her head. "There is no such person, Madame. We have many bad rumors on this island, words of ignorance. I have told Zara not to listen to this talk."

"Oh." Penelope paused a moment, confused, and plucked at her fingers. She'd given up wearing all those rings she used to have, Marguerite noticed, and her polished fingernails were short and bare now.

"Madame wished to ask me something?"

Penelope looked up at her, blue eyes squinting, and she did, for a moment, look young. She rubbed her brow but seemed unable to speak.

Marguerite put the pineapple in the larder and pulled out a chair. She sat opposite Penelope, her sturdy knees apart, the skirt of her fading blue dress stretched between them, and rested her hard, dry hands in her lap. "Forgive me if I have not understood, Madame." She paused, taking note of Penelope's embarrassed expression, which was as transparent as a child's. "But if it is love advice you need, I am very good at this. Because I know this place, it is hard on you English, on your husbands and marriages, *nespa*?"

Penelope shut her eyes, fresh humiliation burning her cheeks. "Yes. You have understood very well."

Marguerite nodded. "I will tell you my story, Madame, and you will see why I understand these things." And she set about weaving her trap.

She told Penelope of Henri, how he had beaten her and how she had left him; of her son Marcel, taken by the sea, wounding her heart so badly she could not feel or cry for a year; and of how his death had made her so dead inside that she had walked away from her firstborn, Lucille, without even a tear.

Penelope reached out to squeeze Marguerite's hand. "How awful," she breathed. "How terrible it is to lose a child. We almost lost Chloe, you know, on the ship coming here. She disappeared for an entire morning. I thought I would die."

Marguerite clucked sympathetically, then told about Joseph, the father of her next three children: Gaston, now grown and gone with his own large family; Fleurange, who worked as a maid in far away Trinidad and kept popping out children; and the sweet Lisette, sixteen and man-crazy. "But Joseph, he was no good, Madame. I found out he was keeping a mistress and giving her all his money. He was drinking my *kalou* also, instead of selling it. So I told him he was a lazy *kouyon* and I kicked him out."

"Good for you," Penelope said, for she couldn't imagine having the courage to kick any husband out, even one like that. "But then who is the father of Francis?"

Marguerite hesitated, taken aback once more by the directness of the question. Before replying, she took a moment to censor the story until she reached the version she wished Madame to hear.

"He was my third husband, Madame. His name was Antoine Dupuis, and he was very handsome, with a head as strong as his muscles. He was wise and kind, so good, so good." She leaned forward in her chair, her long plait falling over her shoulder, and for the first time Penelope saw that she was beautiful. "He was the man of my heart, Madame, as none ever was or ever will be again. It is always the way, I think. The man you love most is the man who must leave you, is this not so?"

"I hope not," Penelope replied, trying in her crisp way to cover the panic caused by these words.

"Henri, my first, this one I never loved. He was old and ugly as a tortoise, I was a little girl. He bought me. There was no love."

Penelope raised her eyebrows. "What do you mean, 'bought' you? How could that be allowed? I thought you were under British law here. It can't be legal!"

Marguerite gazed at her a moment, then began to laugh. She laughed for some time, in short, cackling wheezes, her tea-colored eyes squeezed tight in merriment. Penelope giggled, too, although she didn't know why.

When Marguerite had composed herself, she blotted her face with her apron, crossed her arms again and shook her head, still chuckling. At times Penelope reminded her of the local cattle egrets, stalking around on spindly yellow legs, eyes wide and empty, with no clue as to what they were really seeing. If one had to work for fools, Marguerite often told herself, one might as well enjoy a good laugh at them.

She decided to pursue her point. "The man, he gives presents to the bride, or to her parents, yes?"

Penelope hesitated. "Well, I suppose Rupert did buy me an engagement ring. Emerald. He couldn't afford a diamond. Wedding ring, too."

"And the bride's parents and the groom's parents, they meet and they talk, *pa vre?*"

"Sometimes."

"And the bride, she brings money or goods to the marriage, yes?"

"Oh, I don't know. I mean, we don't have a dowry anymore, if that's what you mean."

"But who pays for the wedding, Madame?"

"Um, well, the bride's family, normally."

"So, you see? What else is this but the selling and buying of a wife, eh?"

Penelope frowned in disagreement, but she couldn't help thinking of the Hurlingham Club, where all her set had gone to learn tennis in the summer, ballroom dancing in the winter and to find a spouse. Nor could she forget the conferences between Rupert's ghastly parents and her mother. "Not exactly," she replied, disconcerted. "I mean, we fall in love first and then we . . . um . . . negotiate."

"Ah yes, Madame, of course. It is different for Englishwomen." Marguerite turned away to hide her smile.

"But tell me, if you don't mind—what about this man you loved?"

Marguerite fell silent a minute, her gaze fixed on her work-worn hands. "My Antoine, yes, my heart's blood." She looked back up at Penelope, who was leaning toward her in eager curiosity, her plain white shirt and brown shorts in striking contrast to her usual fancy getups. Even her hair was pulled back in a simple ponytail, no teasing, no hairspray. She wore no makeup, either. Maybe that's why she looks younger than usual today, Marguerite thought—long-faced and sad, but young as a girl.

"I met Antoine at my friend Josette's wedding dance, Madame. I was still pretty and strong then, with a good income from my domestic work and my *kalou* tree. I had just sent Joseph away and I did not want another man, except for sometimes the comfort in bed, you understand? I had my children, I had my work and my own house. I did not need more trouble." She sighed. "That, of course, is when it always happens, yes? It is as if God is watching to fool you."

Or to humble you for believing you can do without a man, Penelope thought.

"My Antoine, oh, he was beautiful. Dark like takamaka wood, yes, but big-shouldered and strong. And he had such a way with making money! He was the catch of my life. Every woman at that wedding dance was after him, even the bride!" Marguerite chuckled. "But it was me he wanted, Madame, and for that I thanked God.

"For ten whole years, he was a good man. He did not drink my *kalou* like Joseph, but he drew it and sold it so fast, the money, it poured in. And he had a gift for the garden as well, and with animals. He grew cassava and yams, papaya, sweet potatoes. We had bananas and a mango tree. And he kept chickens and ducks who laid fat eggs, and a pig with a belly like a whale. Madame, I thought I had gone to heaven! And then he gave me Francis—you see what a fine boy he is? He does not drink *baca* or beer like his friends, he is smart and good at school, he does not chase the girls when his mama needs him. He is a good, religious boy, with God in his heart, just like his papa."

Penelope could see that Marguerite was getting worked up now, twisting her hands, her voice rising to a tremble. So, reverting to her British training, she offered her a cup of tea.

Marguerite accepted, tickled that Madame was serving her for a change. Penelope put the big black kettle on the stove, lit the Calor gas somewhat gingerly with a match (she was always afraid of blowing herself up) and returned to her chair.

Marguerite peeked at her wonderingly. What could have made Madame turn so considerate? Was it Zara's sorcery? For who knew what that mysterious child could do with her books and her strange knowledge?

"But what happened then?" Penelope said, opening a tin of the digestive biscuits she had brought from London and offering some to Marguerite. (Tea and biscuits, the most comforting food in the world—how Penelope missed them! They tasted all wrong here, the biscuits moldy and damp, the tea too heavy with condensed milk, just as everything in this place seemed moldy and damp: Toynbee, her marriage. Oh God.) "Why did you lose him? Or . . . oh sorry, would you rather not talk about it?"

"No, no Madame, *sava*," Marguerite said, amused at her clumsy politeness. "I was not a young girl anymore. I'd had six babies—this is not easy on a woman's beauty, you know? So he found another woman. Young and pretty, with a good family and money. And so he left me and married her."

What Marguerite did not tell Penelope was that she had conferred once more with the *bonnonm dibwa* (a new one by now, as France Puissance had died), a Monsieur Adonis, who had grown to become the most powerful sorcerer in Seychelles. She had clambered up the mountain yet again, followed by mosquitoes and the smells of pigs and outhouses, and had begged him to help her keep Antoine. He had given her spells and a little square packet of the familiar black powder. "Put the powder in his shoes and he will have bad dreams about the girl that will turn him running back to you," Adonis had told her. But Antoine had found her out, and he had been so angry that he'd left her forever. "I would have stayed with you, if you had asked me," he had said with a coldness that chilled her to the marrow. "I don't care about this girl, it is only a marriage my mother wants. I would have stayed with you and Francis if you had not tried this dirty devil magic on me. You are ungodly, Marguerite, and I cannot love an ungodly woman." If only he hadn't found out, the spell would have worked! Such bad luck! Such misfortune! It had broken her heart.

"I'm so sorry," Penelope was saying to her. "I know how hard it is to lose somebody you love. My father, you know, he—he died very suddenly, the week before I met my husband."

Penelope flushed, surprised at herself. She had never told anyone but Rupert about her father's death before—for just as Marguerite had her secrets, so did she.

"That is sad about your father. But now, Madame, I have talked long enough about my own concerns. What is it you want me to tell you?"

The kettle began to boil, so Penelope made a pot of tea for them both. She wasn't sure how to begin. She had come to Marguerite in loneliness and desperation, needing to talk and curious about the *bonhomme du bois*, but now she had a new idea.

She put the teapot on the table, offered sugar and condensed milk to Marguerite, who accepted both, and poured her a cup. Then she sat down and with a painful and self-conscious nonchalance said, "Do you happen know a Joelle Lagrenade?"

Ah, so she has found out, Marguerite thought, dipping her face down to her cup to hide her expression. The mere mention of the Lagrenade name made her heart race. Not only had the eldest Lagrenade sister, Charité, tried to ruin her marriage to Henri with *grigri*, but the second sister, Alphonse, had seduced Joseph so he would give her all his money. And worst of all, she was still convinced that her beloved Marcel would never have drowned if it hadn't been for the Lagrenade curse. Oh yes, Marguerite knew Joelle Lagrenade all right. She had loathed those jealous, man-stealing, child-murdering sisters for twenty years.

"I am not sure, Madame. I think I have heard the name."

"She works in Mr. Weston's office. As a secretary." Penelope gazed inquiringly into Marguerite's face, but saw nothing except her usual polite pretense of interest. She forged on nonetheless. "I realize this sounds odd, but I was hoping you might, well, know of a way . . ." she paused, flushing. "Well, to put it bluntly, I was wondering if you might know how to get her sacked."

Marguerite took a sip of tea. So, it is as I hoped, she thought. Madame and I have the same enemy now.

Penelope was awakened the next morning by a blood-freezing shriek. She jumped out of her solitary bed, heart pounding, and belted upstairs to the children's room before she could even think. There, she found Chloe huddled in a ball under her sheets and Zara standing in her pajamas, cackling.

"Get it off, get it off!" Chloe screamed. "Off, off, off!"

"What is it? What's the matter?" Penelope cried, rushing to Chloe's bed. "Good Lord."

For there, lumbering about on the sheets below Chloe's hunched-up little body was an enormous and hideous beetle, the

size of a baby's shoe. It had the claws of a crab, a greasy brown cara-
pace and a huge horn on its head.

Penelope reached out and, in one deft movement, picked the
beetle up by its middle. "It's all right, darling, Mummy has it now.
It won't hurt you. You can stop screaming."

Zara ceased her cackling and stared at her mother in amazement.

"Zara," Penelope said firmly, "come with me." And holding the
squirming beetle out in front of her, much as one would hold a live
lobster, she marched out of the room.

Zara followed her mother down to the back veranda and over to
the glass-topped cocktail table. "Sit," Penelope commanded. Zara
clambered into one of the grasshopper chairs. "Now, do you know
what this is?"

Zara shook her head.

Her mother stood tall and fierce, holding the monstrous creature
out in front of her. "Did you consider whether it might be dangerous before you put it on your poor sister's bed?"

"It isn't dangerous. I know."

"How?"

"Because I tried it."

"What do you mean?"

Zara stood up and put her finger right into one of the insect's
fearsome claws. "See, it only tickles."

Penelope squatted down and placed the beetle on the table. "Fascinating, isn't it?" she said in quite another tone. "Where did you
find it?"

"Under the house. Loads of insects live there. I find them all the
time, but this is my favorite. If you put two together who look like
this, they fight with their horns!" Zara looked at her mother happily.

"Well, I happen to know what it is," Penelope said, lowering her
voice to a conspiratorial whisper. "It's a giant rhinoceros beetle. And
do you know something marvelous about it?"

"What?" Zara was watching her mother in fascination. My *grigri* must be working, she thought, and maybe Chloe's worm medicine, too. I haven't seen Mummy like this since we got here. Maybe we can collect animals again, the way we used to. Because silkworms were not the only creatures she and Penelope had hunted—they'd dug in the garden for earthworms, too (Zara had cut the head off one, just to see what would happen), and found a hedgehog under a bush, which they'd fed with dishes of milk all winter long. Penelope had bought her Stubby, the golden hamster, and Pinkerton, the short-lived guinea pig. She had adored Kitty, even with her naughty habits of clawing the sofa and leaving dead mice in their beds. And then there was that thrilling night when she'd brought home a microscope, and the two of them had spent hours examining the antennae of a bumblebee and a strand of Zara's own hair.

"The marvelous thing about the rhinoceros beetle," Penelope was saying, "is it can carry eight hundred and fifty times its body weight. You know how ants can carry things much bigger than they are?"

Zara nodded, remembering the ants in the kitchen hauling away their dead.

"Well, the rhino beetle can, too. It's as if an elephant were carrying eight hundred and fifty other elephants right on its own back."

"What about if it was me?"

"If it were you, darling, you would be strong enough to carry eighty cars all by yourself without even stumbling. And you could fly in the dark, very fast, like an airplane."

Zara laughed. Maybe the rhinoceros beetle was just what she needed to make her spells stronger. Maybe, if she needed to, she could grind it up and put it in her mother's food, and it would make the demon worm crawl away forever.

"Now, take the poor thing back to its home. And Zara, listen to me." Penelope stood up and took the child by her bony shoulders. "You must stop torturing Chloe like this. Making her eat that earth was awful enough—and now this. I shall have to punish you. I shall tell Marguerite and Sylvie—oh, I know how sneaky you are—that you're to have no sweets at all for a whole week. No ice cream, not even a spoonful of sugar, you understand? And if I see you do one more cruel thing to your sister, I'll spank you."

Zara scowled. "I didn't know it was going to make her scream like that. She's such a baby."

"That's no excuse," Penelope said, standing up. "No more teasing her, understand?"

Zara nodded sullenly.

"Good. Now I'm going up to talk to poor Chloe."

As soon as her mother was gone, Zara picked up the rhinoceros beetle and carried it inside. She was going to put it into the bamboo cricket cage Francis had made for her, and keep it in case Mummy's worm came back.

That afternoon, Penelope drove to the post office in Victoria and sent a telegram to her near-forgotten mother. "Send insect books. Soon. All well." Then she drove up the mountain to Bel Air, the privileged enclave of Europeans, which commanded a spectacular view over the ocean, and parked in front of Vicious Vicky's sprawling white house.

"Oh, hello Penny," Vicky said upon opening the door, her blackened cleavage bursting out of a hideous salmon-pink sundress. "What a lovely surprise. Do come in." She flashed her trademark cobra smile. "Would you like a drink, darling?"

Penelope declined. "I only have a minute, I'm afraid, but I was wondering if I might borrow a pair of binoculars. I've taken it into my head to go bird-watching and explore a bit. You know, look at all the flora and fauna this place is famous for."

Vicky narrowed her beady black eyes. "I didn't know you were interested in all that."

"Yes," Penelope said a mite too quickly. "I've always been fascinated by insects and birds. I was all set to read natural science at Oxford, you know, had I not married Rupert." Damn, she though, blushing. Why did I have to bring him up?

"Really? You, a bluestocking at Oxford?" Vicky chuckled. "Do stay and have a drink. We ought to have a chat."

"Another time, all right?" Penelope said, backing away. "Thanks so much, but I must dash off." And, clutching the binoculars Vicky handed her, dash off she did, certain that Vicky thought she'd borrowed them to spy on Rupert.

If my husband must insist on falling for native girls, she told herself on the way home, I'll just have to find a way to win him back. No more complaining about being bored; instead I shall inform myself until I'm too interesting to resist. I'm sure it won't take him long to see he's not really cut out for those ignorant island girls. I'm sure he'll get over this childish infatuation, or whatever it is, and come back to me. He has to.

Zara, meanwhile, was crawling about under the house, choosing a place to hide her beetle until she needed it for *grigri*. She knew a lot more about *grigri* than even Marguerite suspected, thanks to Lisette and Francis, who couldn't resist a fascinated audience, and to the gossip she heard among the women in the market when she went with Nana. She knew you had to possess a piece of a person to put a spell on them, such as hair, nail clippings or blood—or at least a piece of their belongings—and she knew you had to be passionate about what you wanted. Halfhearted magic, the kind you didn't feel or care about, never worked; Francis had told her that. But she also knew that for magic to accomplish anything bigger than causing a little worry here or a little sickness there—for it to have any true power, such as curing Mummy and making Daddy stay at home—you had to own Ti Albert's spell book and you had to have the black powder made of human bones. And the only person who owned the book and the black powder was the *bonhomme du bois*.

The problem was that Zara had no idea how to find the *bonhomme* and Francis swore he didn't either. He said Nana knew, but he couldn't ask her or she would beat him, having forbidden him to talk about the sorcerer ever again, especially within hearing of Zara.

"Mama hits me hard on my hands and my legs when she is angry," he said. "She hits me with a switch made of bamboo."

Zara nodded. "They used to hit the boys like that in my school. The boys used to cry."

"Do you promise not to say anything to *Manman* then?" Francis said, for he truly feared Marguerite when she was in a temper.

Zara put a hand over her heart. They were having this conversation in the colorful back garden where the spider lived. Francis was clipping some flowers for Penelope: magenta bougainvillea off a bush and frangipani from a tree, those yellow and pink flowers that looked like whirligigs and smelled of lilies.

"I, Zara Weston, swear I will not tell Nana anything you tell me, cross my heart and hope to die," she said solemnly, drawing a big *X* on her chest. "Because I love you and I don't want you to be hurt."

Francis was so touched by this he had to look away. "Good," he said. "Now, help me pull out these weeds."

"But Francis?" Zara stood hovering on the grass, scratching the back of one mosquito-bitten brown leg with the foot of the other. "Is the *bonhomme* good or bad? I don't understand."

Francis squatted by a round flower bed, filled with orchids and bordered by a row of split coconut husks. He pulled at the weeds a few minutes before answering, the sinews in his arms flexing with the movement. His coppery skin glowed so warmly in the sun it made Zara want to hug him.

"It is hard to say, *ti koko*," he replied finally. "The *bonnonm* claims he does only good, but I think he does bad sometimes, too. My papa, he says all magic is bad. He says it is against God and it makes God angry. The nuns at my school, they say the same thing. They say all magic is the work of the devil and godly people will have nothing to do with it." Francis glanced at Zara to see if she was listening. She was, her scrawny body still with attention.

"My papa, he left *Manman* because he caught her doing this magic. He told her she was ungodly."

"Your daddy left?" Zara felt a pain in her chest. "Is he gone forever?"

Francis shook his head. "He is gone from my mother, yes, but not from me. But even now, he asks me if *Manman* is still visiting the *bonnonm* and doing ungodly things. He is very religious, you see."

Zara studied him a moment. "Are you very religious?"

Francis nodded and crossed himself, much as Zara had. "I know Jesus and Mother Mary, they look after us here on earth if we are good and take us to heaven when we die. But if we are bad, if we play with the devil and magic, then we go to . . ." Francis had been taught never to say the word *hell*, so he stopped himself there. "We go to a bad place. Do they not teach you the same things in your school back in your Englishman's country?"

"Yes. Though not the magic part." Zara looked down at the red dust squeezing up between her toes. "That means I'm not good. What will God do to me?"

Francis laughed. "You are only a baby. You are innocent in the eyes of the Lord. But," and he raised his finger, "if you mess with that *grigri*, then God for certain will send you . . . down."

"You mean to hell?"

"Shh! It is bad to say that word." Pursing his lips prudishly, Francis scooped up the pulled weeds and stood.

"I'm going to hell, I'm going to hell," Zara chanted, hopping around his feet the way she had at the foot of the *kalou* tree that day she had almost killed him. She couldn't resist because the look on his face was so funny. "What's that?" she said, stopping and pointing to his bare chest, where she had just noticed three small symmetrical scars on his breastbone, right over his heart.

He covered them with his hand, looking around to make sure he and Zara were alone. Then squatting down again, he whispered, "Mama, she took me to the priest to be baptized when I was born, and then afterwards she took me to the *bonnonm* as well. He put the marks there to protect me from *grigri* and *dundosya* my whole life."

"What's *dandosya*?"

"You do not know?" Zara shook her head. "It is a person who has died of *grigri* without absolution from a priest. He walks at night, looking to rest, but he cannot lie in his grave without the magic of a *malfeter*—an evil sorcerer—to help him rest. I think you call him *zombie* in English."

A shiver went through Zara. The idea of a walking corpse with its eyes staring and its flesh rotting had terrified her ever since she'd seen a picture of one in a film magazine. "Can I get those marks, too, to protect me?"

Francis straightened up and shook his head. "No, no. Papa, he said it was a very bad thing to have done because the *bonnonm*, when he made the marks, he rubbed into them the evil black powder made of burnt human bones. Papa said he wanted to beat *Man-man* when he saw them."

"Does he think Nana will go to hell now?"

Francis scowled. "I told you, do not say that word! But . . . well . . . I do not know. Perhaps my father, he is not right about this. She was giving me both the priest's and the *bonnonm*'s protection, and . . ." He looked again over his shoulder. "I think that is correct for a mother to do, no?"

"You're going to hell, you're going to hell," Zara chanted this time.

Francis winced.

Then she stopped. "Mummy tells Daddy to go to hell sometimes," she said gravely. "That's why I do magic. I want to take away her demon worm so she'll stop saying those bad things."

Francis could see her point.

The monsoons began later that week, bringing thick clouds that rolled down from the mountains like great billows of steam, and fat drops of rain that slashed sideways through the air, driving through clothes and screen windows as if determined to soak everything in sight. The children were forced to spend more time inside and quickly got on one another's nerves. Marguerite and Sylvie grew irritable and unkind, disinclined to even slip the girls treats from the kitchen. But most affected of all was Penelope. She spent hours each day now sealed off with a book, smoking one cigarette after another until Rupert came home. And when he did, divesting himself in the hallway of his useless and wind-mangled umbrella, she couldn't stop herself picking at him, in spite of all her vows. "Where have you been?" she would say, unable to keep the accusation out of her voice. "I can't imagine they need you at the office this much." And, "I don't suppose you're planning to grace us with your presence for supper this evening, for a change?"

"Oh, for Christ's sake, shut up!" he would bark, and stride into his study, slamming the door.

Mummy and Daddy never used to talk like that at home, Zara thought, huddled upstairs as she listened. Never.

So in spite of Francis's warnings, she crawled out into the rain one day with a mortar and pestle she had stolen from the kitchen, and ducked under the house to fetch the cricket cage she'd hidden behind the front steps. There, she settled down to murder the rhinoceros beetle. She had decided the time had come to pound it into powder and feed it to her mother, hoping its strength would kill off the demon worm for good. God wouldn't mind if she used a little *grigri* for that, would he? After all, she only wanted to make her mummy brave and nice again, the way she had been that day she'd picked up the beetle. She only wanted to make Mummy kind so Daddy would stop snapping and slamming and stay at home and tell his stories. But the second she brought the pestle down with a loud *crack* on the beetle's back, Marguerite peered under the house and caught her.

"Ai, what are you doing?" she cried, dragging Zara out by a foot. "Is it evil magic, is that it?"

"No," Zara stammered. "It's not evil. It's for—" but Marguerite wouldn't listen. Seizing Zara by the ear, she pulled her all over the garden and into the house, forcing her to take out all her little boxes from their hiding places and show her what was inside. Zara wriggled and kicked and even tried to bite Marguerite on the shin, but Marguerite only pinched her ear all the harder and dragged her around in the rain until she obeyed. And after Zara, who was sobbing hard by now, had spread out all her kapok boxes in the kitchen, all seven of them—some filled with powdered ant, some with human hair, some with bits of gecko tail and some with three-inch-long sticks and the red seeds from the necklace—Marguerite made her take them all, along with their contents, even the precious rhinoceros beetle, and throw them into the stinky rubbish bin outside, which a man with a cart took to the dump that very day.

"What you are doing is filthy and disgusting. This is not real sorcery, this is the stupid game of a child!" Marguerite hissed. "And if I catch you at this again, I will beat you the way I beat Francis."

In truth, however, Marguerite was not so much angry as frightened. The content of those uncannily expert *grigri* boxes had given her a turn. How had Zara known? The insects were nonsense, of course, but the hair, those little sticks—this was the work of someone with the Gift. And as for the jequirity seeds—where had Zara found those? Why, those seeds were so poisonous even one could kill a baby. Suppose Zara had fed Chloe one of those seeds, the way she had fed her the worm-laden dirt? Marguerite cursed herself for not having paid more attention. Had she not sworn weeks ago to save this child from going the Evil Way? She could not allow Zara to know her own powers. She had to belittle and destroy them so Zara could remain innocent—and most of all, so she could remain harmless.

But Zara was devastated. Worse than being pulled about by the ear were the derisive words Nana had used about her magic. For Zara truly believed she was curing her mother, making her better so Daddy would like her again. Now, without the boxes she so loved because Francis had made them for her, without the powders she had carefully mashed and hidden and saved for weeks, she felt stripped; helpless to stop her mother's storming or her father's absences; powerless to protect her family from catastrophe.

She crept off to her nest at the base of the kapok tree, curled up under the pelting rain, and wept.

Monsoons

PART TWO

8

Joelle could not understand her bad luck. Three months in Rupert's bed, three months of his seed in her at least twice a day, of praying to the Virgin Mary with offerings of fruit and the best of the duck's eggs bought from her sister, yet her flow was coming as regularly as ever. Why? With the other men she had not wanted this. She had made them pull out early, or had washed and taken a *tizann*, a special tea, that Madame Hélène, the fortune-teller, had given her because she was determined not to be like her older sisters with fourteen children between them and no money. But with Rupert she had prayed for a baby more than she had ever prayed for anything, yet her belly was flat as a palm leaf.

Joelle often went to the fortune-teller, or *bater kart,* as she was called in Creole, because she was less expensive than the *bonnonm dibwa* and not as frightening. She was also old and wise; people said she'd been a *bater kart* for a hundred years. She knew everything about everybody on Mahé, and had helped the Lagrenade family countless times. She had helped Alphonse get Joseph away from that Marguerite Savy, so stuck-up with her Indian hair and her papa a policeman. She had helped Charité win a man away from his wife, although it had done her no good in the end. And she had helped Joelle, both by giving her the *tizann* to stop the babies and by slipping her another for her men so they wouldn't want anybody else. This last was a tea she made by boiling water with shredded cassava root, three small sticks of cashew bark, several dried and fragrant leaves and a stick of incense. It had worked so well on Rupert he'd confessed to her only the other day that he hadn't slept with his wife once since they'd arrived in the Seychelles.

Joelle had used this man-binding *tizann* so often she was expert at it now, and even made a few rupees on the side by selling it to her friends (something she hoped Madame Hélène would not find out). The trick was to boil the concoction for a count of exactly five, then quickly strain it and make the man drink it as hot as possible. If you boiled it any longer, Madame Hélène had warned her, it would make the man sick and listless. The tea, one was supposed to tell the men, was to aid digestion.

The reason Joelle and her sisters had consulted Madame Hélène so frequently was not only because of their love troubles, though, but because the family had been plagued by misfortune. Joelle's mother had begun well enough, marrying a sober yellow-skinned man with a steady job on a coconut plantation and producing three daughters and two sons, every one of them a beauty. But soon the bad luck had started. Joelle's father came down with an infection in his foot that no doctor or witchcraft could cure. It ate its way up first through his heel, then through his leg until, at the age of twenty-nine, he died of a fever so high he burned to the touch. Then Joelle's eldest sister, Charité, moved in with a man who beat her, gave her nine children and deserted her to go back to an earlier wife. Charité lived high on the mountain now, with a series of men who passed through her house like cockroaches, leaving nothing but their shit, as her mother liked to put it. The next to fall was Alphonse, the middle sister, who might have done well for herself with her buxom flashiness had she not stolen Joseph from Marguerite Savy and become the victim of the woman's revenge. Now Alphonse was worn and bent, and spent almost every evening searching the streets for Joseph then dragging him home, drunk, while he vomited in the road. After that were Joelle's brothers. One became a fisherman, despite his mother's pleas to choose something less dangerous, and so, predictably, died at sea.

The other, a day laborer, survived but refused to go near any of his relatives, not even for Christmas or New Year's, claiming the whole lot of them were cursed. And finally, driven beyond endurance by all these misfortunes, Madame Lagrenade herself descended into drunkenness, complicated by heart disease and diabetes.

Only Joelle, the baby of the family, had been able to pull herself above all this bad luck. She knew having been born the lightest had helped—Rupert said she was more pink than brown—but she also knew it had taken hard work and cunning. She had studied typing, had come first in her class, and had risen, at the age of twenty-four, to being one of the only secretaries in Seychelles, earning seven-and-a-half rupees a week.

Three months into her relationship with Rupert, however, Joelle decided that the old *lizann* wasn't enough, not while he still had a wife and she had no baby. So she determined to go once again to Madame Hélène, this time to ask for help in getting pregnant and to buy medicine that would make Rupert's wife sick enough to have to go home. She had no wish to kill the wife; Joelle was a good Catholic and that would be the work of the devil. She only hoped to make her go away and take her children with her, for what did Joelle want with two children by another woman? Anyway, she reasoned, she was doing the wife a favor, for Rupert had told her how the woman complained all the time about being bored and homesick. And then, when she was gone, Joelle and Rupert would be so happy! For Joelle was certain she would never find another man like him, rich and white, yet so sweet her throat swelled at the thought of him. Nor would she ever have such a good opportunity to help her family escape the Lagrenade fate.

So, on a Saturday morning, she arose early, careful not to awaken her mother, dusted her underarms and full breasts with talcum powder and clambered into the nicest dress she had ever made for herself, an orange poplin with a tight bodice, full skirt, puffed sleeves and a V-shaped collar of black lace. Her hair, which she'd straightened the day before, she pulled into a becoming bun on the back of her head, but she put on her best hat anyway to protect her freckled complexion from the sun. She peered into a bit of broken mirror on the wall. She looked pretty and respectable, and most important, prosperous, and that was what counted when one went to see a fortune-teller.

Before she left, she crossed herself and curtseyed in front of the little plaster Madonna hanging by the door. "Forgive me, Mother Mary, for what I do, but it is for the love of a man and the happiness of my family. Protect me and give me a baby. Amen."

Joelle made her way to the fortune-teller, passing a series of wooden huts, their floors raised on stilts, their courtyards occupied by scratching chickens and snuffling pigs. A wind blew through the palms, sending them rustling and clacking, making her shiver; the monsoon rains were due again soon. But then the morning church bells began to ring and a cock crowed twice: signs of excellent luck. Her spirits lifted.

Madame Hélène lived in an ostentatious two-story house on the outskirts of Victoria. Officially, she made her money from her well-kept vegetable garden and her embroidery—she sold her decorated pillows and handkerchiefs through the shops on Market Street—but everyone knew that most of her income came from fortune-telling and her curative herbs. Her front yard was festooned with unfamiliar potted plants, and her house was bordered by all sorts of mysterious bushes that Joelle was certain produced the illegal but potent medicines that had made the fortune-teller so rich.

Joelle stepped up onto the veranda and knocked. In an instant, the door was opened by a servant girl in her teens whom Joelle vaguely recognized. (It was Lisette, but Joelle didn't remember that until afterward, when it was too late.) The girl was shoeless, one foot strapped to a coconut husk smeared with red polish, on which she'd been skating over the floor to wax it. Lisette's pretty face splashed into a smile.

"*Bonzour, Manmzel,*" she said to Joelle, not letting on she knew her. "Enter, please. I will tell Madame you are here."

Joelle stepped in, her skin tingling as it always did when she came to see the fortune-teller. She could sense the power of the woman's Second Sight permeating the whitewashed rooms.

The house itself made her skin tingle as well, for nowhere else had Joelle seen such opulence. Embroidered doilies covered every table, cushions buried the straw chairs, lace curtains dangled over the pink bamboo window blinds and, most striking of all, the biggest mirror she had ever seen hung opposite the doorway in a heavy gold frame. Joelle's own family shack boasted no decorations but tattered magazine covers and the piece of broken glass into which she had peered that morning. And as for the government office where she worked, that was nothing like Madame Hélène's luxurious abode. Being a place of men—and Englishmen at that—it was bare and austere, without a soft thing like a cushion or a doily in sight. The floors and walls were plain wood and the furniture nothing but clumsy desks and upright chairs (most uncomfortable when it came to making love with Rupert). An old fan revolved in the ceiling, papers and books were stacked haphazardly on a set of wooden shelves, and that was it. Yet the government men didn't seem to care. They spent most of their time out on the veranda anyway, or at the Seychelles Club down on the pier, drinking and talking about women. The only work they ever seemed to do was take an occasional telephone call, or file away a petition from some worried islander or another, who had come clutching a few hard-earned rupees in the hope of buying justice. Joelle's main duties as secretary were to shoo these people away if they arrived after eleven in the morning or before three in the afternoon while the gentlemen were at lunch. Otherwise, she was expected to fetch the beer from the Chinese shop down the road and type out the letters the Englishmen liked to dictate in the afternoons, when they were drunk.

"'To Her Majesty's Department of Sexual Relations.' Ha-ha. No, seriously, Joelle: 'To Her Majesty's Department of Foreign Affairs.' Get it?"

Englishmen could be very stupid.

After standing for some time in Madame Hélène's front parlor (she was not invited to sit) while three girls skated around her on their waxed coconut husks, Joelle was at last summoned by Lisette. She followed the girl through a curtain of wooden beads into a room on the side, still trying to place her familiar face, and was ushered to a straight-backed chair with a seat of woven straw. She sat, the chair creaking under her weight—Joelle, although not hefty, was tall and amply endowed. Opposite her, Madame Hélène was lounging in a wide wicker armchair, fanning herself with a palm leaf and smiling enigmatically. Joelle greeted her nervously.

(Lisette stood out of sight on the other side of the curtain, polishing a lamp.)

Madame Hélène was certainly old. Back when she had first made her reputation some thirty years earlier, she'd been in her forties, not a wrinkle on her, with seven children, a large stomach to show for it and a long, queenly neck, but now she had shriveled and shrunk. Her eyes had closed to mere slits, through which only the smallest glimmer of black pupil could be seen; her former royal bearing had hunched to dwarfish proportions and her previously rich mahogany skin had mottled to leopard-speckled brown. She was hideous indeed, but this, along with her blood-red turban and the necklaces of cowrie shells and seeds dangling from her neck and arms, only added to the power of her presence. Joelle found herself trembling.

"Ah, so it is Joelle Lagrenade," the old *bater kart* cackled, her voice sharp and nasal. "I sensed you would come today. My mirror, it told me." She shifted her tiny body to the edge of her seat and gestured to a clouded mirror lying on a sewing table in front of her, covering the hole where the machine had once sat.

"Let me see, *zoli* Joelle, what you have come about? No, do not tell me." She held up an arthritic hand, gnarled as ginger root, her eyes scanning the tight waist of Joelle's orange dress and her black lace. Not pregnant yet, despite that man she had in town—that must be it. Madame Hélène knew all about the peccable Rupert and his family, just as she knew all about Marguerite and hers.

"So, my dear, how is your mother?"

Joelle answered courteously, as the occasion demanded. "Not so well, Madame. She ate some octopus, cooked by her mother-in-law, and now it walks in her stomach."

"Ah. I shall give you a *tizann* for her. It will make the octopus sleep. And Alphonse, your pretty sister?"

Joelle shook her head and told of how Alphonse suffered from Joseph's reputation as the village drunk. They chatted this way for some time, Madame Hélène disarming and distracting Joelle, gathering her material.

(Outside the bead curtain door, Lisette yawned.)

Finally, the fortune-teller put a finger on a worn coin resting on the mirror and moved it in a circle around two silver rings. Joelle followed the movement helplessly.

"You are what now, about twenty-four years of age, no?" Madame Hélène said, not waiting for an answer. "It is time for a man's heart to be your own." She glanced at Joelle. "My mirror shows me you have a man who is good. He will give you a house and money. This looks like the love of the heart, not of sorcery, yes?"

Joelle flushed. "Yes, Madame."

"We do not want to lose this precious gift, correct?" The fortune-teller picked up a deck of well-worn tarot cards, told Joelle to cut it and laid out the result. She peered at the cards a moment in ominous silence, then coughed three times, her throat rattling phlegm, a cough that Joelle was sure signified something sinister.

"Ah," the *bater kart* finally said. "I see something tall, thin as bamboo. Sharp, like a stick." She looked at Joelle. "A woman?"

"Yes. A white woman." Joelle found her heart thudding.

Madame Hélène closed her eyes and began to sway her shrunken body from side to side. "I see a picture," she moaned in a singsong voice that sent chills up Joelle's spine. "I see two little petals in the sea. Little, pale petals, like that of the jasmine flower, tiny and weak. But wait!" (Joelle jumped, her heart lurching.) "These petals are tied to a piece of black lace, pretty floating lace, and light as they are, they are dragging it down and down, to the bottom of the sea. . . ."

The hair stood up along Joelle's arms. "The children," she whispered.

Madame Hélène's eyes sprung open, and Joelle swore later she saw a deep purple flame shoot out of them. Instantly, though, they were back to their catlike slits. "These obstacles, they are a danger to you and your love. We must help, yes?"

"Yes, please." Joelle leaned forward eagerly.

"Ah, but no." The fortune-teller paused. "No, alas, I cannot. It is too expensive." Heaving a sad sigh, she slumped back into her armchair, suddenly looking like a withered child. She crossed her baggy arms, the bumpy flesh hanging off them like the skin of a scrotum, and shook her head. "Sorry, but I cannot help you. It is too much."

"How much? I can pay. I am not like other women. I make very good money as a secretary!" Joelle was indignant.

"Ah, but you must come four times, and it will be . . ." Madame Hélène took another quick look at Joelle's dress and the ring Rupert had sneaked out of Penelope's drawer. "Today is three rupees, but after it must be four each visit."

Joelle sagged. Added together over four visits, that was half her monthly wages. How was she to buy food and drink, pay for her mother's doctor and come up with the rent, never mind the usual amount she gave to Charité and Alphonse to help feed their hoards of children? Every rupee Joelle made went for food and her family; the poplin for her dress and her nice hats she only possessed courtesy of various gentlemen. She frowned. She would have to swallow her pride and ask Rupert for the money. That amount of money was nothing to an Englishman.

"I can manage it," she said, sitting upright. "Tell me, what should I do first?"

(Lisette yawned again and allowed her eyes to float to the far window. She brightened, suddenly alert, and stood on tiptoe to see better.)

"Very good," Madame Hélène was saying. "First, we help the

bamboo stick go away, yes? And then those little petals, we must take care of them as well. And, of course, my pretty Joelle, we get you a baby."

"You can make the bamboo stick go away?"

"But of course. We can make it bleed to death the next time it has its monthly time, if you wish."

"I can't do that!" Joelle cried, shocked. "I'm a good woman, Madame, I can't—"

The fortune-teller held up her hand. "Calm yourself, *cherie*, do not worry. I, too, am a good woman. I was only testing you. I am here to help, and help you I will. My work is to spread happiness."

Joelle sat back warily, but she listened to the fortune-teller's instructions with care, after which she handed over the first of her payments, along with the guava and juicy red tomatoes she had brought in her handbasket. She hid the cloth sack Madame Hélène gave her in return in that same basket, underneath a handkerchief, then thanked her with respect and took her leave. On her way out through the garden, she passed the girl who had ushered her into the house and nodded farewell. The girl didn't notice, however. She was too busy leaning against the fence, flirting shamelessly with that strapping young man who taught at the school.

"This is a mighty sorceress, no mere fortune-teller," Joelle thought on the way back to her house. "Although, when I think of it, I am sure she made up that dream about the petals and my black lace. But I will do what she says. It would be dangerous not to."

A few days later, Penelope stood alone in the dining room, planning how to decorate the table for Rupert's thirty-first birthday party, her most elaborate attempt to win him back yet. She had tried conversing with him about the fauna of the island and her explorations with Vicky's binoculars, but he hadn't heard a word she said. She had struggled to sweeten her temper, too, despite the nerve-shredding monsoons, but he hadn't noticed that, either. And all her efforts to seduce him had met with the same rebuffs as the first one, leaving her so humiliated she could hardly talk. So she had thought in her despair that if she threw him a party, invited all the important people he needed in Seychelles and served superb food and good wine, he would be touched enough to wake up out of this insane intoxication and remember at last that he loved her.

She had also, in a careful way, tried to make him tell the truth about Joelle, but each time she brought her up, he either lied or shouted. Penelope didn't know which hurt more, that he'd fallen for another woman, that he was lying to her, or that he shouted at her like that—for in all their nine years together in London he'd never raised his voice to her when they quarreled but had only grown icy and sardonic. And when she'd shouted at him, he would shut his eyes and say, "Please stop. You sound like my father," which would silence her immediately. She had seen enough of his father's bellowing furies and the hurtling cups and saucers to make her unwilling to remind him of that, ever.

Penelope had accused Rupert of dalliances in those days, too, but he'd told her not to listen to gossip and not to stoop to mistrusting him. "You know I'm not like that, darling. Have a little faith. Anyway, I adore you." How happy they had been in London compared to now! Especially in the early days, when the children had come along, for Rupert had turned out to be one of those rare fathers who cared about nappy rashes and first teeth. Zara had been born a year into their marriage, Chloe five years later, and he had so enjoyed watching them grow, comparing notes with Penelope over how Zara had rolled over or Chloe taken a step. But what Penelope had loved most about their London life together were the winter evenings, when the whole family would cuddle up on the sitting-room carpet in front of the gas fire for tea and games—Monopoly, usually, or gin rummy. Rupert would cheat outrageously, tucking cards under his bottom or popping Monopoly hotels in his mouth to make the girls laugh. Chloe would lie against Penelope's legs, sucking her thumb, too young for games but still wanting to be part of the family circle.

And Zara would immerse herself in the competition, leaping to her feet each time she won a point and hopping about in triumph before settling back down to continue. Then, after an hour or so, after the biscuits were eaten, the tea finished and the fire had made them sleepy, the au pair of the moment would come in—some sullen Belgian girl, usually, or a pimply Swiss—take the children off to supper and bed, and leave the parents to themselves. Those evenings were the quintessence of family life to Penelope, of everything she'd been denied in childhood—they hadn't felt like playacting at all, when she thought about it now. For her idea of family life had been born of a people who had learned to live with bombs and shortages and sorrow. One didn't need luxury, that's what they'd learned. One didn't need ostentatious houses like Michael Toynbee's or swimming pools like Vicious Vicky had here. No, all one needed was a winter fire, a cup of tea, two children and a spouse.

There had been rough spots, of course—there always were in a marriage, or so her mother had warned her. The time, for example, when Rupert had accused her of being frigid in bed. When he'd said that, Penelope had taken the children and fled to Richmond in tears, refusing to come home until he'd apologized for a week. Not that going to Richmond was much of a respite, mind you; not with her family. Her mother was suffering from some sort of nervous disorder that had come on after her husband had died, causing her to take to her room for days at a time. (I wonder if I've inherited that? Penelope thought as she picked out the linen for the party.) And her brothers had turned into the most appalling sorts of teenager imaginable. James, then seventeen, had become a teddy boy, greasing up his hair into a ridiculous pouf and dressing in obscenely tight trousers, a clownish jacket with enormous shoulders and great ugly shoes, like car tires. His idea of fun was to roam sleepy Richmond with a gang, slashing up bus seats. And the other brother, Roddy, who'd just turned sixteen, spent his time listening to pop music on a phonograph in his room and "wanking off," as he liked to tell her as she was biting into her morning toast. Then there was Uncle Keith.

After her father's death, Keith had lost control completely, shivering all day in one corner or another and shitting himself. They'd had to put him in a home, where Penelope had felt compelled to visit him every day she was in Richmond and make bright conversation while he stared at her in ghoulish silence.

At the end of that trying week, when Rupert had finally apologized enough, sworn he didn't mean it and driven all the way to Richmond to fetch her back, she had taken the children and, without a word, climbed into the car and ridden all the way home with her eyes closed in relief.

"Madame?" It was Sylvie, rolling out of the kitchen to ask a question. Penelope looked up in surprise as she smoothed a green linen tablecloth over the table. Sylvie almost never initiated a conversation. "It is eight people, Madame, yes?" She had on a food-smeared white apron, under which her vast stomach bounced and jiggled.

"Eight guests, yes, but ten people, including Monsieur Weston and me."

"Then we have not enough rice, Madame. The fish, it is good, and the rest, it is good. But the rice, no."

Penelope was about to ask why Sylvie hadn't realized that before—such as that very morning when they had all gone to market—but she stopped herself. It didn't do to quarrel with the cook an hour before the guests were to arrive.

"Is Francis still here? Perhaps we can send him to get some."

"Yes, Madame, I will go see."

Sylvie waddled back to the kitchen while Penelope watched her suspiciously. Marguerite had warned her to be careful of who prepared her food. "Do not take any food from a stranger, or from anybody who knows the Lagrenade family," she'd said. "Do not even take food in your friends' houses because their cooks, they might know this Joelle and they might poison you." Penelope thought this absurd. How could she refuse the food at Hannah's, for example? But she couldn't help worrying about Sylvie, who was in control of all they ate and yet barely uttered a word. Marguerite had promised to ask around and find out if Sylvie was in cahoots with Joelle or her sisters, but had reported nothing to Penelope as of yet. She had also promised to look into this business of evicting Joelle from the government office, but nothing had come of that, either.

Feeling uneasy, Penelope turned back to laying the table. She knew the servants were supposed to do this sort of work, but none of them had her style. Anyway, in London, she'd done everything herself and had not had a servant at all, except for those sulky au pairs, who were usually no more help than a banana.

She opened the silver drawer, lined with brown felt to prevent tarnish, and selected ten soupspoons, ten dinner and salad forks, ten knives and . . . what to use for the pudding? Sylvie was going to make pineapple flambé, slices of sugared pineapple drenched in brandy and set dramatically aflame just before serving. Penelope chose a set of spoons for eating those. But she had also planned a surprise, one not even Sylvie knew about: a fluffy yellow birthday cake for Rupert, iced with a mix of tinned butter and condensed milk, flavored with the local vanilla he adored, and filled with good English raspberry jam, a jar of which she had brought all the way from home. She'd made the cake herself that afternoon (not easy to get it to rise in this tropical heat), and had hidden it in the larder inside a lobster pot to protect it from ants and children. She set out a row of cake forks.

The other time that had been awful with Rupert was when his father had died. You would think he might have been relieved, so monstrous was that man, but then, of course, he could remember what his father had been like before the war. I wish I'd known him then, Penelope thought, it might have helped. For when she did meet him, it had been one of the most horrible moments of her life.

Rupert had been taking her to his flat for sex for several weeks by the time the meeting occurred, but he would not to introduce her to either of his parents. She couldn't understand it. After all, he'd warned her that his father was legless and difficult and she'd said she could cope. "I'm used to that sort of thing—look at my uncle," she'd told him. But Rupert kept making excuses, saying he liked the secret love nest they had made in his room and that his parents would only interfere and spoil it.

He was certainly right about spoiling it. Penelope shuddered at the memory. She and Rupert had been up in his room, the cold brown bed-sit with the fecal wallpaper, and he had just warmed up his hands by rubbing them on his flannel trousers, laughing, so he could take off her brassiere without freezing her (how sweet he'd been before the beard!), when they heard an almighty crash from below and a bloodcurdling howl of rage.

Rupert turned pale and rushed out the door, leaving her to struggle back into her tight green pullover alone.

"Get me up, you fucking wankers!" a deep and enraged voice bellowed up the stairs. "You stupid cow, dropping me like that!"

More diabolic curses, along with the sounds of struggles and grunts.

"Penny!" she heard Rupert call, his voice strained. "We need a hand, please."

And so the way she'd met Rupert's parents was by helping to pick up his father, who had fallen down the steps in his wheelchair and cut open his head, and by ducking when he'd seized a carpet rod and thrown it like a javelin at his wife.

Penelope shook her head as if to rid herself of a fly and went over to the china cabinet to take out the wineglasses. Mustn't think about that. No point. The man had gone mad with pain and helplessness, that's all. Just another war tragedy, and weren't they used to that? In fact, he'd been so mad that when an infection had started up in one of his stumps—this was two years ago—he had refused to go to hospital, preferring to blame the doctors, rather than the Nazis, for the loss of his legs. And so he had died in roaring and violent misery in the privacy of his own home.

Rupert had been beside himself. "I can't believe my idiot mother didn't get an ambulance and a couple of strong blokes to force him into hospital!" he'd moaned night after night, pacing up and down their hallway, their sitting room, their bedroom. "All he needed was some penicillin, for Christ's sake! This isn't the Middle Ages!"

At first Penelope had been sympathetic; she knew about dead fathers. But Rupert had kept on about it for weeks, blaming his mother, even blaming Penelope, until she was at her wit's end. "Rupert," she finally said, "if you don't shut up about your father, I'm going to sleep with Ian Winslop."

Ian Winslop was one of Rupert's office chums, a fuddy-duddy young fellow with thick glasses and a tall man's stoop, who happened to be extraordinarily intelligent. Penelope had never understood why he had married that bony Susan, though. Susan had no more brains than a doorknob.

Rupert had shut up immediately and stared at her with his puppy brown eyes. "Are you serious?"

"I am." Penelope pinned on her hat, pink straw with a graceful rim that curved down over her brow. She was on her way to meet a friend at the National Gallery to see this new thing called Pop Art. "He asked me to, you know. I said I'd think about it." She picked up her gloves—pink, to match the hat—and with the tiniest of smirks, marched out the front door.

Rupert had never blamed her for his father's death again.

The table was ready. Penelope stood back to survey it, pleased. It was a pity, though, that so many of her Minton plates were broken. She'd had to put out some ordinary dishes instead, plain white with an unfortunate green splotch in the middle that was supposed to be a flower but looked more like a bit of stuck spinach. Still, the room did look impressive, not only because of her pretty table, all in green and silver, with a vase of fragrant scarlet hibiscus in the middle, but because the open doors and shutters on every side gave it the look of a glamorous tree house. If only I liked the guests better, she thought, plucking at her fingers. Just the idea of the guests made her stomach twist. She'd had to invite the Talbots, of course, Edith and her odious husband Roger, the toad in the orange toupee, because he was Rupert's superior. Then there was Vicious Vicky and her mate, Hugh Hubert (yes, really, what a name), who was as thick as she was sharp. Hannah was coming by herself because her husband had fallen sick with some tropical parasite and had been shipped off to a Mombasa hospital, so the poor woman was alone with her children, quaking with anxiety and in need of company. Hannah's absent husband was to be replaced by a newly arrived American anthropologist named Paul Leland, whom Penelope had met only once; Leland was married but had traveled here ahead of his family to find them a house. And then, worst of all, there were the Toynbees, both the crowning glory and ultimate humiliation of this whole horrible event.

I'm doing this for Rupert, she told herself. I'm doing it to remind him that I love him. I shall help raise him up so we never have to mix with such pernicious people again. I shan't look Michael Toynbee in the eye, that's all.

"I'm home, darling. Not too late, I hope?" It was Rupert's voice in the foyer. They still kept up this calling of each other darling and dear, only now it had a sharp, teeth-tingling sound to it, like the scraping of nails along a tin wall. "I'll just pop in the shower and get dressed for the dinner. Everything all right?"

"Did you remember to pick up the candles?" Penelope called, walking out to meet him. She looked up into his face. "Oh God."

Rupert had shaved off his beard.

9

Half an hour before Rupert had burst into the house beardless, he had been in bed with Joelle, on the verge of a mighty orgasm. They were lying in her hot and shabby bungalow on a straw mat, the only bed available to them at the time, and Joelle was astride him like some hefty fertility goddess, earthy, voluptuous and so redolent of powder and perfume he felt drunk. He strained against her, his climax mounting, and pulled her down to him for a kiss. He wanted to devour her, to have as much of her touching him, surrounding him, swallowing him as he could.

"Ugh," she said, and drew back.

He blinked, his orgasm ebbing. "Ugh?"

"It is your beard, *cheri*. It smells like a crab."

His orgasm, and his erection for that matter, drained away completely. "Joelle," he groaned, "how could you?"

She rolled off him, panting. "I am sorry, but a woman cannot kiss a crab."

"Shall I wash it for you?" Rupert said meekly. "I do think I had crab soup for lunch."

"Yes, I would like for you to do this." Joelle turned on her side to face him, her great breasts lolling with her. Rupert's penis began to perk up again. He turned on his side, too, his pudgy belly puckering, and started to lick her nipples.

She pushed him away. "That is very nice, but your beard, it tickles and scratches and it makes me want to laugh."

"Does it really?" Rupert scrunched up his brow a minute. "That sounds rather bad. My love, you know I would do anything for you. Shall I cut the beastly thing off, crab smell and all?"

Joelle smiled. "You would do this for me?"

"Immediately. The damn thing's too hot in this climate anyway."

So he jumped up, his penis waving like a train signal, and strode over to the piece of broken mirror on the wall. And there, after Joelle had dressed and run to a neighbor's to borrow a razor and a pair of scissors, and to fill a bucket with water, he soaped it up and cut and shaved the whole shaggy bundle off, down to the last whisker.

Joelle gathered the heap of brown curls off the floor—they felt much softer than they had on his face—and shoved them under her pillow, next to a chicken bone. The bone she had put there earlier because Madame Hélène said it would help her retain Rupert's affections. "I keep this," she said, "because I love you."

Rupert washed the soap off his bare chin, which felt painfully raw. "What do you think?" He turned to face her.

Joelle stared. His jaw was a blaring white, much whiter than his cheeks and brow, which had bronzed in the sun—it was as white as the flesh of a newly plucked chicken. But even so, his brown eyes looked wider and kinder than ever, his cheeks rounder and more boyish, and his chin turned out to be finely shaped and adorably dimpled.

"You look, *cheri*, like a little boy."

Rupert grimaced. "Precisely. That's why I grew the damn thing in the first place."

"But no, you are beautiful." Joelle meant it. She had genuinely hated his beard. The fact that Madame Hélène had told her to get hold of some of it was mere coincidence.

Rupert approached her once more and lifted off her dress.

"Rupert, my heart?"

"Yes, darling girl?" He nuzzled her neck, cradling her breasts in both hands.

"No. No, never mind. I cannot tell you."

"What it is, sweetness? You know you can tell me anything."

"Well . . ." she sighed, lying down again naked on the mat. "It is only that Mama's birthday, it is coming this week and I have not the money for a present. I was going to buy her a new radio, you know? Because the old one, it does not work. But I paid for it and the man at the shop, he pretended I didn't and he would not give it to me."

"The bastard! We should call the police."

"No, no, it is no use. They would not believe me. But I feel so sad now, for I have nothing for my mother."

"Darling, ask and it is yours." Rupert plucked his shorts off a chair, where he'd flung them earlier in mounting passion, and took out fifty rupees from his wallet. (Fifty! Joelle calculated quickly in her head. That would not only cover Madame Hélène but allow her to buy the sugar and medicine her mother needed, along with enough food for three weeks!) He also shyly handed her a silver necklace wrapped in tissue he'd bought off Edith Talbot the night before, who was selling it to raise money for some sort of charity.

"You did not take this from your wife, I think?" Joelle said, stowing the money and the necklace under her pillow with his beard and the bone. She yawned as if it didn't matter.

"No, don't worry. I bought it for you, fair and square."

"But that little scarf you gave me, the blue—that was your wife's, was it not?"

Rupert had the grace to blush. "Well, yes. I hope you don't mind. It was rather shabby of me to give it to you, wasn't it?"

Joelle chuckled and pulled him down to the mat, stroking his newly bare chin. "No, no, I do not mind at all, *monnamour*. Anytime you wish to give me something of hers, you can. It only makes me feel I have your love."

"Really?" Rupert looked at her, puzzled.

"Come," she said, lying on her back and opening her legs. "Let us finish."

The first course, served by Marguerite, who was looking crisply professional with her plait in its crown and a starched white apron over her customary frock, was chilled cucumber soup. This had been achieved only at the cost of a battle with Sylvie, for the cook had scoffed at the idea of a dish so bland and had suggested turtle soup instead, followed by curried fruit bat, which she had insisted were rare Seychellois delicacies that Penelope should be proud to serve. "You expect us to eat a *bat*?" Penelope had said in true astonishment. Sylvie had sulked, Penelope commanded and a cold truce had followed.

"I will make your cucumber mush, Madame," Sylvie had muttered to herself as she'd shuffled back to the kitchen, "but I will put in it a shark chutney so spicy it will burn your little white mouth."

Penelope sat at one end of the sparkling table, smiling with a glassy sheen, Rupert at the other, his chin as pale as Chloe's bottom, and the guests were lined up on either side, a man between each woman. The candles—long ivory tapers, which Rupert had miraculously remembered to pick up in Victoria on his way home from Joelle's bed—flickered as they were attacked by moths (the ceiling fan was turned off to minimize wax splatter), but Penelope ignored that. Insects were a fact of life here and she had long since given up trying to fight them.

"So, what is it, exactly, you're planning to do here?" Michael Toynbee was saying to the American anthropologist two chairs down from him. Toynbee leaned forward in a menacing manner, his beaky nose reflecting the candlelight. "Is it only the natives you're proposing to study, or is it we Britons who are to be your specimens?"

The company tittered politely.

Penelope looked down at her soup, which was oddly pink for cucumber. Whatever had possessed her to think that anything at all about Toynbee was attractive? How did poor Kate stand his condescension? She glanced at her, a large, placid women with the commanding air of a head nurse, who was sitting on her left, between the boiled toad Talbot and Vicky's husband, the pea-brained Hugh Hubert. Kate didn't see her glance, however, because she was gazing across the table at the anthropologist with genuine interest.

"My husband doesn't mean to tease, Mr. Leland," she was saying. "In fact, we're most enthusiastic about your project, both in our—I mean my husband's—capacity as governor, and by virtue of having lived here for five years. We have long thought the people of these islands deserved study. But what is it, precisely, you wish to look at?"

So that's how she does it, thought Penelope; she rescues the stupid bugger. At least Rupert doesn't need rescuing, or I hope not, even if he is a pernicious shit of an unfaithful bastard. She took a long swig of wine. Control yourself, Penny. Just because he cut off his beard doesn't mean anything, does it? It isn't any kind of proof. . . .

"Penny darling, do listen." It was Vicious Vicky, two down on her right, opposite Kate. It was impossible not to listen to Vicky, for her voice had a foghorn quality to it that never failed to seize attention. "The soup's divine—very native. I believe your cook's made the hottest chutney on Mahé to go into it!" She fanned her tongue emphatically and the guests tittered again. "But where did you get the wonderful cukes? All the ones I've found here are so disappointingly inerect." She chortled.

Penelope frowned. "Marguerite—I mean our nanny grows them in her garden," she replied unwillingly, and felt a sudden longing to escape to the kitchen with Marguerite and talk again about love and marriage, instead of sitting at that stuffy table, all bound up and sweating in her blue sheath of an evening frock like a moth trapped in its cocoon.

"Jolly good soup. I'm in need of water, please." This was said by Hugh Hubert, who was sitting on Kate's left. Hugh was tall, bald and bony, and so shortsighted he was bent over with his nose almost in his bowl. He had turned an alarming shade of red and sweat was popping out on his brow. Penelope passed the water with an inward heave of despair. She had wanted to seat Hannah next to her so she could ask about her poor husband; at least that was something out of real life instead of the charade being enacted here. But one couldn't put a woman next to a woman at a dinner party any more than one could place a wife next to a husband. Oh hell, what did it matter? Every last person at the dinner table was unspeakable anyway.

But the American was speaking. She must listen, for at least he was new. "Well, in a sense your husband's right," he was saying to Kate. "I am kind of studying you British. I'm looking at former slave colonies around the world." An uneasy shift of attention occurred at these words and the guests turned toward him warily. "I came here because I'm fascinated by what happens to a people when their customs and history have been wiped out. As you know, all the indigenous cultures of the Seychellois have been destroyed, first by the slave trade wrenching them from their homes and then by French and British colonialism. I want to find out what they've built up instead."

How like an American to be fascinated by slavery, Penelope mused, beckoning to Marguerite to offer another round of soup. Nonetheless, she was intrigued. She hadn't given slavery much thought before landing in Seychelles, or ever, come to think of it, but she did remember Rupert telling her that most of the Creoles here had grandparents or even parents who'd been slaves.

"I think that's putting it a bit strongly, don't you?" Toynbee said. "Of course the Seychellois have a culture. It's absurd to say we've stripped them of it altogether."

"Oh, I don't know," Roger Talbot chimed in, blinking his gelatinous eyes and waving his soupspoon in a way no gentleman should. "The French certainly did their best to quash the people. I mean, look at the appalling Roman Catholicism that's taken hold of the place. You can't so much as peek into a school without seeing a nun, and then there's all their claptrap about birth control being a sin. The church should be forcing people to take the pill, if you ask me, not preaching nonsense about abstinence and holy matrimony. Now the place is overrun with blacks, way too many for the island's resources, and it's all because of their damn popishness."

"Roger's right," Vicky hooted, leaning her baggy, sun-cooked face over the table. "We had to import a governess for the children all the way from England because we couldn't bear to expose the poor lambs to these French Catholic schools. By the way, I do believe it's shark chutney your cook's put in here, Penny. Absolutely soaked in tipiman chilies."

Penelope winced. She was finding this American anthropologist interesting, despite his bad hairstyle (too long) and his slovenly manners (he had left his serviette on the table). She wanted to hear what else he had to say without moronic interruptions from her guests.

"I don't think we can blame it all on the French," she said, speaking up somewhat to her own surprise. Rupert blinked at the sound of her voice and looked startled. She was sure he hadn't been listening to a word anybody said. "I mean, we rule over these people as if they're children and keep them in the most terrible poverty. That's what our nanny tells me, anyhow."

"True," said Hugh, mopping his brow with a handkerchief. "Far as I know, not a native soul on this island has ever cast a vote."

"Exactly!' said the American, picking up his serviette at last and swiping it across his mouth. (But then he put it back down on the table—disgusting.) He was very dark, this Mr. Leland, Penelope noticed, with his overlong black hair and tanned, craggy face. He was trim and muscular as a tennis pro, as well. He looked as though he could clamber through jungles and over mountains, notebook in hand, with no effort at all—if that's what anthropologists did, she thought vaguely.

"Why do you say 'exactly,' Mr. Leland?" Kate said. "In what sense?"

Leland pushed away his soup and leaned his elbows on the table, his blue eyes spots of intensity under his bushy black brows. "Well, look at how they live: governed by you, no local representation worth speaking of, bossed around by European priests. What kind of autonomy can a people have under such circumstances? The only Seychellois with real power are those *bonnonm dibwa* they're so secretive about."

"Oh, really," Toynbee blustered, turning pink. "They don't all believe in that primitive nonsense, you know. Some are quite sophisticated and good Christians to boot. Even if they are Catholic."

Leland didn't answer that, only raised his eyebrows and laughed, a high-pitched cackle that rather put Penelope off. She preferred the low rumble of the English male.

"But what do you mean about the *bonhommes* having power?" she asked him, leaning forward over her inedible soup. "And do they really exist? Our nanny told me the stories about them are only rumors."

"She had to say that because they've been outlawed," Leland replied, turning his remarkably blue eyes on her. "But they exist, all right. What I mean is, if you believe that your misfortune is caused by curses and spells, then you believe it's possible to reverse it, right? So in the eyes of the Seychellois, a witch doctor like the *bonnonm*, who can control curses and spells, has the power to alter your fate. And that's a lot of power."

"But if everyone's so secretive about them, how are you going to find out anything?"

Leland smiled at her. "That's where my fieldwork comes in. I'll start by meeting the local people and gathering data on their household structures, family trees and so on. Like a census. Then, after I've built up some trust, I'll go out and talk to them for as long as it takes to get what I want. My wife Lily's going to help when she arrives."

Penelope blinked. He was going to let his wife work with him? "But what do you want them to tell you? Aside from about the *bonhommes*, I mean."

"How they run their households and manage money, how they regard marriage and love, politics, religion—all that. Later, I'll compare what I find here and in other former slave colonies to the Negro condition back home."

"Well, Mr. Leland, you have your work cut out for you," Kate said, sitting back and folding her hands over her matronly stomach. "The people here won't answer your questions, you know. They loathe direct questions of all kinds, but especially those about their private lives. Haven't any of you noticed?" She looked around the table with a teacherly air.

"Oh, absolutely," Vicky hooted. "It's impossible to get a word of truth out of them. All one gets is evasions and lies." She downed the rest of her red wine, pushed her glass forward suggestively and lit up a cigarette.

Penelope glanced at Marguerite, who was clearing the soup dishes at last (one taste had burned Penelope's tongue so badly she hadn't been able to eat the rest at all), hoping her limited English had prevented her from understanding this part of the conversation.

The American was unperturbed. "Yeah, I know. It's like that in all former slave cultures—in the States, too. But if you'd been blamed and punished without anybody considering your point of view for generations, would you answer a question directly? Every question is a trap, right? A way to get you into trouble. No, I'll have to take it slow until Lily and I can win enough trust to be let into their confidence. I've found an interpreter to help, of course."

Penelope listened thoughtfully. She had noticed how reserved Sylvie was, and Marguerite as well before that tête-à-tête they'd had in the kitchen, but she'd assumed it was merely their way of keeping a polite distance, just as servants did in England. She had never seen their evasiveness as protective before.

"I'm sorry, old fellow, but that's nonsense," Toynbee said, leaning back while Marguerite lifted away his barely touched soup. "You're only seeing an imitation of the manners they've learned from their French and English masters. After all, we don't go around revealing our secrets at the drop of a hat, do we?" Penelope flushed, thinking of the many secrets crowding the table. "As you probably know, Leland, we English are legendary for our reserve, and the French aren't much different at heart. We've simply passed the habit on, so to speak. It's nothing to do with slavery. That's a lot of socialist bosh."

"Um, Mr. Leland, would you care for more wine?" Penelope said quickly, hoping to blunt the ever-burgeoning offensiveness of Toynbee. She glared at Rupert because, as the man of the house, he was the one who was supposed to be pouring the wine. But Rupert was off in a dream.

"No thanks," the anthropologist replied with another smile. "One glass is all I can take in this heat. And please call me Paul."

"My goodness, are you both adorably earnest *and* totally incorruptible?" boomed Vicky with a phlegmy laugh as she drew on her cigarette. "I gather you don't even smoke. We shall have to work on desanctifying him, shan't we, Penny?"

Penelope blushed, too mortified to even send Leland an apologetic glance. If she didn't want so badly to please Rupert, she'd tell every one of these poisonous drones to bugger off home.

While the dinner party limped along, the tension between Toynbee and the American thickening every minute, Joelle was alone in her house a mere two miles away, working on the fifth of Madame Hélène's spells, the one to get rid of Penelope. She had already used Rupert's beard to strengthen her possession of his heart, sewing a handful of it to the inside of her dress so she could have him with her at all times, just as she'd used the chicken bone. She had also taken a pinch of the chunky gray substance the fortune-teller had sold to her, mixed it with talcum and doused her hands in it, so that when she touched him his spirit would be captured. Finally, after he had left her bed, she had dropped a thread into a bottle of magic syrup and flicked it against her stomach three times. No man, Madame Hélène had told her, could resist that.

To deal with Penelope, however, Joelle had to use the blood of her own menses.

She waited until her mother and sister had left for the Saturday-night dance at the church hall, then got down to work. Pulling out the blue silken scarf Rupert had given her, she ripped it into shreds and put it inside a clay cooking pot. Then she took the pot behind the house to the toilet shed, squatted over it and allowed a spill of urine and menstrual blood (still no baby, she lamented) to fall inside, as Madame Hélène had instructed. To that she added a clump of Rupert's beard and the fortune-teller's lumpy powder. (Joelle was not privy to the ingredients of this powder; one had to be a sorcerer to know that. Not even Madame Hélène was sure what was in it, but she had bought it, guaranteed, from *Bonnonm* Adonis, who had assured her that it contained the necessary ground bones and testicles of fruit bat, along with a helping of his own excrement. It also contained a fair bit of another concoction he had obtained from a lesser *bonnonm* in the neighboring island of Praslin, the contents of which were a mystery.)

Taking a stick from the ground, Joelle stirred all these ingredients into a gray powder, which she poured into a cotton sack she had sewn out of a handkerchief. Then she built a fire out in the court-yard. As the smoke rose, she threw in a pinch of the powder, bent over the fire and chanted, fanning the flames so the smoke would carry her incantation far into the night.

"He is mine, not yours," she whispered in a harsh hiss. "He is mine, he is mine, not yours, not yours." She added more beard and a crushed cone of incense to the fire, and as the pungent smell rose to her nostrils, she stood up, stamped three times and turned a circle. "You will sicken, sicken, go away, away." Spooning out the now blackened contents, she poured them into a little bottle, along with a watery blue brew Madame Hélène had given her. The sackful of mysterious powder she tucked into her bosom.

Now she only had to find a way of getting the bottle into the white woman's house, and the powder into her food.

By the main course of the dinner party—Sylvie's usual fish curry and rice (the only dish she'd agreed to cook, having been denied fruit bat)—Penelope was feeling disconcertingly blurred. Every time she raised her eyes to her husband, off in his daze at the end of the table, and saw his fresh-shaven face, such pain seared through her that she could only quell it by taking a long gulp of wine, and by now she'd had too many to count. He looked so appealing over there in the candlelight. He looked the way he had when she'd first seen him at the Hurlingham Club, as if the last ten years had not marked him at all. The ruddy freshness of his cheeks, that sweet little dimple on his chin, the broadness of his shoulders and those brown eyes with their thick lashes, luxuriant as a babe's. Penelope felt a great rush of desire for him, stronger than she'd felt for months, and it made tears spring to her eyes. Oh, why hadn't he shaved off the beard before? For now it seemed to represent all that had gone wrong between them, all the ways he had changed. For years she had begged him to remove it, but he kept saying he felt ashamed of how callow he looked without it—like a clueless schoolboy, he'd insisted. No, he'd wanted the beard, he'd needed the beard. And now, this woman, this Joelle Lagrenade, whom Penelope had still never seen, had whisked it off him in no time. He was under that woman's spell, and the cut went so deep Penelope could barely breathe.

Meanwhile, the dinner conversation had run into trouble. Seeing that her husband was making things unpleasant for Leland, Kate Toynbee had wrested control of it away from him and was now drawing the wives out about which cooks on the island they liked best, a topic that managed to bore every last person at the table catatonic. She then dissected the fish curry (kingfish, she announced, flavored rather deliciously with the local curry leaf—*pile*—ginger and onions, turmeric and garlic), examined the breadfruit (marinated in coconut milk, pepper, malt and sugar, then simmered in oil under a banana leaf) and analyzed the salad (a mix of grated white cabbage, tomatoes and onions, carrots and green mango, shredded and soaked in salt water and dressed with olive oil and lime juice). It didn't help that both Rupert and Penelope had dropped out of the conversation. Rupert was staring at the flickering candles, neither eating a bite of his food nor hearing a word that was said to him (not at all the way a host should behave) and Penelope was drunk. So Kate took over, as she so often took over, bringing her matronly competence to the rescue.

While all this was going on, Talbot decided to liven things up by making a pass at his hostess. He had fancied her ever since the governor's cocktail party where he'd first seen her, and thought it high time the silly tart gave him a response. She really was a beauty, if not exactly sexy (something a bit too stiff about her for that), but still, he could imagine releasing a firebrand in bed. He did like her long, fine-featured face, that aquiline nose and the baby-blue innocence of her eyes. Not to mention her little slip of a mouth. She had that delicious child-whore combination he found so appealing, a sort of snide dirtiness behind the naïve gaze. He put his hand on her knee and slid it up to the soft inner part of her thigh. Ah, one of the many pleasures of tropical life—bare legs on a woman.

Startled, Penelope drove her fingernails into his hand and knocked it off her. Then she leaned forward, that same little mouth rather sloppy with drink, and with excruciating volume and precision said, "Roger Talbot, don't you dare put your clammy toad hands on me."

Silence, as if a huge and muffling fire blanket had dropped over the table. Everybody stared at Penelope.

"*Madanm tou dimoun in fini?*" Marguerite said quickly, bending over Penelope. She had been watching from the wings and saw that Madame needed help.

"Yes, we're finished, thank you, and Marguerite, could you please tell Sylvie we're ready for the flambé now? And would you get the cake out of the larder and put the candles on it, the way I showed you?" Penelope said all this in a low-voiced Creole—she was speaking it quite competently now—and sent Marguerite a grateful glance. The guests again looked at Penelope in surprise. They rather made a point of not speaking Creole but sticking to proper French. Everything about their hostess was turning out to be embarrassingly gauche.

Marguerite nodded and hurried out of the room, her sandals flapping. Penelope stood up unsteadily. "Carry on," she said to her gaping guests. "I must see to something in the kitchen."

When she had left, weaving a little as she went, Rupert woke up at last and poured everybody more wine, which they knocked back with some desperation, then asked a few inane work questions of Toynbee and Talbot (who was still blushing all the way up his receding hairline), while the women cast meaningful looks at one another. Vicky was wondering whether Kate knew that her husband had probably screwed every woman there, and if not, whether it would be amusing to tell her. Hannah, whom nobody had addressed all night, was at last remembered and asked about her sick husband, but turned out not to be able to talk about him without crying, so was quickly returned to Coventry. Edith was preparing a searing lecture to deliver to Roger on the evils of making passes at other people's wives. Leland promised himself never to dine with any of these bigoted Brits again, except perhaps his poor hostess, who seemed to be having a rough time of it. Hugh tried to join in the office conversation with the other men, but was too drunk by now to do much but burble. (He, like Rupert, was besotted with a village girl, and all he wanted to do was go back to her bed and put his tongue in her vagina.) And Toynbee was entertaining himself by comparing the women in the room, their various bottoms and moans of lust. Hannah had whined with guilt after each time until he'd had to let her go. Penelope had been the best looking, but that feistiness of hers was terribly off-putting. Edith had been dull and dutiful. No, Vicky, he decided, had been the best, even if she was lumpy and sun-damaged. Quite a lustful woman, really, ready for anything, wagging that great white moon of a derriere at him. She had even let him bugger her.

He did not think about his wife. He never let himself think about his wife.

Suddenly the lights went off and a glow of fire was seen at the dining room door. "Surprise!" Penelope sang out, and in she came, staggering slightly, bearing a large cake ablaze with candles. Marguerite followed, looking small and wary beneath a great tray of flaming pineapples.

Both were put down in front of Rupert, who was now very glad he'd shaved off his beard or surely it would have been set alight.

"Happy Birthday, darling!" Penelope said carefully, trying not to slur. "Wake a mish!"

Rupert stared at the cake, his stomach turning. Cake, in this climate? He didn't even like sweet things, but especially not cakes covered in gloppy icing. And all those hundreds of candles, or at least it looked like hundreds—could he have grown that old? He glanced up at Penelope, who was standing beside him, tall and shiny in her blue case of a dress, smiling like a barracuda.

"Go on," she said.

Rupert closed his eyes, and as he did, he thought he smelled a curious whiff of burning hair. His hand flew to his chin involuntarily, but no, nothing there anymore. The last he'd seen of his beard, it was tucked under Joelle's pillow.

"Wish, go on," Penelope urged him again.

He shut his eyes tighter and tried to concentrate. And, gradually, words flowed into his head: "Joelle, I am yours," the words said. "I am yours forever. Free me, my love." He blew as hard as he could, then opened his eyes.

Every one of the candles was out.

"Bravo!" cried the guests, applauding.

"How sweet of you, Penny," Kate said pointedly, thinking these words surely should have been spoken by Rupert. "Did you bake it yourself?"

"Yes, I'm afraid I did," Penelope said with a hiccup, and everybody smiled politely. "Go on, darling, here's the knife. Cut us all a slice." She hiccupped again. "Then we can have the flambé on the side."

"My, you really have outdone yourself," someone else said—Penelope didn't notice who—and the others joined in with similar inanities. Rupert didn't say a thing. He only picked up the knife and began cutting the cake like an automaton.

Penelope wove back to her chair, hiccupped again, and sat down. She couldn't touch either the pineapple or the cake, for she felt terribly full all of a sudden, as if her stomach had been stuffed with those fluffy kapok balls the Seychellois used to fill mattresses. She wanted, very badly, for every last person at the table to disappear.

What she didn't know, due to six glasses of wine and her state of despair, was that the entire time since she'd brought in the cake, her face had been running with tears.

10

After the party was over, the guests had staggered out to their cars
and Madame and her husband had gone to their separate rooms
without a word, Marguerite sat in the near dark of the kitchen, eating the leftover cake. Some of it she had wrapped and put away
for the children, but she'd kept a fat slice for herself and was now
relishing the rare opportunity to eat such a treat slowly and alone.
Sylvie had lumbered home in her usual cryptic silence the minute
she and Marguerite had finished washing up, her yellow cotton
dress hitching up her vast thighs as she walked and her good shoes
balanced on her head in common island fashion, to save them from
wearing out.

Marguerite licked Penelope's buttery vanilla icing off a spoon
and watched a moth burn to death against the hot glass of the paraffin lamp. She felt sorry for Madame, making a fool of herself in
front of the guests like that, because ever since their little chat her
heart had gone out to Penelope. She'd been wrong about the snake,
she decided; Madame had no sting in her. She was merely a lost
woman with a bruised soul, in need of comfort and love. And it
was all that evil Joelle's fault. Thanks to Lisette, whom Marguerite
had cleverly planted in the fortune-teller's house as a spy, Marguerite knew all about the spells. (She did not know, however, that the
moment the fortune-teller had moved from love spells for Rupert
to a potion against Penelope, Lisette had been outside, flirting.)

Why, that scheming Joelle was doing to Madame just what her sister Alphonse had done to Marguerite: stealing her happiness out of envy and greed.

I must find a way to help Madame, Marguerite thought, standing up to wash off her spoon and douse the paraffin lamp. Her husband is already *anmare*—too tied up by magic to even see his wife. Is it not one of the most evil tricks of *grigri*: to make men blind and deaf to their wives? Yes, I would like to help Madame get her man back, and at the same time bring at least one of those thieving Lagrenade sisters to her knees.

Meanwhile, however, Marguerite had another matter to attend to, for Lisette had also come up with good news: Madame Hélène had let slip that a man in the village was interested in Marguerite—a good man, with money.

Marguerite knew who the man was: Philippe Chanson, the barber. He was a little old, sixty or so, and he'd lived with two other women already, but he had left them both over one dispute or another and was now single again and there for the taking. Marguerite had known him for years, often stopping to chat with him as he cut men's hair out in front of his little wooden shop, and she thought him sober and wise. He had made a success of his business—a rare quality among the men she knew—and also brought in a profit from his secret and illegal still, where he turned sugarcane juice into liquor. The trick now was to secure Monsieur Chanson before some other fast-eyed woman got to him first.

So the next morning, she released her hair into its long, sexy rope, made Zara and Chloe change into matching white sundresses and walked them to the village. "We must go to the Chinese shop to buy soap for your mama," she told them. "If you are good and do not make for me trouble, I will get you some sugarcane."

The village, Bois Rouge (named after a towering species of local tree with a rusty red bark) was only a small distance down the mountain from the Weston's house in northwest Mahé and it was a fine day for the walk, the air sparkling and the season's stickiness

alleviated by a breeze. Marguerite took the children on a path alongside a mountain stream, where the village women washed clothes
while they laughed and talked, scrubbing them with a mix of coconut soap and grass, slapping and pounding them on a rock, then
spreading them out by the road to dry. (The sun bleached out the
grass stains, Marguerite explained to the curious Zara, but Zara still
thought it scandalous to scatter your underthings about like that for
anybody to see.) The sky blazed and Marguerite hummed one of
the hymns Lisette was always singing around the house. Zara and
Chloe held hands and skipped behind her, cocks crowed in their
yards and even a waft of Madame Bonnetard's ill-kept pigpen did
not spoil the freshness of the morning air.

Zara was being sporadically kinder to Chloe these days, partly
because of Penelope's threats but mostly because Francis had
shamed her into it. She had been in the back garden with Chloe and
was just bending her little sister over her knees to give her another
spank, pulling down her knickers and getting that tickling feeling
between her legs again, when Francis had walked around the corner
and caught them. Zara jumped up, spilling Chloe onto the ground,
guilt crowding her dark little face.

"*Mon dye*, what are you doing?" he'd exclaimed. "You are torturing your sister again?" He'd lifted Chloe off the ground, pulled up
her knickers and hoisted her onto his shoulders. Then he'd turned
his magnificent eyes on Zara, the whole of him so tall and strong and
wonderful, and said in a voice of deep disappointment, "I thought
you were more noble than this. Nobody with a good heart hurts
those who are weaker than he." And he'd strode off, Chloe riding
in triumph, leaving Zara crushed and knowing she would never
spank her sister again.

They reached the village just as the market was getting going,
along with the gossip of the street. Children clad in nothing but
ragged shorts or shifts crouched in the dusty road, playing marbles
with takamaka seeds, and a cluster of women gathered around the
few stalls, their dresses bright and clean and their faces shaded by

straw hats. Marguerite stopped at a small wooden stand and bought the girls a bottle of papaya juice each, then strolled past Monsieur Chanson, chatting to Chloe and pretending not to notice him.

Philippe Chanson was a thin gentleman with teak-brown skin and a gaunt, high-boned face, who rarely smiled and never took off his straw fedora. He kept his barbershop open all morning—it was nothing but a wooden shed, really—and tended his customers in front of it, where they were shaded by a sheet of corrugated tin propped up on spindly bamboo poles. He would sit them in an old wooden chair, tie a white towel around their necks and cut their hair and shave their chins with a straight-edge razor while absorbing and disseminating the news of the village. Like barbers everywhere, Monsieur Chanson knew everybody's business, from gossip about the Swiss priest, who was as pink as a pig and had a predilection for inviting young virgins to his house, to who had lost their brothers and husbands fishing at sea. This was the main reason Marguerite liked him, aside from his talent for making money. She thrived on gossip and nobody besides the fortune-teller knew more gossip than a village barber.

"*Bonzour zoli*," he called out as she strolled by with the children. "How is it going, my little morning flower?"

Marguerite pretended to look affronted at this saucy greeting, but sauntered over to him anyway, as if she were only approaching him for lack of anything better to do.

"Not bad," she said, with a shrug. "Life is hard, as always. And you?" And they began chatting. Zara soon lost interest, so she wandered over to Chloe, who was standing on her sturdy little legs, her tongue thrust deep into the bottle of juice, trying to lick every last drop of sticky orange papaya from it.

Out of sheer boredom, Zara snatched the bottle away and lapped up the rest of the juice herself.

"Mine!" Chloe screamed, and then she did something she had never done before. She leaped onto Zara's back, wrapped her arms and legs around her, pinning Zara's arms to her sides, and dug her little chin as hard as she could into her sister's neck.

"Ouch!" Zara yelped. "Get off, damn you," a phrase that would have earned her a slap from Marguerite had she been paying attention. But Chloe would not get off. She only sunk her chin in deeper and tightened her hold.

Zara dropped the bottle, shook herself and ran in circles, but could not dislodge her sister. Chloe clung like a barnacle, digging her chin into Zara, silent, determined and vengeful.

Marguerite glanced at them, chuckled, and kept on flirting with the barber.

"Let go!" Zara yelled, turning in circles. "Get off!" Unable to budge Chloe, she hobbled up to Marguerite, doubled over with her sister's weight and the pain. "Make her get off me. She's hurting!"

Marguerite ignored her.

Finally, Zara lay on the ground and rolled until she knocked Chloe off. But Chloe was on her feet instantly, still enraged, her chubby face streaked with dust and tears. She hurled herself at Zara, flailing wildly, eyes closed, fists clenched, not caring what she hit or how hard.

Zara could have fought back but something stopped her, some thing about Chloe's vulnerability, her smallness, along with a wriggle of guilt inside her own belly. So she lay curled up in a protective ball on the ground while Chloe kicked and pummeled her with all her strength. Zara didn't uncurl until her sister threw herself down face-first in the road, spent and crying.

Zara sat up and looked at her. She felt bruised but not terribly hurt. "Serves you right, you beastly monkey," she said, but Chloe was sobbing too hard to hear.

"La la la, you two are like dogs, fighting in the street like this," Marguerite said, picking Chloe up and setting her on her feet. She dusted down her now filthy white dress. "You should be ashamed."

"Do all the children of the English act like this?" Monsieur Chanson asked, his deep voice disapproving.

Marguerite glanced at him and laughed, which made her eyes sparkle and her teeth shine. Chanson looked over her sturdy form appreciatively. Yes, she is a good one for me, he thought. Strong in the leg and the money, with a pretty little face and that lovely rope of hair. He imagined it running over his body and grew hot.

"I am going to the dance at the church hall next Saturday," he said. "Perhaps you would care to accompany me?" He pushed his fedora back on his head and glanced over Marguerite's shoulder in a show of nonchalance.

"If I am free," Marguerite replied airily and took Chloe by the hand. "Come, *ti dyab*, it is time to go home." She sauntered away, her plait swaying over her buttocks, the children trailing after her miserably.

"But you promised to buy us sugarcane," Zara objected. She loved to chew on the cut cane, sucking out the sweet juice from its stringy fibers, and had been looking forward to it all morning.

Marguerite laughed. "Wild animals do not get sugar cane, *kopran*? Your sister, she has shown you at last, eh? Stealing her juice like a thief—I saw." And to rub it in, she bought Chloe an ice lolly and wouldn't let Zara have even one lick.

A few days later, while the girls were at the beach with Lisette, who had the day off from the fortune-teller's, Marguerite approached Penelope for a talk. She was worried about Madame, for ever since the birthday party, the woman had sunk once again into an inertia that was doing neither her nor the children any good. She ate almost nothing, pushed the girls away whenever they approached and spent hours poring over fat books full of pictures of insects that had just arrived from abroad, while smoking one cigarette after another.

"Madame, you must eat," Marguerite said once she'd found her on the veranda. "You had no dinner last night, and now you have not touched your breakfast, either. Are you still not well?"

She wondered if Zara had slipped her mother some of those red jequirity seeds before Marguerite had made her throw them away, for who knows what the child would do with her mysterious fixation on that demon worm? I must make the girl understand there is no such thing, Marguerite told herself. The demon that is troubling her mama is no worm.

"No, no thank you, I'm fine." Penelope looked up from her book with a weak smile, a cigarette between her fingers. She was sitting in the shade on the breezy side of the house, but she still looked depleted from the heat. "My stomach is better now. I'm just not hungry."

Perhaps it wasn't Zara's seeds making Madame ill like this but some magic by Joelle, Marguerite thought. That *pitan* might well be doing *grigri* against Madame as well as Monsieur. But how? Joelle could not be reaching her through Sylvie. Lisette had checked with Madame Hélène and found only what Marguerite had already suspected: that Sylvie was a good woman. She supported seven children and her mother-in-law, went to church every Sunday and had no known link with either the Lagrenade family or *grigri*. No, Sylvie was safe. Moreover, Madame had refused to go out and see friends since the party, so she had not been exposed to the potions of other, more untrustworthy cooks, either. Marguerite lingered in the doorway, looking at Penelope thoughtfully. Madame was wearing nothing but a flimsy white nightgown and her hair looked distinctly unwashed. Lisette must have missed something.

"Madame?" Marguerite said. "I would like to ask you a question please."

Penelope put a marker in her book, closed it, and looked up again with repressed irritation. "What is it?"

Marguerite replied hurriedly. She did not like to interrupt somebody's reading, for she believed that books were the path to wisdom and advancement. Nobody she knew in the entire island owned a book, except the *gro blan*, the piggy priest, the teachers at school and the *bonnonm*. The sight of someone reading always filled Marguerite with awe.

"I only wish to ask if Madame has noticed anything missing."

Penelope drew on her cigarette, regarding Marguerite through the smoke. "Missing? Why?"

"Madame, you should know there are people on this island, evil people who might wish to do *grigri* against you. And for this they need a thing that belongs to you."

Penelope felt a chill at these words but quickly suppressed it. "Oh really, you don't expect me to believe that, do you?"

"You can believe what you wish, Madame, but it makes no difference. If someone puts *grigri* on you, it will work. I know of many white families who have suffered in this way. My old master, two families before yours—he tried to dismiss his cook and he died the next week. The white children, too, they are very vulnerable. If somebody is angry, if you cheat them or pay them too little, or if you insult them . . . oh, there are many reasons for *grigri*, Madame."

Penelope's skin prickled. She didn't believe any of this nonsense, but Marguerite's fear was strangely catching. "Marguerite, are you trying to frighten me?"

Marguerite stepped closer. She didn't care what this English-woman said to her; *gro blan* always turned defensive and stupid when you warned them about sorcery. "Madame, you should understand that with *grigri* it is wise to trust nobody, not even your very best friend. I am thinking of the children. I do not wish them to be harmed."

Penelope leaned over her long legs, scabbed now with mosquito bites, and stubbed out her cigarette. She was touched by Marguerite's concern, for it was obvious she was sincere. Marguerite was a good soul.

"Of course. I'm sorry, I shouldn't have been so short with you. I'm not . . . I'm not in the best of moods. But now that you ask, yes, I have noticed a few things missing. I didn't want to make a fuss or accuse anybody as they weren't very important, but I do seem to have lost a silver ring and a blue silk scarf. One or two other things as well, come to think of it."

Marguerite clucked her tongue. "This is not good, Madame. Of course you know that Sylvie and me, we would not take anything of yours, yes?"

Penelope had wondered otherwise but succumbed to the pressure of Marguerite's earnest gaze. "No, of course not."

Nodding, Marguerite lowered her voice. "I will see what I can find out and then I will tell you what to do. But please, Madame, when you comb your hair, you must take all the hairs from your brush, wrap them up and burn them. It is very important you do not let any other person find them. I leave you to read now."

Penelope gazed after Marguerite as she disappeared inside the house, the snap of her rubber sandals echoing. I shall never get used to it here, she thought with a heave of misery. How can one go through life expecting to be robbed or poisoned at any moment? And once again she yearned for home, for the familiar rules of behavior—for a place where she felt anchored.

During the rest of the morning, while the girls were still at the beach with Lisette and Penelope remained paralyzed in her reading chair, Marguerite went hunting for *grigri*. She scoured the house, peering under beds and into drawers and cupboards; she examined the back garden, the outside doors and the edges of the building; and she crawled around the front steps looking for sprinkled chaff, patterns in stones or sticks, or little square packets containing the lead, needles, nails or bones that signified a curse. She even peeked under the house, its damp and murky shadows making her cringe. But she found nothing.

I must wait for Zara, she told herself. The child can find signs of *grigri* much better than I, with her gifts and her Sight. I am sure Madame has been cursed by a Lagrenade, and a Lagrenade curse is dangerous. She shivered in real fear, thinking of Marcel and his fate. Who knew what that evil Joelle would do to Madame—or even worse, to the poor children? Yes, Marguerite decided, I must make Zara help.

• • •

Zara, meanwhile, was on the beach with Chloe, building a huge sand castle. She had already spent a whole hour in the turquoise ocean, snorkeling among her royal subjects, and Chloe had paddled about in her own rubber ring, trying to swim like Zara while Lisette lazily held her—a rare day when the teenager had consented to enter the water, at least up to her knees. Now Lisette was asleep in the shade of a rock the size and color of an elephant, and the two children were squatting in the sand, protected from the sun in shorts, shirts and floppy white beach hats, building a home for the sand fairies.

"I'm making a turret for the queen," Zara said, carefully placing an upside-down bucket of sand on top of the castle, which the girls had already encrusted with blue-tinted cowries and some pretty polka-dotted shells they'd found on the beach. She brushed away the flies that were tickling her foot. "Queen Zara, Empress of the Sea."

"I got a flag!" Chloe announced, holding up a tongue-shaped takamaka leaf, dried and browned by the sun.

"Oh good. Put it there." Chloe stuck the leaf on top of the turret and they both let out sighs of satisfaction. The girls were getting on better since Chloe had rebelled.

"Let's make a moat," Zara said.

"What's a moat?"

"It's a big ditch full of water and monsters, so if an enemy comes he falls in and gets his legs eaten off like Granddad's, and then he can't swim so he drowns."

Zara often referred to her legless grandfather, for she remembered him only too well, having been forced to see him every weekend of her life until he died. Penelope had tried to protect her from the roaring man, suggesting more than once that a mad amputee was a bit much for such a small girl, but Rupert had insisted on claiming what family he could by visiting them every Sunday. His mother would sit in the fading salon, which smelled of old people and cigarettes, tremulously offering tea and cakes. Penelope would sit as far back in a corner as she could, hoping to be forgotten. Rupert would run around like a lapdog, trying to please everyone. And his father would either stay slumped in his wheelchair, looking sad and tired and refusing to talk, or shout at his wife, his stumps waggling in rage and frustration. Worse, he would sometimes try to stand up, only to fall to the floor with a heart-stopping crash. Zara so feared that he would shout at her, too, or fall again, that even the sweetest of cakes would turn to dust in her mouth.

Chloe pouted and sat back on her heels in the sand. "I don't want a moat. I don't want the fairies' legs eaten off like Granddad's."

Zara patted the tall sides of the castle with her small brown hands. "We have to have a moat. All castles have moats. Don't worry, it's only for the bad fairies."

"What's a bad fairy look like?" Chloe squinted at Zara, her blue eyes the exact color of the sea behind her. Chloe had hardly adapted to the climate at all, even though the family had been in the Seychelles now for four months. She was always peeling on one shoulder or another and her blond curls had turned almost white. On the other hand, she had stopped lisping, as if she had at last freed herself from babyhood.

"It looks like a good sand fairy, except it has a horn on its nose, like a rhinoceros beetle," Zara replied.

Chloe puckered her brow, trying to reconcile her image of a fairy—a tiny, delicate lady with gossamer wings—with the idea of anything so ugly as that beetle that had scared her on the bed.

"Oh la la, what a very pretty castle you have made."

Startled, the girls looked up. A tall woman with freckled, reddish skin was standing over them, wearing a bright fuchsia dress and a straw hat in the shape of an upside-down bowl. She was carrying a *tant* and her feet were bare.

She squatted beside them. "Who lives in this pretty castle?" She spoke in English but with a heavy Creole accent.

Zara wouldn't answer. She didn't like grown ups who talked to children as if they were idiots. But Chloe wasn't so cautious.

"Queen Zara! That's her bedroom there, where she sleeps. She's a sand fairy but the bad ones have horns on their noses like rhi—rhi—" Chloe gave up.

The woman bent down to have a look, the brim of her hat hiding her face. "Oh yes, I can see. A tiny princess with yellow hair, yes? She is asleep in the bed."

Zara scowled at this condescension and glanced around the beach for Lisette, but the girl had disappeared. Probably fallen asleep in the shade, as usual.

Joelle fell silent. She sat on the sand, drew her knees up under her skirt and gazed over the sea. She was prepared to wait out Zara's suspicion as long as was necessary.

Two days earlier, Joelle had finally had a stroke of luck. She'd been at the harbor market, haggling for a fish head to bring to her mother for soup, when she'd spotted the fat cook Sylvie Ballon, whom she knew worked for Rupert, laughing with some friends. Joelle had bought the fish head and sidled over to eavesdrop.

"Yes, these white children I cook for, they are very amusing," she heard Sylvie saying, her voice as big and deep as her girth. "The oldest one, she thinks she can do *grigri*. She thinks her mother has a 'demon worm,' so she grinds up the beetles she finds under the house and she feeds them to her own mama!"

The other women howled. The idea of a white woman eating beetles tickled them no end.

Joelle looked around at the collection of women she had known all her life, big women and scrawny women, dark women and light women, dressed in bright prints or faded cotton, in head wraps or straw hats, all of them pretending not to be as poor as they were, and she smiled, too. But for a different reason.

The girls kept working on their sand castle, but the fun had gone out of it now that this stranger was watching. Uneasy, Chloe stood up and trotted off to find Lisette. Zara remained squatting in the sand, her skinny brown knees sticking up to each side of her like a cricket's. She poked at the castle moat listlessly with her spade, wishing the woman would go away.

"I hear your mama, she is sick, yes?" Joelle said at last.

Zara stopped poking and eyed her suspiciously. "Who told you that?"

"Oh, the news here in this island, it flies like the mynah bird. Your mama has the demon worm, I hear, is this not so?"

Zara's heart began to thud. She thought of how sick her mummy was looking, sitting in her nightie all day, smoking and not even brushing her hair, and the image filled her with both anxiety and shame. It mortified her that stranger should know about this, so she kept silent.

Joelle pretended to yawn. "I know all the secrets, you see. The mynah birds, they talk to me. They listen in your garden, they fly to me and they talk. You have heard them talk, yes?"

Zara returned to digging in the sand, deepening the moat. She didn't believe a word of this rubbish. Did the woman take her for a baby?

"So that is how I know about your mama's worm," Joelle continued, trying to sound casual. "But do not be afraid, little miss, because nobody else knows, only me. And I can help you."

Zara paused in her digging, eyeing Joelle again. "Are you a *malfeter*?"

Joelle was startled. How did an English girl know such things? But she recovered herself. "Come now, do the birds talk to evil wizards? The pretty, good birds?"

"They might." Zara studied Joelle a moment. "Why do you want to help my mummy anyway? You aren't her friend."

Joelle shifted on the sand. "Well, no, it is true, I do not know your mama directly. But I do want to help her. Now tell me, what is your name?"

Zara didn't answer. She returned to her digging.

"Me, I am Claudine. Your castle, it is very nice, yes?"

Zara remained silent. A gull flew overhead, wailing mournfully, and the waves swooshed beside them. Zara picked up a scallop shell and placed it over the moat as a gangplank. Down the beach, a coconut plopped off a tree.

Joelle decided to take a risk.

"You see, I know your papa. He is such a nice man. And he is worried about your mama, for he loves her very much, yes? And that is why I want to help him."

Zara looked up quickly. "You know my daddy?"

"Yes. And I think he is the kindest man I have ever met. He told me about the stories he tells you. Flappy Flopbottom, yes? This is very funny. He tells good stories, your papa."

Zara gazed at her appraisingly, then resumed her digging. A long moment passed. "How will you help?" she finally muttered between her knees.

"I have some special medicine." Joelle lifted a handkerchief off her basket, revealing a red *jamalac* fruit, the shape of a strawberry but the size of a lime, and a bunch of tiny bananas. She rummaged underneath them and drew out a small white bag. "It is medicine especially for the demon worm. But it is very strong. You must give it only to your mama, you understand?"

Zara eyed the bag. "How does it work?"

"It works only on people with the worm. Anybody else it makes sick, which is why you must not eat any yourself or let your papa or anybody else touch it. You understand?"

"How do you know it won't make Mummy sick, too?"

"Because I have tried it on my own mama when she had the worm."

"It worked on your mummy?"

"Yes, it worked so well! She is strong and happy now. But perhaps you do not want this medicine, eh?" Joelle began to put the bag back in the basket.

"No, I do want it!"

Joelle hesitated, as if trying to decide. "All right," she said, handing the bag to Zara. "But you must hide it where nobody, not even an animal can find it. You know a place to hide it like that?"

Zara nodded.

"Good. Now listen. You open the bag and you take a little pinch, like this pinch of sand, see?" Joelle demonstrated. "Every morning, you put the pinch in your mama's coffee or tea, whichever it is she drinks, and stir until it dissolves. Once a day is enough. Do not let her see it, though, or the medicine, it will not work. It works only when the demon worm does not know it is coming, you understand?"

"Yes, I understand." Zara felt excited now. She was going to cure her mummy all by herself! This was much better that the potions Nana had made her throw away. "Will the magic work fast or slow?" she said, pushing the bag deep into the pocket of her shorts.

"It will work fast. Now, promise you will say not a word to anybody about this, yes? Or the magic, it will fail. You promise?"

Zara nodded solemnly. "I know about magic. I'm going to be a *bonnefemme du bois* when I grow up."

Joelle glanced at her, startled, and stood up to go. "Good luck, little one," she said, "I must leave you now."

What a repellent child, she thought as she walked away. It will be a good thing when her mama takes her back to England.

The minute Zara got home from the beach, she checked to make sure Marguerite was nowhere near, crawled under the house to her usual dark spot in a corner and took the little bag out of her pocket. Dipping her finger into the lumpy substance inside, which had the texture of dust filled with pebbles and sticks, she tasted it, then quickly spat it out. It tasted of wood and of something rotten—it was disgusting. It will never work like this, she thought, Mummy will taste it right away. That woman is a stupid witch. I'll mix it with sugar and coconut until it tastes good, then I'll put it in Mummy's tea.

So as soon as Sylvie had hauled herself off for her regular afternoon nap on the back veranda, Zara sneaked into the kitchen and took from the larder jars of vanilla bean–flavored sugar, shredded coconut and cinnamon. Dumping Joelle's medicine into a bowl, she mixed up her own version, put it back in the bag and carried it up to the bedroom. There, she tucked it into Kangy's pouch and shoved the kangaroo under the other soft toys on her bed. Zara knew that Nana was constantly spying on her now, trying to stop her from doing magic, and that she'd discovered all of her hiding places in the kitchen and the garden. But she doubted Nana would ever think to look there.

That evening, shortly before dinner, Zara heard Marguerite calling her from downstairs, but ignored her. She was crouched inside the long passageway behind the bedroom wall, reading by torchlight, and she didn't want to leave. Zara loved reading in there, where Chloe and Nana were afraid to follow her and where she could be alone among the dangling, forgotten clothes from London: coats and cardigans and long, woolen scarves that still smelled of home and comfort and of when everything was normal.

Zara's favorite book of the moment was *Pippi Longstocking*, even though it filled her with unrealizable longings. Pippi lived all by herself in a house with no grown-ups and never went to school. Both her parents were far away, her mother in heaven, her father a pirate at sea, but she didn't seem to miss them. And she was strong enough to throw bullies and burglars right over her roof.

"Zara, come quickly! Hurry up!"

This time Nana sounded so upset it ruined Zara's concentration, so she reluctantly put her book aside and crawled out of the closet, brushing cobwebs from her face. She found her nanny standing in the bedroom, her crown of black hair gleaming in a sunbeam.

Marguerite took hold of Zara's thin arms and squatted down to her eye level. "Listen to me," she said, lowering her voice.

Zara looked steadily into Marguerite's warm brown eyes, her mind still full of Pippi. "Nana, can I cut off your hair?"

"*Kwa*? Why?"

"I want to use it for a rope."

Marguerite chucked her under the chin. "Pay attention. You wish to protect your mama from *grigri*, yes?"

Zara grew serious, nodding solemnly. "The demon worm."

"I am not talking about your stupid worm, *koko*, I am talking about something much more serious. I am worried that a jealous woman has put *grigri* on your mama, you understand? I have heard things in the market. . . ."

"A woman jealous of Mummy? Why?"

"Some women here, they are often jealous of a white woman."

"Really?" Zara squinted a moment. "I know who it is—Mrs. Hubert!"

"Hubert? Who is she?"

"You know. That big lady with the shiny hair who comes here for dinner. She's always shouting at Mummy. She's not nice."

"But she is not jealous, *choux choux*."

"Yes, she is."

Marguerite was about to argue, but gave up. "Listen, Zara, it is serious. I need you to help me look for signs of *grigri*."

"The stick patterns and the little packets and the blue bottle?" Zara said, sounding scared.

Marguerite nodded, surprised by the child yet again. Where did the girl learn all this?

"I want to look now!" Zara tried to pull out of Marguerite's hands, but Marguerite tightened her grip.

"Wait. You must tell only me what you find, yes? Nobody else, understand?"

But Zara wasn't listening. "Let me go!" she hissed, straining to break free. Then, like a frightened dog, she bit Marguerite on the wrist.

"Ai!" Marguerite yelped, letting go. Zara dashed out of the room.

Marguerite stood up, rubbing her wrist. She felt a twist of remorse, for she had clearly terrified the child. But what else could she do? Only somebody with the Sight could find this *grigri*. Zara was necessary.

Outside on the veranda, Penelope was still in her nightdress, reading and smoking, as she had been all day. Marguerite was right about her; she had descended into the same state of passive despair she'd been in that first week in Seychelles.

Ever since the night of Rupert's disastrous birthday party, she had been unable to talk to him. He looked right through her when she spoke, and now he'd taken to disappearing for entire nights without even bothering to manufacture an excuse, making it impossible for her to deny any longer that she was losing him to that secretary. Penelope had continued to try everything to win him back: Funny stories about the children, reminiscences, wine and candles over dinner, expressions of love and even several more attempts at seduction, but Rupert had shrugged it all off as if she were a bothersome fly. The hurt of it had gone beyond humiliation, beyond anger; it sat in her like a smoldering coal, burning out everything but pain.

"Madame?" It was Sylvie's gruff voice. "The dinner, it is ready."

Penelope gazed up at the cook from her lounge chair, cigarette smoke circling her face. Supper time already? But she had only just arisen, hadn't she? She felt frightened. Had she lost even her sense of time?

"Madame?"

"Yes, sorry. Are the children here?"

"They are in the garden, Madame." Sylvie turned to go, her buttocks jiggling under her tentlike dress.

"Sylvie?" Penelope ground out her cigarette in a scallop-shell

ashtray and forced herself to her feet. "Do you remember I wanted
to have a dinner on Friday for the Americans?"

Sylvie turned back, shifting her eyes away from Penelope, as
she always did when about to be asked to do extra work. Her great
bosom rose and sank in a sigh.

Penelope girded herself for battle. The problem with planning
meals with Sylvie lately was that Sylvie had stopped cooperating.
She listened politely, her face round and smiling, and then went
ahead and did whatever she wanted, regardless of what Penelope
had said. Perhaps she had grown tired of cooking the bland meals
Penelope and the children insisted upon, but matters had been getting out of hand lately. Last night, she'd served them local *tec-tec*
clams so glutinous and spicy that Penelope hadn't been able to
stomach more than one bite. But she tried to prevail once more.

"Now listen, Sylvie," she said sternly. "Our guests have only
just arrived in the Seychelles. They come from a country where
people eat hamburgers and peanut paste. Do you know what a
hamburger is?"

Sylvie nodded, still smiling, as she did to everything Penelope
said.

Penelope sighed. "My point is they've only just got here—the
wife and children a mere two days ago—and they can't be expected
to eat curried octopus or turtle, let alone that stuff you gave us last
night. So please, just grill some fish—kingfish is nice—and put it on
a bed of rice with a simple green vegetable. Do you understand?"

Sylvie nodded, her grin broadening.

"Are you laughing at me?"

"No, no, Madame. *Mon riye akoz lavi i gou.*"

"What?"

Sylvie shrugged, still chuckling. "*Mon riye akoz lavi i gou*, Madame.
I must return to the kitchen, yes?" And she plodded back into the
house.

Mon riye akoz lavi i gou? What on earth was she saying? Penelope stood alone on the veranda, repeating it to herself several times. This Creole was peculiar, sometimes so near French it was easy to understand, at other times quite incomprehensible, especially when spoken fast, as if its Malagasy and Hindi elements were bubbling to the surface. *Mon riye akoz lavi i gou.* Ah! I've got it! It's a mix of French and English: "I laugh because life is good." Oh, Penelope thought as she entered the house to dress for dinner—oh, to laugh because life is good.

"Mummy, Mummy!" Zara came hurtling across the room and threw herself against Penelope's legs. She was panting so hard she could barely talk.

"What's the matter, darling?" Penelope said, holding her steady.

Zara tried to control her breath. "Mrs. Hubert—" she stammered, "Mrs. Hubert's trying to kill you!"

"What are you talking about, silly goose? Of course she's not trying to kill me. Where do you get these ideas?"

Sylvie and Marguerite appeared in the hallway to see what the racket was. But the minute they caught sight of Zara, their eyes grew wide and they both backed away from her.

Disconcerted and a little frightened herself now, Penelope disentangled Zara from her legs and bent down to look into her face. "Now, take hold of yourself and tell me what's the matter," she said, trying to sound calm.

Mute now with crying, Zara held up her fist. In it was a small, earth-covered medicine bottle, filled with blue water.

II

Penelope told Paul and Lily Leland all about the bottle of blue water when they came to supper the following Friday. Although Zara's notion that Vicky was trying to kill her mother with *grigri* was really quite funny, Penelope found it disconcerting that her child was so prone to believing in curses and spells and wondered if the Lelands would, too. On the other hand, she could see where Zara was getting it from, for the bottle had badly frightened the servants. Marguerite now refused to stay in the house for even a minute after dark, and as for Sylvie, she had taken one look at the damn thing, waddled out of the front door like a panicked duck and hadn't been seen since.

Sylvie's desertion had at least compelled Penelope to action, however, so the morning before the supper she had put on outdoor clothes for the first time in days, gone to the market to buy fish and vegetables and set about cooking the meal herself.

"Madame, this is serious," Marguerite said to her in the kitchen. "You must go to *Bonnonm* Adonis. He is a good man, he is a powerful man. He will undo the curse of the bottle."

"Why, Marguerite, I seem to remember you telling me there's no such thing as a *bonhomme*."

Marguerite chose to ignore this. "If you do not go to him, Madame, this fortune-teller sorcery, it will make you lose all you love. I know. It has happened to me. *Bonnonm* Adonis is the only one who is strong enough to take off the curse."

"Oh, do stop, you're frightening Zara. Anyway, you know I don't believe in this nonsense. I'm a Christian, as are you, I might add. And as Christians, neither you nor I should have anything to do with this poppycock, blue bottles or otherwise."

"Don't call it poppycock, Mummy," Zara said urgently. "It's real. I've seen it work."

Penelope paused at her snapping of beans on the kitchen counter and turned to look down at her daughter, who was standing close by her left leg. Zara had barely left her side since she'd dug up the bottle from behind the front steps. She followed Penelope everywhere, peering at her from around doors and sitting at her feet while she read. And whenever Penelope tried to detach her, she would say, "No, Mummy, I'm protecting you."

"Zara darling, there's no need to be frightened. The bottle doesn't mean anything. And I've told you not to tell fibs. Of course you haven't seen it work."

Zara fixed her eyes on her mother in one of her discomfiting stares. "It's not a fib. I have seen it work. I've seen it work on you."

Penelope sighed and turned back to the beans. It was difficult enough managing supper for these Americans with no Sylvie or Rupert in sight without having to deal with the murky reaches of Zara's imagination as well. She would have to have a serious talk with Marguerite and tell her to stop filling Zara's head with this nonsense.

"Marguerite, would you mind cutting up the fruit over there for a salad?" She pointed to a passion fruit, a grapefruit, two mangoes and three papayas on the wooden kitchen counter. "Thank you so much. No more word on the whereabouts of Sylvie, I suppose?"

Marguerite picked up a spoon and set about scooping out a papaya. "No, Madame. Sylvie, she is a good woman and does not like the work of the devil. When she hears you have protection, she will return, I am sure of it."

I suppose I walked into that one, Penelope thought. "All right. I'm going to lay the table. They'll be here in half an hour. And thank you so much for all this extra help."

Penelope had at last learned that politeness and indirect requests tended to get one much further among the Seychellois than any command, no matter how firm.

The Lelands arrived on the dot, which flustered Penelope, who was used to the British habit of fashionable lateness, but at least she and the table were dressed: she in a blue poplin frock that matched her eyes, tight at the waist and springing into a full skirt; the table in an ivory cloth and a large vase of delicately suggestive passionflowers, their heads ringed in vulvate red. Zara and Chloe, on the other hand, looked like street urchins, their shorts and shirts grubby and their feet dusty and bare. Zara's hair was sticking out like a golliwog's and Chloe's curls had grown so long they were flopping into her eyes. Penelope was embarrassed that the children weren't more presentable, but she was too distracted to dwell on it for long. She went out to the veranda to join the girls, who were jittering about excitedly, eager to meet the Lelands' two sons—playmates at last.

When Paul Leland climbed out of his rented Land Rover, dressed in rumpled brown shorts and a white short-sleeved shirt, his physical presence took Penelope by surprise. He was much shorter and springier than Rupert, and she was struck by the energy that seemed coiled within his compact frame. Rupert moved with the gangly lope of the tall and long-legged, whereas Paul seemed to bounce. His wife, on the other hand, looked like a creature from another planet. Tiny and spry, with cropped blond hair and a pixie face, she was dressed as casually as Paul, wore no makeup or jewelry and, in spite of her diminutive size, strode across the courtyard with the assurance of a man.

"Welcome," Penelope called to them from the veranda, feeling suddenly dowdy in her frock and drop earrings. She smiled nervously as they approached. She had invited Paul by telephone, so hadn't seen him since Rupert's hideous birthday party, and the memory of it mortified her.

"Hi there," Paul said, bounding up the front steps. "Meet my nutball family. This is my wife, Lily." Lily winked. "And these are our two rascals, Pete and Rory. Boys, say hi to Penny. It's okay to call you that, I hope?"

"Um, yes, of course," Penelope said, a little taken aback at this sudden familiarity, and looked down at the boys, both stubby and small with hair so short it stood up on their heads like newly chopped grass. She was about to greet them when Zara stepped in front of her.

"You better watch out in our house," she said, staring at the boys solemnly. "We've been cursed." And so Penelope had to explain about the bottle.

"I must say it worries me how seriously Zara takes all this super-stition," she said as she ushered Lily and Paul to the veranda over-looking the back garden and served them each a gin fizz. "I told her to throw the bottle away and not give it another thought, but she seemed genuinely frightened. I couldn't calm her down at all until we'd taken it to the beach, emptied it and thrown it into the sea, and even then she was sure it would somehow make its way back to our house."

"Kids'll believe anything at this age," Lily said in her flat, nasal voice, perching on the edge of one of the grasshopper chairs. She was so small that if she'd sat all the way back in it, her legs would have dangled off the ground. "Pete only stopped believing in Santa Claus last year and he's almost eight. Does your daughter go to a religious school?"

Penelope took a seat opposite her and smoothed back her hair. She had given up entirely on back-combing and spraying it, the monsoons and Rupert's neglect having taken care of that. Now she always wore it in a simple knot, which made her blue eyes look startled and her face long and naked. "Yes, in England she does. Only Anglican, though, not Catholic like they have here. Why?"

"Oh . . ." Lily paused, running her green eyes over Penelope as if to take her measure. "I just think that once people have been raised to believe in one kind of religion, they're pretty much open to believ-ing any kind, 'specially when they're kids."

"But surely not witch doctors and curses?" Penelope exclaimed. "Zara's been brought up to believe in the Holy Trinity, not fairy stories."

"Well, I don't mean to offend, but to me there's no difference."

Penelope lit a cigarette to cover her shock, then leaned forward to squint at this tiny, bold woman through the smoke. What must God think of this blasphemy? Yet, far from feeling offended, she was thrilled by the daring of Lily's words. In all her years of bedtime prayers under the watchful eye of Nanny, of hymns and Bible readings every morning at school and mumbling grace over cold mutton and cabbage, Penelope had never given her faith much thought. Like everybody else she knew, she'd moved through the rituals of worship with yawns and a sense of virtue, finding them vaguely reassuring without ever taking the time to examine why.

"No, I'm not offended. But do you really mean Jesus is no more credible to you than Zara's *grigri* bottle?" she finally said, blowing her cigarette smoke to one side. Lily smoked, too, she was glad to see, even if Paul was a purist.

"Yup. But that doesn't mean I'm not sympathetic. We all need some kind of religion to explain our lives. Some people do it with witchcraft, some with religion. I guess I do it with science."

"I like witchcraft best myself," Paul interjected with a wink. He was lolling in a chair beside his wife, hairy knees akimbo.

Penelope gazed at the tangled green jungle beyond the garden, which was rapidly falling into shadow. She understood what Lily meant, but she couldn't quite agree with it. Her belief in God felt much deeper than merely a way of trying to explain life. In fact, to her it was the opposite—it was about not being able to explain it at all. She found it comforting to think of something out there that was wiser than she, more powerful; if not God, then something that knew everything she did not. She liked the mystery of it, the sense that there were reasons for what happened in the world she would never understand, reasons beyond science. It made her feel innocent, somehow, like a child; innocent and free.

They drank three cocktails each on the veranda, while the sun slipped into the sea behind them, turning the garden gold, then violet, then a deep purple before Penelope gave up on waiting for Rupert to come home. She rose to her feet. "I'm sorry. I seem to have been rather abandoned tonight." She let out a little laugh. (She'd told Rupert to be home on time for the guests—how could he do this to her?) "My husband must have been kept late at the office and my cook has disappeared because of that silly bottle. So please excuse me while I finish making our supper. I'm awfully sorry. It's not very polite of me, I know."

Lily and Paul both jumped up at once. "Hey, don't worry about us," Paul said. "We'll come help you. I'm getting bitten to death out here anyway."

"Oh no! You can't do that!" Penelope was aghast. One didn't make one's guests cook their own supper—she'd never heard of such a thing.

"Don't worry about it. We do this all the time at home. Put me to work and we'll get dinner ready in no time."

Lily chuckled. "Don't look so dismayed, Penny, it's okay. Paul's a good cook, you'll see. I'll go check on the kids, then I'll join you." She hopped off the veranda and disappeared into the waning light, following the voices of the children out in the garden. Somewhat stunned, Penelope led Paul into the kitchen.

"Do you really cook?" she said, tying an apron around the tight waist of her dress. "Rupert can't at all, although I've no idea why not. He lived by himself for years, starting at fifteen, but all he knows is how to boil an egg and open a tin of baked beans. He might fry a kipper, if pressed."

"I learned from my dad," Paul said, walking over to the sink to wash his hands. "He was an army cook in the war." He rolled up the sleeves of his shirt. "Lily's too busy most of the time with her work and the kids, and it bugs her not to be able to do everything perfectly. I, on the other hand, don't give a damn about making mistakes. Speaking of which, you better tell me what to do."

"Oh." Penelope gazed at him, a little dazed. Are all American men like this? she wondered. Or is this something modern I've somehow missed? "Um, can you fillet fish?"

"You bet."

"Well, I have some in the larder. *Bourgeois*—that's red snapper in English. I thought I'd steam it. I've already done the vegetables and the salad. I hope you weren't counting on having a Seychellois curry, or perhaps hamburger? Those are beyond my capabilities, I'm afraid."

"Nope, we didn't come all this way to eat hamburger. Steaming the *bourgeois* sounds great, just what they deserve. Now tell me, how come your husband lived on his own at fifteen?"

Before long, the three adults were sitting at Penelope's pretty table, deep into a second bottle of French white wine (bought at the local Indian shop, which truly carried everything) and laughing. The children were playing upstairs, Lily having fed them so fast they were finished before Penelope had even dressed the salad, leaving the adults to themselves, and Penelope felt more relaxed than she had in weeks—so much so that she was able to overlook the Lelands' rather plebian table manners: the way Paul poured the wine for himself, for example, and then pushed the bottle over to the women. The food was a success even without Sylvie, the fish on a bed of spinach, along with sautéed sweet potatoes and string beans tossed with almond slices, followed by fruit salad spiked with mango liqueur. Even better, the Lelands weren't acting in the least bit whispery or shocked about Rupert's absence. Paul had been darling with the children earlier, inviting Zara to show him her collection of shells and praising Chloe while she demonstrated her lopsided somersaults all over the room. And afterward he had questioned Penelope about life in England during the war so guilelessly that she found herself talking about Uncle Keith, a subject she usually tried to avoid. (She did not mention her father, though; that was still too painful.)

Yet Lily, too, was an astonishment. When Paul went upstairs to check on the children, Penelope learned that Lily held a doctorate in natural science, just as she had once hoped to, and was planning to write a book on the Seychelles' insects. A woman writing a science book? Penelope was in awe. "Mahé and a few of the other Seychelles islands are the only mid-ocean granite islands in the world, you know," Lily told her with enthusiasm. "All the others are either volcanic rock or coralline, so that makes this place a dream for us naturalists."

"You mean you came here to do your own work?" Penelope asked. "I thought you were only here to help Paul."

Lily lit up another cigarette before replying, which, given her size, made her look like a child sneaking a smoke. "We made a deal. I get to study my insects, as long as I help him gather interviews. He gets to do his fieldwork as long as he gives me time to write my book."

"You lucky thing," Penelope said wistfully. "I'd love to do something like that. I find insects so fascinating. Sometimes I think I prefer them to people. But do come, I have something to show you I think you might like."

Jumping up from the table, she led Lily into the sitting room—a formal parlor of white walls, upright cane chairs and teak side-tables—where she took out the luxurious volumes her mother had shipped from London and spread them out on the bare wooden floor. The two women settled down, each with a fresh glass of wine in hand.

"These are beautiful!" Lily breathed happily, leafing through a meticulously illustrated book on moths. "Where did you get them?"

"My father found them for me in an antiquarian book shop when I was seventeen." (They'd been the last birthday present he'd ever given her, but she kept that to herself.) "I've been fascinated by insects ever since I was small, you see. I was sent to live in Devon during the war and there wasn't much to do but roam the fields, seeking out butterflies and so on. And my father liked to encourage me. It was the one thing we had to talk about."

Lily leafed through a few more pages. "Well, these were quite a find—he has a good eye. Did you know that there are more than three-and-a-half thousand species of insects here? My dream is to catalogue every single one of them in a book like this, then add a few new ones nobody's named before."

Penelope gazed at Lily in admiration. "Could I possibly help you, do you think?"

"Of course." Lily looked up at her with a smile. "I'd love that!"

"Really? Oh, thank you!" Penelope blushed at her own enthusiasm. "You know something, Lily?" she added a moment later. "I've been stuck on Mahé for nearly five months. I have to get off."

And so, early the next Saturday, Penelope found herself crowded onto a small government-run launch with the Lelands and eight basket-laden Seychellois, bumping over the waves toward the outlying island of Praslin. She was thrilled that Paul and Lily had invited her, for she had long wanted to visit Praslin, the island *of coco-de-mer*, as the horrid Toynbee had told her, the coconut so blatantly sexual that General Gordon had thought it the apple of Eve. Rupert had once wanted to see Praslin, too—they had talked about it back when conversation had still been possible—but of course he hadn't come, just as he'd never shown up that night with the Lelands. He never went anywhere with Penelope anymore, which had turned her into an object of derision and pity in the eyes of Vicious Vicky and her gang. No matter, Penelope tried to tell herself, I shall have a better time without my phantom husband, because even when he is at home he stalks the house like a ghost. But then a pang of missing him clutched at her heart. What fun they would have had together on an adventure like this if everything hadn't gone so wrong!

"What's the latest on Zara and her magic?" Lily called over the wind in the open boat. "Is she still fretting over that bottle?"

"I'm afraid so," Penelope shouted back, steadying herself with a hand on the gunwale, wishing the damn dinghy wouldn't leap about so. "Neither she nor the nanny will give me any peace until I visit a *bonhomme* with them. The cook won't come back, either. They're all convinced our house is under a curse and that I've got to ask this witch-doctor person to lift it." Catapulting four inches into the air, she landed back on the bench with an unpleasant *thwack*.

"I think you should go," Paul yelled above the wind, balancing on the narrow plank opposite her. Lily was squeezed between him and a large Creole woman with a baby. "Think of it as anthropology. It could be fascinating."

Penelope squinted into the warm wind and sea spray, her brown hair whipping into her eyes. She was dressed like Lily now, in pale khaki shorts and a simple white shirt. "I suppose so. I just don't want to encourage Zara to believe any more of that rubbish than she already does." But this was not the whole truth. The truth was she was afraid. Now that she'd learned this *bonhomme* was considered truly powerful, a sorcerer capable of both good and evil, the idea of putting herself in such a person's hands made her shudder. Why, he might be truly maleficent, or even insane.

"Bring the kid along. Maybe she'll learn something," Paul was saying. "I'm planning to go myself if I can get an introduction."

"You don't think it could be dangerous?"

"Not unless you want it to be." He winked. "Nah, it'll be a great adventure."

Oh, to be so brave, Penelope thought, and smiling wistfully, she turned to gaze at the island they were leaving behind.

From a distance, Mahé looked like the head and shoulders of a vivid green giant, its arms rising out of the sea as if to embrace them. Clouds tumbled down from its crown, dissipating as they reached the ocean, and a few small islands were sprinkled around it like offspring. But soon all that disappeared over the horizon and the boat was surrounded by nothing but water. The ocean was no longer turquoise out here but an opalescent black so dense it looked solid, its surface cut by a wide path of flashing silver leading to the high, pale sun. The boat headed right into this path, as if sailing to the heavens, so Penelope found herself having to squint against its dazzle, barely able to see the flying fish leaping about her or the occasional dolphin curving through a wave.

Praslin was only twenty-one miles away, but in this launch— nothing more than a large rowboat with an outboard motor—the trip was going to take more than three hours.

For a while Penelope and the Lelands tried to keep talking, but the effort of shouting above the wind and coping with the heaving vessel soon exhausted them. Lily leaned her head on Paul's shoulder and actually managed to fall asleep. Paul stared fixedly out at the water, turning greener by the minute. And Penelope, whose stomach surprised her by handling this bucking boat much better than it had the SS *Kampala,* gazed, mesmerized, at the dips and hollows of the black waves, her mind drifting back to an earlier time she had been on the sea like this, in the Isle of Wight, during her first family holiday after the war.

It was 1946, and she was home for the summer after her initial year at boarding school. Twelve and gawky, she was at that age when she never quite knew what to do with her spindly limbs or dark hair, which tended to dangle in lanky, unfashionable strands. Even less did she know what to do with her family, whom, she had realized by then, she barely knew. Her father, with his narrow, disappointed face, was withdrawn and unreachable. Her uncle Keith, newly out of hospital, followed him everywhere, trembling and unable to speak. Her mother was commanding on the surface but brittle underneath. And her little brothers seemed bent on proving to Penelope that she was neither big sister nor friend.

The day the family arrived at their rented cottage, they deposited their bags in the kitchen and headed out to the beach for a walk, Penelope trailing behind them, her cold hands thrust into the pockets of her anorak, the damp English wind rushing up her skirt and making her nose run. She had been living away from home for half her life by then, so the role of daughter and sister was a puzzle she could not fathom any more than she could fathom why she had been the only child to have been evacuated during the war, and why nobody spoke to her much or seemed to know what to say when they did. So she turned for comfort to the wonders of the seaside: the damp beige sand filled with treasures and the gray sea lapping at her feet like the tongue of a vast and happy dog.

For a time, she explored the tide pools along the craggy coast. Scrambling from rock to rock, over slippery green lichen and pale limpets like crowds of tiny Chinese hats, she found periwinkles and snails in delicate dawn colors, sea urchins as prickly as curled-up hairbrushes and miniscule fish swimming frantically about, looking for escape. In one pool she spotted a tiny crab, whose claws tickled her palm; in another a pink sea anemone, which closed into a tight, fleshy ball the instant she touched it. Penelope was happy like this, alone with nature, and still liked to collect its treasures, just as she had during her solitary years in the war. Her bureau drawers at school were full of the stones and dried moths, conkers and carapaces she had collected from the school grounds. Now she would be able to add shells and crabs, maybe a starfish if she were lucky . . . and then she saw it: a glinting red jewel lying at the bottom of a tide pool. Forgetting even to push up her sleeve, she plunged in her hand and snatched it up: a luminous red stone, the size of a baby's tooth. She wasn't sure what it was, but knew it had to be precious—a garnet perhaps, or even a ruby. She quickly set about hunting for more, among the rocks and along the beach, in the tangle of glutinous seaweed and in the messy sand. She found a green one, then a yellow and a white one, and then, most thrilling of all, a fingernail-sized disk of sapphire blue. She quite forgot about her troublesome family, so absorbed was she in her hunt, for every treasure Penelope found made her feel a little safer, as if it were part of a nest she was building in which to hide from the world.

"What've you got?" her brother James interrupted.

She looked up from where she was crouched at the edge of the sea, clutching her treasures in her hand. "Nothing. Go away."

James squatted his five-year-old self beside her. He was one of those boys who always looked grubby and mischievous, with a knowing face, spiky dark hair and a challenging glint in his blue eyes. His thin mouth was twisted into the sneer of a bully, as if he already knew of his Teddy Boy future. "Let me see."

She jumped up. "Leave me alone." She walked away from him, her bare white legs striding in their worn Wellington boots. But James ran up behind her and before she even knew he was there, hit her hand hard enough to knock the treasures flying.

"Ooh, look!" he crowed, diving for the colorful jewels in the sand.

"Those are mine! Give them back!" Penelope shouted. She shoved him over and fell on him, prying open his fingers while he writhed and kicked. Roddy trotted up then, four years old and pudgy, utterly under his brother's spell. He dived in, too, and began pummeling Penelope as a matter of course.

"Children!" their mother called, and strode up, her gum boots sucking at the wet sand with a strange, hollow *pop*. "Stop that this minute. Penny, leave your little brothers alone."

"I'm not—" Penelope pushed off James's hand, which was clawing her face. "I'm not—they're trying—"

"Oh, really." Mrs. Clarke pulled the boys off Penelope and placed them like skittles behind her forbidding brown curtain of a skirt. "Get up and explain yourself."

Penelope struggled to her feet, covered in wet sand, her hair dangling into her eyes. The precious contents of her pockets, the shells and crabs, had spilled to the ground, half buried by the scuffle, and when she opened her clenched palm only three jewels were left.

James chose this moment to cry. "Those are mine!" he wailed. "She took them all! Selfish cow!"

"None of that language, please," Mrs. Clarke said. "Now what are you talking about?"

"He's lying! I found the jewels! He tried—"

"What jewels? What is this nonsense?" Mrs. Clarke seized Penelope's hand and examined her find. "Oh, really, it's only sea glass. It's all over the beach. Plenty for everyone. Penny, you're too old to treat your little brothers this way. Give the glass back—one to Roddy, too, before he kicks up a fuss. We have to go home for tea. You can find some more tomorrow."

"But I'm the one who found them!"

"Be quiet!" Mrs. Clarke held out a palm, true anger mottling her face, until Penelope, crying herself by now, was forced to hand over every one of her precious finds, even the treasured sapphire.

The next day, when they went back to the beach, she looked and looked, but could find nothing. The day yielded no more than one piece of sea-worn brown glass, no longer a jewel at all in her eyes but only a piece of junk, no more interesting than a pin. And so it went for the rest of the holiday, for it turned out sea glass was not so easily found after all, unless one had luck and love on one's side, and by then it had become clear to Penelope that she had neither.

The hours of sick-making bumping came to an end at last and Praslin rose into sight. This island, Penelope saw as the boat approached, was much flatter and barer than Mahé, its mountains set further back along a plain. The sea had changed again, turning from black to a brilliant sky blue, lit from beneath by pristine white sand. And all around her, huge gray boulders thrust out of the water like sea monsters, some in the shape of dinosaurs, others resembling mammoth heads, their surfaces looking as velvety as moleskin. Penelope gazed about in wonder. How extraordinary this is, she thought, and how astonishing that I am here to look at it. And she realized that for the first time, here in the company of the easygoing Lelands, away from the children and Rupert, away from her mire of jealousy and regret—for the first time, she could really see.

The boat at last chugged into the harbor of Grande Anse, Praslin's only jetty, where a pair of black pirogues, the graceful canoes of the fishermen, drew alongside to carry the passengers ashore. Two

men on each pirogue loaded up with supplies from the launch—
packages of food and bundles of letters, huge tins of paraffin and
sacks of rice until the slender canoes were so low in the water that
Penelope was sure even one passenger would sink them. But they
climbed in anyway, she and Lily in one, Paul rather greenly in the
other, leaving their Seychellois companions to wait patiently for
their turns. With only half an inch between the gunwale and the
water, they were rowed safely, if wetly, to land.

Once disembarked, they were met on the beach by the guide
Paul's interpreter had hired for them, a Monsieur Cadeau, who
explained in Creole that he would drive them to the little restaurant
he ran with his wife, where they could have a drink before going on
to the Vallée de Mai and the forest of *coco-de-mer*. He ushered them
into the back of his dilapidated Renault, which was as tiny as a golf
cart, with no sides and nothing but a tattered cloth for a roof. Paul,
whose color was returning now that he was on land, squeezed in
between Penelope and Lily, leaving Monsieur Cadeau alone in the
front. "I wonder where these people get their silly names," Penelope
whispered in English as the car took off. "They're so funny when
you translate them. Our driver is Mr. Present, my cook is Sylvie Bal-
loon, which quite suits her, actually, and I've met a Mr. Soap and a
Mr. Song, too."

"Slave names," Paul said abruptly, and Penelope was silenced.
"The French liked to give them stupid names sometimes, just to
make fun of them. I've come across a Monsieur Mustache and even
a LaBlague, which means a joke, as you know. That reminds me. I
found an amazing old guy yesterday who says he was born a slave.
He was about ninety-eight, and he had some kind of red stone in his
earlobe. He told my interpreter that a few former slaves are still here
and you can recognize them by the stones or rings in their ears."

"He'd have to be a hundred and twenty-five years old, by my
calculations," Lily said drily. "I think you've been bamboozled,
honey."

"Maybe." Paul smiled at his wife. "But slaves didn't disappear overnight, you know. Pirates and Arabs kept trading them for years after emancipation. The British Navy was still arresting traders and freeing slaves up till about sixty years ago and they dumped thousands of them right here."

It was lucky they were talking, Penelope realized just then, because the drive was terrifying. The road was no more than a narrow rutted track, the mountain was much steeper than it had appeared from the sea, and their journey featured so many hairpin turns, precipitous drops, potholes and fallen rocks that she was surprised the three of them hadn't been tossed out of the open car like salt from its cellar. She tried to squeeze her eyes shut to spare herself the vertiginous view, but that only made her queasy and more nervous than ever. She wished the damn jalopy had a side.

"Here we are!" Monsieur Cadeau called out in Creole as he slowed down at last. He parked in front of a palm-thatched cottage, the dust puffing up around them. Penelope half climbed, half fell out of the car and brushed herself down. Her mouth was full of dust.

"A drink for *medamzemesye*?" he said then, nodding at them pleasantly. He was a tall, sinewy man, no longer young but strong, with toffee skin and Chinese eyes. "Come with me, please." Penelope thanked him, translating once more for the Lelands, and the three of them followed him onto the wooden veranda of his restaurant, which was shaded by a roof of woven green palm leaves.

"My mouth's all gritty," said Lily with a laugh, settling her compact little body into a rough wooden chair. She ran her eyes over the cottage behind her, its walls made of overlapping palm leaves and its silvery roof thickly thatched. "What a cute house. Makes me think of Peter Pan. Oh, wow, look at that view."

Taking a chair beside her, Penelope did. And the view before them was indeed spectacular. Below them stretched the mountainside, giant trees and sprouting palms cascading downhill in a thousand raucous shades of green. At its foot was a crescent of beach, white as flour, and beyond that was the sea, an expanse of blue silk shimmering all the way to the horizon. In some areas the water was so clear as to be invisible, in others it gleamed brilliant turquoise or aquamarine. How have I not noticed all this until now? Penelope asked herself. How have I not seen that Seychelles is the most beautiful place in the world?

"*Bonzour imsye madanm.*" A plump Chinese woman appeared (Madame Cadeau, Penelope assumed), a flowered apron tied over her belly, carrying a tray laden with three green coconuts and a plate of breadfruit fritters. "*Vwala*, the cocktail of Seychelles." She set a coconut before each of them, in which was drilled a hole. "*Bon swaf.*" Nodding, she shuffled back inside.

"What's this?" Paul said with a laugh. He extracted a chair from the jumble of furniture on the terrace and sat opposite Penelope and Lily, a square wooden table between them.

Penelope picked up her coconut with both hands and gave it a sniff. "I suspect it's going to be a trifle inebriating." She took a sip. Her taste buds were flooded with a startling mixture of coconut water, both tart and sweet, and what was obviously a healthy dose of gin. "Oh my."

Paul picked up his coconut, too. "Bottoms up." Tipping back his head, he poured a long swallow down his throat. "'Oh my' is right." He wiped his lips with the back of his wrist and helped himself to the breadfruit fritters, which tasted like parsnips, sweet and earthy. "That's better. I was feeling pretty sick on that boat."

Just as they were polishing off their cocktails, Monsieur Cadeau popped up on the veranda. "Excuse me, but it is time to leave. We must go now because early evening, it is the best time to see the black parrot, and I was told Monsieur's wife wants very much to see this, yes? And after, when we come back, we will cook you the finest dinner you have had in Seychelles."

"Black parrot?" Penelope asked Lily after translating.

"Yes. It nests in the upright trunks of dead *coco-de-mer* trees and doesn't exist anyplace else in the world. Pretty thrilling, huh?"

Hiccupping from the coconut gin, Penelope nestled back into the rickety car, pressed up once again against Paul's leg.

Somehow, the drive this time didn't seem so bad.

While the adults were guzzling coconut cocktails in Praslin, their children were playing on Mahé's Beau Vallon beach under the reluctant eye of Francis. Marguerite had gone off to dress for the dance with Philippe Chanson and Lisette was on duty at the fortune-teller's, so it had fallen to Francis to babysit and he was not pleased. It was Saturday afternoon, when his friends played football and then went into town to scrounge beer and flirt with girls. He didn't want to be stuck on a hot beach with a bunch of white children.

So having made sure they would not drown or kill one another, he lay down in the shade of a takamaka tree, his hands behind his curly head, and gazed up into the spotless sky, dreaming of a pretty girl he knew named Emmaline and what he might say to her at school if he dared. Before long, he was asleep.

Zara and the two boys spent a couple of hours splashing in the waves, burying one another in the sand and collecting shells and coral, some of it shaped like brains and some like tiny white branches. Finally, they decided to dig a hole to the other side of the world. Chloe, who had been unsuccessfully trying to join in their games all day, grew fed up at this point and trotted off to find Francis.

"First one gets to Australia wins," the older boy, Pete, said, after they had been digging for some time.

Zara looked at him with scorn. "It's not Australia on the other side of the world, stupid, it's China."

"No, it's not!" Pete replied. Neither of them knew, not having learned to orient themselves from the equator, that the real opposite end of the world was in the middle of the Pacific Ocean.

Having exhausted themselves with digging, they gave up on reaching Australia or China, dipped once more into the sea to cool off and settled under a takamaka tree, whose branches grew so close to the ground they formed a roof. Zara squatted in the sand among its twisty roots, looking dark and stern, despite her smocked blue bathing suit with its hated frill of a skirt, and the boys crouched in front of her, not unlike hedgehogs in their bristly American crew cuts. They watched her expectantly, for Zara, they had learned, was mighty interesting.

"Would you like me to tell you about the *dandosya?*" she asked.

"What the hell is a *dandosya?*" said Pete, who, at seven, liked to talk tough. "Sounds like a dodo bird to me."

"It's a zombie," Zara said gravely. "Do you know what zombies are?"

"Sure," said Rory, who was five and knew everything. "Dead people who walk around. I saw a movie once about zombies. I'm not scared of dead people."

"Even if they walk with their arms sticking straight out and their eyes stuck open?" Zara crawled out from under the tree and stood up to demonstrate, and soon the boys joined her. They stalked over to Chloe, who was lying beside the snoozing Francis, sucking her thumb and rubbing the ear of her ratty toy lion to make herself sleepy.

"We're zombies coming to eat you," Zara intoned in a spooky voice, forming a ring around her with the boys, their arms held out stiffly, their eyes wide and staring. Chloe gazed at them indifferently.

"We're coming to eat you," Zara tried again. "We're dead and we're going to make you dead."

Chloe took her thumb out of her mouth with a wet *pop*. "You look silly. Go 'way," and turning onto her side, she snuggled up against Francis.

Zara shrugged and led the boys back to their spot. "Anyway," she said, recovering her dignity as she sat down again under the tree. "The *dandosya* are people who've been killed by black magic. When that happens, a *malfeter*—he's a bad wizard who can turn himself invisible and do evil things—he makes them get out of the grave, puts a rope around their necks and leads them into the forest to dig and plant for him for eight days. *Malfeter* are always looking for people who've died of magic so they can turn them into slaves like that." The boys stared at her, fascinated.

She leaned forward, lowering her voice to a whisper. Zara had been listening to these stories for months now—from Francis, from the women in the market, from Lisette—but she'd never had the chance to tell them herself before (Chloe being too young to understand), let alone to an audience as rapt as this. "You know what you have to do to stop a dead person you love from turning into a *dandosya*? It's really horrid."

"What?" the boys said eagerly.

"You have to stick seven crosses made of pins into seven different bits of his dead body. Then you've got to find a *malfeter* to dig a fresh head out of a grave and scoop out its brains."

"Ooh, yuck," said Rory in a thrilled voice.

"That's not all. After that, he has to mix up the brains with seven rotten black bananas, all mushed up, some earth from the grave and seven drops of water he steals out of a flower vase on somebody's tomb. Then he has to put the whole mush back in the grave before the body is buried. If he does that, then no evil wizard can ever call the body out of the grave and get him to be a slave or anything."

Zara pointed up at the mountain looming behind them, its crown obscured that day by heavy gray clouds. "See that forest? It's full of *dandosya*. They kill children, you know, because they want to drink their blood. Francis told me a girl's head was found yesterday in the forest and all the blood had been sucked out of it. They never found her body."

"Were her brains scooped out, too?" asked Pete.

"Of course."

Pete swallowed. He was slight, with Paul's dark complexion and Lily's pixie face. "You scared?" He tried to snigger.

"Who, me?" Zara shook her head. "Oh, no. But that's because I'm older than you and I've learnt to do magic to protect myself. I protect

Mummy and Chloe, too." She lowered her voice. "My nanny says I have the Sight."

The boys were impressed.

"You two better watch out," she continued. "You're American children, and the *dandosya* love to eat American children because you taste all buttery."

Rory squeaked, then coughed, trying to cover up. "What kind of magic do you do?" he said. Rory was as blond as Pete was dark, totally Lily's child, but unlike Chloe's pink and burnable blond, he was the kind who turned a golden caramel under the sun. He did indeed look buttery.

Zara frowned at him. "You sound funny. You talk as if you've got cotton wool up your nose."

"Nah, I don't. You're the one talks funny. C'mon, tell us about the magic."

Zara shrugged. "All right. It's called *grigri*. I learnt it from Francis and Lisette. I can protect both of you, too, if you want. But it won't work unless you do something first."

"Oh, yeah? What?" Pete said warily.

"You've got to give me something precious that belongs to you."

"Like what?"

"What have you got?"

"Nothing. Just my bathing suit."

"Me, too," said Rory.

"Didn't you bring anything to my house before you changed?"

The boys glanced at one another.

"All right, if you're going to be like that, never mind," Zara said with a shrug. "But you better not go outside at night, and you better close all your windows in your house. The *dandosya* wait till children fall asleep, then they sneak in the windows and breathe on them. Their breath is cold, like ice, and it freezes you stiff. And then they carry you away and cut off your head and suck out the blood and crunch up all the rest of you for supper."

"I brought my taxi," Pete said quickly.

"And I got a—um—I got my tiger," Rory added.

Zara paused a second. "You really like those things?"

The boys nodded.

"All right." She stretched and yawned. "When we get home, you give me those. And you have to do one more thing, too, because *grigri* is powerful and I am powerful and you better be careful."

"What do we have to do?" both boys asked, their little mouths hanging open.

"You have to show me your willies."

When Monsieur Cadeau reached the top of the Vallée de Mai, he parked on the side of the pin-thin road (God help anyone who needs to drive past, thought Penelope), helped the women out with old-fashioned courtesy and led the party down a narrow trail into the valley's ancient forest. After the rattle and bang of the jalopy, the sudden silence was so eerie it made Penelope's skin prickle. She looked about in amazement. This was like no forest she had ever seen. Rather than the dense jungle she had expected, the trees here stood far apart from one another, like sculptures in a museum, with nothing between them but the odd sapling and the forest floor. Yet their leaves were so huge they met above to form a solid roof, turning the forest into a vast, still room.

The trees, she realized, were less like trees than like plants swollen to gargantuan proportions: palm leaves as big as carpets, grass as tall as a barn, *coco-de-mer* nuts like giant black acorns, each the size of four heads. Weird pandanus surrounded her, too, the screwpines that looked like upside-down trees balancing on their bare branches, with wild yellow wigs sprouting out of their feet. And all over the ground lay a deep jumble of dead leaves, each the shape of a blade of grass, only as long and thick as a leg.

Penelope gazed at the golden-green light filtering around her, at this forest so enclosed it seemed removed from sun, weather and time, and understood completely why General Gordon had taken this place for the Garden of Eden. It looked prehistoric, more suited to dinosaurs than humans, and for the first time since reaching Seychelles, she had a sense of its history stretching back to long before mankind ever existed. There was no domestication here, no soft grass or fluffy vegetation. The leaves here were so tough they felt like rubber and sounded like wood if you knocked against them, and the trees were clearly designed to last long after Homo sapiens had become extinct. It was humbling. I am in a place purer than I have ever been or ever will be, she thought. Ancient and virgin, gigantic and wise, it puts all the efforts of we humans to shame.

Nobody talked for some time. They all sensed they should fall silent in reverence for the forest and feel as miniscule as they really were. So they walked down the path without a word, the crunch of their footsteps on the dead leaves the only sound. Every now and then Monsieur Cadeau stood still and held up his hand, commanding them to listen: a high-pitched whistle echoing through the trees, which he whispered was either the black parrot or a mynah bird imitating it. A burst of monkey-like chatter from a quarreling fruit bat. The creak of enormous leaves rubbing against one another, like a groaning ship. The *thud* of a fallen leaf, heavy as a plank. A breeze running through the treetops with the sound of rain tapping on glass. But most of the time, a silence so profound it felt sacrilegious to speak.

Eventually, they crossed a small stream at the bottom of the valley, its clear water tinkling timidly between monstrous boulders, and wound their way up a steep hill on the other side, where Monsieur Cadeau had told them they would have the best view of the oldest *coco-de-mer* palms in the forest. And when they got to the clearing, there the trees were, up to a hundred feet tall, their trunks as straight as spears, their giant, fan-shaped leaves sprouting from their crowns like feather dusters. The trees tended to stand in couples. At the top of the females were clustered the massive nuts, their husks smooth and black, dangling like teats among their gigantic leaves. And on the even taller male palms sprouted three-foot-long brown catkins, each shaped exactly like a phallus, covered with tiny white flowers and smelling vaguely of seminal fluid.

They took their time on the return hike to the bottom of the valley, for there was much to see. Penelope reached out to feel a baby *coco-de-mer* leaf—big as a bed—and found it so thick and stiff she could have propped it up like a wall. Lily pointed to a Praslin gecko nibbling on the florets of a *coco-de-mer* catkin, its bright green back decorated by a row of red dots. And Monsieur Cadeau spotted a pale gray tiger chameleon, which, he whispered, would turn yellow or black if frightened. They stood and watched it for some time as it moved robotically along a branch, swiveling its gummy eyes in opposite directions, reminding Penelope of Roger Talbot. They found a bronze gecko, too, decorated with spots and bars, which Penelope knew could shed not only its tail if attacked but its entire skin. And at last, as the afternoon slid into evening, Lily got to see her black parrot, which was not black but brown, hoisting itself up a guava tree with its gray beak and claws.

By the time they reached the bottom of the valley it was dark, the forest canopy having blotted out any remaining light. Now making their way back out would not be easy, despite the guide's electric torch. The mess of spiky pandanus leaves underfoot became slippery, the serrated edges cutting their ankles and the long blades catching at their feet; boulders rose up in the dark as if to attack; and the roots on the forest floor seemed to come alive, turning into trip wires. The quality of the darkness was unlike anything Penelope had seen, viscous and tangible, as if a black ink had bubbled up from the heat of the day to envelop them. And as the dark thickened, so did the silence. Penelope had thought a tropical forest would wake up at night and fill with jungle noises, the cries of strange birds and the calls of monkeys, but Seychelles had no monkeys, the birds were no longer speaking and even the insects kept quiet, as if they, too, were struck dumb by the majesty of the forest.

They walked slowly along the narrow path in single file, Monsieur

Cadeau in front with his torch, Lily behind him, Penelope next and Paul bringing up the rear. Penelope stumbled at one point, scraping her knee on the invisible edge of a rock, and only just managed not to fall. Paul reached out to steady her. "You okay?" he murmured. She nodded, heart hammering. "Don't worry, I'm right here," he added. Her heart refused to calm itself for the rest of the hike, partly from fright, but mostly from the gush of gratitude she felt at being shown such consideration by a man. How pathetic I've become, she scolded herself. Or rather, how pathetic I've allowed Rupert to make me.

When they had at last climbed out from under the dense forest canopy, Penelope was surprised at how light the sky was still, as if they'd stepped out of a dark cinema into afternoon. They turned for a last look at the canopy stretching below them like a nubby green blanket, the *coco-de-mer* palms poking above it like huge, open parasols. The black silhouettes of fruit bats, wingspan three feet long, flapped their way creepily over the trees.

Monsieur Cadeau drove them back to his restaurant just in time to catch the last greenish-gold rays of the sunset. They sat on the terrace again, each cradling another coconut cocktail, which felt more like holding a head than a drink, content to remain silent as the ocean blushed a luminous rose, then darkened to amethyst before disappearing into the black of the sky. And as the gin-laced coconut water coursed through her, Penelope was seized by the same sort of thrilling humility she'd felt in the forest, a fleeting moment when she knew that she and her little troubles didn't matter at all.

"I'm so glad we came here, aren't you, honey?" Lily said then, her voice hushed, and turned to caress Paul's cheek. "I've never been anywhere so beautiful."

"Yes, but don't spoil it, Lily," Paul said quickly but gently. "Don't spoil the beauty by trying to give it words."

Penelope couldn't have agreed more.

Madame Cadeau appeared then, bearing a tray. She laid out

cutlery and napkins for them all, placed five small votive candles around the wooden table and turned to Penelope, whom, she'd already realized, was the only one who could understand her.

"Madame, welcome to my humble home. We have tonight octopus fritters and *tec-tec* soup for the appetizer, for the main dish we have our famous turtle curry with mango chutney, accompanied by a most rare treat, *palmiste* salad. Dessert is breadfruit custard with *jamalac* jam."

After the hostess had left to see to their dinner, Penelope translated for the Lelands, who were sitting opposite her cuddling, which made her feel a pang of loneliness. "They have to kill a whole baby palm tree to make that salad," she added. "Very extravagant."

"What's *tec-tec* soup?" asked Lily, her blond head on Paul's shoulder.

"It's those little clams you see people digging up on the beach. They cook them with garlic and onions and ginger. My cook made me some the other night." And it almost killed me, Penelope was about to add, but didn't. She wanted to be a good sport with the Lelands. "Don't worry about the octopus, though. They marinate it in papaya juice, which dissolves protein, so it's beautifully tender, nothing like that chewy stuff you get in Italian restaurants. I've heard they throw in a cork, too, though goodness knows why."

"Yum, corked octopus," Paul said with a smile. "Hey, let's have another cocktail."

Penelope ordered another round, then raised her coconut to her friends. "To the loveliest people I've met in years." Her voice trembled, for she truly meant it. Paul and Lily may well have been the most openhearted and generous people she had ever met in her life.

"Why, that's so sweet of you," said Lily. "We're glad we found you, too, aren't we Paul?"

"Agreed," he said, raising his coconut as well. The three of them clacked their nuts together, which made a satisfying *thunk*. "To new friends," he added, tipping back his coconut, and over its edge, he sent Penelope a wink.

• • •

Back at the house in Mahé, Zara and the boys were arguing over the sacrifice of their treasures. Francis had hosed the children down after the beach and made them change, and now he was inside with Chloe, fixing her a snack, so Zara had taken the boys out to the back garden. "All right, hand over your things," she commanded. "It's that or die. Pete, give me your taxi."

Pete fingered his Matchbox toy. "Do I have to? It's my favorite."

"It's that or die," Zara repeated, crossing her arms. She was standing on the grass in shorts and a T-shirt, her thin brown legs planted solidly on the ground.

Reluctantly, he held out the taxi, a little yellow car with a checker pattern around its edges.

"That isn't a taxi," Zara stated. "Taxis are black."

"No, they're not!" Pete's voice wavered. "That's a New York taxi and I love it."

Zara snatched it and slipped it into her pocket. "Rory?" she said sternly, looking down at the pudgy little fellow. "Where's your tiger?"

"Don't know." His lip quivered.

"All right. The *dandosya* will get you, though."

"No, no, I got it here." He pulled out a small plastic tiger from his pocket and handed it to her. "It keeps me safe," he added, his voice squeaking.

"Not as safe as I will. Now, follow me." Zara led the boys to the jungly vegetation at the edge of the garden, so dense it was like a green wall. "You have to find one stick each, about as long as your finger." The boys scrabbled about and found them pretty quickly.

"Good. Now come under the house with me and take off your clothes."

"I don't take my clothes off in front of girls," said Pete. "It's dirty. Mommy told me."

"You want me to do the *grigri* or not?" Zara said with a grown-up sigh. "When I show you how, you can do some yourself, you know."

"Oh, yeah?" Pete said more eagerly than he meant to.

"Yes. I can teach you how to put a spell on somebody and how to protect people, too. But you've got to be really brave, so brave the *dandosya* won't dare hurt you."

"I am brave," he said quickly.

"Me, too," Rory added.

So the boys crawled under the house, where they reluctantly disrobed. Zara squatted down and squinted at their stubby little penises.

"They look silly," she said. "They look like worms with their heads cut off. Now lie down."

Naked and embarrassed, the boys did as they were told. Zara took the sticks, muttered a made-up spell and on the chest of each boy, Pete first, Rory second, scratched three little marks like the ones she'd seen on Francis, scraping just hard enough to make them bleed.

Pete took it stoically but Rory started to cry.

"Don't be a baby," she said. "*Dandosya* eat babies."

"But where's your mark?" Pete said suddenly, his voice jeering. "I've never seen one on you. We're safe but the zombies can get you now."

Zara looked at him a moment, and the thrill of power she'd just been feeling melted into fear. It was true, she realized, for all her boasting she had no real protection against *dandosya* at all, nor against evil spells, either.

"All right," she said, setting her jaw. "I'll do it, too." She unbuttoned her shirt and, with a wince, scraped her chest three times till it bled.

Rupert was also naked at that moment, but his penis did not in the least resemble a beheaded worm. He was in Joelle's bed, where he spent most of his time these days, hovering over her delectable body and shuddering with desire.

"Joelle, my love, I do believe you have the most beautiful nipples in the world," he gasped. He licked first one, then the other, and eased open her muscular thighs, licking there, too. "Let me in, darling," he whispered, moving back over her. "I want you so badly."

Joelle grunted as she took him in, and while he thrust in and out of her, moaning with pleasure, she reached under her pillow, doused her hands in powder of ground human bones and bat testicles and rubbed it over his buttocks. "Give me a baby," she whispered in Creole, biting his earlobe while she was at it. "Give me, give me, give me a baby."

Marguerite stood opposite Philippe Chanson at the church-hall dance, beating a rhythm with her feet. They were dancing the *camptolet*, a style of French contra dance in which the men and women lined up facing one another, never touching, and stamped their feet to the rhythm of drums and the clapping of hands. (A few years earlier, they might have been dancing the *moutia*, a dance with African roots that was always held outdoors, but that dance was banned from Victoria and everywhere else after nine at night, as the Church considered it lewd and the government a disturbance of the peace.) The night was drawing to an end, so most of the men were already drunk and lying against the walls or in their women's laps, sucking on beer bottles like babies. But Marguerite wasn't even tired. She loved to dance. Dressed in her best silk frock of dusty rose, her hair woven and pinned to her head in its crown, she stamped in slow solemnity as she faced her lover. For Philippe would be her lover, she had decided upon it—she had even told Lisette and Francis to sleep elsewhere in preparation. But first, she would make him pass all her tests. He had passed two already: he had arrived at the dance decently dressed in a clean white shirt, ironed and starched, even if it did dangle off his bony shoulders like a curtain; and he had not fallen drunk. Now she wanted to give him the third test: He had to dance, old man or not, until the first cock crow of dawn.

Penelope and the Lelands didn't get home from Praslin until past midnight. The children were already in bed when they arrived, Zara and Chloe in their own room and the two boys in Rupert's, as he, of course, wasn't there. Francis was pacing the veranda impatiently, a paraffin lamp swinging in his hand, furious because he'd been kept there so long he'd missed an entire Saturday night's fun.

The Lelands scooped up their sleeping boys and stowed them in the back of their Land Rover, while Penelope dismissed Francis with a generous three rupees and a thank-you. But as she stood on the veranda, waving Paul and Lily off, she became so aware of Rupert's absence in the house behind her that it was all she could do not to call them back. When their car drove out of sight, she felt marooned.

To stave off the awaiting loneliness, she went up to the children's room to check on them. Chloe was asleep, a tiny mound under her sheet, so Penelope kissed her lightly and straightened the mosquito net around her bed—the poor child suffered so from bites. But Zara was still awake, reading by an inadequate hurricane lamp.

"Enough of that now, Zouzou," Penelope whispered, gently taking the book out of her hands. Zara lay down and Penelope tucked her in, running her fingers over the girl's sea-sticky hair. "You shouldn't read by such a weak light, darling. It's bad for your eyes."

"Mummy? Will you go to the *bonhomme* tomorrow?" Zara's brow was furrowed, her face a brown nut against the pillow.

"Goodness, will you never let up?" Penelope kissed her daughter's salty cheek. Zara smelled of the sea all the time now.

"Please say you'll go, Mummy."

"We'll see. Now go to sleep."

"Please, Mummy, please go. You have to. I've got a feeling if you don't something really bad is going to happen."

"Don't be silly, poppet. I wish you'd stop going on about all this magic nonsense. You'll be telling me you're a witch yourself next." Penelope doused the lamp.

"Francis says I almost am," Zara replied seriously. "He says Nana told him I have the Sight. He says I have the power to protect people from evil sorcerers and *dandosya*. But I'm not sure. That's why you've got to go, Mummy. Please!"

"Oh really, what rubbish. Francis has been filling your head with claptrap. Now go to sleep, and tomorrow we'll do something fun, all right?"

"No, please, let's just go to the *bonhomme*."

"Shh, you'll wake Chloe." Penelope drew the mosquito net closed. So it wasn't only Marguerite and Sylvie who had frightening Zara but Francis, too. She must tell him to stop. "We'll discuss this in the morning. Good night, muffin."

"Where's Daddy? I want to say good night to him, too."

Penelope closed her eyes. "Daddy's not home yet."

"He's never home. He never tells us stories or says good night or anything. Where's he go all the time, Mummy?"

"He's at work, darling. I know, I'm sorry. He's very busy. I'll speak to him about it in the morning."

"I don't think Daddy likes us anymore."

"Of course he does!" Penelope replied, shocked. "I'm sure he just doesn't realize how much he's been out. I'll tell him to stay home more, all right?"

Zara shook her head. She didn't believe that Daddy would agree to stay at home. Not while Mummy might still have the demon worm, and certainly not after the blue bottle.

"Go to sleep now, darling. Good night."

"'Night, Mummy. Please be careful. I love you."

"Thank you, sweetie," Penelope whispered, an ache in her throat. "I love you too," and gently she closed the bedroom door.

Downstairs, she stepped into Rupert's room and stood over the empty single bed. How his absence yawned. It was palpable, insistent, as concrete as a presence. Oh, why didn't he just stay here and stop hurting them all?

Glancing up, she caught sight of herself in the mirror across the room and stared at her long, stork-like reflection critically. I wonder if I could fill my life with purpose as Lily has, she thought. I wonder if I could learn how to matter.

12

Rupert awoke early on Sunday to the clanging of Victoria's church bells. He lay beside Joelle's slumbering form, his arms behind his head, listening to her mother and sister whispering in the adjoining room as they dressed for church. Nothing but a bamboo partition separated them and he felt unpleasantly vulnerable lying there naked, his crotch sticky from sex and sweat, his buttocks chafed by something gritty. I wish Joelle would stop using that damn talcum powder, he thought. It smells revolting and it irritates my skin. I shall have to buy her a finer brand.

The whispers soon escalated into chatter and bursts of loud laughter. Rupert frowned. Were he and Joelle to have no peace? The two women had come back wailingly drunk from the church hall dance, waking him up in the middle of the night, and now they were at it again, as clamorous as a market. They were always loud, these Lagrenade women, and it was even worse when Alphonse brought her crowd of brats home, or when Charité, the eldest, labored down from the mountain, shabby and desperate, to borrow money from Joelle. Furthermore, he could not abide how they all treated him, one minute with embarrassing obsequiousness as if he were a prince, the next appraising him with calculating eyes as if he were a wallet.

Poor Joelle, how hard she worked to uphold her family. For he had come to see how much they all depended on her, the price she had to pay for being the family's only success. Her mother was drunk every day by noon, her sisters were wanton and slovenly and her remaining brother never showed up at all. What a burden the poor girl carried. Yet she never complained. When Rupert had expressed sympathy, she'd only looked surprised and said, "But it is my duty, *cheri*. My sisters and mother, they have been cursed with bad luck. It is only I whom God has seen fit to help." Rupert admired her no end.

I shall rent a bungalow, he decided, somewhere much nicer than this bare wooden shack, which is more like chicken coop than a proper house. I shall find a place where Joelle can live in peace and where I can visit her in privacy whenever I please. I'll start looking for one today.

Joelle stirred, muttered something and sank back into sleep, while inside her, two of Rupert's sperm doggedly made their way up her left fallopian tube. One carrying an X chromosome, the other a Y, they pushed past the crowd of punier sperm and battled on. Most of Rupert's spermatozoa had grown somewhat lackadaisical since he had reached the tropics, the combination of heat, beer and sitting too long in his hard office chair having rendered them weak and lazy. These two, however—urged on, possibly, by testicle of bat—were doing just fine. Pushing past their inferior brethren, some of which were stupid enough to be heading in quite the wrong direction, they swam valiantly upward, straining toward the lovely round sun of Joelle's patiently awaiting egg.

Marguerite, too, awoke to the sound of church bells, and lay for a moment listening to their sonorous chimes, while memories of Antoine crowded into her head. Normally, she was adept at pushing them away, four years having passed since he'd left her, but this morning, like every other morning after she'd been with a new man, she had no strength to resist them. Philippe's body felt so bony compared to Antoine's, his skin so loose, his old man's breath so sour and stale. The minute the old barber had climbed on top of her, she'd had to close her eyes and turn her mouth away, struggling to quell her body's call for the man she truly loved. She didn't blame the barber. It wasn't his fault. He couldn't know that being with him only made her yearn for somebody else.

She stared blankly at her shuttered window, sunbeams seeping through its cracks, dust motes swirling within them. A cock crowed, blending with the church bells and Philippe's hoarse breathing beside her. The loss of Antoine had been as devastating to Marguerite as the loss of hope. It had made her helpless with grief, weeping for weeks, praying to God, begging Mother Mary to bring him back. It had made her heart shrivel up until it felt as dry and unyielding as sand in the soil. And her heart felt that still.

Philippe yawned to show he was awake, grunted, and squeezed her fingers to signal that he would like again to indulge. Marguerite closed her eyes, rolled toward him and placed his hand over her breast.

If love is no longer to be mine, she thought, I will make do with this old man. It is better than no one.

On the far side of Victoria, the bells also reached Paul and Lily Leland, who were likewise lying naked in bed. Paul was on his back, Lily's head on his shoulder, her pale skin vivid against his dark tan, and they were talking quietly so as not to awaken the boys in the other room of their rented bungalow.

"I feel sorry for Penny," Lily was saying. "Her marriage is obviously in trouble. She's in for a pretty bad time, if you ask me."

Paul gazed for a moment at their mosquito net, which was filtering the morning sun into a mist of sparkling dust. He liked this boxy room, with its rough wooden walls and floor, its slatted shutters and the little veranda in front. He enjoyed the monkish simplicity of it, the living out of a suitcase without the luxuries of American modernity, the humility of a corrugated iron roof. The nomadic life appealed to Paul, who, at heart, was something of an ascetic. He felt free like this, liberated from the physical and moral burdens of material possessions.

"Yeah, I know," he said eventually. "What a jerk her husband is. I didn't like him at all at that party she gave him. The whole night he acted like he couldn't stand the sight of her. It was pretty embarrassing."

"I wonder how she'll support herself if he leaves? She's never had a job in her life."

"Oh, I don't know. I've got a feeling she's tougher than she looks."

"You think so?" Lily turned onto her side to face him and propped herself up on an elbow, her little breasts peeking out over the sheet. "You like her, don't you?"

He shrugged. "She's okay. Kind of stuffy."

"Come on, I know you like her. She's very lovely. And very tall. You better watch out, Professor Leland."

"Come here, baby," Paul said, pulling his spry little wife into his arms. "No stick of a Brit is gonna lure me away from you. Don't you worry."

"I'm not sure about that weird little girl of hers, though," Lily said, staving him off a moment. "She's spooky. I don't like what she did to the boys."

"They'll survive." Paul nuzzled his wife's neck and slipped his fingers between her thighs.

"Mmm. But she hurt them, Paul. Those scratches she gave them are infected already."

Paul grunted, turned Lily over, and pulled her up on her knees. "No more talking," he said, crouching over her from behind. "Now concentrate, Mrs. Leland. This is gonna feel very good."

Penelope didn't hear the church bells because she was fast asleep and caught in an erotic dream about Paul Leland. He was standing in a green glade of some sort, a mixture of the Vallée de Mai and the familiar woods of Devon, removing her shorts while he nibbled her ear. She felt the tickle of the hair on his arms and the brush of his lips, his hands running delicately over her breasts, which, when she glanced down, were curiously like the shell of a *coco-de-mer*. It bothered her that her breasts should look so brown and crusty, and she worried that he would draw back in horror at their rough wooden texture. Yet he didn't seem to mind. He only knelt at her feet and kissed her woody nipples, pulling her down to the forest floor beside him, spreading her legs as she trembled and moaned . . .

"Mummy!" Zara landed on her with a thump, startling her awake.

"Oh God." Penelope blinked, trying to clear her head. Where was she? The light around her was curiously steamy and out of focus, as if she'd awoken on one of those cozy mornings at home, when the whole of England seemed swaddled in fog. Oh, the mosquito net.

"Zara, this is not a kind way to wake a person up."

"Mummy, pay attention." Zara climbed onto Penelope's chest, her sharp little buttock bones digging into her mother's ribs. She put her fingers around Penelope's eyes, forcing them open and holding them there, the way she had that odd time before, which prevented Penelope from being able to blink.

"Listen, Mummy. We're going to the *bonhomme*. He's going to make sure you're safe from the blue bottle. Promise?"

Penelope glared helplessly at her dark daughter, who, at that moment, resembled a little black imp more than the English girl she putatively was. "I can't even blink, let alone go anywhere. Please get off me, darling."

Zara peered into her mother's eyes a minute. No more red thread. Maybe the worm really had gone!

"Zara, please."

"All right, I'll get off. But you still have to cross your heart and promise to go." She released her mother and rolled off.

Penelope closed her stinging eyes and remembered the dream. Was she really that attracted to Paul or was her mind playing tricks?

This won't do, she told herself, I cannot become the sort of woman who lusts after other women's husbands. Toynbee was mistake enough. I must get my own husband back, no matter what it takes. If Rupert were here in bed with me, where he belongs, instead of with that damn secretary, I wouldn't have to dream about Paul Leland or anybody else. And the dream came back to her, the woods and his breath and the tickle of his tongue. . . .

"Mummy!" Zara clambered back onto her stomach, making Penelope grunt. "You haven't promised to go yet. You've got to. Come on!"

Penelope gazed absently at her daughter. Should she try this *bonhomme*? It would certainly appease Zara if she did, and Paul might be right, it could be an interesting adventure. If Marguerite came as well, it shouldn't be overly frightening. Perhaps this witch doctor person could even proffer some advice, if he were as wise as Marguerite said. At the very least, he might tell her how to get Sylvie to come back.

Penelope tickled Zara until she fell off her, giggling, and sat up in bed with a stretch. "Has Nana arrived yet?" Zara shook her head. Penelope glanced at the sun streaming under the bedroom shutter. "Odd, she's not usually this late. Well, darling, if I do consent to visit this *bonhomme* of yours, Nana shall have to go with me."

Zara bounced up to her knees on the bed. She was wearing nothing but a baggy pair of navy blue knickers, and with her ashy brown skin, ribby torso and disheveled short hair, she looked more like an imp than ever. "I'm going, too."

"You most certainly are not." Penelope swung her legs off the bed and stared at them groggily—they felt terribly long and heavy, as if they belonged to somebody else.

"But you can't go without me. You won't know what to do."

Penelope rubbed her temples, which were aching horribly. Those coconut cocktails were more dangerous than she'd thought. "And I suppose you do?"

"'Course I do." Zara jumped off the bed. "I got it out of Francis.

For ages he pretended he didn't know, but then he told me." She planted herself in front of Penelope, her knickers drooping around her tiny hips. "He said you've got to bring lots of money and presents. And you've got to go early early in the morning or right after sunset. Those are the only times."

"Why?" Penelope said, smiling. But Zara was dead serious.

"Because that's the time no one will see you."

Penelope could see the sense in this. The Seychellois didn't much like the dark. Unless they were at a celebration or dance, they tended to disappear into their shacks the minute the sun sank and stay there until the full light of morning.

"Anyway," Zara added, "Francis said if the police catch us visiting the *bonhomme*, they'll put us in prison."

"In that case, I think we better talk to Nana before we go anywhere." Penelope rose from the bed. "What happened to your chest, by the way?"

Zara's hand flew to cover the scratches, just as Francis had covered his. "Oh, nothing. Just some scrapes. They don't hurt."

"They look a bit infected. I'll tell Nana to put some iodine on them. I'm going to have a bath now. Go get dressed, darling, and let me know when she arrives."

"But Mummy, you will go to the *bonhomme*, won't you?"

"Goodness, you are relentless. All right, I'll go."

So the very next morning it was Penelope's turn to toil up Morne Seychellois at dawn, a basketful of offerings in her hand; only, in this case, as she was white and knew what was expected of her. Her offering was money. Marguerite was ahead of her, showing her the way, Chloe was back at the house with a sleepy Lisette, and Zara was trotting at Penelope's heels, thrilled, nervous and gravely earnest at the same time, her mother having utterly failed to prevent her from coming.

Although the sun had barely peeked above the horizon and the

sky held only a glimmering of pink light, the air was already so
steamy that it clung to their skins like a sweat, making it impossible
to tell whether the dampness came more from inside or out. Wet
patches were seeping through the back of Marguerite's blue dress
and Penelope could feel her shirt and shorts sticking to her like
polythene wrap. It was at times like this, when the heat was suf-
focating and the air hostile, that Penelope felt most aware of the
proximity of the equator, as if it were running like a hot iron poker
right through her chest.

Marguerite led them high up the forested mountain, a steep and
grueling climb far above their village of Bois Rouge. Soon they
were on a small trail of red earth that wound past the poorest of
the island's houses, most of which were ramshackle huts built of
palm leaves, scraps of tin or wood, and sheets of cardboard fortified
by magazine pages that had been glued all over them in a haphaz-
ard collage. Penelope supposed that *Bonhomme* Adonis lived this far
up because he had to hide his business, it being illegal. Nevertheless, she wished it weren't so much of a trek. Rupert had taken the
car with him the last time he'd left (five days it had been now), so
they'd had to walk all the way from the house, even along the road,
which at this point was almost two miles ago. Anger stirred in her
yet again, but with it came genuine bewilderment. It was so unlike
Rupert to be this inconsiderate, especially of the children. He had
indeed become a stranger.

A bloodcurdling scream tore the air just then, making them all
jump. Penelope and Zara froze in their tracks.

Marguerite glanced over her shoulder, saw them both staring at
her in terror and burst out laughing. "It is nothing," she said when
she could speak. "They are killing a pig. They do it early in the morning so the heat of the sun, it does not spoil the blood." Still heaving
with laughter, she turned her stolid back on them and plodded on.

This mountain forest was much denser than the Valleé de Mai,
more like the jungle Penelope had expected, with vines hanging
from branches, huge trees, bizarre roots springing out from tree

trunks and crawling along the forest floor, and that same deep rubble of dead pandanus leaves shin-deep along their path. The angry squawk of a bulbul sounded nearby, followed by the whistle of distant frogs, but otherwise this forest was also quiet, its rustling leaves often the only noise. Penelope tried to name the trees around them: cinnamon was everywhere, so she scratched off a piece of bark and gave it to Zara to sniff. She recognized the *lagatia*, too, tall, with fern-like leaves and bean pods that split open to spill shiny red seeds, the size of peas. A banyan, its roots dangling from its branches like snakes. A sang dragon, its pale trunk huge and fat— this was the tree that bled if you cut it. And then her favorite, albizia, a silver tree that reached up like a fountain to form a feathery flat canopy, like a bright emerald carpet in the sky.

They walked for nearly an hour more, the sky lightening from its gentle pink to a searing blue, but nobody talked much, each too sunk in her own thoughts for conversation.

Marguerite was contemplating Philippe and whether it was too soon to ask the *bonnonm* to give her a spell to secure him. Maybe I should find out first if he is as against *grigri* as my Antoine was, she thought. She did not want to risk losing another man because he found her ungodly, for who knew whether, at her age, she would ever find a lover again. No, I will stay natural for now and wait to see what happens, she decided. Perhaps my *kalou* and my house will be enough to keep him.

Penelope was experiencing one of those disconcerting, out-of-body moments when one sees oneself from afar. Look at that foolish Englishwoman, she thought, clambering up a tropical mountain to see a witch doctor. Who would have guessed it? Penny Clarke of Denbigh Road, Richmond, trying to save her marriage by consulting a sorcerer in the middle of a jungle. She wanted to laugh it was so unlikely. She would have laughed, and given herself a good ribbing, too, had the whole enterprise not seemed so desperate.

As for Zara, she was filled with such a mix of excitement and fear she barely noticed the long, steamy climb at all. She couldn't believe she was on her way to meet an actual wizard. This wasn't a fairy story, this wasn't a book—this was real! She shivered a little at the thought. What was the *bonhomme* going to be like? Would he really be able to protect Mummy from the blue bottle curse? Or would he be bad and frightening, like Francis said he could be, and set a *dandosya* after them? And what would he look like? Big and scary in a tall, pointy hat? Evil like the devil, with a long black cloak and red, burning eyes? Or would he be nice, like Merlin, with a woolly white beard and an owl in his hair? And what would he think of her? Would he laugh at her the way all the other grown-ups did when she spoke about magic, or would he agree with Nana and say, *Yes, little daughter, you have the Sight. I shall now teach you the Ways?* Oh, if only that would happen! She would be like Pippi Longstocking then, strong and heroic. She would make magic adventures for herself and Chloe, she would protect her family from *dandosya* and *malfeter*, and she would be nice to everyone, even those American boys—so nice that Daddy would never go away again.

When they reached the *bonhomme*'s house, Penelope was surprised. She'd expected to find the usual wooden shack, scruffy chickens pecking about in its dusty courtyard, but this house was as grand and white as her own. What's more, it was surrounded by a spectacular garden of bushes and fruit trees. She recognized cassia, the candle bush, so called because its upright yellow flowers looked like melting candles; rows of coffee plants, their dark green leaves drooping like scarves; and a stand of cashew trees, sprouting red apples at the ends of their branches, each with a solitary green nut curling out of it like a fingernail.

The side yard was equally impressive, with a wide vegetable patch, several beehives and a shed of remarkably clean pigs and cows. It also contained an official looking kiosk of thatched wood, like something one would find at a tourist site, where a crisply dressed woman was selling honey and coffee beans, fruit juice and bananas, and small, tortoiseshell picture frames. Most surprising of all, though, was a sort of bus-stop shelter in front of the house, with a thatched roof and walls of layered palm leaves, which Marguerite told her was the waiting room.

"The waiting room?" Penelope said.

"But of course, Madame. *Bonnonm* Adonis is the most important doctor in all of Seychelles and he is very busy. We must wait here with the others, until the nurse, she comes to fetch us."

Maybe there really is something to this fellow after all, Penelope thought. Why else would he command such respect?

"Come, let's sit," Marguerite said, and led her inside the shelter, where seven men and women were waiting in their best clothes, each with a hand basket filled with goodies. They were lined up on two facing benches, flipping through magazines and fanning themselves like patients in waiting rooms all over the world. Somewhat dazed, Penelope sat next to a buxom woman in a flower-print frock, making room for Marguerite at her side. Zara, who was the only child there, wandered off to look at the animals.

Presently, a nurse arrived to call the first patient. The nurse was dressed in starched white and had the same irritable manner of nurses everywhere. Penelope was struck by how much more organized and prosperous this waiting room was than the one at Dr. Panyal's clinic, with its worm-ridden children and gonorrheal young men. "Next, please," the nurse snapped, and an elderly man heaved himself off the bench and hobbled after her across the courtyard, clutching his basket to his stomach. They didn't go into the main house, however, but to a raised wooden bungalow on one side, which Marguerite said was the doctor's office.

While they waited—and the wait was long, for each person took between a quarter and half an hour with the *bonhomme*—Penelope studied her fellow patients. All were Creole and all studiously avoiding looking at her, but before long they were chatting to Marguerite, who had a knack for drawing people out. One handsome woman in a bright yellow dress said she was there because a tree had been growing in her stomach and was sticking out below her ribs and hurting. Another, thin and half toothless, said her daughter was having a baby and she was worried that the curse of a rival would make it come out wrong. A third, who was wearing a wide-brimmed straw hat that swooped coquettishly over her plump face, said her son had fallen in love with a dark-skinned girl from a poor family and she wished to put an end to this most undesirable romance. And a fourth, dressed smartly in a blue dress with a white collar, admitted that she was there because her husband's eye had wandered one too many times. Penelope was curious to know what the three men in the waiting room were there for as well, but they were more reticent, trying to look as if they weren't listening to the women. Meanwhile, with every patient who was called away, two or three more arrived, until the waiting room was bursting with patrons. *Bonnonm* Adonis was so popular, one of woman said, that people came all through the night to see him, braving their fear of *dandosya* and the dark. No wonder he's so rich, Penelope thought, for not only did the patients bring him their brimming baskets, most of them stopped at the kiosk to buy something, too.

Penelope had to wait for two hours before it was her turn with *Gran* Adonis, as she heard the other patients call him, which gave her plenty of time to grow apprehensive. She had embarked on this adventure out of curiosity and to appease Zara (and, she had to admit, to prove to the Lelands she wasn't a complete coward), but now she felt shaky, as if she really were about to meet a person with inexplicable and frightening powers. She was also dying for a ciga-rette, but Marguerite had told her that decent women did not smoke in Seychelles, and certainly not in public, and that if Madame did so it would shame her. So Penelope sat limp and wilting in the heat, nicotine deprived and horribly nervous.

When the nurse called Penelope at last, Zara jumped up and inserted a trembling hand in her mother's. The nurse, however, glared at Zara and said in a firm, business-like tone, "No children, Madame. The doctor, he forbids it."

Zara let out a cry of disappointment. "Please, Madame nurse," she pleaded in her impeccable Creole. "Please, I won't make any noise." But the nurse was impervious. Nodding briskly at Penelope, she turned her back on Zara and marched across the courtyard.

Zara was crushed. How was she to learn anything from the *bonhomme* now, let alone become strong and magical? How was she to find out whether he was evil or good, or how to get her daddy back? She stood at the edge of the shelter, staring after her mother in dismay. Then she had an idea. Marguerite was deep in conversation with her neighbor again, her back turned, so as soon as the nurse had led Penelope inside the bungalow, Zara scuttled after them, ducked into the crawl space underneath and wriggled out of sight. She wouldn't be able to see the *bonhomme* like this, which was terribly disappointing, but at least she'd be able to hear him because, as she had long ago learned, the floors of Seychellois dwellings were made of nothing but wooden boards, and between every board was a sound-leaking crack.

Above her, the nurse opened an inside door and ushered Penelope into the *bonnonm*'s presence.

The first thing that struck Penelope about *Gran* Adonis was that he looked like an elderly African businessman. She hadn't exactly expected grass skirts and masks, but neither had she anticipated the dignified and modern appearance of this short, portly gentleman, dressed in an ironed white shirt and gray trousers. His face was dark, with a broad jutting chin, and his springy hair white, under which his brow was etched with deep lines. His sunken eyes were narrow and watchful. A thin white mustache bristled over dry, silvery lips. And his manners were exquisite.

"*Bonzour, Madanm,*" he said in a clear and mellifluous Creole, standing as she entered and bowing slightly. "Forgive me, for I speak no English and my French, it is not very good." He waved the nurse away. "But I can see already that you understand me perfectly. Please, Madame, take a seat." He gestured to a chair facing a battered wooden desk.

Relieved that the man seemed neither mad nor malevolent, Penelope sat down with her basket on her lap and took a quick look around. The office was a simple wooden room with one window beside the desk, a gray electric fan on the floor and three rows of rough, plank shelves stacked with jars and tins. On every wall hung a huge and garishly colored poster of the royal family. The *bonhomme* coughed discreetly, sat at his desk and offered her a toffee from a Quality Street tin. She shook her head, smiling nervously.

"I am honored that you have come to see me," Adonis said then, his voice cracked and rumbling. "It is not usual for Europeans to seek me out. They do not, as a rule, respect my work."

How quickly he gets to the point, Penelope thought with some admiration. What she didn't know was that Marguerite had visited Adonis some time ago to fill him in. She had told him all about Rupert and Joelle and Zara's misplaced attempts at *grigri*. She had also assured him that Penelope was not a spy, even though she was friends with those suspicious Americans who were asking too many question. (The whole island was worried about the Lelands, certain they were spying for the government, for rumblings of opposition and independence were increasing by the day. "You are sure this white woman is not coming to spy and report me to the police?" Adonis had said. "No, no," Marguerite had replied. "Madame is too thin in the blood to be a spy. She is not—" and at this she had leaned toward the *bonnonm* and dropped her voice—"she is not very sharp.")

For some time Adonis kept Penelope chatting about minor matters. They complained of the heat and the unreliability of servants, and wondered whether the queen had been right to put twelve-year-old Prince Charles in a school rather than have him privately tutored, as every prince before him had been since the beginning of time.

"I think it's going to make him awfully common, mixing with ordinary people like that," Penelope said, warming to the subject. "On the other hand, perhaps it will make him a kinder king, sort of like Prince Hal and his friendship with Falstaff."

"Me, I wish it was Princess Anne who would be the queen, not this ugly boy with a big nose," said Adonis, stroking his mustache. "I like queens. The queen mother, for instance, she is a perfect lady."

Penelope smiled in delight. "Yes, dear old queen mum. She was so brave during the war."

(Why are they talking about the queen? Zara wondered impatiently, brushing a line of ants off her knee. Why don't they get to the magic?)

This went on for some time, Penelope losing her self-consciousness as she sank into familiar English gossip, Adonis studying her. She quite forgot to marvel anymore that she was in the middle of a tropical jungle chatting with a witch doctor, so when he said, in the same chuckling voice with which he'd been discussing Prince Charles's nose, "And so, Madame, how can I help you today?" she felt caught.

"Oh. Well, I'm having a little trouble with . . . um . . . my cook. You see, my daughter found a bottle of blue water buried by the front steps, and the woman fled. I haven't seen her since."

Ah, so this white woman has a worse enemy than she suspects, Adonis thought. But all he said aloud was, "I will give you protection, and if you ask Marguerite Savy to tell this cook I have done so, I am sure she will come back. But now, Madame, let us be honest. This is not why you came all the way up the mountain to see me, is it?"

Penelope pretended to laugh. She felt like a schoolgirl caught cheating on an exam. "Well, no, I suppose not." She flushed again. Damn my white skin, she thought, it's so mercilessly revealing. She struggled to speak for a moment, then fell silent and looked at the *bonhomme* helplessly. It was simply too embarrassing. She was not brought up to spill her marital secrets to perfect strangers, doctors, sorcerers or otherwise. The words would not come.

"Madame, I respect that it is difficult to speak," Adonis said gently. "So, perhaps I can help, for I have the Sight, you know, and I can see into the hearts and minds of my clients."

(Zara's skin tingled at that. Here it comes, she thought, and strained toward the floorboards to listen.)

"Oh, really?" Penelope replied skeptically, but at the same time she felt oddly lightened by his words. "And what is it you see, Monsieur?"

Adonis fiddled with his window shade a moment, peering out at his waiting clientele. Then he turned back to Penelope with a kindly expression that reminded her of her father in one of his rare companionable moods.

"I see a man in your life, a man whom you love with all your heart, who is drifting away, Madame, like a pirogue loose from its moorings."

Penelope swallowed. Did she wear her heart on her sleeve as obviously as this?

(Is he talking about Daddy? Zara wondered with growing panic. Why does he say Daddy is like a boat? Does he mean he sailed away? Is that why he hasn't been home for so long?)

"You wish my help to retrieve him, Madame?" Adonis continued.

"Um, well, I suppose so. Yes." Penelope's cheeks burned again.

"Ah, but you must be sure this is truly what you want. Is it his love you miss, Madame, or is it only the life he gives you?"

The question caught Penelope up short. Adonis spoke again. "I ask because my medicine, it will not work unless you truly want what you say you want. You are sure, Madame, that you want this man's love for your own, forever?"

"Oh yes," Penelope said with a lurch of the heart, but she did wonder, just for a second, if she were able to separate Rupert from what he gave her. Respectability, safety, a home, a life—a role. All these came with a husband and was it even reasonable to separate them out? Of course it was, don't be ridiculous, she told herself, her eyes darting about the room as the *bonnonm* watched. Of course Rupert's love is what matters most, his love for me and for the children. After all, it's for them, even more than for myself, that I must win him back, isn't it? Oh, I'm in such a muddle!

"Very well, Madame," Adonis said gently. "One minute, please."
He pulled toward him the very same sort of dim and blotchy mirror
Madame Hélène had used for Joelle. Peering into it, he moved three
white pebbles around it in circles with his dry and wrinkled fingers,
then darted a look at Penelope.

"Madame, I must make for you a very strong spell. Your husband, he is caught like a fly and it will take a mighty struggle to
free him."

(Daddy caught like a fly? Zara thought of the spider in her garden and shuddered. Stupid me, she thought angrily. I was so busy
protecting Mummy I forgot to look after Daddy, too.)

"Caught like a fly?" Penelope repeated. "Yes, I suppose that does
sort of sum it up. What is it you propose to do against this . . ." she
almost spoke Joelle's name, but stopped herself, partly out of discre-
tion but mostly to preserve her dignity.

"Madame, for the . . . um . . . spider, if you follow me, I will give
you a spell to chase her away. But for your husband, it must be the
cockerel, and that is both very secret and very expensive."

"The cockerel?" This is getting awfully silly, Penelope thought,
yet her curiosity was piqued. She drew her chair nearer. "Go on,"
she whispered.

(Don't whisper! Zara ground her teeth in frustration, tried to
stand up and knocked her head against the floorboards.)

Adonis froze. So did Penelope. Then he nodded sagely, his old
eyes crinkling, and smoothed his mustache again.

"The spirits, they are listening, Madame. They know this is
important. Now, the cockerel. For this to work, I must make you
a potion. To do so, I must go to the cemetery at midnight and take
with me a black cockerel. There, I shall seek the grave of a young
virgin, upon which I must lie and pleasure myself."

Penelope started back. "Is that strictly necessary?" she said,
blushing bright pink.

(What's a cockerel? Zara wondered.)

The *bonhomme* continued, ignoring the question. "I must catch the product of this act, if you follow me, and then I must cut the bird's throat and drink some of the blood. The rest of the blood I mix with the semen and some herbs I shall have ready. This I dry out in the sun until it is powder. The powder I give to you. If your husband touches it or eats it, he will never wander from you again. *Vwala*. This satisfies you, Madame?"

Penelope stared at him a moment. "Very nice, thank you," she finally said. "But I'm still a little uneasy about the, you know, grave part. Couldn't we do without that bit?"

Penelope had been taught never to walk on a grave, let alone lie on it and desecrate it in this blasphemous manner. If one did such things, both her mother and Nanny had told her, one would disturb the soul within, who would then rise in protest and haunt. Anyway, what the *bonhomme* had proposed was disgusting.

"No, Madame, I must use the virgin and the grave. I am sorry, it is essential. And it will cost you twelve rupees, if you please."

(Zara was in heaven. She hadn't followed all of the spell but she thrilled to the part about the grave and midnight and drinking blood.)

Penelope hesitated. She wanted, of course, to say, "Nonsense! I neither believe in all this codswallop nor have any intention of using your vile spell." But her own despair stopped her. Why not see what happens, she thought. After all, none of her other efforts to keep Rupert had worked—neither love nor charm, shared history nor seduction, not even her appeals to consider the children. Why not try this ancient remedy? It would serve Rupert right to ingest a bit of this revolting stuff. And even if it didn't work, at least she would have proved to the Lelands that she could be adventurous, too.

"All right," she said eventually. "But I don't want the bit about fending off the . . . uh . . . spider. I wish to do no harm, even to that . . . person."

The *bonhomme* screwed up his eyes in amusement. "Very well. In that case, I will give you only the potion and a protection against the blue bottle. But I do no harm, Madame, never fear. I do only good."

(I knew it! Zara exulted. Francis's daddy was wrong. I knew the *bonhomme* was good!)

"And if I use this . . . 'potion' on my husband, you're sure it won't make him sick?"

Adonis raised his hands in shock. "Madame, why would I give you something to harm the man you love? No, this is an ancient remedy. It will bring back his love to you, just as it brought love back to so many men and women among my ancestors." He smiled with grandfatherly reassurance. "Do not worry. I have not risen to be the most trusted and beloved *bonnonm dibwa* in all of Seychelles by making people sick. And remember, if you need me again, you know I am here, always ready to help you. Now, this is what you must do."

Penelope listened distractedly to his instructions, paid, then said her good-byes and left. She was in too much of a daze to notice the red dust smeared on Zara's frock or to wonder where the child had been, for she could not rid herself of the image, abhorrent as it was, of this nice old man masturbating on a grave.

Spells

PART THREE

13

Three weeks after Penelope's visit to the *bonhomme*, Rupert drove home from the office, determined to tell her he was leaving forever. He felt terrible about the children—it was only because of them that he went home at all—but he simply could not tolerate his wife's company any longer. She was the only thing that stood between him and Joelle and he couldn't even feel sorry for her, this angered him so. Once she's got the message, he thought, it should be easy to persuade her to pack up and go home.

He arrived at supper time, which was not unusual for him those days. He had developed a routine over the past fortnight since he'd moved into a spanking new bungalow in Victoria with Joelle. Every couple of days he would show up at seven, share an awkward cocktail with Penelope, refuse to answer her questions about where he'd been and why he was never home, play with the children, gulp down a meal and drive away again as soon as he could. Sometimes he would return later to creep into his study bed, just to keep up appearances. But now he'd had enough.

Nevertheless, this time he approached the house with trepidation. He loathed domestic disputes, thanks to his bellowing father, so dreaded not only Penelope's reaction but the children's. Zara had become increasingly difficult during his visits, staring at him in doleful reprimand until he squirmed, while Chloe attached herself to him like a limpet and cried heartbreakingly every time he left. I'll just have to teach myself not to mind, he thought. After all, children grow used to anything eventually. Look at what happened to me: sent to live upstairs like a servant, invited down for supper no more than once a week. Even I got used to that in the end. No, the girls are so young they'll probably forget all about me when they return to England. And no doubt Penny will find another father for them soon enough—perhaps old Ian Winslop. He was always keen on her and I'm sure Susan's chucked him by now. And then if I do miss the girls too unbearably, I can always go back for a visit.

Neither the children nor Penelope were home when he arrived, which didn't surprise him. He had heard from Edith Talbot that Penny had turned quite eccentric lately, and that she and the children were spending most of their time now with the American anthropologist and his family, running about with butterfly nets. So he took advantage of their absence to fill a bag with a few books and some of Penelope's neglected perfume for Joelle, and sat down in the sitting room with a sigh of exhaustion to read. If I weren't so bloody tired all the time this wouldn't be so difficult, he thought. This damned job is draining me.

It was true that Rupert had been working hard of late. The week before, word had come from above that he was to produce his economic report in publishable form within the month and he was at his wit's end about it. If anyone at the Colonial Office had a clue, he'd grumbled to Joelle, they would know the colony was in no state to be accounted for by anybody. Corruption was rife, half the economy worked by barter rather than money (how was one to assess the payment of three duck's eggs for a spell?) and the whole place was in debt to the *duka*, the Indian shops whose keepers gave out loans and sold everything on credit until even the French *gran blan* were in hock up to their eyebrows. Rupert had made Joelle type endless letters home, pleading for time, money and understanding, but they had met with a resounding silence. It was enough to make any man wilt.

He was just opening Evelyn Waugh's novel, *A Handful of Dust* (perfect description of my marriage, he mused), when the children catapulted in from the beach, still in their bathing suits and covered in sand.

"Dada!" Chloe cried in delight, hurling herself at him. She clambered onto his lap, shedding sand all over his bare and hairy shins. (Rupert had taken to wearing baggy cotton shorts and sandals like the Seychellois men, the climate being too damned hot for all those dashing safari outfits he'd bought in London.) She planted a kiss on his nose. "Give me a ride on your foot."

Zara crouched in the corner of the room, eyeing him sulkily.

Rupert bounced his youngest daughter listlessly while he kept an ear out for Penelope. He found Chloe oddly heavy and his leg muscles ached. Not only was he tired all the time lately but peculiarly weak. In fact, for almost a month now he'd been feeling awful, suffering bouts of diarrhea and chills, along with the most excruciating stomach cramps, and his appetite was virtually nonexistent. He couldn't understand it.

"Zara," he finally said, "I do wish you'd stop glaring at me like that. What's the matter?"

Zara muttered something in Creole, which Rupert had still not learned to understand.

"Pardon?"

"I said, what do you care?"

"Don't be silly, muffin. Of course I care. Come here so I can talk to you."

Zara got up and trailed over. She stood in front of Rupert, scowling, her bony brown limbs sticking out from her bathing suit with the gawky grace of a foal's. He was about to pull her past Chloe and onto his lap, but something stopped him. He gazed at her a moment, confused, until he realized what it was. She was beginning to look unnervingly like Penny.

"Now," he said, mastering his dismay, "tell me what's wrong."

Zara's mouth trembled but she swallowed and forced out an answer. "You never stay at home anymore."

Rupert cringed. "I know, darling. I've been terribly busy at work. I'm sorry."

"I think you've stopped liking us. I think that's why you go away all the time and never tell us stories."

"That's not true!" Rupert said, startled. "I love you and Chloe very much."

"Then why are you being so horrid to Mummy?"

"Am I?" Rupert tried to smile, but it came a grimace. "I'll try not to be horrid anymore, all right? Grown-ups are horrid sometimes, aren't we? It's your job to tell us not to be."

"All right. Then don't be."

"Yes. Quite. I'll try. Anything else?"

Zara stood and contemplated him while he continued to bounce Chloe halfheartedly on his foot. She could not fathom why *Bonhomme* Adonis's potion wasn't working better. She knew her mother had been feeding it to Daddy each time he came to supper (she'd been spying on Penelope quite a bit), but nothing had changed. Perhaps the *bonhomme* wasn't such a clever wizard after all. Mummy had said he looked perfectly ordinary, like a fat little man—no pointy hats, no beards or owls, not even a wand—which had disappointed Zara no end. Perhaps the *bonhomme* was wrong and the trouble with Daddy wasn't that he was sailing away on a boat (he hadn't sailed anywhere, as far as Zara could see) or trapped in a web like a fly. Perhaps the trouble with Daddy was that he'd caught the demon worm.

She bent close to look into his eyes, just as she had with her mother.

"What are you doing?" Rupert said, drawing back.

"Your eyes have gone yellow."

"They have not," he snapped. That was another symptom he'd noticed in himself lately, irritability. At least with everyone but Joelle.

Zara stared at her father a minute. Not only were his eyes yellow, but the whole of his face, so thin now he'd shaved off his beard,

looked sallow and strange. I should give Daddy the medicine from
that silly witch on the beach, she thought. She hadn't used the medicine yet, the worm having gone from Penelope's eyes, so it had
been sitting in Kangy's pouch for weeks, growing stale. I know,
she decided. I'll fix it up and give it to Daddy next time he comes.
Mummy may not need it anymore, but Daddy does.

"Daddy?" she finally said. "Are you ever going to come home
again to stay?"

Rupert became flustered. He'd forgotten how canny Zara could
be. She was almost nine by now, after all. He stuttered and stood up,
spilling Chloe onto the ground.

"I hear Mummy coming," he said. "It must be time for supper."

"Halloo girls!" Penelope called as she walked into the house and
dropped her books on the hallway table, along with a special net for
capturing insects. (She and Lily were collecting insects by the hundreds in the hopes of finding some unclassified wonder they could
claim as their own.) She nodded a frigid greeting to Rupert and went
into the kitchen to start supper. Sylvie had never returned after
her fright over the blue bottle, regardless of the *bonhomme*'s spell to
neutralize its curse. (He had given Penelope a stick to shake over the
threshold of the house while chanting *mon demare*—"release me"—
three times. Zara and Marguerite had insisted she do this while they
watched and she'd never felt so silly in all her life.) Now Sylvie had
gone to work for Vicky Hubert, the thief, who'd snapped her up in
spite of that tongue-searing soup the cook had made for Rupert's
birthday. And because Marguerite still insisted on going home before
sunset, apparently no more reassured by the *bonhomme*'s stick than
Sylvie, Penelope now had to make all the suppers by herself.

Rupert stayed in the sitting room, playing an unenthusiastic
game of tiddledywinks with Chloe. Zara went into the kitchen.

"What's your father doing?" Penelope asked as she put Zara to
work grating coconut. She poured some rice into a pot and glanced
at her watch to time it.

"Nothing. Playing with Chloe. He's in a bad mood."

Of course he's in a bad mood, Penelope thought. The perfidious shit.

"Mummy," Zara went on, "Daddy's eyes have gone yellow. His skin, too."

Penelope darted a look at her. "It can't be that bad, darling. Tell him supper's ready, would you?"

A few minutes later, all four members of the family were seated dutifully around the dining room table. "I know it looks peculiar," Penelope said, piling their plates with rice and something goopy and odd, "but I'm hoping it's chicken curry." She served Rupert an extra large helping, to his alarm, because to him the curry looked like stewed worms. He took two bites, then had to stop.

The contrast between this family dinner and their first in Seychelles six months earlier was striking, although everyone was too preoccupied to notice. The children were still in their bathing suits, sandy and dusty, with unwashed hands, which would never have been allowed in earlier times. Penelope was wearing crumpled shorts and a stained shirt, her hair long and loose. The table was set with nothing but mismatched forks and soup spoons. Marguerite and Sylvie were absent. And Rupert was beardless, thin and, as Zara had said, yellow.

"Sorry," Rupert mumbled as he pushed his dish away. "I don't seem to be hungry. I'll just nibble a little fruit."

"Oh," Penelope said, sounding put out. "Have some rice, at least."

So he tried the rice, which was sticky and overly sweetened with coconut, and after a few forkfuls moved with relief on to a banana. All the while, he was aware of Penny watching him like a cat on the hunt.

After a tense and interminable meal, during which the only person to speak was Chloe, who burbled on about some shell or other she'd found on the beach, Rupert sent the children upstairs and told Penelope, in what he considered a calm and reasonable voice, that he had something to say to her.

Penelope waited until the children were out of earshot—Chloe crying at the banishment, Zara back to her sulking—before she replied. "All right, what is it?"

He took a deep breath. "Penny, I've decided to move out. As you must be aware, our marriage dried to dust some time ago (thank you, Mr. Waugh), so I believe this is best for both of us. I'll pack up a few things tonight and fetch the rest later. I don't need much."

Penelope regarded him with an icy gleam. She was looking extraordinarily unkempt, he noticed. Disheveled and inelegant, hair dangling all over the place, not a dab of makeup in sight. Nothing like the groomed and poised London wife of whom he'd once been so proud.

"How odd," she said. "I was under the impression you already had moved out. I was under the impression, in fact, that you had deserted the family, broken all your vows and, in effect, shredded the marital contract."

"Now don't be difficult."

"Before we go into all that, however," Penelope went on in quite another tone, "I have to say you don't look at all well. I'm worried about you, and so is Zara." For a moment there, Rupert thought, she sounded like the old Penny, the nice one from long ago. "You've lost an awful lot of weight and you're a terrible color. Are you all right?"

He had to confess he wasn't. "I'm tired all the time. My stomach's delicate, too, and I feel damnably weak. I wonder if it's overwork."

Penelope suppressed a snort. Rupert might be guilty of many things but she was certain overwork was not one of them. "Perhaps you should stay home and rest," she said, trying to keep the irony out of her voice. "I'm sure they'd understand at the office."

For one second—only a flickering of a second, mind—the idea of lying in bed while Penny nursed him appealed. It made him think of the hot porridge his mother used to serve him when he was small and sick, and of the tea and biscuits she would bring on a rattling tray to his bed and feed to him while they chatted. That was before the war, of course, before his mother became sad and downtrodden and unable to love him.

But Joelle would do that just as well, wouldn't she? Even better. She would make a much more patient nurse than Penny. Penny would probably tire of the role in one day, the way she always had with the children when they were sick. "Oh, stop lying about like an old cushion," she'd say. "Snap out of it and get up."

"No, it's all right, thanks. I must go. I'll just pop a few things in a bag first." Rupert rose unsteadily from his chair.

"But aren't you going to have your usual postprandial pipe? Or a drink?"

"No, thanks. Doesn't agree with me anymore."

No drink? He must be sick, Penelope thought. I hope to God my love potion isn't poisoning him. *The bonhomme* did say not to give Rupert more than two doses a week, didn't he? And that's what I've done. I never see Rupert more than that anyway. She squinted anxiously at her husband. Adonis had sent the promised powder (cockerel blood, semen, cinnamon leaves and a mix of unnamed ingredients) by messenger—a little boy—and Penelope had been administering it to Rupert every time he came for dinner with all the conscientiousness of a nurse. She still didn't really believe it would work, but as the old sorcerer had sworn it would do Rupert no harm, she had decided to go ahead anyway. Perhaps the medicine would serve as a sort of antibiotic against infidelity. After all, as Adonis had said, the Seychellois had been relying on it for generations. Who was she to say there wasn't something to it? At best the potion might bring Rupert home, at worst it would be ineffectual.

"How long have you been feeling like this?" she said, trying not to sound guilt-stricken.

Rupert headed for the door. "Don't know. Quite a while. Thanks for supper. I'm off to pack now."

Penelope jumped up from the table. "Don't go yet! We have to talk. What about the children?"

"Nothing more to say, old girl. I'm off."

"Rupert, wait!" Penelope cried, her voice faltering. "Please don't leave me."

Without looking at her, he went to his study to pack.

On the drive back to Victoria ten minutes later, Rupert managed to quiet the disturbing echo of Penelope's plea by thinking about Joelle, which filled him with a much more pleasant sensation. He was having such a lovely time setting up home with her in their pretty new bungalow, cooking together, decorating, working out their routines. She was so even-tempered and affectionate, so delighted with everything he did. She was always darting across the room to give him a kiss and looking at him with adoration. Why, just the other night, she had not only grilled him a mild fish even he could stomach but taken him for a walk along the harbor pier at moonlight, holding his hand and urging him to talk about England. She loved to hear about his life outside the Seychelles: his years in the crowded and sooty streets of London, which he was sure she could barely imagine; his days at school during the war; his booze-sodden sojourn at Cambridge. But she especially loved to talk about the books he'd managed to smuggle out of the house, which she read at a dazzling speed, for she said she wanted to learn all about the world so she could be as educated as he. What a terrific girl! No, he had never had such a pleasant time of domestic life as he was having with Joelle, and he was certain now that Penny had been a youthful mistake, a wife taken on before he knew who he really was. Joelle, on the other hand, was perfect, a true companion—clearly the woman destined just for him.

Not that his role as her full-time man was without its problems. For one thing, nobody would accept them. His office friends refused to see her as anything but a Creole mistress, so never invited her to their homes or introduced her to their wives. Her mother and sisters were still treating him as if he were a prince or a wallet—oh, there were a million obstacles, and they all made him wonder how he was going to cope with living on this island forever, as he was now determined to do.

Rupert had decided to stay forever in Seychelles not only because of his love for Joelle or even his wish to escape Penelope but because it had finally become clear to him that he had always hated England. Perhaps if his formative years hadn't been spent under Hitler's bombs he would have felt differently, but the combination of terror and dreariness that characterized wartime Britain had given him the same feeling about his homeland as one might have about a joyless and sadistic headmaster. Perhaps he might have even loved England had he been able to cauterize his memories.

His father absent one morning over breakfast. "Where's Daddy? Isn't he coming down?" His mother blowing her little nose, her eyes red around the edges. "Your father's gone to war, darling. He's going to fight that bully Hitler. We must be brave."

A petrifying night, when something had screamed in the sky and he'd been seized, half asleep, and dragged under the earth, where it was so cold and black he'd thought he was in a grave. "Mummy?" he'd called, terrified. "Mummy!" "I'm here, hush now," her voice had replied, and he'd felt a rough blanket drawn over him. Other people were there, too; he could hear and smell them, clumps of them all around him in the dark, their stinks thickening the air: cigarette tobacco and whiskey breath, damp wool and old boots, the acrid scent of fear. People began talking, saying strange things. "I 'ope to God those Jerries spare the church," a woman said in a cockney accent. And a man with a voice like a policeman's: "Is that a little boy you've got there, mudum? It isn't right, you know. You should've had him evacuated." And another: "They got Sally's house last week, blinking Huns. She went out for a pint, came back, every last brick of it gone." And a fourth, the voice trembling: "Bits of bodies all over the street. I trod on a foot. A foot, just lying there, like a bloody fat sock. What sort of God would let this happen?" Another scream. Instant silence in the hole. The air still, bodies frozen. A long, fearful wait. Then a giant *thud*, as if someone had kicked his chest clear through his body.

"Bend him over, go on, now!" The words of the head boy at school, standing over Rupert with a white cane in his hand. The humiliation of being doubled over, held down, his arse sticking out for all to see. And the *whack, whack, whack* of the whistling cane, coming down on him so hard that his legs buckled and he weed in his trousers.

"Darling?" His mother on the school telephone. "I think you'd better stay at school for the holidays. It's not safe here for children."

"No, Mummy, please let me come home, please don't make me stay—"

"Darling, there's a war on." And again, "Be brave."

And when his father had finally come home at the war's end: "See what they did to me, Rupert! Look at me! *Look at me.* Don't flinch, boy! See what they've done to your father?"

"Monnamour?"

Rupert lifted his head from his desk and gazed bleary-eyed at Joelle. It was the morning after he'd broken his news to Penelope and he felt more depleted than ever.

Joelle studied him with concern. He looked a different man than when she'd first met him, and it wasn't an improvement. His beardless cheeks were no longer ruddy or boyish—they were sunken in now, making his chin look unattractively sharp—and his skin had turned an unhealthy urine color. Even the whites of his eyes looked stained. Is it Madame Hélène's love potion, she wondered. Is it too strong? Am I making my poor man sick? For Joelle had been giving him quite a bit of it over the past few weeks, sprinkling it in his soups and teas, not to mention rubbing it over his buttocks while they made love, to make sure he wouldn't go back to his wife. I better stop, she thought. I do not want to poison the man I adore.

"Yes, my love? What is it?" Rupert's voice was so fond it made Joelle's throat swell.

"*Cheri,* I have some news I hope will please you."

Rupert blinked at her. "Really? A glimmer of sense from the Colonial Office, perhaps?"

"No, it is not that. I hope this will not make you angry."

"Nothing you do could ever make me angry." Rising from his chair, Rupert hobbled to her side of the desk and sank down next to her, taking her long fingers in his. Joelle looked more beautiful than ever to him these days, her sloe eyes tender, her rosy skin aglow, her body shifting with magnetizing grace under her simple cotton dress. He couldn't even glance at her without feeling helpless with love.

For a time they sat in silence, he waiting for her to speak, while the fan creaked in the ceiling and a wasp buzzed indignantly at a shuttered window.

"What is it, darling? Don't be afraid," Rupert said at last.

"Rupert?" She swallowed. (He loved the way she said his name. The soft, purring *R*, the *U* like a coo, the ending like a sigh: *Rrooperrr* . . .) She brought his hand to her belly. "I have just come from the doctor and, *mon cheri,* I am going to have our child."

Rupert's yellow eyes widened. "Joelle, my love!" he cried, gathering her in his arms. "I'm so glad! Oh, darling, I am thrilled! Our own baby!"

Holding her close, he felt buoyant with happiness. Yes, he thought, this makes me complete. I'm not cut out to be a career type, not really. I don't give a damn about economic reports or impressing my superiors. I want to be a lover and a father, and I want to be with Joelle. I shall devote myself to her for the rest of my life, to our children and our home. To hell with ambition and the English. Joelle and I will stay in this paradise forever, and I shall never, never have to go back to England again.

• • •

Half an hour earlier that same morning, twelve hours or so after Rupert had officially given notice as a husband, Penelope had telephoned Lily Leland. All night long she had stormed in anger and wept with humiliation, but by morning she was simply afraid. What was she to do, stranded on this godforsaken island with two children, no job and no husband? How was she to hold her head up, pay for food, run her life—how was she to cope?

Lily answered on the fourth ring, sounding a little out of breath. "Hi, Penny. What's up?"

Penelope felt the tears rising again, but she managed to tamp them down enough to speak. "Good morning, Lily," she said, her voice trembling. "I hope I'm not disturbing you."

"No, no, I was just playing ball with the boys. What's the matter? You sound upset."

"Well, I don't wish to be melodramatic or anything, but Rupert appears to have left me." Penelope emitted a strange little laugh. "It sounds absurd, I know, like some sort of bad play, but I believe he might really mean it. He's even taken his clothes and half my books. He's got the car and all the money, as well. It's left me rather marooned."

"Jesus! The bastard!" Lily paused a moment, gathering her thoughts. "Listen, Penny, I'm going to send Paul to talk to him. Right now. Rupert works at the Queen's Building in Victoria, right? At least we should get the car back for you."

"Oh dear, please don't do that! It's much too much trouble for Paul. I didn't mean that at all. I was only looking for a lift to town, when you have the time."

"Penny, we're your friends and we're going to help."

So, when Paul stormed into the government office to confront Rupert, it happened to be just at the moment Joelle had confessed her pregnancy. Rupert had been easy enough to track down, but Paul was quite taken aback when he found him. For one thing, the strapping and chubby man he remembered from the birthday party now looked gaunt and yellow. And for another, he was sitting beside a stunning Creole woman, holding her hand and staring adoringly into her eyes.

Oh boy, Paul thought. Poor Penny.

"Excuse me," he said. "Rupert?"

Rupert rose painfully to his feet. "Who are you?" he said with less than British politeness.

Paul was disconcerted. "You don't remember me? Paul Leland?"

Rupert gazed at him blankly. "Are you an American? What on earth are you doing here?"

God, the guy's in some kind of trance, Paul thought. He doesn't remember me at all. "We met at your house the night of your birthday party. I was there for dinner. How are you?" Paul held out his hand and Rupert shook it automatically.

"Oh right, you're that anthropologist Penny's been hanging about with. Sorry. Um . . . this is my . . . this is Joelle Lagrenade, my . . . um . . . secretary."

Joelle began to stand up but Paul stepped forward to stop her. "No, no don't get up," he said, and shook her hand, too. "Pleased to meet you." Her hand was as soft and voluptuous as the rest of her. Paul felt a shiver of desire.

"What can I do for you?" Rupert said then. He tottered a little and balanced himself against the desk with one hand. Sweat broke out on his brow. "Sorry, not feeling terribly well. Must sit." And he plopped back into his chair.

"Are you okay?" Paul said. He thought the guy might be about to faint.

"Don't know," Rupert replied, looking about the room vaguely, as if he expected somebody else to answer for him. "May I help you in some way?"

Paul took a deep breath. He was already feeling sympathy for this befuddled man, when only a moment ago he had been furious at him. "I wonder if we could speak in private? It's kind of important."

"In private?" Rupert said, blinking, as if he'd never heard the phrase. "Well, I suppose so, yes. I don't see why not. Shall we pop over to the club for a drink?"

The last thing Paul wanted was a drink—it was ten in the morning—but he couldn't see any other way of excusing himself from the presence of this achingly desirable secretary. "Okay, fine. That'd be great."

"Very well." Rupert heaved himself up again and patted Joelle on the shoulder. "I shan't be long, darling. Hold the fort. And we'll celebrate tonight, all right?"

Joelle nodded and pursed her lips. Something was happening here she didn't like. She decided to use the office telephone to call ahead to the club and ask her friend Albert, who was a waiter there, to eavesdrop.

The two men walked out of the office, Rupert hobbling slowly, and made their way down to the British Seychelles Club on the pier. A squat, disheveled building that had long since misplaced its paint, the club was nonetheless so exclusive that Rupert had some trouble getting Paul in, even as a guest. Facing it was another club, the Tobruk, used only by upper-class Creoles. This is just like Jim Crow, Paul reflected. He and Rupert took their seats on the terrace and ordered a Tiger beer each.

"So, Mr. Leland, how are you liking life on our island?" Rupert said, picking up his beer with a shaking hand and taking a swig.

Paul ignored the question, along with his drink, which he had no intention of touching. "Listen, I have to go back to work, so I need to get right to the point. My wife and I, as you seem to know, have become friends with Penny, and I have to tell you that you can't—"

"Did Penny send you here?" Rupert interrupted with a frown. "Not very discreet of her. This is our private business, Mr. Leland."

"You've left her and the kids with no car and no money, Rupert. What the hell's she supposed to do? How can she get to Victoria to shop? What if the kids get sick? How's she supposed to get around?"

Rupert looked startled. "Oh. Oh, yes, I hadn't thought of that."

Paul opened his mouth, then shut it again. He had steeled himself for argument, even a shouting match. He hadn't expected Rupert's blank astonishment.

Rupert coughed and rubbed his brow. He looked seasick and feeble. "I've been feeling a touch unwell lately and I suppose I haven't thought it all out. Of course I'll send some money her way. But I'm not sure I can afford to rent two houses and two cars, even though everything here is so cheap." He swallowed another gulp of beer, then pushed his glass away. Even beer was making him feel nauseated these days. His stomach cramped unbearably and he gasped.

"I tell you what," he added, his voice strained. "Take the car keys and drive the damn thing over to Penny, will you? I can manage without it for now. My new house is walking distance from the office." He fished in the pocket of his shorts and pulled out a set of keys, which he tossed on the table in front of Paul. "Excuse me," he said, and staggered off to the lavatory.

Paul didn't know what to think. He half sympathized with Rupert—what man could resist a beauty like Joelle? And he half suspected the guy was so sick he didn't know what he was doing. So when Rupert reappeared and sat down again, looking more drained than ever, Paul studied him curiously.

"Have you seen a doctor?" he said. "You look sick as a dog."

"Do I? I must say, I'm not surprised. I haven't felt this under the weather since I had scarlet fever as a boy. Yes, I went to Dr. Malavois at Victoria Hospital. Don't know if you've met him yet, that scuttling little Frenchman? Always reminds me of a crab. Anyway, he said it was most likely I ate some shellfish or other that didn't agree with me. He gave me something to settle the stomach, but I can't say it's done much. I think all I need is a rest."

"Perhaps you should get another opinion," Paul ventured, but Rupert waved the idea away.

"Joelle says that, too. She wants me to go to the local clinic where she's always gone, but I'll be damned if I'll put myself in the hands of some Seychellois crackpot. Half the time they send their patients off to see witch doctors, anyway, for Christ's sake. No, I'll be all right. To be honest, I think it's work and all this strain with Penny. Now we've sorted things out, I suspect I shall get a lot better." Rupert smiled bashfully and shrugged, and Paul didn't know what to say. There was something endearing about Rupert, in spite of the terrible things he was doing. He seemed almost helpless.

"Okay," Paul said, pushing back his chair and standing up. "Thanks for the beer. I didn't expect you to be so reasonable, to tell the truth."

Rupert laughed weakly. "Oh, we English believe in being reasonable. Tell Penny she can keep drawing from the bank account for now, but encourage her to be parsimonious, if you would. I don't have endless resources. She used to be a fiendish spendthrift in London, you know. Couldn't stop surrounding herself with useless knickknacks. But there's nothing much to buy here, so she's more under control." Chuckling, he rose creakily to his feet, shook Paul's hand and tottered out of the club.

When Paul pulled up at Penelope's house in her Mini, she ran out to greet him with astonishment. "My goodness, you've got it already!" she said as he clambered out of the tiny car. "You're a miracle worker!"

He smiled and handed her the keys. "I didn't have to do anything much. Your husband was surprisingly amenable. He says there's money in the bank for you, too, or at least some. He didn't make any fuss at all."

"Thank God!" Penelope clutched the keys to her chest. "Come in and have a drink. That's the least you deserve."

"Okay, thanks, but no alcohol. It's too early."

"Oh, come on, one beer won't kill you. You've earned it. Please?"

Paul was about to refuse again but her face was so pleading he couldn't. "Okay, just one." He followed her into the house, surreptitiously checking his watch. It wasn't even noon yet. These Brits seemed to float through life on a river of booze.

"The kids here?" he said as Penelope opened two bottles of beer in the kitchen and handed him one.

"No, they're at the beach with Marguerite. I do hope Rupert has enough money to allow me to keep paying her. I can manage with Sylvie gone, but without Marguerite I'd be lost. Let's go to the sitting room. It's cooler in there with the fan."

The sitting room was pleasantly cool, with a sea breeze wafting through the open shutters and two wicker fans whirring in the ceiling. They each took a seat, Paul on the cane sofa, which was hard and stiff but at least covered with cushions, Penelope on a matching armchair opposite. Lily had dropped Paul off at Rupert's office straight from his morning interviewing, so he was still wearing his usual work outfit: short-sleeved white shirt, brown shorts and the sunglasses he'd tucked into his shirt pocket when he'd come inside. Penelope was freshly bathed and in a plain blue cotton dress. She looked healthy and tanned but for the rings under her eyes from her sleepless night of weeping.

"I can't thank you enough for going to Rupert for me," she said, her voice forcedly cheerful. "I hate to ask people favors, but he simply refuses to talk about anything practical. He ran off last night without even allowing a discussion. But it's awfully embarrassing to have involved you at all. I'm most terribly sorry."

"Hey, don't be," Paul said. "You didn't ask any favors anyway. It was my brilliant wife's idea."

"She is brilliant, isn't she? I admire Lily so much. I wish . . . oh, never mind."

"You wish what?"

"Nothing, really. I just wish I could be more like her. How's your fieldwork going, by the way?"

Paul leaned forward, his elbows on his hairy knees, rolling the beer bottle between his hands. "Slowly. We've got about fifty families so far, but I need at least two hundred more."

"Are they talking to you, though? Are you managing to cut through that famous reserve we were discussing at my horrible dinner party?"

He shrugged. "I think so, little by little. Lily's specially good at getting the women to talk. The problem is we can't tell whether what they're saying is true or whether they're just telling us what they think we want to hear. And then I suspect they're all too worried about their neighbors finding out what they've said to tell us much anyway."

"Yes, I know what you mean. I've become fairly close to Marguerite, but I still get the feeling she never quite tells me the truth. Oh, I forgot, have you had any lunch? Would you like some?" Penelope jumped up from her armchair.

"No, no, sit down. I had a late breakfast. I can't eat lunch in this heat, anyhow. I wait for dinner."

"But that's terrible! You must eat. All that toiling up and down the mountain—Lily's told me. You must keep up your strength."

Paul patted the seat beside him. "Sit down here and relax, Penny. Take a deep breath, a long swig of beer and relax, okay?"

She hesitated, darting a haunted look about the room and did as he suggested. "I suppose I am rather jittery, aren't I?" she said with a little laugh, and looked down at the beer in her hand. Then she began to cry.

"Hey, hey, it's all right," Paul said gently. He took away her bottle and gave her his handkerchief, which she pressed to her eyes while she wept.

"Oh God, I'm such a fool," she said between sobs. "I didn't see it coming, I really didn't. I pretended I did but I didn't. I thought this was just a little fling. I thought he'd get over it and come back. We'd always agreed to keep the family intact—it was our promise to one another because of the war. I was sure he would stay for the children, at least, if not me."

What a bleak view of marriage, Paul thought, but all he said was, "You haven't been a fool, Penny. Don't blame yourself. He's being a bastard, that's all."

She wiped her eyes. "I've been like a leaky tap I've been crying so much. Pathetic." She let out a watery laugh, glancing into his face. "Do you really think Rupert's being a bastard?"

Paul thought of Joelle, so headily desirable, and of Rupert's befuddled state. "Of course I do. But the problem is, I'm not sure he can help it."

"I know. That's what I think, too." Penelope wrung Paul's handkerchief in her hands. "He's been like another person since we got here. In England he was never like this—well, almost never. He was a good father, then. He was lovely." Her voice trembled again and she fell silent, twisting the handkerchief in her lap. "I mean, I was dreadfully angry at him when he made us come here. He didn't consult me at all, you know, he just forced us to pack up our home, give everything up—our flat, friends, oh, everything. But before that . . ." she trailed off, her eyes running over Paul's face without seeming to see him. "They say men become bewitched in places like this, and I must say, if I wasn't so sure that sort of thing was stuff and nonsense, I'd be inclined to agree. Does he . . . does he seem to be acting at all odd to you?"

"He does seem kind of distracted, yeah. He looks pretty sick, too. He did tell me he's seeing a doctor, though."

"Did he?" Penelope looked frightened. "What did the doctor say?"

"He said Rupert's eaten some bad shellfish or something, and that he needs to rest."

Oh Lord, Penelope thought, I have poisoned him!

"What's the matter?"

"Oh, nothing. It's just that I'm worried. I . . . I heard the most frightful thing from Hannah today and it's given me quite a turn. Do you remember Hannah, the woman who kept crying at my dinner party? Anyway, her husband came down with some sort of tropical disease and went off to a Mombasa hospital weeks ago; he was already gone the night of the party, as a matter of fact. And he hasn't come back. She telephoned me this morning and apparently he's either at death's door or he's run off with an African nurse. But Hannah can't find out which."

Paul laughed. He couldn't help it. "I'm sorry, forgive me, I shouldn't laugh," he said, still chuckling. "It's just the way you put it."

Penelope looked surprised. "Yes, well, I suppose that did sound rather funny, but I didn't mean it that way. I feel very sorry for Hannah. I only hope Rupert doesn't meet the same sort of fate. Would you like another beer?"

They had several more beers, it turned out. Paul could tell how badly Penelope needed company, so he relinquished his plans for that afternoon's work and tried to keep her talking.

"Penny," he said at one point, "did you ever go to that witch doctor you were telling us about?"

She shifted nervously on the sofa. "Um, well, as a matter of fact, yes, I did. I went with Marguerite and Zara. It was quite a trek."

"And did he help with the blue bottle?"

"Not really. He was a terribly nice man. Quite ordinary, though. But it was an awful lot of rot."

"What did he do?" Paul was interested in this, his anthropologist antennae up.

"He moved some stones around on an old mirror and muttered about spells and so on. It was just the same sort of mumbo jumbo you'd get from a circus gypsy, if you ask me. He told me to shake a stick over the threshold, which made me feel ridiculous, and he gave me a potion made of cockerel blood and . . . other revolting things." And it didn't do a jot of good, she added in bitter silence.

Paul sat up. "He did? What were you supposed to do with it?"

"Oh, you know, sprinkle it around," she said, avoiding his gaze. "I threw it away, naturally."

"That's a pity. I would've liked to see it. Do you remember any of the spells?"

"Not really. They were gibberish anyway. Are you sure we shouldn't be eating something with all this beer? Or shall we just say to hell with it and keep drinking?"

"To hell with it and keep drinking, of course," Paul replied, disappointed at her lack of information. He would have liked to know more about the *bonnonm* and his methods, for a local priest had told him that the witchcraft here was just as European as it was African, which would fit in nicely with his theories.

"More beer?" Penelope was saying. "Or would you prefer something stronger?"

"Stronger. I wish we could make those coconut bombshells we had on Praslin."

"Yes, they were scrumptious, weren't they?" Penelope got up and walked unsteadily over to the drinks cabinet to mix two very strong gin fizzes. "Here, this should be almost as good." She handed Paul the drink and sank back down next to him.

What a brave act she puts on, he thought. Poor thing.

Penelope kicked off her shoes and slid down the sofa, her legs sprawling in front of her. She held up her gin. "All right. A toast."

"Oh yeah? What to?"

"A toast to sending Rupert on his way, and good riddance."

Paul looked at her in surprise, but raised his glass as well. "Okay, then. To your new freedom."

"Right. To hell with Rupert Weston and all his sins. I shall become a new woman, modern and daring and . . . whatever it is new women are."

They clinked glasses and took a few deep swallows. But I don't really mean that, Penelope added silently. That's not what I want at all.

"Where did you and Rupert meet, anyhow?" Paul asked then.

"Oh, God, you don't want to know. Much too dull."

"Sure I do."

Penelope gazed at her toes, dusty now and scruffy with half the red varnish rubbed off. "Well, if you must know, we met at a tennis club where all our parents sent us to find a spouse. I would have gone to Oxford if Rupert hadn't been there. I wanted to be a naturalist, like Lily. I might have if my father hadn't died and left us rather poor. That's what propelled me into marriage, really."

"It's not too late. You could always go back to school."

But Penelope wasn't listening. "You know, Paul," she continued, sipping her drink, "I've been a creature of habit far too long. Following all the prescribed paths, never wavering. I was brought up enslaved to habit, really. Never even saw how much of a trap it was. Do you know what I mean?"

"No idea," Paul said with a smile. "Explain."

"I mean I was trained to conform and obey without questioning anything. I believed in the God I was told to believe in, married when I was expected to marry, had the children I was supposed to have, learnt to think about clothes and jostling for social position instead of interesting things like rhinoceros beetles and moth larvae. In boarding school, we were watched every moment. We had to sleep sixteen girls to a room, as well, and even there they were constantly checking on us. I hated it. All that snoring and weeping, everyone miserable with homesickness."

"It sounds like Dickens."

"Well, it was rather, minus the whips and gruel. Anyway, looking back on it, I think it was an attempt to turn us into obedient citizens by stifling our imaginations."

"Not to mention your sexuality."

"What?" Penelope turned her head to look at him. She was a little taken aback at how close Paul's face was. His eyes were an astonishing blue, the exact color of that sapphire sea glass she had found and then lost as a girl on the Isle of Wight.

Paul decided to drop it. There were certain subjects, he had discovered, about which Penelope was impenetrably naïve. "Never mind. What were you saying?"

"Oh, I don't know. It's just that they did it to my father, too. He was so much the obedient citizen and so guilt-ridden all the time. He killed himself, you know. Gas in the car on Christmas day."

"Jesus!"

"Yes." Penelope sighed. "I was the one who found him." She fell silent, gazing into her gin glass. "You know something? I've complained like mad about being dragged away from London, but there is one good thing that's come out of it, aside from the marvelous luck of meeting you and Lily. It's allowed me to escape my whole dreary past, and most of all, my family. The entire Clarke clan is quite bonkers, you know. I mean, Daddy tried to sleep with me, Mummy's had one nervous breakdown after another, my poor uncle was driven mad by the war and my brothers are juvenile delinquents. You probably think me just as bad, but I assure you I'm the sanest of the lot."

"Penny, you're something else," Paul said, and pulled her toward him.

"Am I?" she said, pleased. "Thank you . . . mmm," for Paul was kissing her, really kissing her, with the very sort of kiss she'd dreamed about that night after Praslin. His hand was running over her breasts now, his tongue probing, his fingers playing with her nipple through her dress. And—oh God—for she felt a wash of desire, a breathless hot wave of simply wanting him that made her shudder. Yes, this is what she needed, what she craved. She ran her hands over him desperately, feeling the muscles in his strong back and shoulders. This was like nothing she'd ever felt with Rupert, nor with Toynbee, either. It was like nothing she had ever felt in her life.

Paul was on top of her now, his hand hitching up her skirt. She raised her hips a little to make it easier for him, so he could slip off her underwear and open her up. She longed to feel him plunge into her, longed to melt around him. Her head was swimming, her eyes closed, her body singing—

"Shit," Paul said suddenly and pulled away from her, sitting up quickly. "Christ, what the hell am I doing? I'm sorry, I'm sorry." He was standing up already, pulling his shorts straight, pushing the curls back from his eyes.

Penelope struggled upright, too, her skirt bunched awkwardly around her waist. "What?" she said. But she knew.

"I'm sorry, Penny. I'm real fond of you, you know that, right? Lily is, too. We're your friends, okay? Don't forget that."

"Paul, please don't go."

But before she could say another word, he scooted out of the door and down the hill, literally running away from her.

14

Joelle stared angrily into Madame Hélène's crumpled old face. "But he is truly ill!" she cried. "Your potion, it has poisoned him, Madame! You gave me medicine to make the wife sick, but she isn't sick at all, only my man is. I don't know why my mother has trusted you all these years! You must give me the antidote or I'll report you to the police!"

The fortune-teller looked at this belligerent *rouz* with distaste. Marguerite Savy was right, she thought, these Lagrenade women are nothing but trouble. I should have sent this arrogant hussy away the first time she mentioned her cursed love potion. She shifted to the edge of her enormous armchair and riffled her tarot cards to buy a little time, straightening the ropes of cowries coiled about her wrinkled and splotchy neck.

"Calm yourself, Joelle," she said at last. "Your man is not seriously sick. I've seen him in the street. This has nothing to do with my potion. He only has the white man's disease of too much luxury and love. And now you are giving him a baby as well—thanks to my help, do not forget. Is there anything this man cannot have?"

Joelle frowned at this and laid her hands protectively over her womb. "I don't understand. Why do you say I give him too much?"

Madame Hélène narrowed her already half-closed eyes until they looked like little grimaces.

"Think, *cherie*. Is there anything he wants that you deny him? Your body, your love and now your child? He is turning yellow from a surfeit of indulgence. To cure him, you must cross him, just as you must cross a child to teach him discipline. It is not good for any human being to have everything he wants, and especially not for a male human being. It swells him with laziness until he falls sick."

Joelle twisted the silver ring on her finger, the one Rupert had stolen from Penelope. "But I like giving him what he wants. I love him. How can I go against this feeling?"

"Ah, but remember, it is for his own good. You must do it in little ways. When he asks for curry, give him breadfruit. When he asks for breadfruit, give him fish. When he wants to make love one night, say no and make love in the morning. And make him give you what you need, my girl. Does he give you what you need?"

Joelle thought of the report from her waiter friend, Albert at the Seychelles Club: that Rupert was still allowing his wife free access to his money.

"Not everything, no. I don't wish to sound greedy, but she has the big house and the car like a *gran blan,* while we live in two little rooms and must walk everywhere like servants."

"Ah, so you see?" Madame Hélène chuckled, her throat rasping until she coughed. She fiddled with the strings of shells around her wrist, her speckled hands wrinkled and arthritic, and straightened the tottering red turban on her head. Joelle made her think of an old Seychellois proverb she used to hear as a child: being clever does not prevent you from being stupid.

"Do not forget you have the right to take from him, as well as give," she said then. "Make your demands. This is not so hard."

"But it *is* hard, Madame!" Joelle clutched at her skirt in distress. "We have never quarreled and this will make him angry with me! I do not want him to be angry."

"Ach!" Madame Hélène spat on the ground. "Listen to yourself! Have some dignity. Tell him no, make him struggle a little. Otherwise, watch him die."

This frightened Joelle. "You have no herbs for him, Madame, no special *tizann* to help?" she said more humbly. "He suffers so! And now he has developed a fever that won't go away."

Madame Hélène stalled. By the sound of it, Joelle's man had either really been poisoned or had caught a disease and ought to go to Dr. Panyal, who could cure almost anything. She was certain her own love potion would not have poisoned him, but it was possible the man's deserted wife was doing it. On the other hand, she didn't want to lose Joelle's business by sending her to somebody else just yet. Anyway, Marguerite Savy had slipped her a few extra rupees to make mischief between Joelle and this stolen white man, and Madame Hélène could hardly let her down.

"You follow my instructions for two weeks, *zoli* Joelle," she said eventually. "Cross him and make him work for your favors. And if your man is no better by then, or if he gets worse, come back and we will discuss this further."

She stood up, her shriveled face tiny beneath her turban, her shrunken body lost in its loose, red cotton dress. She held out a mottled claw. "Three rupees, please."

Joelle hesitated. She didn't like the sound of this advice at all, and certainly didn't want to pay for it. On the other hand, she was afraid to push the powerful fortune-teller any further, for who knew what she might do if angered. So she opened the little chain-link purse Rupert had given her and handed over the money.

That will teach you to threaten me with the police, greedy girl, the fortune-teller said to herself as she sent Joelle away. You've taken a white man from his wife, you are carrying his baby, you have one of the best jobs on the island—and still you are not satisfied? It is time to bring you down a peg or two.

She peered through the slats of her window blinds, chuckling, and watched Joelle plod unhappily down the street.

• • •

Far up the mountain at that same moment, Marguerite was also in consultation with a purveyor of spells, only in her case it was *Bon-nonm* Adonis.

"Doctor, I'm worried that I cannot keep this barber's heart," she was saying, while perched on the hard wooden chair in his office, fiddling with the handle of the yellow *tant* on her lap. "Already he tells me he must stay down in the village two, three nights a week for his work. I think he is trying to escape me."

Adonis suppressed a yawn. "Marguerite, we have known each other many years, yes?" he said in his kindly voice.

She nodded, her long plait wobbling in its coil upon her head.

"This is why you must trust me when I say that I think you are overly anxious. Give Monsieur Chanson a little more time, *cherie*. Give nature a chance to work." He leaned over and patted her hands.

"But I have tried nature already, *Bonnonm*. I do not think she is strong enough."

The old sorcerer clucked disapprovingly, fiddling with his mustache, and dropped his gaze over Marguerite. He had always thought her pretty, with those warm brown eyes and that lively little face, so young for her age, even if her brow was too often pinched with worry. He liked her squat body, too, strong but feminine, with breasts round as grapefruits.

"You are an attractive woman, Marguerite," he finally said. "It is time you trusted your own charm to keep a man, not always my spells."

She frowned. "But there are many charming women and they all want my Philippe. I do not wish to see him stolen away, like that Alphonse stole Joseph. And I do not want to lose him the way I lost my Antoine."

Adonis shook his head. It pained him to see a good woman like Marguerite doubt herself so. She always had, and it had only led her into trouble and lost her the great love of her life. He tried again to dissuade her.

"You don't see your own beauty, my dear, or the appeal of your own kind heart. You do not need my magic to keep this barber. He likes you well enough. I know, I have looked into my mirror and I have seen. And the emotions of love are much better without the interference of the spirits, are they not?"

Marguerite squinted at him dubiously. She had never trusted flattery, especially not from this old *bonnonm* who probably used it on all the women.

Adonis leaned forward in his desk chair and took her hand in his. His palms felt surprisingly soft, she noticed, like little pillows; a sign that he hadn't needed to do any physical labor for a very long time.

"Marguerite," he said, "I have watched you with many men now and I know your mistakes. 'Tell me whom you love and I'll tell you who you are,' as our old saying goes, yes? I know you well, my dear, and I see you worry too soon, you grasp and you plot. You frighten your men away. But this time it can be different. The barber is a steady man. He will not stray if you keep him happy. Think about him, not your spells."

He let go of her hand and stood up. "The way to keep a man's love is this." He plucked her basket off her lap and cradled it in his arms, kissing and fondling it lewdly. "You have no need of any other sort of magic." He winked and handed it back to her. "So go, my dear, go give your Chanson what he needs. And I will not charge you today."

Marguerite thanked him and left, but all the way down the mountain she was furious. The old charlatan! she thought. All those sweet words just to cover up that he is losing his powers. Look at that fancy potion he gave to Madame to help her keep her husband—it didn't work at all!

While Marguerite and Joelle were consulting their sorcerers, Zara and the two American boys were planning how to kill Philippe Chanson. Zara had disliked the barber for some time now because whenever Marguerite brought the girls with her to visit him in the village, he scolded and snapped at them, so she had decided to tell the boys he was a *dandosya*.

"How do you know?" Pete said. "He looks like a regular guy to me." The children were crouched in Zara's favorite spot under the house, taking shelter from a sudden rain, and were already covered in a fine red mud. Chloe was wandering alone in the house, left out as usual.

"No, he doesn't. He never smiles or says anything nice. And look at how thin and tall he is, and how his eyes are all boogly and evil. I think we've got to get rid of him before he eats one of us or does something terrible to Nana."

"How?" Pete looked at her warily while his little brother shuffled his feet in the earth. Pete could never quite tell how serious Zara was about this magic stuff, which was why she was sometimes thrilling and other times as scary as a *dandosya* herself.

"Francis told me how. He said it's a really powerful spell that only a wicked sorcerer should do, but I think it sounds easy. All you do is take a piece of wood from a cross in a graveyard and another piece peeled off a jasmine tree in the forest. Then you take a handful of sand he's stepped on and bury all of it together along a path where he always walks. Francis says if he's really a *dandosya*, he'll get sick and die. And if he's just an ordinary man, nothing will happen. So we might as well do it."

"You sure?" said Pete. "You sure it won't kill him if he's just a regular person?"

"I'm sure," Zara said with authority. "Francis knows about things like this, don't worry. He'd never teach me to hurt anyone who didn't deserve it. Francis is good."

"Okay," Pete said. "But how are we gonna find a cross?" He was tickled with the whole idea now, especially as it didn't involve anything painful, like that time Zara had scratched their chests.

"We can go to the cemetery the next time Nana takes us to the village. She never watches us anyway when she's talking to him." Marguerite's obliviousness to the children when she was with Philippe was another reason Zara had decided to exact her revenge.

So later that week, when Marguerite took all four children to Bois Rouge, they were ready and excited. "I got the jasmine wood," Pete whispered proudly to Zara on the way down the hill. "Mom and I went for a walk in the forest, so I asked her to tell me which was the jasmine tree and I pulled off a piece." He held up a strip of light brown bark.

"Well done!" Zara said, and Pete beamed. A remark like that from Zara was high praise indeed.

"I got the sand!" Rory said quickly, eager for his own share of the limelight. He opened his shorts pocket and showed Zara the mound of loose sand inside.

"Are you sure he actually walked on it?" Zara had learned that Rory tended to be somewhat cavalier with the truth.

"Yeah! I scooped it up from right behind his feet one time when Dad was getting his hair cut."

"All right, good. Now all we've got to do is get the piece of wood off the cross and bury it all outside his shop."

"You sure we won't kill any of his customers by mistake?" said Pete.

"I told you, it's only for *dandosya*." She rubbed the scratches on her chest with her little brown hand. Every time she thought of *dandosya*, they itched.

"And you really think we can do this without a bad wizard helping us?" Pete whispered then. "I mean, suppose we get it wrong and make something bad happen?"

"Don't be such a worrywart. Francis told me how to beat a *malfeter* if he annoys you, by the way."

"How?"

"You hit his bottom with a stick because that's where his face is when he turns invisible."

When they reached the barbershop, Marguerite went over to

Philippe to give him the bottle of *kalou* she had brought from her tree, shooing the children away as usual, so Zara and the boys scooted across the road to the village cemetery, a weedy plot on the side of a hill filled with a mix of old and new graves. The new ones didn't suit the children at all, for they were made of raised cement slabs and headstones, like concrete beds. The old ones were perfect, though: crumbling and overgrown, with nothing but a wooden cross to mark them.

Chloe trotted behind, a thumb in her mouth, her other hand clutching her toy lion.

"Let's pick a grave at the back, where no one will see us," Zara whispered. "Follow me." The four of them dropped to their knees and scuttled between the headstones, hiding and darting like mice. The boys loved it. They felt like spies. Zara was always creating adventures for them like this, which is why they both feared and adored her.

"I'm hungry," Chloe said. "I want Nana."

"Shh!" Zara hissed, and dropped back so Chloe could catch up. "This won't take long. Then we'll get her to buy us some ice lollies, all right? Just keep quiet."

Chloe pouted but crawled obediently behind her sister, dragging her lion in the dust. Her knees were getting bruised by the grit and stones on the ground, and they hurt. She whimpered.

"Here," Pete said, "what about this one?" They had reached the back of the cemetery by now, where a few graves lay half-hidden under the shade of a huge breadfruit tree. Splats of the tree's fallen fruit were scattered over the ground like cow patties, their smell yeasty and rotten, flies buzzing over them. Zara only just avoided putting her hand in one, and gagged. She hated the smell of breadfruit, and was disgusted by the way its shell split open like a skull, spilling out a sickly yellow pulp. She refused to eat the stuff, even when it was sugared and served as a dessert.

Pete stood up and tugged at a wooden cross in front of them, which was planted at the head of a caved-in grave. The cross was deeper in the earth than he thought, though. He couldn't even wiggle it.

"Just strip off a splinter, that should be enough," Zara whispered. But the cross was too smooth for his fingers to get a hold.

"Wait, look what I got," said Rory. He pulled a Swiss Army knife from his pocket. "I stole it from Dad."

"Good, give it to me." Zara stood up, opened the knife and scraped its blade along the edge of the cross. A long sliver of wood peeled off into her hand.

"I've got it," she said with satisfaction. "Now, all we have to . . ."

"What are you doing, *move dyab!*" a deep voice bellowed behind them.

Zara whirled around just in time to see a giant figure bearing down on them. "*Dandosya!*" she screamed and, dropping the knife, she took off, the boys tearing after her.

Chloe, forgotten and frightened, stumbled to catch up, but her legs were much too short to outstrip the giant. "Zara!" she wailed, "wait for me!" But it was too late. She felt herself grasped around the waist and lifted high into the air.

The minute the children reached Monsieur Chanson's barbershop, they darted into his doorway and dropped to the floor. Crawling into a dark corner of the shed, they huddled together, panting as quietly as they could. For a long time they crouched there, listening. But they heard nothing.

"Do you have my dad's knife?" Rory finally whispered.

"Shh!" Zara did not, but she didn't feel like telling him that just yet.

They waited again.

"What about the wood from the cross?" Pete whispered then. "You got that?"

Zara held up the strip of wood proudly. "Yes, can you see it?" She handed it to him then peered around in the dark. "Where's Chloe?"

The boys looked, too, but now their eyes had adjusted it was perfectly evident that Chloe wasn't there.

"The zombie got her," Rory said. "You think he's eating her brains?"

Zara dashed out of the shack.

"Chloe!" she called, but her sister was nowhere to be seen. Nana and the barber were gone, too, his chair empty, his razor put aside in a chipped enamel bowl. Even the street was bare of people under the noonday glare.

Zara was afraid now. Where had everyone gone? She ran up and down the hot dirt road, panting and sweating, but Chloe and Nana were neither at the fruit-juice kiosk nor at the market stand, where the only visible person was a man taking a nap with a hat over his face. They weren't by the cemetery, either, nor in the little church beside it. Zara found nothing but dust, flies and silence.

Swallowing her fear the best she could, she ran into the graveyard and peered behind every stone big enough to hide Chloe, trying not to think about the man who had loomed up out of the graveyard so suddenly like that. But nothing was there, aside from the stinky breadfruit patties. "Chloe?" she called in a hoarse whisper. "Chloe, where are you?" No answer. Suppose the *dandosya* was eating her? How was she going to explain that to Mummy? This didn't feel like a game anymore.

Finally, she ran up the sun-drenched street again, toward the only small shop of the village. She tore inside and stopped dead. There, sitting in front of an electric fan and laughing over some sort of fizzy drink was Nana with her barber and a very tall man, who was holding Chloe on his lap and feeding her ice cream.

"Zara, you little devil!" Marguerite exclaimed. "What were you doing in the cemetery, eh? Kind Monsieur Souf here, he told me he saw you desecrating a grave! Do you not know how evil this is? Do you not know that you awaken the souls of the dead if you disturb their resting place? You are a bad, bad girl. I will have to tell your mama."

Zara looked at the scuffed wooden floor of the shop and scraped at it with her sandaled foot, her chest heaving from all her running and her back damp with sweat. "We were just playing hide-and-seek," she said when she'd caught her breath. "I didn't mean Chloe to get lost. And I didn't hurt a grave." All of a sudden she felt stupid, convincing herself like that that the barber and the tall man were *dandosya*. It was obvious they were just ordinary.

Marguerite narrowed her eyes. She knew Zara was lying—she could always tell when the child lied. She also suspected that Zara was up to her *grigri* mischief again. What else would she be doing in a graveyard?

"Come," she said, lifting Chloe off the tall man's lap. "Let us find the boys and take you home. You, Zara, must explain to your mama what you have done. I think you will be in very big trouble."

All the way home, Rory complained to Pete nonstop about the lost knife, but Zara said nothing. She felt too ashamed of her silly game to even look at Pete.

When they got to the house, Marguerite gave the children a quick lunch, put the boys to work on a puzzle in the sitting room and took Chloe upstairs for a nap. Zara she sent in to see her mother. "I will give you one chance to tell her the truth," she said sternly. "But if you lie, I will know. And I will punish you."

Zara knocked on Penelope's bedroom door in a funk. Inside, she found her mother sitting cross-legged in shorts on the bare wooden floor, surrounded by a jumble of jewelry, makeup and knickknacks.

"Oh good, it's you, darling. You can help me sort these things out."

Mummy looks strange, Zara thought. Her eyes are all puffy. "What are you doing?" she asked.

Penelope sighed. "I'm getting rid of my rubbish. See that tissue paper over there? Bring it to me, would you, love? You can sit here and wrap up the things I give you, if you'd like. All right?"

"Yes, all right." Zara liked this sort of task, especially when it meant being close to her mother. She nestled down next to Penelope and was soon wrapping earrings and necklaces, lipsticks and bangles, and some pretty silver pillboxes her mother had kept on her dressing table for years.

"Are you really getting rid of all this? I thought you liked these things."

"Not anymore," Penelope replied crisply. "Sometimes in life, darling, one realizes one has simply accumulated too much." Too much bile and regret, too much uselessness, too much memory and sorrow. "How was your day, muffin?"

"Bad."

Penelope glanced at her. "Bad?"

Zara nodded. "Nana took us to Bois Rouge and we were playing in the graveyard and we lost Chloe and a giant man caught her and I was scared."

"Slow down!" Penelope said with a smile. "But I heard Chloe come in just now, so she's not lost. What giant man? You're confusing me, darling."

Zara explained again, with a somewhat doctored version. "I was playing in the graveyard with Pete and Rory and Chloe, and then a tall man came and shouted at us, so I ran away and Chloe got left behind. Nana's awfully angry. She says I did a bad thing."

"And so you did, leaving your poor sister like that. Was she very frightened?"

"Yes. Me, too. I'm sorry, Mummy."

Penelope patted Zara's head. Her hair was growing out now, making her look less like a boy than a mop-headed urchin. "You're a good big sister, darling. We can't expect you to be the perfect little mum all the time. You're only eight."

"Nine in a fortnight," Zara said proudly.

"Yes. I wonder what we should do for your birthday?" Penelope's heart sank at the thought of the two weeks ahead. Two more weeks of bearing up under Rupert's bad behavior, of facing Paul and Lily. And who knew whether Rupert would even remember Zara's birthday, given the state he was in. How much it would hurt the poor child if he didn't!

Zara was growing fidgety. "Can I go now, Mummy? I want to play with Pete and Rory."

"*May* I go, darling, not *can*. I didn't realize the boys were still here. Yes, off you go."

What Penelope hadn't told Zara was that she was on a grim mission to purge herself of Rupert, not to mention make a little money at the same time. When she had visited the bank that morning, she'd found barely enough for the rent and the evening's food, and none whatsoever left over to pay Marguerite. So she had decided to sell all the jewelry and ornaments Rupert had ever given her, most of her London makeup (who cared anymore?) and also her perfumes, or what was left of them. (Was it the children or Sylvie who'd been pinching her perfume? Maybe that was why Sylvie hadn't come back, not the blue bottle at all.) She might even sell some of her frocks, if she could find anyone to buy them. But where was that clever little chain-link purse Rupert had given her eons ago, the Art Nouveau one with the lovely marcasite clasp? That would fetch a good price. She hadn't seen it in ages, come to think of it. Might Sylvie have taken that, too? Penelope got up and rummaged everywhere in the room, but was unable to find it. Frowning, she tossed everything into a plastic bag and put it in a drawer. Early next week, when she could face it, she would take every last bead and bauble her shit of a husband had ever given to her, drive it over to Hannah, who had agreed to buy it all to help out a sister deserted wife (for Hannah had decided that her husband had indeed run off with a nurse), and say good-bye and good riddance to the whole lot of it, forever.

Upstairs, Chloe was curled up in bed for her nap, missing Daddy, missing Mummy, and singing her usual little chant while she tried to go to sleep. The bed felt wide and empty to her, the room scarily big. She wished somebody would come and tell her a story to make the emptiness go away. "Daddy, daddy, daddydaddydaddy," she sang quietly. "Mummy, mummy, mummymummymummy." But nobody heard.

Downstairs, Zara discovered that Marguerite had left to take the boys home, so there were no playmates to be had. Disappointed, she tiptoed up to the bedroom, where Chloe had now fallen asleep, picked up Kangy and went back to the kitchen. There, she pried Joelle's medicine out of the kangaroo's pouch, dropped it into a small wooden bowl and sniffed it. It smelled worse than ever now it was stale, and it even had a little mold on it. She scraped off the mold as best she could, threw it in the sink and poured a spoonful of vanilla sugar over what remained, along with a mound of shredded coconut, a dose of cinnamon and a helping of Golden Syrup, which helped it all stick together. Then she rolled it all up into a lumpy gray ball, coated it in confectioner's sugar and tasted it. Not bad, this time. Quite good, in fact, all nutty and sweet, like those yummy coconut balls Sylvie used to make. It had a slight almond smell that was quite nice, as well. She wrapped it in a piece of wax paper she found in a drawer, the way she'd seen Sylvie wrap dough, stuffed it back into Kangy's pouch and took it up to her bed. She couldn't wait for the next time Daddy came to visit. She would give the magic medicine to him disguised as a treat, kill off the demon worm, and then he would never go away again.

At that moment, it so happened, Rupert could have done with a treat, for nothing was going his way. He had failed to make any progress on his report for the Colonial Office. Everything he ate disagreed with him. He'd developed a fever he could not shake, in spite of Dr. Malavois's endless doses of revolting diarrhea medicine and, now, antibiotics. ("I am not sure what ees wrong, Monsieur Weston, but zese should take care of eet," he had said in his music hall Parisian accent.) And, for the first time since he'd known Joelle, she had turned contrary. Perhaps it was the pregnancy—he remembered Penny getting rather peevish when she was carrying Zara and Chloe—but Joelle's previous delight in everything he did had quite reversed. Just the other night, for instance, when he had suggested another moonlight stroll along the pier, she'd said no, she wanted to go to bed. But as soon as he'd undressed, turned off the light and lain down in his now customary state of depletion, she'd sat up and declared that she absolutely had to go to the pier after all, and at that very moment. She was like that with their meals, too. For weeks she had been solicitous about his increasingly delicate stomach and loss of appetite, cooking for him only the most mild and enticing of meals. Now she was bringing home all sorts of repulsive things to cook. Octopus was the worst, but just the other evening she'd brought back a great horny leg of turtle and boiled it up with marrow and onions—it had been impossible to eat, let alone digest. Whatever he asked for, she refused. She had never been like this before. What had happened?

Finally, after more than a week of putting up with this capriciousness, Rupert decided to have it out. He sat Joelle down—if anything, her pregnancy had made her lovelier than ever—took her by the hand and looked into her eyes.

"Joelle, my love, I know it's awfully dull to be hooked up with such a sick man as I. But please remember this is temporary. I am already getting better"—this was a lie—"and by the time the baby comes, I shall be my old self again. Can't you have a little patience?"

"It is babies, not baby," she snapped.

"What?"

"We are having two babies, not one. We are having twins. The doctor at Victoria Hospital, he told me."

"Oh."

"Aren't you pleased?"

"Uh, I suppose so. Yes, of course. Twins? It's just a bit of a shock. I mean . . . twins? Where are we going to put them?"

"It is necessary to get a bigger house, of course."

"A bigger house? But I can't afford one, dearest. I can barely make the payments on two houses as it is. My bank account is virtually drained and I'm not due for another rise until Christmas. Even Zara's birthday present was a stretch. I bought her some flippers, by the way. Good idea, wasn't it?"

Joelle looked at him scornfully. "Why are you talking about flippers? Do you not see how serious this is? You are a white man, you can get a house. I want the house your wife lives in."

"But . . ."

Joelle stood up. "You love me, yes? You love our baby—babies?"

"Of course I do, darling. You know that."

"Then get me the house or I will not sleep with you." And she stalked away, swinging her behind insolently in his face.

And so it was that the very next morning, Rupert appeared once more at Penelope's door. She had just returned from a most humiliating visit to Vicious Vicky, for Hannah had not been able to buy her things after all, having just heard that her husband hadn't run off with an African nurse but had, in fact, died, and that she had to leave for Mombasa immediately with her children to arrange to have his body shipped back to England. Poor Hannah! So, in desperation, Penelope had been forced to sell to Vicky, while enduring the woman's patronizing pretense of charity and barely disguised glee.

"You must be bloody hard up to want to sell all this," she'd hooted in her foghorn voice. "Even your makeup. My, my."

So when Rupert arrived at the door, Penelope greeted him with less than warmth. "Christ, you look worse than ever," she said drily. "You better sit down."

He followed her into the sitting room and sat gingerly on the cane sofa, like a man with a bad case of piles. "Penny, I've come to ask you an important question."

Penelope's heart sped up. Was he going to beg her to let him come back? For that's what she still wanted, still prayed and cried for. That, and to undo the excruciating memory of her encounter with Paul.

"Did you remember Zara's birthday present?" is all she replied.

Rupert handed over the flippers. "Could you wrap them for me? I haven't had the time."

Penelope nodded, relieved that he had at least remembered this. "She'll like these," she said. "Good choice." She sat cross-legged on the floor, the way Lily often did, and gazed up at him. She didn't realize it, but lately she'd fallen into imitating Lily in all sorts of ways. "Well, what's your question?"

But now that he was here, Rupert was reluctant to speak. He didn't want to ask any more favors of Penelope, or give her any more ultimatums. It wasn't in his nature. He wanted matters to take care of themselves. But of course, matters wouldn't.

He sighed. "Well, you see, I've got rather a pickle on my hands."

"Do you now? Who would have thought?"

"Penny, please." He shut his eyes.

"You know, Rupert, you should go to hospital. I mean it. You look even worse than last time I saw you. You must have lost nearly two stone in the last month."

He opened his eyes again. "Have I? Oh dear." He passed his hand over his sweaty forehead. "No, I'm sure it's all right. I have gone to hospital, several times, as a matter of fact. To Dr. Malavois. He's keeping an eye on me."

"Are you sure?"

"Yes, yes. He says it's the diet and all my worries. Speaking of which—"

"What diet?" Penelope said in alarm. "Did he say anything in particular about that?" I wonder if they'd arrest me if they knew? she thought. Or if they'd arrest *Bonhomme* Adonis? Or maybe both of us? That would be just like my life now. One long chain of humiliations, all the way down to being thrown in jail with a witch doctor for poisoning my husband.

"Listen, Penny, do stay on the subject. I'm going to have a baby. Two, actually."

Penelope looked at him steadily.

"Well?"

"Funny, you don't look pregnant."

Rupert shifted irritably on the sofa. "Oh, really. You know perfectly well what I mean."

"As a matter of fact, I don't."

He stood up and actually shouted. "Joelle's having twins! My twins! For God's sake, Penny! I need the house. *This* house. I want you to go back to England with the girls. Now!"

Penelope stared up at him in shock. But all she said was, "Shh. The girls will hear you."

"Sorry." Rupert sat back down with a plop.

For a moment the two of them were silent, Rupert gaunt and yellow, folded up like a deck chair; Penelope huddled on the bare floor, waiting for the painful swell of fear and jealousy to subside enough to free her tongue.

"And where do you think we'll live back in London?" she said at last. "Do you expect me and the girls to move in with my lunatic family?"

"I don't know. I'll send you money to get a flat, I suppose."

"Rupert, there wasn't enough money in the bank last week even to pay Marguerite, let alone buy tickets back to England and rent a flat. And what about the children? Twins or no twins, you happen to already be the father of two little girls who need and love you, in case you forgot."

Rupert rubbed his brow again, hard. God, this was agonizing. Maybe he should give up on this going-native business and go home with Penny. Maybe he wasn't cut out for tropical adventures and Seychellois wives after all. He certainly wasn't cut out for all this drama.

Penelope rose to her feet, oddly calm now, and with her hands on her hips looked down at him. "You've got yourself in an atrocious mess, haven't you, Rupert? But I want you to understand something. I am not going back to London unless you come with me.

And I am certainly not leaving until you're better. You are seriously sick, and I think you're having a nervous breakdown to boot. So I shall, as the saying goes, stick by you."

"But I don't want to be stuck by," Rupert said plaintively.

"Of course you do. Now go tell that secretary of yours to stop making unreasonable demands. Tell her you're going back to England and will send her money for the babies. That's what women expect here, you know, Marguerite told me. It happens all the time with white men like you. Then we'll get you home and to a proper doctor." She thought of poor Hannah's dead husband and shuddered. "And the sooner, the better."

"But I love her! I can't leave!" And to Penelope's astonishment, Rupert started to cry, actually cry, great, fat male tears spilling over his sallow cheeks, catching in his trembling mouth, dropping onto his blue shirt, making perfect round stains. "Oh God," he moaned, "I don't know what to do!"

While all this was going on in the sitting room, Chloe was wandering aimlessly upstairs, sucking her thumb and twisting a blond ringlet around her pudgy finger. Zara had retreated behind the bedroom wall to read and wouldn't play with her, Mummy and Daddy were shouting again and Nana was out at the market, so she was alone and bored. She looked at some picture books for a while and made a game with her toy animals, but quickly tired of that, so climbed onto Zara's bed to feel safe and less lonely. Creeping under the folds of mosquito netting, she pulled the pillows around her to make a nest and lay down, putting her thumb back in her mouth. She liked the way the room looked through the netting, all fuzzy and misty, like the middle of a cloud. Zara had told her a story once about a family living in the clouds, jumping from one to another as if they were trampolines. Chloe loved that story. She loved to lie there with Zara and pretend they lived on a cloud that tasted of marshmallow, which they could eat whenever they felt hungry, or sleep or bounce on. Chloe sniffed, took her thumb out of her mouth and sniffed again. She did smell something sweet, in fact, although it was more like almond than marshmallow. It smelled like one of those yummy sweets Sylvie used to cook when she was still in the house. Chloe sat up and rummaged around the pillows and toys, following her nose. She smelled almond and coconut and something else delicious and gooey. Her mouth watering, she picked up Kangy and opened its pouch.

As soon as Marguerite returned from the market, Penelope asked her to stay with the children while she drove Rupert back to his office. She had another two errands in mind, as well. She was going to confront that old fraud Adonis and demand to know if his medicine could be poisoning her husband. Then she was going to visit Paul and Lily to prove she could act as if nothing had happened. So she bundled Rupert into the Mini and set off.

Rupert had subsided into some kind of shock. He'd dried off his tears on the back of his wrist—like a snot-nosed schoolboy, Penelope thought—and was now slumped in the passenger seat in a daze, as if he'd only just awoken from an anesthetic.

"Are you all right now?" Penelope asked him. "In good enough shape for the office?"

No answer.

"Rupert?"

"What? Oh, yes. The office."

"I need some money before you go. Have you any in your wallet?"

Rupert pulled his wallet from his pocket with a grunt and opened it. "Yes, I've a bit here. I'll telegraph my bank manager at Barclays this afternoon and see if I can get a loan wired to our account. Here, take this." He dropped a bundle of rupee notes into Penelope's lap. "Just leave me on the corner, thanks. I can manage the rest of the way."

"Are you sure, darl—" She stopped herself. "Are you sure?" she said again.

"Yes, thanks. Sorry about all that." Rupert smiled at her weakly and pushed himself with an effort out of the car. Penelope watched in horror as he shuffled away. God, I hope I didn't really do this to him, she thought. He's moving like an old man.

She turned the car around and drove back in the other direction, up the mountain toward the *bonhomme*'s house. She would have to park and walk for at least an hour through the forest to reach him, she realized, and by now it was glaring mid-morning. Perhaps she shouldn't go now, perhaps it was too risky. Zara had said she might get arrested if she went in broad daylight, especially being white and as conspicuous as she was. I better wait, she thought. I better go tomorrow at dawn again, when it's safer. So she turned the car around once more and headed, with trepidation, for the Lelands.

Penelope had tried not to give the event with Paul much thought, being preoccupied with Rupert and her finances, but of course every moment of it was still there, searing her with humiliation. She didn't know which felt worse, the fact that Paul had rejected her, leaving her pleading, or the fact that she had been willing to betray Lily. Lily, of all people! The woman she most liked, most wished to emulate of anyone in the world! Oh, God, Penelope thought with an inner groan, I've grown as depraved as my husband.

She pulled up at the Leland's bungalow just in time to see Paul arriving home for lunch, looking dusty and hot and achingly handsome. Lily was in the side garden with the boys, examining something on the ground.

"Hi, Penny," Lily said cheerily as Penelope approached. "Look what we found. A jewel beetle. Isn't it gorgeous?"

Penny crouched down beside her, trying to control her trembling. She sensed Paul walking up behind them and it made her sick with longing. "Yes, it's lovely," she said, her voice shaky.

"Where's Zara?" Pete said. "Did she come with you?" He stood up and looked toward the car.

"No, I'm afraid not. She's at home. I'll bring her next time."

Lily glanced over Penelope at Paul, who had come up to them by now, and the two exchanged looks. They had decided to keep the boys away from Zara for the time being. She was too much of a bad influence. Both their sons were having nightmares about zombies, and only the day before, Lily had caught Pete slipping a crushed worm into her lentil soup. "What the hell are you doing?" she'd asked him, dumping the soup out with disgust. "It's *grigri*," he'd told her. "Zara taught me. It's gonna protect us."

"Hi, Penny," Paul said then, his voice only a touch forced. "How's the beetle collection going?"

Penelope stood up without looking at him and brushed some red dirt off her bare knees. "All right, thanks. But I've found out the Seychellois despise my beloved giant rhino beetle because its larvae attack baby coconut palm."

"A giant rhino pest?"

"I'm afraid so."

The three of them stood for a moment in silence, pretending to be absorbed in the boys, who were still on the ground examining the jewel beetle. And at that moment, Penelope knew it was over. This marvelous friendship, the best of her life, shattered by one act.

"Well, I just dropped by to say a quick hello. Have to run off now and do a million errands." Penelope backed away from them, avoiding their eyes.

"Bye," Paul said. "See you later."

She got in the car and fled.

When she reached the house, she sat in the car, unable to move. Her hands were shaking and the inside of her chest was iced with despair. She closed her eyes. Now Penny, she said to herself, stay calm and think this out. How much of this mess is your fault? One: Rupert having left you. Your fault—you've been inadequate and clueless and dull. Two: Rupert being sick. Yes, that one's yours, too, as you seem to have poisoned him. Three: No money. Well, that one is mostly Rupert's, but surely I could have found something useful to do, some way of making money so I wasn't such a drain. Four: Paul and Lily. Now that one is more difficult. Oh, be honest,

Penny, of course it's your fault. You shouldn't have led him on, you shouldn't have pushed him to have all those drinks and you shouldn't have accepted his advances. He was drunk—and he's a man who doesn't drink much. He didn't know what he was doing and you did. And you not only didn't stop him, you begged him to stay.

She dropped her face into her hands.

When she'd pulled herself together enough to get out of the car and into the house, she found Marguerite in the kitchen, preparing an egg salad lunch for the children, who were still upstairs. "Don't worry, I'll do that. You can go home," Penelope said, for she badly needed to be alone. Her life had taken on a disturbing resemblance to a shattered windshield, she realized, or perhaps a puzzle with half the pieces missing—whichever, it was a hideous jumble and she was determined to sort it out. I shall conquer this, she thought fiercely as she watched Marguerite's back disappear from the courtyard. I shall not succumb to panic or passivity. I shall not lie in bed for days or sit on the veranda, reading and forgetting to dress. Not this time. No, I shall find a way to win back Rupert and Paul and Lily, too. I must.

She sat down at the kitchen table, overwhelmed again, when she heard Zara shouting from upstairs.

"Nana! Mummy! Come quick!"

Something in her voice made Penelope jump up immediately and run to the foot of the staircase. Zara was standing at the top, dressed in nothing but her knickers, her face wild with fright.

"What's the matter, darling?"

"Mummy! Chloe's shaking all over and she can't breathe!"

15

Joelle loosened the belt of her Sunday dress and sat back carefully on her sister's rickety chair, legs spread, to accommodate the twins within her. The contrast between her fine orange poplin, which she'd worn to church before climbing up the mountain to visit Alphonse, and her sister's ragged blue dress pained her, as did the difference between the lovely bungalow she had with Rupert and this shack with only one room and two chairs. She ran her eyes over it in distress: Patched-up walls made of tin and wood scraps; a bare, uneven floor; a single window half nailed over with a rotting plank. And, as bad as this was, Charité, her eldest sister, had a home higher up the mountain that was even worse. The sight made Joelle unhappy, for although she was grateful for the luck she'd had in life, she would have been more grateful still had she been able to share it with her sisters.

Joelle had come to see Alphonse not only to give her food and money, as she did every Sunday, but to seek advice about Rupert. "He refuses to see Dr. Panyal," she told her sister once they'd exchanged the usual news of children and health. "He won't listen to my advice, no matter what I tell him. He goes only to the white doctors at the hospital and they understand nothing, as you know."

Alphonse nodded. Her face was thin, her mouth collapsed around missing teeth. She had once been a beauty like Joelle, voluptuous and flashy, but five children and a drunken man had worn all that away. Now, at thirty-nine, she could have passed for Joelle's mother. Her formerly rich, dark skin had turned ashy, and her spindly body was already stooped from work and malnutrition. She spent all her time now trying to scrape up enough food for her children and chasing down Joseph before he could drink away his meager earnings. Nevertheless, she fastened her weary eyes on Joelle and listened, for Joelle was not only her sister but her closest friend.

"But this is the way white men are, no?" she said gently. "Did you go to Madame Hélène for help?"

"I did. And you know what she said? She advised me to quarrel with him until he was miserable. And she gave me a potion that made him so sick I'm afraid he will die. That woman is a fraud and a cheat."

Alphonse pulled her exhausted frame upright on her wooden chair. "Yes, I've been thinking the same for some time. She helped me take Joseph away from Marguerite Savy, as you know, but look what it's come to." She sighed, bending over to rub her bony knees and the shrunken calves beneath them.

Joelle took a handkerchief from her basket to wipe her sweating face, not wanting to let on that she had always thought Alphonse foolish for going after Joseph when he was such a drunk. "You know what else?" she said. "The little girl who showed me into the fortune-teller's house? I finally remembered who she is: Marguerite's daughter. That woman must have put her there as a spy. They are all against me, Alphonse." She sipped from a glass of water to cool herself down. She felt overheated all the time now, as if the babies were a fire within her. "But what am I to do? Rupert is very sick. You should see him. He looks like a yellow pole. And he smells—poo! He smells like the grave." She flushed, feeling she had overstated the case. "Well, it's not that bad. But I'm so worried! What if he decides to go home to England? That's what these whites usually do. Or suppose he stays but becomes an invalid, and then I have to look after him and my twin babies and *Manman* and . . ." she didn't finish, not wanting to be tactless.

The smallest of Alphonse's children ran in then, five-year-old Georges, naked but for a scrap of shorts around his loins. His eyes were rheumy and his stomach distended. Joelle gazed at him sadly. That her own nephew should look like a child of the poor, diseased and worm-ridden, made her heart hurt. She tried her best to help her sisters, giving them all she could spare, but she knew it wasn't enough. She must get more money from Rupert.

She glanced out of the open door at the sky. It was almost noon and he was expecting her, but she hadn't finished yet. "Tell me," she said quickly, "where do you think I should go for help? I've prayed in the church, I took a communion wafer to use in a tea for Rupert, and I got the priest to bless a candle for one of the fortune-teller's spells. I've done everything that old fraud Hélène told me to, and nothing has worked. What do you think I should do?" She rubbed her pregnant belly anxiously.

Alphonse picked up little Georges and set him on her knee, cradling him in her thin arms. She nuzzled his sickly body with affection and Joelle again felt a pang. She loved Rupert with all her heart, but she loved her family more.

"You must go to the *bonnonm dibwa*," Alphonse said quietly.

"But he is so expensive! And I'm not sure I trust him any more than I do that Hélène."

Alphonse shrugged. "You must, little sister. What else is there?"

Joelle picked up her now empty basket. "Perhaps you're right," she said, sighing, and stood to kiss Alphonse farewell. "We will have to see."

Down the mountain, Marguerite quietly opened the hospital-room door. "Madame?" she whispered. "May I come in?"

Penelope raised her head. She was sitting in a chair beside Chloe, holding the child's limp hand. She gazed absently at Marguerite under the glaring hospital light. "What? Oh, yes, of course."

Marguerite tiptoed through the door and up to the bed. She put her hand on Chloe's pale forehead, leaning over to smell her puffs of shallow breath. Penelope watched helplessly.

"Madame, we must get Chloe better help than these stupid doctors," Marguerite said in a low voice. "I went to see *Bonnonm* Adonis this morning, and he said this is *grigri* and that your white medicine, it is not enough. He said she has been poisoned, Madame."

Zara, who was crouched on the floor in a corner, winced at this and bit her finger. She had refused to budge ever since they'd rushed Chloe to the hospital the day before, no matter how much Penelope had tried to coax her. She had sat and slept in her corner all day and night, never moving except to go to the toilet or to replace Chloe's toy lion beside her on the pillow whenever it fell off. She had also piled all her favorite belongings at the foot of Chloe's bed, which she had asked Marguerite to bring from the house: Pippi Longstocking and some other books both her grandmothers had sent from London, a beautiful kite Francis had made for her and the now empty cricket cage. (She would have given Chloe Pete's little taxi and Rory's tiger as well, had she not returned them because of feeling so stupid about the *dandosya*.) When Penelope had asked her what she was doing, she'd only said, "These belong to Chloe now."

"But that's no different from what the doctors told me," Penelope said to Marguerite. "They say she's eaten something dreadful, raw cassava root and perhaps something else toxic." She swallowed, unable to continue. The doctors had pumped Chloe's stomach and administered antidotes, but they were not optimistic.

"But who would do this, Madame? I have tried and tried, but I cannot think who would harm our Chloe."

Zara squeezed her eyes shut. She knew who it was: the bad witch she'd met on the beach. I must tell them, she thought for the hundredth time. I must tell them the woman tricked me and that she wanted me to poison Mummy, not Chloe. But she could not speak. For a whole day and a night now, Zara had been unable to speak about what she knew.

"It doesn't make sense," Penelope replied. "It must have been a mistake, some ghastly accident, like the way the poor darling picked up those pinworms."

At those words, both women looked at Zara.

"Zara?" Marguerite walked over to the corner to crouch beside the child, who was still curled in a knot on the floor. "Little one, did you ever see Chloe eat any raw cassava? In my garden, perhaps, or from the market?"

Zara shook her head, her knowledge still imprisoned in her mouth.

"Come," Marguerite whispered, leaning closer. "You do not have to be afraid of your Nana. But you must tell me what you can because it might help to save your sister."

Zara looked up at Marguerite, her small face pinched tight with guilt and fear. Finally, with a great effort, she made herself nod.

"What? What is it, little bird?" Marguerite said.

Penelope looked on anxiously.

Zara opened her mouth to blurt out her secret, but before she could speak the door swung open and Paul and Lily came in, bearing bags of drinks and snacks. The minute they'd heard what had happened, they'd rushed to Victoria Hospital, and had been bringing food and sitting with Penelope and Chloe ever since. The awkwardness between them and Penelope was forgotten now. Chloe's danger overshadowed everything.

Lily tiptoed up to the bed, while Paul hovered in the background. "Any changes?" she asked. She didn't want to use the word *progress* because the last time she'd said it, Penny had begun to weep.

Penelope shook her head. "The same. They say her vital signs aren't improving at all, even with the IV." She spoke calmly but her voice shook. "It's cyanide, you know. The human digestive system converts raw cassava into cyanide. They told me. Who would have thought? Everybody here cooks and eats so much of it."

"They're sure that's what it is?"

"Yes. They did tests. They say it's lucky she only had a small amount or . . ."

She fell silent and all of them gazed at Chloe's still face. It was unspeakably sad to see a young child lying so quiet and still, with needles in her arms and tubes in her chest. Her skin had turned glossy and pale, like a waxwork's, and her springy curls were now limp with sweat. Her eyes were shut, her face devoid of expression or suffering.

Marguerite was still crouched beside Zara, who had dropped her head on her knees and was visibly shivering. She reached out to stroke her back. "Come, little one," she whispered, "come with me." And taking her by the hand, she led her from the room. In the stark hospital corridor, she turned to Zara and lifted her chin. "Look at me now. I can read in your face that you know something, and the something is giving you pain, yes?"

Clenching her mouth against tears, Zara nodded.

"Come then, tell me. I will not be angry. I know you wish to help Chloe."

Zara stared at her, her eyes wide and serious with fear. Finally, after another long struggle, she found her voice. "Nana," she said, and then stopped again, swallowing. "Nana, is it true that the person who puts a curse on somebody is the only one who can take it off?"

"I have heard that, yes, although sometimes a *bonnonm* can as well. Why? What is it, little cabbage?"

"Because I know who did it."

And at last, with tears and gulps, Zara confessed the whole story: how a woman named Claudine had found her on the beach, had promised her medicine to kill off her mother's demon worm and how Zara had made it into the sweet, mushy ball that had tempted Chloe.

"I didn't know," she said, her voice tight. "I thought it was good medicine. I was going to make Daddy better with it so he would come home. I didn't know Chloe would eat it."

"But how do you know she ate it, little one?"

Zara's lip trembled. "Cause when Mummy was carrying Chloe to the car to bring her here, I found Kangy on the floor and its pouch was empty, and that's where I'd hidden the medicine. Oh, Nana, what if she dies? It will be because of me! If she dies then I'll run away and jump in the sea and never never come back."

Marguerite shut her eyes. *Mon dye*, she thought, I always knew this girl had powers, but those powers have gone beyond her now. She has been used by the devil!

She squatted down and took Zara by the arms. "Come," she said. "It is good that you told me this. I think I know who this Claudine is, so now you and I, we will go find her. I am sure even this *fanm sal* did not mean to poison a baby. We will find her and make her tell us what was in the medicine and how to call off the curse."

So Marguerite told Penelope she was taking Zara out for some food and air and the two of them left the hospital. Marguerite was certain this Claudine was Joelle. Who else would want to poison Madame, and who else would seek out Zara to use like this? She also knew where Joelle lived with Rupert, as did the rest of Mahé. It was twenty minutes away from the hospital, but Zara walked the entire way without saying a word.

They reached the house just before sunset, and the minute Marguerite saw it she was jealous. It was a perfect square, raised high on concrete blocks, and everything about it was elegant and new. The walls were freshly whitewashed, the tin roof was a pristine pink, and it had no less than four windows and a finely carved white balustrade around the veranda. To top it off, a grand stone staircase descended to the ground and trimmed bushes surrounded the whole compound like a fence. It was as good as the house Marguerite had lived in with Henri and it made her furious.

She took Zara's hand and walked angrily up the steps to the front door, which was propped open to catch the evening breeze. "Call your papa," she said, her tone grim.

"Daddy?" Zara's voice sounded small and frightened. "Daddy?"

Joelle appeared at the door, looking puffy. She'd grown quite hefty between the twins and eating all the food she cooked for Rupert that he wouldn't touch. The minute she saw Marguerite, she raised her hands as if to ward off an attack.

"*Bonzour*," Marguerite said icily. "Is Monsieur at home?"

Joelle looked with dismay from Marguerite to Zara and back again.

"Joelle, who's that?" a feeble voice came from inside.

"Daddy!" Zara cried and darted around Joelle into the house. "Daddy, it's me! Where are you?"

"Here. In the bedroom." His voice sounded shaky.

Zara blinked in the sudden darkness and peered around till she could make out the bedroom door. She ran inside. There was her daddy, lying in bed. She took one look at him and stopped.

Rupert had grown so thin that, lying down, he reminded Zara of Nana's barber. His skin was more sallow than ever, his eyes were the color of saffron and even though he was shiny with sweat, he was piled up with blankets. He smelled horrible.

"Zara, my pet! What are you doing here?"

She was too frightened to reply. She backed away.

Rupert reached out a damp hand. "Don't go. Come nearer, where I can see you. Are you here with Mummy?"

Zara shook her head, hesitating. She took a step forward but she didn't touch his hand. Why did he look like this?

"Come, Zara, answer me," Rupert said impatiently. "Is Mummy here?"

"No," she replied at last. "Mummy's in hospital with Chloe."

Rupert struggled to his elbows. "Hospital? Why, what's happened?"

Zara opened her mouth, but the thought of Chloe made her throat swell up again. She shook her head. No words would come.

"Zara, speak up," Rupert said sharply, reminded of the way she'd behaved on the ship that day her sister had gone missing. "What's happened to Chloe?"

Zara swallowed her tears until she could speak. Then she pointed out the door toward Joelle.

"That lady poisoned her!"

• • •

Half an hour later, Marguerite and Zara were plodding back to the hospital, more upset than ever. Marguerite had gotten nowhere with Joelle. The cursed woman had confessed to nothing, denied everything. She'd even said that she had never seen Zara before, that the child was lying and that all this was only more of Marguerite's mischief against her.

"I know what you are doing," she had said, glaring at Marguerite. "You are making *grigri* against me, just like you did against my sister. But I see through it and I know you will never succeed."

Marguerite had glanced away guiltily. It was true. She had paid Madame Hélène to ruin Rupert's love for Joelle—in fact, she and the fortune-teller had spent quite a bit of time cackling over their plot. ("Make her pick fights with him," Marguerite had suggested. "Yes," said Hélène, chuckling, "and I will tell her to beg him for money, as well. Men always hate that.") Marguerite felt she'd had to do it, not only to help Penelope but because she could not stand the sight of yet another Lagrenade successfully stealing a man.

Rupert, too, had been unreceptive to Zara's accusation. "Of course Joelle wouldn't harm Chloe," he'd said to Zara indignantly. "The very idea! But poor darling Chloe! Tell Mummy I'm coming as soon as I can, would you?"

Zara promised she would, but she left as miserable as Marguerite. She had never seen a grown-up lie so unfalteringly as Joelle. The witch had even lied about her name! It made her wonder which other grown-ups she knew lied like that. *Bonhomme* Adonis? Nana? Perhaps even Mummy? How was she to know?

After they left, Joelle went out into the courtyard to escape Rupert's sickly smell and to plan. This was a new blow. She had not meant to harm the little girl. When she had crept up to the Weston's house that night and buried the blue bottle behind the front steps, it had been intended for the wife, not the children. And hadn't she told Zara not to let anybody eat the medicine but her mother? Stupid child! Dangerous, too, with her fantasies about becoming a *bonnfamn dibwa*—who had ever heard of a English girl with dreams like that? Now Joelle not only had to find a cure for Rupert but a way to protect herself from that Savy woman, too. Marguerite's reaction had betrayed her: she really had done *grigri* against Joelle, and probably against her growing babies as well.

Alphonse is right, Joelle decided. I will have to go to the *bonnonm*.

"What are we going to do now, Nana?" Zara said as she followed Marguerite back to the hospital. "That woman is a bad witch and a liar and now she won't help us."

"Yes, she is very bad, little one. We will have to find another way. But Zara, you must make me a promise." Marguerite stopped in the road and frowned down at her charge.

"Yes, Nana?" Zara looked up, her face somber.

"You must give up this *grigri* forever. You are too young to know its power and look at the harm you have done with it. What do you think Francis would say if he knew?" Marguerite was well aware of how much Zara adored Francis and how crushed she would be if she displeased him.

Zara thought of Chloe, of how she lay there not speaking or moving. She thought of her mischief with Philippe Chanson, and of how she'd scratched Pete and Rory, made them show her their willies and taken their toys. I will go to hell, just like Francis says, she thought. I will go to hell and burn there forever.

She looked into Marguerite's eyes. "I promise. I promise I will never do *grigri* again. Please please don't tell Francis what I did!"

Marguerite nodded and walked on. She believed Zara. The child was clearly chastened.

Back at the hospital, matters were no better. Chloe was still lying flat and unmoving in bed, her breath fast and shallow. The doctors were still discussing how much damage the cyanide had done and what other poisons the child might have ingested. Lily and Paul were still bringing in food no one ate and drinks no one drank. And Penelope was praying.

"Rupert, *cheri*, I am going out. I shall be back in a few hours."

"A few hours?" Rupert looked up at Joelle, who was standing above his bed. She had on her Sunday hat, one of her best frocks, loosened now at the waist, and was carrying a large basket, which was clearly very heavy. "But it's dark, my love. You can't go anywhere now."

"I know it is dark, but I must go to find some help for us. For your daughter and for you. For our babies, as well. It is too urgent to delay."

"I know what that means," Rupert grumbled. "That means you're going off to one of your crackpot witch doctors, doesn't it?"

Joelle put a glass of water by his bed. "Sleep and do not worry. I shall be back soon." And she left.

Rupert fell back on his bed with an exasperated groan. Telling him not to worry these days was like telling a bee not to buzz. All he did was worry: about his two houses and the work at the office, about Penelope and Joelle, the children and what was going to happen in the future—and now this horrible news about Chloe! For Rupert had decided he was dying. He had checked into Victoria Hospital for a few days but none of the doctors had done him the slightest bit of good, and it was so irritating being bossed about like a child that he'd hobbled out in a huff. Now he was obviously wasting away. He felt as if he were being eaten from the inside out, as if a poison had blossomed in his heart and was coursing though his body, killing off his organs one by one. Maybe it's my conscience, he thought in his delirium. Maybe it's my dastardly deeds (Susan Winslop came back to him, as did that blonde on the ship). The saddest thing, though, wasn't that he was leaving this world, for what use was he, really, except to bungle things with women and children? No, the saddest thing was leaving his two daughters and Joelle's twins without a daddy. If only he had money to give them all, he thought. But he had not even that.

And poor Chloe! She was seriously ill, Marguerite had told him once he'd commanded Joelle to let her into the house. The child had eaten cyanide! Not very much of it, thank God, but because she was so small it was dangerous. Cyanide smelled of almonds, he knew—perhaps that's what had attracted Chloe to it. But where on earth would a three-year-old find cyanide? Was it in one of those bottles Penny kept in the bathroom cupboard, some concoction against wrinkles or blemishes? However it may have happened, it wasn't Joelle's fault, of that he was certain. What nonsense these Seychellois believe, accusing one another of all sorts of sorcery and hocus-pocus when it was perfectly obvious that the ills of life came about because of germs or God. But sweet little Chloe! He must go to see her! He would have to find somebody to help him to the car and drive him there—for Rupert could no longer walk. My little bubble-head, he moaned, tossing in bed as his fever mounted again, my little muffin! And he dozed off into a dream about frolicking in the heavens with Chloe, both of them dancing with angel wings in the shape of ceiling fans whirring on their backs. "Did you know we're dead, darling muffin?" he said to her. "Yes, Dada," she replied, and giggled as if he'd given her a lollipop.

Getting up the mountain in the dark was no easy task for a woman pregnant with twins. Joelle took a taxi as high as the road could go and extracted the rest of the directions from the driver (Adonis's address was hardly a secret in Mahé), but she still had to face a long and steep walk through the forest. Nevertheless, she was determined. She was young and strong and had swiped Rupert's electric torch to light the way. She wasn't afraid, either. As a girl she had often shocked her family by roaming the mountains by herself until sunset, walking alone beneath the great blanket of forest, the mahogany and banyan trees, until she came upon a clearing overlooking the ocean: a shimmering azure stretching to the sky. Over there is Africa, she would say to herself. Over the other way is India. And above me is the rising moon. I might have been born on one tiny island, but I am still part of this world.

She reached *Bonnonm* Adonis's house at midnight, panting and thirsty, and found it annoyingly busy, with several people already waiting in the shelter by lantern light, murmuring among themselves. She asked for some water at the kiosk and took a seat, but had no wish to converse with the other patients. Joelle knew the power of gossip and did not want to feed it. She looked about while she waited, noting how prettily the garden was lit with lanterns and the size of the *bonnonm*'s house. When I move into the white woman's home, she thought, I will light up the garden like this myself.

When at last it was her turn to sit with the *bonnonm*, she wasted little time getting to the point, for her anxiety about Rupert and her babies made her unusually candid.

"You have many troubles," Adonis said with raised eyebrows after she had finished speaking. "I can help you easily with the curse from Madame Savy. Do not worry, your babies, they will be safe." (He chuckled inwardly, for of course he knew Marguerite's history only too well and understood just what had happened. Marguerite might seek revenge against a Lagrenade, but she would never curse innocent babies. He would give Joelle a harmless spell—the same one he gave Madame Weston—which should rid her of anxiety.) "But I sense there is something else you have come about, something you have not told me." He scanned Joelle's guarded face; a pretty face, but a sly one. "Is there something more you have come to say, *zann fiy*?"

Joelle shifted uneasily under his gaze. She had been putting off telling him about Chloe because it made her feel so guilty. "*Wi, docteur,*" she said at last. "It is the other reason I have come. My man's little girl, she is sick and maybe dying. And I am afraid it's from the potion the fortune-teller gave to me for the wife."

Adonis closed his eyes. When Marguerite had told him about the child's illness, he had feared it might have been caused by some mischief like this. "You were trying to poison this white woman?" he said severely to Joelle.

"No, no, I would never do such a thing! And I told this to Madame Hélène. No, it was only to make the wife want to go home."

Adonis studied Joelle again, and this time decided to believe her. "And what did the old witch tell you to put in this potion, eh? Wait, I can guess. Your monthly blood and urine?" Joelle nodded. "What else?"

"I burned a piece of silk, *Bonnonm,* and some of my man's beard, and then I mixed it with the medicine she gave me. I do not know what was in that."

Adonis clucked his tongue. "Stay away from that Madame Hélène from now on. She is dangerous. She is not a *bonnfamn,* not *bon* at all, in fact, but she tries to have the same powers. And look at what happens."

I wonder if it was I who gave her that evil medicine, he thought unhappily, for he did sell Madame Hélène his potions for a nice little profit. He tried to think back to the transaction they'd had a few weeks earlier. He knew the contents of his own potion, but had he also mixed it with that mysterious substance he'd been given by *Bonnonm* Gacher over in Praslin? Yes, it was possible. And who knew what that second-rate *malfeter* might have put in it? Cassava that had been neither cooked nor grated and washed? That would be poisonous. Or maybe jequirity seed, by the sound of what had happened to the child. Perhaps Gacher had even given it to him in the hope of ruining his reputation and dispensing with a rival! He must be more careful in the future.

"But what about my man?" Joelle urged. "I think he is dying, *Bonnonm.* He can no longer even walk."

"This is not my medicine that did this," Adonis said emphatically, rubbing his mustache in distress, for he was displeased with himself now. "I do not give out any potion that would make mischief like this. So unless there is something more you have not told me"—and again he narrowed his eyes at Joelle—"something you have fed him, you must take him to Dr. Panyal."

"I have fed him nothing!" Joelle lied. "I tried to make him go to Dr. Panyal, but he won't do it. He only trusts the white doctors at the hospital."

"Then he is a fool." Adonis paused, remembering the cockerel blood and semen he had given to Madame Weston. But that would never make the white man sick like this.

"Tell him he must go to Dr. Panyal. This doctor is the best in Seychelles. He knows the white man's body, the Creole's and the Indian's. He is wise and he is knowledgeable." And he also sends his patients to me, Adonis could have added, as I do mine to him, for we both know that the body, mind and soul must be treated as one.

"And if he still won't go?"

Adonis shook his old head. "You women, you never know your own powers. You are extraordinarily beautiful, *Manmzel* Lagrenade. You can make him do what you want."

"Penny, it's late, you must sleep," Lily said. "Lie down on the cot there and I'll watch Chloe."

"I can't, I just can't."

"I know it's difficult. But the doctors say she's stable. You'll get sick yourself if you don't sleep and eat something. And she needs you to be strong."

"Lily's right," said Paul. "You haven't eaten or slept for two days. You have to rest. We'll wake you if anything happens."

Penelope bent forward in her chair, resting her head on the bed beside Chloe's chest.

"I can't," she whispered. "I need to see her breathe."

• • •

Zara curled into a ball on the hospital-room floor, her face in her hands, silently pleading. "Dear Baby Jesus and dear Father God. I will never do any bad magic again, I promise. I will never say the word *hell* again, I promise. I will never do *grigri* or grind up a beetle or make a spell again, I promise. Please please please let Chloe live. And if she doesn't, please let me die, too."

"I think Penny's fallen asleep," Lily whispered to Paul. Penelope's head was still beside Chloe, her long back curved over the bed. "Should we move her?"

Paul looked down. He could hardly stand it. Every time he looked at Chloe he saw his sons. Every time he looked at Penelope he saw himself as a grieving father.

"Leave her be," he said hoarsely. "Leave her be."

Marguerite was at church, kneeling in front of a statue of the Madonna high on a marble pedestal behind a grate. She had lit a votive candle for Chloe and was now praying fervently, her head bowed, her small jaw clenched. On one side of her was Francis, on the other Lisette. And just behind her knelt Philippe Chanson.

"Mother Mary, for the love of God save this child," Marguerite prayed. "Take the soul of my little Marcel, drowned in the sea so long ago, and give it to Chloe. Please Mother Mary. Give it to little Chloe to save her."

Francis was rocking back and forth, muttering his own prayer, a terrible ache in his chest. He couldn't stop thinking of Chloe's dimpled little face smiling up at him, and of all the times he had dried her tears, put on her clothes and held her because no one else would. "Please, oh Madonna, save this child," he prayed. "She's only an innocent baby. Save her and save her sister, and deliver them from evil."

Lisette was weeping. "She is such a little child, dear Mother. She cuddled me so much, she's never done any harm. I will give up my hopes for Michel Deschamps forever if you will save her."

Philippe had his head bowed and his long back straight, his hands perfectly aligned, palm to palm, under his chin. "For the sake of my love for Marguerite, save this unfortunate child, oh Mother of Christ. Marguerite is a good woman and she has had enough pain."

Up on the mountain, by the light of the waning moon, *Bonnonm* Adonis was standing by his house, gazing into the sky. He had sent his patients away and his servants to bed, and now he was alone in the deepest hour of the night. In one hand he held a mirror, in the other a wooden crucifix. Slowly, he raised them both and held them facing one another, so that the cross was reflected in the mirror and lit from behind by the bright, unforgiving moon.

"Oh great powers that be," he chanted in a deep, rasping voice. "Oh gods of the sky and sea, of the soul and the heart, oh gods of my ancestors the slaves, witness here that I mean only to do good. Take from me the last years of my life and give them to the child. Absolve me and save her, dear gods. For she is young and blameless, and it is not her time to die."

16

Dr. Panyal bent over Rupert and shook his head. "Look at the state you are in, sir," he said, moving his stethoscope over Rupert's bony chest. "Why didn't you send for me before?"

Rupert flushed, which made his face look a greenish mud color. He was lying in the bed of his bungalow, dressed in the blue striped pajamas that Joelle had ironed and insisted he wear out of respect for the doctor.

"Don't know, really. Sorry. Thought the hospital doctors were the thing, you know?"

Dr. Panyal nodded. He knew. Opening his battered doctor's bag, he took out his ophthalmoscope. He did not usually make house calls until Fridays, but Miss Lagrenade had come to him in such a panic that he'd closed his clinic and rushed over, although it was only Tuesday. He didn't like to make a pregnant woman anxious.

"Miss Lagrenade was quite right to call me, sir. You are very unwell." Dr. Panyal shone his instrument into Rupert's pee-yellow eyes. "Have you any pain anywhere in your body?"

"Course I have. Every damn part of me hurts. What do you expect?"

"Just list the pains for me, if you don't mind."

"Oh, all right. My stomach, my back, my legs, my neck and my shoulders. Oh, and my head. Satisfied now?"

"Which shoulder, sir?"

"What's my bloody shoulder got to do with it?" Rupert shouted. I knew it, he thought, another crackpot.

"Just answer my question, please."

Rupert thought. He really did hurt so much all over that it was hard to sort out what he felt where. "Well, now that you ask, my right shoulder has been aching quite a bit from my lying in bed for so long."

"Liver," Dr. Panyal said flatly, and rubbed his brown hands together in what looked to Rupert suspiciously like glee. "Pain from the liver is referred to the right shoulder, sir. It is just as I thought. If you had come to me months ago, I would have cured you in a flash. I must take a stool sample, but I can guess what it is already. Have you been taking anything for your diarrhea, sir, such as kaolin or Pepto-Bismol?"

Rupert nodded. "Yes, repulsive stuff. Like cooked toothpaste. Dr. Malavois gave it to me, along with some other useless pills."

"Pity. That will disguise the test results. Never mind. Take this little bottle and send it over to me with a stool sample as soon as you can, so I can take a look at it under my microscope. We should check your blood as well, of course. I will write you a prescription now and give you a ring as soon as I have confirmed my suspicions."

"A prescription for what?" Rupert said warily.

"Metronidazole."

"Never heard of it." Rupert felt rather dazed.

"It is also known as flagyl, sir. But never mind, it is quite safe. Take eight hundred milligrams three times a day for ten days—that will be a pill with each meal. Then come back to see me. No alcohol whatsoever, please, and drink a lot of fluids. And you must not take any other medicine until you hear from me. That has to be a promise."

"Can't I even take a little spell here and there?" Rupert mustered up a chuckle.

Ignoring him, Dr. Panyal pushed his spectacles up his nose, scribbled out the prescription and put it on a side table. Dropping his instruments into his doctor's bag, which looked as if it had been run over by a bus, he shut it up with a snap. "I will ring you as soon as I have the results, sir."

"But what do I have?" Rupert said plaintively. "What's wrong with me?"

"I believe it is an *Entamoeba histolytica* infection, sir. Probably known to you as amoebic dysentery. It is very common round here, only the amoeba usually lodges in the intestine or the bowel, not in the liver, as I suspect is the case for you, which is probably why the other doctors did not catch it. That, and the Pepto-Bismol. Most unfortunate. Anyway, you are lucky, really, for it can, of course, lodge in the brain, which would be a great deal more unpleasant."

Probably already has, Rupert thought glumly. "You mean to say all I've got is some common parasite?"

"Yes, sir. A common parasite in an uncommon way, with a touch of consequent jaundice, by the look of you." And, he added silently, if your stupid wife had listened to me when I told her about *Entamoeba histolytica* all those months ago, you would have been spared this suffering altogether.

"Do you mean I'm going to be cured?" Rupert said, his voice breaking. "I'm not going to die?"

Dr. Panyal kept his face impassive. "Not this time around, sir. Good day." And he left.

"Joelle!" Rupert called. "Joelle, you can come in now!"

She stepped into the bedroom, kneading her hands in worry. "What did he say, *mon cheri*? Are you going to be well again?"

"He says I'm not seriously sick at all, my love! He says I'll be cured in under two weeks. Darling, I'll be better for the babies!"

Dr. Panyal arrived back at his clinic to find fifteen people lined up outside, waiting for him to reopen. For the rest of the day, he had no time at all to think about *Entamoeba histolytica* or Rupert's liver, for he was too busy ridding people of worms and diagnosing the malnutrition, gonorrhea, elephantiasis and tuberculosis that were the curses of the Seychelles islands. But finally, at eight in the evening, he locked his office door, took off his now sweat-stained and wrinkled white doctor's coat and sat down to write a paper on Rupert's case. It would be a labor of love, he was sure, because all the other times he had sent papers off to London about one tropical disease or another, he had never been acknowledged. Nevertheless, he had to do it, for the sake of science.

He wrote deep into the night every night for the next five days—long after Rupert's stool sample had confirmed his hunch—and at last sent the paper off with satisfaction. It took two months and six days to arrive at the Hospital for Tropical Diseases at St. Pancras in London, where it sat on somebody's desk for another half a year.

"Hmm, interesting," mused one Dr. Robert McKenzie, reading it over at his office desk on a Wednesday afternoon. He took a sip of whiskey-laced tea and a bite of jam tart, then turned the paper over and read the name of the author. Oh, one of those Indian chappies. He put it in a drawer.

It stayed there for fifteen years.

Four days after Rupert had started his metronidazole pills, Paul Leland drove up to his house just after lunch. He parked the Land Rover beside an open drain in the road, climbed out and stood facing Rupert's front door. His hands fiddled nervously with the keys in his shorts pockets and his brow dampened in the still afternoon heat. A mosquito buzzed at his sweaty neck.

He dreaded this, but it had to be done. Shit, he thought. A million shits.

Pushing his sunglasses up on his head, he took a deep breath, walked up the stone steps and knocked on the closed wooden door. "Rupert? Are you in?"

Rupert had been sitting with a book in the salon, admiring his nest when Paul knocked. He was proud of the way Joelle had done up their bungalow. Postcards of local scenery decorated the unpainted wooden walls, a large framed mirror hung between the windows (she had been so excited by that!), pretty embroidered doilies graced the backs of the chairs and a simple square table sat in a corner. A typical Seychellois house, really, with not a trace of old England about it. None of that leftover Victorian fuss he had so hated at home, porcelain knickknacks, grannies in picture frames and depressing things like tea cozies and poufs. None of that postwar shabbiness, either: the linoleum floors and nasty little gas fires, with their rows of tiny flames that did nothing but burn one's socks or cause chilblains; the endless brown pots of tooth-staining tea; the dull routines of suppers and church; the gawky Englishwomen with red noses and cold feet; the vicars and how-do-you-do's and Scotch eggs and pork pies and mackintoshes and gum boots and trifle and gooseberries and rain and rain and rain. . . . Could there be a more dispiriting country in the whole world than England? Rupert had decided some time ago that he'd been misplaced at birth, like a changeling. He wasn't supposed to have been born an Englishman at all. He was supposed to have been born a handsome and cocky Creole.

At the sound of Paul's knock, Rupert pushed himself feebly out of his chair and hobbled to the door, leaning on a cane, wondering if it was Talbot or Hugh Hubert, who came over once in a while to gawk at Joelle. (Everybody at the office was being terribly nice to Rupert about his illness, assuring him that his work could wait until he was well again, no matter what the Colonial Office said, because the Colonial Office, as they all really knew, didn't give a horse's arse about the Seychelles.) He was feeling better, but still not strong enough to leave the house. The amoeba had eaten seven-eighths of his liver, Dr. Panyal had told him, leaving no more than a rupee-sized piece to cope with all he consumed, and it would need some time to regenerate. The jaundice apparently would take care of itself as the liver healed.

He struggled for some time to open the door, Joelle having taken to locking it lately with a great, heavy bolt. He had no idea why, for it only made the house dark and stuffy and nobody else in Victoria kept their doors locked all day. But when he'd objected, all she would say was, "*Monnamour*, you are very sweet and innocent. But you and I, we have enemies now. Leave it to me."

He finally succeeded in unfastening the bolt and threw open the door a little harder than he meant. "Why, hello, it's Paul Leland!" he exclaimed breathlessly. "See, I remember you this time."

"Good. Listen, Rupert, I have to talk to you."

"Not another goodwill message from Penny, I hope?"

"No. May I come inside?"

Rupert squinted into the brightness of the street. He did not like the humorlessness of this American, nor his brutish directness, but he especially disliked the way the man wore his sunglasses perched on top of his head, as if he were trying to look like an Italian film star.

"Yes, of course. Do come in." Rupert crept back to his chair.

"Are you any better?" Paul said. He was shocked at how much Rupert had deteriorated since he'd last seen him for that drink at the club. He sat down and pulled at his collar. The room was stiflingly hot and a little stinky.

"On the mend, thanks. Joelle's splendid, though. She would say hello, but she's at the clinic at the moment for a checkup. She's due in November. We're awfully excited. Did you know we're having twins?"

"Rupert, I'm afraid I have some pretty bad news."

Rupert came to his senses. "It's Chloe, isn't it? I was going to visit her as soon as I could walk anywhere. Oh God, what's happened?" He looked at Paul with real terror.

Paul stared down at his legs, hairy and brown under his shorts. He felt so masculine and clumsy at this. He should have sent Lily.

"I don't know how to say this, so please forgive me if it sounds pretty blunt. But I'm afraid . . . I'm afraid she's in a coma, Rupert. It happened this morning, at dawn. She just kind of slid into it."

Rupert slumped. He didn't just slump, he collapsed.

"Please don't tell me this," he whispered, his voice cracking.

"I'm sorry, I'm real sorry. But I think Penny needs you right now."

"Yes, yes, of course. I should have gone before." Rupert stood up and patted the empty pockets of his trousers for his car keys, looking around vaguely.

"You don't have a car," Paul said. "I'll drive you."

When Paul ushered Rupert into the hospital room, Penelope gazed up at them with a blank stare. She had grown haggard in the last few days, her hair stringy, her eyes ringed by brown stains. She kept licking her lips, over and over, and now they were cracked and flaking.

"Rupert," she said.

Rupert shuffled over to the bed, leaning his tall frame on his cane, his gaze fixed on Chloe. He was too shocked to speak. Chloe looked so tiny lying there, no more substantial than a rag, so dwindled was she by the tubes and machines all around her. She was barely a bump in the bed.

"What happened?" he finally managed to croak.

Penelope shook her head, unable to speak, so Lily spoke for her.

"The doctors say a coma happens sometimes with cyanide poisoning. It's not hopeless, though. She's breathing on her own and her heart seems okay. It's just that her blood pressure is dangerously low and they're not sure, they're not sure . . ." Lily stopped. She couldn't say it.

"Who are you?" Rupert said, staring at her glassily.

"I'm Lily Leland. Paul's wife."

"Oh. Oh yes, sorry." Rupert bent over the chair where Lily was sitting and shook her hand. He reminded Lily of a Don Quixote statue she had once seen, tall, thin and stupefied. "What were you saying?" he asked.

"She was saying they're not sure Chloe's brain is all right," Penelope replied in a flat voice. "Cyanide can damage it, apparently, or maybe it's the coma. Oh, God I wish we were home! I just can't be sure these people know what they're doing. Think of poor Hannah's husband. If he'd gone to back to England instead of to Mombasa . . ." she trailed off.

"Well, Dr. Panyal cured me," Rupert said. "It was only a simple parasite in the end. Did Hannah's husband ever go to Dr. Panyal? He's an expert on these tropical beasts, you know."

Penelope didn't hear him. She had turned her attention back to Chloe.

"What are all these horrid tubes for?" Rupert asked then, and at last reality hit him and he tottered. Lily saw just in time and jumped up to give him her chair. Rupert closed his eyes and sank into it. He was afraid he was going to vomit.

"They call it irrigation," Lily said quietly. "They're pumping her with water to keep washing out the toxins. And to give her nutrients, too, of course."

Rupert's eyes were still closed, his gorge rising. He felt as he had all those months ago on the ship, tearing through the corridors, calling out for Chloe, imagining her overboard, imagining her drowning. Only this time she had gone overboard, she was drowning. No, he thought, this is not bearable. I cannot sit here and watch my child drown. This is not something a human being can bear.

He slumped forward, head in his hands, elbows on his knees, and for a brief moment his vision seemed to clear, as if a veil had been lifted. What in the hell have I been doing? he wondered in astonishment. Wallowing in Joelle all these weeks, lying in bed feeling sorry for myself just because of a little amoeba, when all along my family has been suffering, needing me, and my child has been dying! Have I been out of my mind?

He felt a small hand on his knee, like a cat paw. "Daddy?"

He forced open his eyes to find Zara beside him. With an effort, he lifted her up and put her on his lap. Wrapping his arms around her stomach, he pulled her to him and buried his face in the back of her head, his entire frame wracked with remorse. Dear God, he prayed silently, if you let Chloe recover, I shall reform. I shall never desert my family again. I swear.

"Daddy?" Zara said. "When Chloe gets better, can we go home?"

Rupert rubbed his nose in her hair, which smelled of sea and little girl.

"Can we, Daddy?"

He drew her to him. "Of course, my darling muffin," he said, his voice breaking. "Of course we'll go home."

EPILOGUE

1961

Penelope gazed perplexed at the suitcases she was going to have to stow away. Not as many as when they'd come to Seychelles, as she had divested herself of so many belongings, but still there were five of them and they took up a lot of room. She looked over the cabin, trying to work out the logistics. Two could fit under the bed. None should go on the shelf above the upper berth—too dangerous. If the ship encountered another storm, a suitcase might fly off and crush somebody's head. The one full of books and beetles she could stow under the sink. And the remaining two she would have to lean against a wall as best she could. When we get to Madagascar, she decided with a sigh, we'll hire a porter, expense be damned.

The ship's foghorn blasted just then, startling her: a long, chilling moan of accumulated departures and farewells. With a shiver she picked up her sunglasses and left the cabin, quickly locking its door behind her—too much lost already—and hurried up to the deck to look for Zara and Rupert.

It took her some time to find Zara among the people milling about, weeping and saying their good-byes: women leaving to visit sick relatives, fathers traveling for who knew how many years to seek work, sons and daughters off the find their fortunes, perhaps never to return. But finally she spotted her, clasped in Marguerite's vigorous arms. Marguerite was weeping, too, the tears coursing down her face as she squeezed Zara to her, then let her go, only to hug her again.

Zara held onto Marguerite with all her might, her head buried in her chest, inhaling her scent of baby oil and curry for as long as she could—the most comforting scent in the world.

"But Madame, this is too sad!" Marguerite cried upon seeing Penelope. "It is too hard!"

"Yes, I know." Penelope grasped both of Marguerite's hands, yet, wrenched as she was, her voice did not tremble. "I cannot thank you enough for everything you've done for us, Marguerite. You've helped us all through this terrible year, and you've been so understanding and patient. You're an angel, you really are. You've been such a good friend to me." She pressed a hundred-rupee note into Marguerite's palm.

"Ah, Madam." Marguerite threw her arms around the Englishwoman. "You will write to me, yes? And you will come back to our beautiful island to visit?"

Penelope returned the hug awkwardly, murmured something vague and put on her sunglasses. The last thing she ever wanted to do in her life was come back.

Zara tugged at Marguerite's plait. "Nana?" she said, her voice anxious. "Where's Francis?"

"Here I am." Francis pushed his way through the crowd behind his mother and picked Zara up, holding her out in front of him with his muscular arms. "You will be a tall and lovely woman next time I see you, *pa vre*?" He pulled her to his chest and gave her a great squeeze, then put her back on her feet. "Take this, *ti ser*." He placed in her hands an intricately carved box of casuarina wood, which had taken him days to finish. "I made it especially for you."

Zara clasped the beautiful box to her chest and looked up at him, her face serious. "You promise not to marry anybody while I'm in England?"

"I promise, little monkey. I'll wait and marry you." He winked.

Zara studied him gravely. "You mustn't tell fibs. It's bad."

The foghorn blasted again, startling everybody this time, and the ship's steward shouted for the guests to disembark. Penelope looked over the crowd anxiously. Where was Rupert? Marguerite hugged Zara one last time, and she and Francis made their way down the gangway to a launch that carried them ashore.

Penelope took Zara's hand and pushed urgently through the other passengers to the deck's railing so they could look out at the people on the jetty. Standing close behind Zara, she surveyed the crowd. Lily and Paul were there, Paul's hand held aloft in a still salute, while Lily waved sporadically beside him, looking from this distance like a little girl. The boys stood in front of them, clowning madly for Zara. "You look like a *dandosya!*" they called, though neither she nor Penelope could hear. "You look like a coconut!" But still no Rupert.

Zara waved back to Pete and Rory; her movements heavy and sad, as if her arm weighed almost too much to lift.

By now Marguerite and Francis had joined Lisette, who was also on the Jetty, waving a handkerchief, her pretty face puffy with tears. They look like a flower bed, Penelope thought, all these people with their colored dresses and straw hats. They look like a bed of pansies. And the handkerchiefs fluttering above them, those are the butterflies.

"Where's Daddy?" Zara said, her voice wavering. "I don't see Daddy."

"I don't know, darling." Penelope tried to sound calm. "Something must have delayed him." She lifted her arm in a wave, then suddenly couldn't anymore. Dropping her hands onto Zara's shoulders, she stood and stared, trying to memorize the faces of these people she had grown to so love and depend upon. She doubted she would see any of them ever again.

With a loud clanging and creaking, the gangway was lifted and secured, and the ship gave a great shudder as it prepared to move. Penelope searched the crowd one last time. Rupert had said he would come, the bastard! He had promised! She set her mouth in resignation, her face half hidden by her sunglasses. She should have guessed he wouldn't bother. He was ensconced in the big house with the pregnant Joelle now, all his panicked vows at the hospital forgotten, back to his smug self and growing another beard. Oh, he had stood about looking guilty enough while they were packing, making all sorts of rash promises about visiting them in England and sending them money, and barely able to even look at Zara as she clung to his knees. But of course in the end he had been too cowardly, too unwilling to face how he'd shattered his family to even come and wave them off. Oh, he had revealed his true colors now. It wasn't the island, it wasn't Joelle or her babies, it wasn't even that he'd never loved Penelope as much as he'd said he had. It was only that this is the way he really was.

The SS *Kampala* let out another tragic blast of its horn, then drew away with an enormous groan, the smell of fish and seaweed rising from the churning water below. Some people cheered from the shore, others wept, their farewells drifting away on the wind.

"Daddy didn't come!" Zara wailed, and she began to cry.

Less than a mile away from the harbor, Rupert was, in fact, trying very hard to come, but just as he'd been about to leave Joelle had picked a quarrel with him. "You go off and leave me here alone when the babies, they are due any minute, so you can run away and see your other family? See, it is as I thought—you do not really care about me at all!"

Rupert glanced at his watch anxiously. "Darling, you know not a word of that is true. I'll be back soon. I really must go."

"And then you will give them all your money and we shall starve!" she went on. "I am already hungry and we have nothing in the house because you forgot to go to the market yesterday."

"Can we talk about this later?" Rupert said, edging a foot over the threshold. "If I don't leave now, I shall miss them. Ships don't wait, you know."

"You see! I know what you are thinking! You are going to jump on the ship back to your precious England and desert me. Yes, leave me and your babies to starve!" And Joelle began to cry, her now enormous bosom shaking with each sob.

Rupert watched her with concern. She had been terribly capricious lately, always throwing one fit or another like this. He knew it was the pregnancy, he was sure of it—she would get back to normal once the twins were born. But meanwhile he had to muster all the patience he could simply to get through the day. He looked at his watch again. Damnation! He pictured Zara's little face looking out for him. He couldn't let her leave without seeing her off—it would break her heart!

"I'm sorry, my love, I must go. I shall be back soon, I promise, and then I'll go to the market."

"And now you are going to leave without even giving me a kiss! It is because I am so fat, now, isn't it? You find me ugly. Oh, I know you white men, what do you care?"

The sound of the ship's horn drifted over the town, sending Rupert into a panic. "Please don't talk like that, darling! I shall be back in a minute, really!" And with a final anxious glance at her, he slipped out of the house and down the steps, her sobs and shouts following him, and hurried to the harbor. Another blast of the ship's horn—damn it, he was going to miss them! He had a present for Zara in his pocket, a beautiful little cricket cage made in India he'd bought at Mr. Raja's shop, and a large check the bank had loaned him for Penny, but it was probably already too late to hand them over. Damn, damn, damn! He broke into a run, cringing with guilt as he rounded a corner and loped off toward the departing ship, for whenever he thought of Penny now he couldn't help but picture her back in her dreary home with her nervous wreck of a mother and no money. She had been remarkably stoic about it, with that new grim efficiency she had developed at Chloe's bedside, claiming that she would find a job somehow and start life anew, but he couldn't see how she would manage it. She had no qualifications to work, no income, no flat. And not for the first time, a chill of apprehension passed through him. Perhaps he was making a mistake, a dreadful, irredeemable, permanent mistake.

Penelope and Zara remained on deck as the ship pulled away. Zara was still sweeping her eyes over the harbor, searching desperately for her father, while she clutched her precious box from Francis to her chest. And Penelope was holding onto Zara's shoulders for dear life, watching Mahé loom above her, as if that same green giant she'd noticed on the journey to Praslin was rising from the ocean to bid them farewell. Rupert wasn't coming, obviously. A wave of despair and anger passed through her. How could he? How could he, on top of everything else, do this to his own daughter?

Unable to bear it any longer, she turned away and bent over Zara. "I'm going inside, darling," she said gently. "Do you want to come?" Ever since Marguerite had told her how the poison had fallen into Chloe's hands, Penelope had felt intensely protective of Zara. She accepted that it had all been an accident, that Zara had been used by that infernal Joelle, who had denied everything, of course, and whom the bewitched Rupert had chosen to believe. But Penelope also knew that it would take years and years for Zara to stop blaming herself, if she ever did at all. "I only wanted the medicine for Daddy to make him stay home," she had said, sobbing, and the confession had pierced Penelope's heart.

Zara hadn't answered, so Penelope asked her again. "Sweetie, do you want to come inside with me?"

"No. I want to stay here."

Penelope hesitated. She knew the poor child was still hoping her father might show up. "All right. But don't climb up on the railing, promise?"

Zara nodded. She understood about risk now, about her mother's nervousness. "I promise."

"And you remember where to find me?"

"Yes, Mummy."

Penelope kissed the top of her head and pushed through the waving passengers, making her way past a tangle of white metal ladders and coiled ropes till she came to the steps leading to the deck below. There, she walked along a bland interior corridor until she reached the third door on the left, labeled *Nurse*. She opened it and stepped inside.

Chloe was lying in a bed by the wall, thin and fragile, her former pinkness turned the sallow white of the sickbed. Penelope walked over to her with the same clutching of the heart, the same mix of dread and hope with which she always approached her daughter now. She pulled a chair up to the bedside, while the nurse lingered behind her, and took Chloe's soft little hand.

"Chloe, love?" Chloe blinked. She did at least seem to be able to hear, although she had not spoken since falling into the coma. But the poison had turned her expression blank. Her eyes were incurious now when they rested on her mother, as if all her concentration were borne upon her inner self. "We cannot assess the extent of the damage, Mrs. Weston," the doctors had said when Chloe had at last awoken. "The child has undergone severe toxic shock and her neurological system is damaged. There is a chance she will recover, but we cannot predict when or to what extent. We wish we could tell you more, but we simply don't know."

"We must take her back to London," Penelope had said to Rupert. "To the top doctors. We're going to fight this every inch of the way. We have to."

"Yes, yes, of course," Rupert had murmured from where he'd sat frozen in his hospital chair, staring with terror at Chloe, at the machines attached to her arms, and at his own body, so strange all of a sudden, and so useless. "No expense spared. Of course."

"Chloe?" Penelope said in the ship nurse's quarters, resting her hand on top of her daughter's limp hair. Her hand looked enormous spread over the child's small head like that, the fingers brown and coarse. She bent over Chloe's face. "We're going home, muffin. We're on a ship and it's going to take us back to England."

Chloe's pale eyes gazed at her impassively. How Penelope longed for something more, anything—a cry, a whimper, the smallest twitch of a smile. A dribble emerged from Chloe's mouth and ran slowly down her chin. With her bare thumb, Penelope wiped it gently away.

Up on the deck, Zara was still grasping the railing, her legs planted on the floorboards, staring fiercely at Mahé. She was determined not to let the island out of her sight for a minute, to watch it without wavering until Daddy appeared. She watched the expanse of water between the ship and the land stretch and deepen. She watched the boats in the harbor, the houses in the distance, and all the people on the jetty—Francis and Nana, Pete and Rory and Lisette—grow smaller and smaller. And then, just as she thought Daddy would never come, she saw him. Tall and thin, much thinner than he used to be before he got sick, he was running toward her. "Daddy!" she screamed. "Daddy!" He was running faster now, she could see him, weaving through the people on the quay, pushing them out of his way till he got to the edge. He lifted his arm and waved madly, his mouth open, calling something, but she couldn't hear. "Daddy!" she cried, waving and waving, the tears tumbling down her face. "Daddy!"

ACKNOWLEDGMENTS

I never would have discovered, let alone lived in Seychelles, had my mother and anthropologist father, Marion and Burton Benedict, not brought me there in 1960. I am indebted to their memories, field notes, photographs and, above all, to their book, *Men, Women, and Money in Seychelles* (University of California Press, 1982). Among the other books I found useful were *Forgotten Eden* by Athol Thomas (Longmans, Green & Co, London, UK, 1968) and *The Seychelles: Unquiet Islands* by Marcus Franda (Westview Press, Hampshire, UK, 1982).

I am also most grateful to Lee Haring, Professor Emeritus of English at Brooklyn College and an instructor in the Graduate Program in Folklore and Folklife at the University of Pennsylvania, who gave me advice and introductions. It is to his book, *Indian Ocean Folktales* (National Folklore Support Centre, India, 2002), that I owe the story of Kader and the Fish Queen, a Seychellois folktale collected by Mederic Adrienne in 1980–1982 under the sponsorship of Seychelles Ministry of Education and Information.

Inside Seychelles, many people gave of their time and knowledge: artist Michael Adams, whose art graces the book's cover, and his daughter Alyssa; Robert Grandcourt; Marcelle Estrale and Erica Fanchette of Lenstiti Kreol; Kantilal Jivan Shah; Michel Rosalie and Janick Bru-Rosalie. I also wish to thank the many kind Seychellois who answered my nosy questions and showered me, unasked, with fruit and coconuts.

Outside Seychelles, I thank Joan Silber and Rebecca Stowe for their invaluable readings and suggestions; Laura and Bronwen Hruska for their faith in this book; the Virginia Center for the Creative Arts for summers of time and peace; the Yaddo Corporation in whose inspiring embrace I made my final revisions; Simon and Emma O'Connor for putting up with the obsessions of a writer mother; and most of all, Stephen O'Connor, who has most generously shared the adventures all the way.

Thanks to you all. I am lucky.